A Stairway to the Sea

by Jeff Newberry

Pulpwood Press
Panama City, FL

Inquiries should be addressed to:
Pulpwood Press
P.O. Box 35038
Panama City, FL 32412

Newberry, Jeff
A Stairway to the Sea / Jeff
Newberry
-----1st ed.
p. cm.

ISBN: 978-1-888146-57-8

Printed in the United States

1 3 5 7 9 10 8 6 4 2

First Edition

Dedication

A lot goes into the writing of a novel, as any writer can tell you. It's doubly hard, I think, to write about a place you love. I wanted to tell the truth as I saw it, so instead of setting *A Stairway to the Sea* in a real place, I created St. Vincent, an amalgamation of several small Gulf Coast towns, places that I love, places that I carry in my heart. I want to thank the landscape and the people for their inspiration, and I beg indulgence for any geographical or historical error.

I couldn't have written this novel without the support of my wife, Heather, who is my first reader, my encourager, and my best friend. Thank you, Heather. I love you.

Thanks to Vince Everett, the best friend I've ever had. A police veteran, he's worked nearly twenty years as a law enforcement officer in Port St. Joe and Gulf County. Vince, this book is for you. Thank you for indulging the late-night phone calls and last-minute emails asking for clarification on police procedures. Any errors in the book are mine and mine alone. Love you, brother. You were the inspiration.

I must thank Russell Pryor, PhD, a professor of history at Abraham Baldwin Agricultural College (ABAC) in Tifton, Georgia. Russell's knowledge about the history of American labor helped me to shape the character of Wayne Childress. Thanks, too, to my colleagues in the Department of English and Communication at ABAC. Don't you all have some essays to grade?

Thank you, Jeremy Flake, for your intimate knowledge of military procedure and the American campaign in Iraq.

Much thanks to those who read early versions of this manuscript and helped me as I wrote it: Sian Griffiths, Tom Franklin, John Dufresne, Matt Forsythe, Michael Lister, Reginald McKnight, Thomas Alan Holmes, Jenn Blair and Laura Valeri and others who offered valuable feedback and insight.

Thanks, Mama. I'm sorry I kept you awake typing on that Tandy 1000 way back in the day.

Jim Kibler, I wouldn't have written this without Larry Brown and Harry Crews. Thanks for introducing me to them.

Thanks to the librarians at the Tifton/Tift County Public Library, where the majority of this novel was written. Vicki, keep my seat warm. Many thanks to the entire team at Pulpwood Press. I appreciate your taking a chance on this book.

And thank you, readers, for picking up this book. I hope you enjoy it, and I hope you'll keep reading. I'm not positive, but I'm not sure I'm done telling Justin's story.

Meanwhile we do no harm; for they
   That with a god have striven,
Not hearing much of what we say,
   Take what the god has given;
Though like waves breaking it may be,
Or like a changed familiar tree,
Or like a stairway to the sea
   Where down the blind are driven.

—"Eros Turannos," E.A. Robinson

1.

The last time I saw Donnie Ray Miles, he was coming out of Harley's Bait and Tackle, a twelve pack of Natural Light under his arm. I'd stopped by before my shift to pick up a pack of cigarettes. It was just past 7:00 p.m. and the sun hung low in the sky, a hot, June day melting to a balmy night. I'd parked the police cruiser at the edge of the lot, the nose of the Crown Victoria pointed at the highway.

I knew him before I recognized him: an uncombed shock of red hair, a scraggly beard that curled in on itself and hid most of his face. We nodded at each other, a slight tip of the head, but we didn't say anything. He got into the cab of his primered Chevy truck and backed away. He looked thin, drawn-up, wrung-out like a dishrag.

Maybe *thin*'s the wrong word. He looked hollowed out and empty, as though something had scrubbed his insides out. I thought of the gourds my grandfather used to hang from his front porch. He scraped the insides clean with a Case knife and purple martins would build nests in them every fall.

I'd not seen Donnie Ray in a good while. He'd come home after a short stint in the Army. He'd been deployed to Iraq. At first, we all thought he was on leave. Given the troop build-up, we figured that he'd be gone again soon. But I kept seeing his truck around town. One night, I ran him and Jimmy Danley off from Tommy Parrot's, a bar on the beach. Jimmy got loud and drunk. Spilling Natural Light everywhere. Yelling at other patrons. Generally being an ass. The bartender called the sheriff's department, and I was dispatched. When I stuck my head in the door, Jimmy narrowed his eyes and shook his head. "I guess old deputy dog here's gonna ruin our fun," he said to Donnie Ray, who didn't pay any attention to Jimmy.

"Probably a good idea for you guys to find a new place," I said, hoping that Jimmy didn't decide to show his ass. I'd known both of them since high school. Jimmy Danley had been a Class-A shithead for as long as I could remember.

"This place sucks anyway," Jimmy muttered and swaggered out of the bar. Donnie Ray sat still, staring at a beaded mug of beer sat before him. Then, he drained it, turned in the stool, and put his feet down hard. He walked past me as though I weren't even there.

Before too long, the town realized that he wasn't going back to Iraq. Something had happened. Some people said he'd gone AWOL. Others said he'd been drummed out for selling pot. I didn't know if that was true, but it wouldn't have surprised me.

In high school, he'd had a reputation as a hell-raiser, the kind of loudmouth jackass who loved to piss in your cornflakes . Then, Donnie Ray was capable of anything. He'd punch you in the mouth as quickly as he'd look at you and mutter, "What's up, man?" His crew—Jimmy Danely, Tater Wilson, Freddy Richards—eased through Apalachee County High like a slow tide. They didn't seem to care about anything other than the next party. Part of me was jealous of that attitude. Part of me found it disgusting.

But that swagger had been beaten out of him. That night at Harley's, he didn't stride by me the way he once did. He walked with a measured step, despite his drunkenness, as though the world were fragile and he might step right through it and disappear forever. And the night he drowned three months later, I guess that's exactly what happened.

Police and sirens flickered silently, casting disjointed shadows over the scrub and slash pines. 3:00 a.m. I coasted the police cruiser down Boat Ramp Way, an oyster-shell road off the main highway. Four Apalachee County deputy cruisers lined the cul-de-sac at Wallace Landing. An ambulance sat backed up to the edge of the Apalachicola River where a couple of EMTs stood near the water, smoking. Other people milled about in a dense early-morning mist.

The boat landing was a crumbling concrete ramp down into the muddy water. The sloughs up and down this section of the river were packed with houseboats, many owned by locals. Most were homemade, little more than a single wide trailer sitting on two pontoons.

The boat ramp was at the very end of the road, a turn-around overgrown with live oak, cedar, and pine trees. Catty-corned across from the launch sat a dilapidated cinder block store with an ice machine and a single gas pump out front. A faded Mobil sign was on top of the building. A clapboard sign hung from the porch overhang: "Last Chance Food & Gas." When I was a kid, my father took me bank fishing out here, and we always stopped at Last Chance for some RC Colas and Lance crackers. But that was another life. My father had been dead for years.

I'd spent my entire life in St. Vincent, Florida, a mill town and fishing village on the Florida Gulf Coast. For all the vacation caché of places like Destin and Panama City, St. Vincent remained relatively undiscovered, a small town that hadn't changed much since I was a kid. I knew these back roads well, knew the cutoffs and blind doglegs that led back to dead-end turnarounds and private hunting leases. I'd grown up fishing these sloughs and creeks. I knew the land the way I knew my own voice—familiar and close, intimate.

I pressed the brake and eased to a stop behind Chris Chambers' cruiser. I opened the car door and squinted out toward the river.

"Who was it?" I said to Chris, a tall, slender guy with thick forearms and broad shoulders. I always felt envious of how he looked in his brown and black department uniform. Even with the bullet-proof vest swelling my chest, I felt small around Chris. He filled out the uniform like a poster model, his chest like a comic book hero. He'd always been fit, even back in high school. Although he never played sports, he jogged and worked out. He had a boyish face and a shadow of a mustache, a thin line across his upper lip that looked like smeared grease.

I felt for a cigarette in my front pocket and yawned. Chris cocked an eyebrow—he'd been after me to quit smoking for a long time—but said nothing. Police radio squelch blended with the sound of frogs croaking out in the bayou. A light wind blew from the southeast. I swatted a mosquito and lit the cigarette.

Chris and I had been on the force for five years. Like me, he'd grown up in St. Vincent. We'd both taken classes at Gulf Coast Community College in Panama City for our law enforcement standards. He was one of my best friends, though I'd not seen him outside of work in a few months, at least not since Janey died. We'd met in elementary school. He was the first guy I knew who owned his own shotgun, a Browning 4-10 his mother gave him when he was in the sixth grade. He loved guns and firearms and was fascinated by the military. He'd planned to join the Marines after graduation, but he was missing the first two fingers of his left hand, lost from a hunting accident when we were teenagers.

He'd set a 4-10 against the side of a cypress tree butt-down, and the gun had fired and blown off the ring and pinkie finger on his right hand. I wasn't with him when it had happened, but I remember the huge bandage that wrapped his hand and the way the accident gave him a gangster-like mystique at school.

When we were seniors, a Marine recruiter told him that because of his missing fingers, he'd never get through basic. He'd never be able to field strip and reassemble his rifle quickly enough. For a while, he flirted with joining the Coast Guard, but he wound up in the law enforcement program at Gulf Coast.

Chris and I were both on duty tonight—Chris on the north end of the county, me on the south end, down in and around St. Vincent. Another deputy, Frank Sutton, was a floater, patrolling Highway 71, the long two-lane road between St. Vincent and Stetson, the tiny town on the north end of Apalachee County.

"Donnie Ray Miles," Chris said.

"Really? I just saw him the other day."

Chris leaned against the side of the cruiser, arms crossed over his chest. "He was on Big Don's houseboat. Looks like he fell in. Probably drowned. They can't find him."

"Damn. What happened?" I said. I'd been sitting in the parking lot of the Swifty back in St. Vincent, sipping a cup of black coffee when the dispatcher, Sheila Sanders, called about the drowning.

Chris shrugged. "Hell if I know. Cowboy said that the call came in just after 2:00 a.m. Donnie Ray and Jimmy Danley and that crew were up here, all of them drunk as Cooter Brown. At some point, they all looked around and nobody saw Donnie. They had to come back to the landing so they could get a cell phone signal."

"Jimmy Danley. Why am I not surprised?" I said and exhaled.

"You never have liked him, have you?"

"Jimmy Danley's an asshole."

"It's been a long time since Apalachee High, old man."

I chuckled without humor. "Yeah, tell me about it. You think he had anything to do with this?"

"What? Donnie Ray drowning?"

I shrugged. "You never know."

"I doubt it, but we'll find out if he did. They're going to grill him later on. Frank drove them all back to the department. I'm sure Malone will talk to all of them. From what I heard, Donnie Ray was crazy drunk. They all were. This is probably a case of morons being morons."

"Maybe," I said.

I took a drag of my cigarette and looked at the river, a thick black blanket that edged the muddy bank. This place would be a mess for the next few days. There'd be an investigation and a lot of questions. God only knew who had to notify the family.

The sheriff, Mack Weston, stood near the edge of the river with his hands on his hips, talking to the county investigator, Davis Malone. Malone was a Yankee who'd grown up somewhere up north, a college-educated guy who had a face like a hawk's bill, all sharp and angular. He'd been the county investigator for about close to ten years. I didn't know the whole story, but I'd heard that he'd grown up vacationing down here with his parents. He seemed like an okay guy if not a bit of a straight edge. He was all business.

The sergeant, Cal Nuegent, stood close by, talking into the radio clipped to his lapel. Nuegent was a twenty-year veteran, a tall barrel of a man with a bushy mustache and a thick head of salt-and-pepper hair. He carried a .357 Magnum revolver slung low on his right hip, a pistol that had inspired the nickname Chris gave him: "Cowboy."

Headlights flooded over the scene as a brown and white Ford pulled

up towing a flat-bottom boat. Search and rescue. Maurice Howard got out
and slammed the door. A tall, thin man built like a cane pole, he wore an
Apalachee County windbreaker.

"You need help launching this thing?" Chris said.

The sixteen foot skiff actually belonged to Maurice, though it was
painted like an official Apalachee County Sheriff's Department boat. We
didn't have the budget to fund a full-time search and rescue unit. Maurice
was an auxiliary deputy who ran an auto garage in town.

"That would be great."

"Maurice," Mack said. "Thanks for coming."

"Do you know what time it is? It's fucking two in the morning."
Maurie yawned. "Jesus, Mack, I was sleeping."

The sheriff ignored him and nodded his head at Chris. "You and
Justin help him." He looked at Maurice. "I know it's early. Thanks for being
here. Look, we're going up the river a mile or so. I'll show you the way."

"Want us to go?" I said.

Mack shook his head. He had steel-gray hair and thick beard the
color of a wolf's fur. "No. the sergeant's got something for you to do."

Maurice backed the truck down to the launch while Mack guided
him. When the boat was in the water, Chris unwound the winch that kept the
boat secured. I stood off to the side, feeling useless. Soon, Mack and Chris
had the boat in the river. Maurice parked pulled his truck beneath a cypress
tree overhang near Donnie Ray's pickup.

I studied Donnie Ray's primered truck. The U.S. Army sticker looked
out-of-place on the rusted bumper. The tailgate was down, the bed empty.
The gun rack in the back window was empty, too.

Tree other vehicles sat next to it—a tiny Ford pickup, a full-sized
Chevy Suburban, and a green Mazda 626.

"Okay," Mack said. "Let's go."

"You sure we don't need to go with you?" Chris said.

Mack pointed over to Cowboy, who was talking with the EMTs.
"Talk to the sergeant."

Maurice got in the boat and Mack pushed it into the water. The
motor coughed to life, its back-firing rattle loud in the early-morning
darkness. Mack sat at the stern, shining a halogen light into the night. Maurice
backed the boat into the water and turned it upstream, toward the Miles'
houseboat. Somewhere up the river, Donnie Ray was beneath the water, lost
in the darkness.

Cowboy told me and Chris that we needed to drive into Bay View and notify Donnie Ray's parents. We stood by my cruiser, and I lit a cigarette and offered one to Cowboy. He shook his head. Up close, you could see the tattoos on his forearms. On his right arm was a large stylized anchor, on his left arm, a topless mermaid with flowing hair. Cowboy had been in the Navy for a long time before he became a cop. He took a cigar from his shirt pocket and put in his mouth but didn't light it.

"Why us?" Chris said.

"Mainly because I told you to," he said and chewed at the edge of the cigar. He grinned at us.

Chris snapped a military-style salute with his left hand. He folded his index finger into his palm, leaving his middle finger sticking out. "Yes sir, Sergeant Cowboy."

I laughed and shook my head. This was typical.

"If I'm the Cowboy, Chambers, you're the Indian. And you know who won that battle."

"We'll take care of it," I said. I opened the car door. "But I've got to be honest. I'm not sure I'm the right guy to do this. I wasn't the biggest fan of Donnie Ray. Maybe Chris should go by himself."

"I still want you two to go. You guys were his age," he said. "You graduated with him. Doesn't matter if you were his buddy or not. There's a connection there."

"We got this," Chris said.

"Radio me when you get done," Cowboy said. He looked at me for a moment, a look I'd come to recognize and expect since Janey's death. No one knew how to treat me. Everyone seemed to expect that I was on the verge of bursting into tears. Given by lack of sleep, I wouldn't have been surprised. The world felt at a distance most days, hazy, more like a memory than the real thing.

Cowboy walked back into the misty darkness. I watched him and felt myself slipping away. I shook my head, trying not to zone out.

"You all right?" Chris said.

"Good as I can be, I guess. I mean, a guy drowned, right?"

"That's not what I'm talking about."

I nodded. The image of Donnie Ray choking on river water was stuck in my mind. A drowning. It seemed the worst way to go—stuck beneath the water, knowing that you're going to die. I'd worked a drowning my second year, but it had been down Highway 98, close to Liberty County. David Cravey, just eleven years old. The Craveys had rented a cabin out at the Duna Blanco State Park for a week that summer. I'll never forget the way his father kept looking out at the water, shaking his head, helpless.

"We love this place. We come here every year," he kept saying, as though the water had betrayed him.

Search and rescue recovered the body quickly. A textbook drowning, kid caught in the undertow, a rip tide famous on the Gulf Coast. Growing up here, you knew about it, how the water would wrap around you and pull you out before you knew what happened. It happened to me once, when I was a kid, swimming off of Cape San Vicente. But I'd known to let it take me and swim parallel to the beach. I knew how to get back to shore. Most tourists didn't.I

I knew when I became a police officer that one day, I'd have to work a drowning. I'd tried to prepare myself, but you're never really prepared for death. Afterwards, I'd walked around in a daze for a week. Whenever I saw a kid somewhere, I thought of David Cravey and wondered about all the things he'd never do.

"You remember that kid who drowned a few years ago?"

"Who?"

"David Cravey?"

"The one from Georgia? Yeah. But this is different. It's different when you know them."

"I reckon."

Chris slapped the top of my cruiser. "Let's go. Let's go do this" he said.

On the drive back into town, I kept imagining the scene: Donnie Ray laughing, a can of Natural Light in his hand. He stumbles away from the conversation to take a leak off the back of the boat. Then, he falls into the muddy water and sinks. He wouldn't have screamed. He wouldn't have thrashed around. Television usually lies. Real drowning is quiet. Real drowning can happen in as little as four inches of water. Real drowning happens while the world spins on, oblivious to you, deep in the cold water, the numbed laughter of friends above you where the moonlight blades through the cypress trees and the world fades to nothing.

They found Donnie Ray's body not long after Chris and I had left the landing. The call came over the radio just as we were cresting the overpass into Bay View, a collection of single-wide trailers and tiny sea shacks that sat just outside the city limits, about a mile west of the paper mill.

At night, the paper mill was lit up like Christmas, red, green, and yellow lights everywhere. When I was a kid, the mill ran at one hundred percent. But now, with the national economy in the toilet and the demand for paper down, only a few cars sat in the parking lot. The mill had been on a three-quarter crew for over a year now. The union had saber-rattled in the local newspaper, but these days, it was basically toothless. Years of constant negotiation with management had whittled their power down. The union was a shadow of what it had once been. My father had once been the union president. He was probably spinning in his grave.

I never drove past the paper mill without thinking of him. A sharecropper's son who'd joined the Navy to escape the oppressive heat of the South Alabama peanut farm where he'd grown up, he spent four years in the Navy before discharging to work at a paper mill in Southern Ohio. There, the union had been strong, fearless, untouchable. When he married my mother, a North Florida native he met by chance when her family was visiting family in northern Kentucky, he moved the family south to work at the mill in St. Vincent.

When Chris turned off the highway onto a limestone street that ran parallel to the main road, I thought about the day Janey had died. Cowboy came by my house to deliver the news. I hadn't known how to feel. Numb? Pained? Angry? All of those. How are you supposed to feel about the death of a wife who'd left you, who'd once told you that you had no motivation, no aspirations, no dreams, who'd told you that you were as boring as fishing, a sport you loved and she hated?

The Miles home was a weather-beaten bungalow surrounded by a chain link fence. Out front was a painted sign, *Miles Taxidermy and Processing*, with a phone number beneath it. Patches of grass and weeds made up the front yard, most of it sun scorched and dying. Big Don Miles' black and chrome Chevy dually sat in the granite-rock driveway.

Chris parked across the road from the house, and I pulled in behind him and got out. The night was silent, save for the constant wash of the waves from St. Vincent Bay, just a few hundred yards behind us. My head was throbbing. I wanted a cup of coffee.

"You ready?" I said.

Chris answered by walking across the road, opening the gate, and going into the yard toward the front door. I followed. He knocked, his knuckles barely scraping the door. It had once been blue, but was faded to an old gray, the paint blistered and peeling.

Chris knocked again. "Mr. Miles?"

I unclipped the Maglite from my belt and tapped the door loudly. "Mr. Don Miles?"

A light came on inside. Stumbling. Muffled voices. "Hang on," someone said. A man's voice, groggy, deep. Big Don. The porch light came on, blinding us. I covered my eyes and winced at the fresh, sharp pain shooting through my forehead.

The knob jerked back and forth before the door opened. Big Don Miles filled up the frame. He was taller than Cowboy. He shared his son's beard, but Big Don's was streaked through with white. He had long curly hair. He wore only a pair of boxer shorts, his hairy beer belly hanging out over the waist band. In his left hand, he held a revolver of some kind—a Colt, maybe.

At the sight of the gun, both Chris and I jumped back, hands on our pistols. "Apalachee County Sheriff's Department. Please put that gun down," Chris said, his voice edged, official.

Big Don studied us for a long, painful second. I thumbed back the release on my holster.

"Mr. Miles," Chris said.

"The hell do ya'll want this time of night?" he said. He let the pistol turn over in his hand and held it forward. Smart. Showed us that he didn't want any trouble. Chris took it.

"I got a permit for that," he said.

"Don? What's going on?" A woman's voice sounded from the back of the house. Donnie Ray's mama.

"Nothing," he shouted. "Go back to sleep."

Chris took the pistol and opened the cylinder and poured the bullets into his hand. Up close, I could see it: a .357. It could put holes the size of pine stumps in a man.

"Mr. Miles," Chris said, "can we talk for a minute?"

Big Don's jaw slacked. I'm sure he turned a shade of gray, too, but squinting in the porch light, I saw only a large shadow of a man who suddenly hunched forward, as though someone had hit him from behind.

"Is it Donnie Ray?" he said, his voice a rasped whisper.

"Can we come in?" Chris said.

I swatted at a moth and Big Don stared at me. "Yeah. Come in," he said and turned around.

The house smelled like cigarettes and beer. The living room was relatively clean, though: piles of newspapers here and there, an overflowing ashtray on the coffee table. Several mounted fish, squirrel, and deer heads hung on the walls. A gun cabinet stood near the hallway. On the wall behind the couch hung a few pictures of the family, all of them sharing the same red or strawberry-blonde hair, all of them with pale complexions.

"What time is it?" Big Don said.

I glanced down at my watch. "It's about a quarter till four."

He yawned and scratched at his chest, his fingers passing through the thick patch of gray there. He had an ornate anchor tattooed on his left arm. On his other arm was a cross. He had several other tattoos, too, some tiny, some large. On his right forearm, he had Donnie Ray's full name, *Donald*

Rayford Miles and a date beneath it. Donnie Ray's birthday. On top of Donnie Ray's name was another name with a date: *Molly Cecille Miles.* Donnie Ray's sister.

We stood in the living room, forming a semicircle around a worn coffee table.

"Mr. Miles, I am afraid that we—" Chris began.

"You boys want some coffee?" he said, his voice monotone.

"Oh my Lord. Oh my God. What happened?" someone said. We turned toward the hallway. Donnie Ray's mama stood there, wrapped in a housecoat. Tears streamed down her cheeks. Graying auburn hair hung down in her face. Her mouth hung open, her words little more than a shaped wail: "Oh my Lord. Oh my God. What happened? You tell me what happened."

I wanted a cup of coffee and felt bad for wanting it. I wondered if I looked as nervous as I felt. "Mrs. Miles," I said, "can we sit down?" That's what Cowboy had said to me when he told me Janey was dead.

She was frozen in place. "No. No you can't. You need to leave. This is our home."

"Shut up, Betty," Big Don said. He scratched himself and looked at Chris. "Is he dead?"

"Yes," Chris said. "We're sorry to have to tell you, but there was an accident."

"What happened?" Big Don said.

"It's still being investigated," I said.

"He drowned," Chris said.

"Were they up at the houseboat?" Big Don said.

Chris nodded. The room stood still. I realized I was holding my breath, waiting on something. I didn't know what.

"Oh my God," Donnie Ray's mama started saying, first under her breath and then louder and louder. Her voice trailed to a whisper. Then, she fell silent, mouthing the words again and again.

"Mrs. Miles," I said. "Why don't you sit down right here?" I took her elbow, tried to move her toward the couch, so the family photos would be behind her.

"Well Goddamn," Big Don said. He put his hands on his hips and took a deep breath. "Well just Goddamn." He turned and went into the kitchen. Water started running. He was making coffee.

"Oh my God," Mrs. Miles said.

Chris and I locked eyes and he gestured at Donnie Ray's mama and went into the kitchen, leaving the two us alone.

I sat down on the couch a cushion down from her and rested my elbows on my knee, laced my fingers, and tried to think of something to say.

I couldn't help thinking of my own mama, the day Dad died, how calm she'd seemed, not like Mrs. Miles at all, who looked as though she might be going into shock. She held her hands beneath her chin and rocked back and forth, whispering, "Oh my God, oh my God, oh my God."

"I'm so sorry about this," I said. I'd never done a notification before. In the movies and on TV, the camera cuts away as soon as the police officers arrive. Sometimes, you hear a scream, hear some crying, see a mama break down into tears. But the movies never stay with the scene, never show you what happens when silence fills the room like salt water.

Chris and Big Don were talking in the kitchen, their voices muffled.

"What happened?" she said after a minute. "How did he—how did—what happened?"

I took a breath. "It looks like he fell overboard." I stopped, started to speak, and stopped again.

"Was he drinking?" she said.

"I don't know. But probably. Yeah." I didn't know for certain, but I'd have been willing to bet that the toxicology report would show that Donnie Ray was blitzed.

"Was Jimmy Danley up there?" It was Big Don. He stood in the kitchen doorway, a blue and white oversized mug of coffee steaming in his hand. Just behind him, Chris stood in the shadow of the kitchen light.

I was about to say "Yes, he was," but Chris spoke first.

"We're not really sure. There were several people up there. The sheriff's department is investigating right now. The sheriff's up at the landing. So is the county investigator."

"Davis Malone? That yankee?" Big Don said and took a sip of coffee. I studied his feet. He wore a pair of moccasin-style slippers.

"That Danley's a troublemaker," Mrs. Miles said and I wanted to laugh. Donnie Ray Miles was a troublemaker, too.

"That boy's always up to no good," Big Don said. He came into the living room and sat in a brown leather recliner.

"They're investigating," I said.

"He already said that," Big Don said, gesturing at Chris with his coffee cup. He took a sip. "Was Wayne up there?" He spoke to Chris.

"Well, it's like I said. We're not sure who all was up there."

We all fell silent for a few moments. I wondered who the hell Wayne was and nearly asked, but Chris said, "Someone from the department will be in touch with you," and stood up.

I was thinking about coffee, and I wanted some. The smell had permeated the house, but we needed to get out of there, let them figure this out on their own.

"I've got to call Molly," Mrs. Miles said.

Chris and I went to the door.

"Seems a Goddamned shame," Big Don said.

"We're very sorry for your loss," Chris said, his voice robotic, trained.

"Boy went all the way to Iraq to fight towelheads and dies right here, right here at home." He took a sip of coffee.

I looked at the photos behind the couch again. Something seemed off about the pictures, but I couldn't place it. My mind felt foggy, distant.

"You all take care. You have our sympathies," Chris said and we walked outside. The eastern sky was beginning to glow just a bit. By six, the sun would be up, and I hoped that I'd be home. I wanted this night to be over. I looked back at the Miles residence and thought about how Big Don made his money—stuffing dead animals, mounting them for people to remember them. He was preserving memories, really, capturing moments in time. I wondered how he'd remember this night.

"I'm headed back up to the north end," Chris said. We stood by the door of my cruiser. The engine rumbled, the governor set low. We rarely turned them off during our shifts. They were made to stay on for hours, if need be.

"You going back to the landing?" I said.

"Probably not. I'd just get in the way. I'll radio Cowboy, tell him we took care of this."

I opened my car door. "All right, then."

"I know this was hard on you, man. I do."

"Why?" I said, feigning ignorance. I didn't want to talk.

"With Janey and everything," he said. I wouldn't look him in the eyes.

"I'm fine. I'm going to get a cup of coffee," I said and put the car in gear.

"All right, man. All right. Take care," Chris said and tapped the top of the car with his hand. I backed up and swerved around him. In the rear view, he watched me pull away.

Inside right now, Big Don and Betty Miles were coming to the realization that their son was dead. I knew the feeling. I'd been dealing with it for months. I kept thinking of Donnie Ray Miles sinking beneath the waters of the Apalachicola. The water wove its way down through bayous and cricks, all the way down to the Gulf of Mexico. The water was older than St. Vincent, older than all of us here. It would be here long after Donnie Ray was buried beneath the sandy soil, a wet earth so different.

When I crested the overpass, it struck me why the pictures in the Miles' living room seemed off. Despite the numerous pictures of Donnie

Ray from high school—his senior portrait, his football shots—there wasn't a single photo of him in his Army uniform. Perhaps it wasn't so strange; perhaps they were ashamed that he'd been drummed out for drug use. But the absence was strange, like a desert with no sand, like a an ocean with no salt.

2

After my shift ended, I radioed the sheriff's department and asked about the drowning. No one knew much. The medical examiner had to drive down from Tallahassee. The autopsy would be that afternoon. Mack had let Jimmy, Tater, and Freddy go. No reason to keep them. I thought that Jimmy knew more than he told Mack or Davis Malone. I thought Mack should have kept him around a little longer. No doubt there was paraphernalia on the houseboat, probably a bag of weed, a roach or two. I'd have played it differently. Jimmy Danley knew something. I could feel it in my gut.

Jimmy was a tall guy with long arms and a long face. He reminded me of an angled toothbrush with his close-cropped hair and hunched forward shoulders. He kept a trimmed goatee and always had a toothpick sticking out of the corner of his mouth. I'd fantasized about punching him and sending that spike deep into his throat. Like Donnie Ray, he'd grown up out in Bay View among the single-wides and one-room shacks along the canal. He had a deadbeat daddy who'd split years ago and a mama who'd gone to jail more than once for selling food stamps. His older brother Timmy was serving time in state prison for an armed robbery. Jimmy was like every other Danley—a first-class loser. If anyone knew what happened on that houseboat, Jimmy knew. And the sheriff had cut him loose. I shook my head and my stomach growled. I was starving.

I'd finished my shift east of town, driving along the highway. I drive through the residential area of town and crossed into downtown St. Vincent, a single road flanked by old storefronts and a crumbling sidewalk. Over the years, many of the businesses had closed. Tyner's Furniture had newspaper in the widows. Rex's TV Repair was open only on Saturday mornings. The Video Den was open, but only in the afternoons. Only the Dollar Store kept full-time hours. I parked my cruiser in the alley behind the Dollar Store and Charlie's Cafe, the one full-time restaurant in town.

I liked Charlie Mason, an older guy who'd worked with my father at the paper mill, running paper machines, turning pulp into corrugated sheets that later become cardboard. This had been in the early 1980s, back when a three-month strike effectively shut down St. Vincent.

My father had been an architect of that strike. As the union president, he'd led the workers in their charge for better wages and safer working conditions. Both Aaron and I had grown up hearing tales of Vince Everson, the union president who saved the mill. Charlie kept a picture of Dad hanging behind the cash register, speaking at a podium in front of the Papermakers Labor Union meeting.

At 7:00 a.m., only three people were in the restaurant eating. Dean Schroeder, who cut meat at the Piggly Wiggly two blocks over, was having pancakes and coffee. Mr. Bobby Platt, a retired architect who lived out on the cape, sat by front window. He always wore white shorts and a loose-fitting t-shirt. This morning, he had on a University of Florida baseball cap. Charile's had a side room with more tables. Somebody was in there reading a newspaper, occasionally flipping the pages.

"How do, Mr. Everson?" Charlie said. He stuck his head through the window into the kitchen behind the register. The place smelled like bacon and syrup.

"Good. I'd do better with some grits and scrambled eggs."

"Be right out. Help yourself to coffee. You want some sausage, too?"

"Yeah."

"I only got patties this morning. I'm out of smoked."

"That's fine."

I walked around behind the counter and poured a cup, enjoying the stream that rose from the strong black brew. Charlie could brew a good cup of coffee. I like his mugs: big, thick, beige, utilitarian. I poured in some half and half and dusted the top with some sugar.

"You work that drowning last night?" Charlie called from the kitchen.

"Yeah," I said and took an open table. Somebody had left a pamphlet for some vacation rentals in St. Mark's, out the other side of Apalachicola. I flipped through the flashy brochure, wondering how on earth anyone could afford such prices.

"People already talking about it?"

"Heard it on the scanner," he said. "Boy was your age, wasn't he, Justin?"

"Yes sir," I said and took a sip of coffee. I knew that I shouldn't drink it before I went home, but I didn't figure that I'd get much sleep today.

Charlie came out of the kitchen. Short and stocky, he was built like a dock pylon—solid, sturdy. He had bright white hair and a thick, western-style mustache. He had a deep voice that reminded me of a boat horn, low and resonant. He set the plate in front of me. It smelled wonderful and salty and fresh. I began to eat, quicker than I meant to, and I started coughing.

"Slow down, big boy," Charlie said. "There's more where that come from."

I stopped and took a long drink of coffee. "Yeah, I know. I know. Long night."

We sat in silence for a few minutes, me eating, Charlie nursing his own cup of coffee. Dean Schroeder chewed loudly and sipped his coffee. Mr. Platt coughed and cleared his throat. Whoever was eating in the side room flipped the newspaper pages. Country music warbled softly from a tinny-sounding radio in the kitchen. No one else came in.

Dean Schroeder broke the silence. "Well, Charlie, I reckon I better settle up. We got a truck coming later this morning, and I need to be there."

Charlie stood up, walked over to the cash register, and punched a few buttons. "Ya'll got ground chuck on sale this week?"

"Yes sir, yes sir," Dean said. "Come on by. I'll set you up a deal."

Charlie took Dean's money and made change from the drawer. "I'll be by later, after Luann gets in."

"Yes sir, yes sir," Dean said again. He turned toward the door and opened it. A tiny bell rang.

"Be good, boys. Be good. Good seeing you, Justin. I still think about your old daddy all the time. How's your mama doing?"

"She's all right. She lives up there where Aaron lives now, outside Atlanta," I said. "Moved up there to be closer to the grandkids."

"How many young'uns does your brother have?"

"Two. Girls. Keeps him busy."

"Tell her come by see me if she comes to town."

I nodded, thankful that he'd not mentioned Janey. "Thanks, Mr. Schroeder. See you soon."

"Bye-bye," Dean said. The door closed behind him.

Charlie came back and sat with me. I'd finished eating. I was resting my head against the wall, thinking of refilling my coffee when something strange happened. Somehow, I saw the restaurant in third person—from a camera's eye view above the entire place. I could see me, sitting there, my fingers laced behind my head. Charlie sat in front of me, leaned forward on his elbows. Mr. Platt spooned up the last of his oatmeal. And there, at another table, sat Donnie Ray Miles, dressed in the same ripped jeans and blue shirt he'd been wearing that day at Harley's Bait and Tackle, the last time I'd seen him. He was drinking a cup of coffee and eating a plate of grits and scramble eggs and patty sausage.

The flash lasted only an instant. Donnie Ray was gone.

I must have jumped, startled. The table rocked and coffee sloshed. "You okay?" Charlie said, cocking an eyebrow.

"I'm fine." I shook my head and rubbed my eyes. I looked over at the table where Donnie Ray had been sitting. Other than a black and white pair of salt and pepper shakers and a greasy napkin box, it was empty. I rubbed my eyes again.

"You sure? Looked like you fell asleep."

"Maybe. Yes. Yes. I'm fine," I said. "I think I need to get some rest."

He studied me. "How are you doing?"

"I'm all right. I'm good."

"You look a lot like your mama, son. Did you know that?"

I nodded. "I've heard that." Aaron looked like my father, tall, broad-shoulder, wide. I was of Cochrane stock, my mother's side—slight, thin, and weedy. I got my father's height, though, so I was built like a telephone pole.

"You hear from her lately?" Charlie said.

"Mama? No, not really. I call her every now and again. She came down for a while after Janey died. I don't know what for. She's good."

"Tell her I said hello."

"I will."

We fell silent for a moment as I ate. "Did you know that boy who died, Donnie Miles?"

"Yeah, but not to know him. Not really. We graduated together."

"He used to hang around down at Tommy Parrot's some nights. Him and his whole crew. Me and Luann was in there one night watching the football game. What's his name, that Danley character? He was drunk as hell. Hollering at the screen. Donnie Ray just sat there, silent but almost shaking, you know? Like he was mad about something. The bartender asked them to keep it down, and they left after she threatened to call you guys."

"That sounds about right. Danley's a first-class dick."

"He should have joined the Army, too."

I laughed, unable to picture Jimmy in fatigues. "He'd have been kicked out just like Donnie Ray."

"Do you know the full story on that?"

I shook my head. "Nope. Everybody says he was dealing pot."

"I heard the same thing. It's a shame. His old man was in the Navy a long time ago. Did you know that?"

I didn't. I thought back to the tattoos on Big Don's arms. The anchor. It made sense. "No. My dad was in the Navy, too," I said.

Three men came into the diner, dock workers or shrimpers. All three had sun-dark mahogany complexions. They looked tired and worn, pulled as thin as frayed rope. Deep-sunk eyes. Sharp cheekbones. Clawson's employees. They sat at a table near the back of the restaurant by a window and took up menus.

"Good morning, fellas," Charlie said and stood up. "What can I get you?"

"Morning. Coffee," one said. "For all of us."

Clawson's Fisheries was the second-largest employer in town, next to the paper mill. Nearly a thousand folks worked for the fishery. It had a fleet of close to thirty shrimp boats to its name. On top of that, a lot of independent contractors shrimped for Clawsons. The place had warehouses in Destin and Pensacola.

Frederick Clawson himself was a bootstrap story that everyone knew, a kind of good old-fashioned American enterprise fairy tale. He'd grown up in nearby Apalachicola and had started the fishery with a single shrimp trawler back in 1965. By the early '90s, he owned a huge fleet of trawlers and had on contract fishermaenn and shrimpers up and down the Gulf Coast, from Destin to Eastpoint. He made tons of money selling redfish, shrimp, and oysters, exporting the catch all over the nation and beyond. A Discovery Channel documentary had shot some footage at the fishery several years ago and used it in a special about commercial fishing. It was the one place my father swore he'd never work and the one man he forbade me to ever work for.

"He's a crook," Dad said on more than once occasion. "Fred Clawson is a carpetbagger. No. He's worse than a carpetbagger because he's from here. He's exploiting the very people who made his money possible."

People said Clawson could squeeze blood from a stone. The company prided itself on efficiency, running shrimp boats on skeleton crews, laying off workers during slow times with little to no warning. Everyone in town knew that Clawson had little tolerance for unions. Even though Florida's right-to-work status kept the union's power in check, he still feared the power of a labor organization. Supposedly, he'd quashed several attempts to unionize the dock workers and fishermen. My father summed up Fred Clawson this way: "He loves money more than he loves people."

Charlie brought the coffee out and took the fishermen's orders and disappeared into the kitchen. I kept thinking about my dad and his dislike of Fred Clawson. I must have zoned out because after a moment, I realized that one of the shrimpers was looking at me. He had a thin face with rounded cheek bones. He had a goatee the color of a deer's coat. His features defied age. He could have been twenty-five. He could have been forty.

"Did we do something wrong?" he said. He didn't have the strong accent I expected. There was an educated clip to his voice.

"No," I said. "Sorry. I just sort of zoned out there for a second."

"Then why are you staring us down?"

"I'm not staring you down," I said. "I'm just leaving." I started to stand up.

No one spoke for a moment. Then, he said, "All right, then." He smiled to himself, amused. I was put off by him, but I didn't have the energy to deal with an asshole.

"I worked graveyard last night," I said and trailed off. The three of them were studying me the way you might look at a child who'd wandered up in the middle of a conversation. One of the men drummed his fingers on the desk. The tops of his knuckles were crisscrossed with scars.

"No problem, officer," the one with the goatee said. He nodded and I looked away. His accent bothered me. Something in the sharp way he broke off words reminded me of a teacher's voice, articulate and pronounced.

I stood up just as Charlie came out of the kitchen with a basket of toast for their table. "I got to run, Charlie," I said.

"Sure thing," he said and put the toast on the table. "Food will be out in a minute, fellas."

At the cash register, I handed over a ten dollar bill. "Keep it," I said.

"Now, hang on, hang on," he said, counting change. "You know I ain't keeping this." It was useless to argue with him. I let him count bills into my hand but refused the coins. He dropped them back in the register.

"Be careful out there," Charlie said. I opened the door to leave and glanced over my shoulder at the three shrimpers. They were sipping coffee and talking quietly. I wondered what their day held.

"Justin?" Charlie said and I looked back at him. "You need to get some rest, son. Have you thought about taking some time off?"

I shook my head. Chris had suggested the same thing. Mack would have given me the time had I asked. "No. I don't think I need it. I like working. I'm fine."

"Well, you might not be the best one to assess that," Charlie said. I could tell he wanted to say more, but he didn't. "You just take her easy, okay? Come back in sometime. Next breakfast's on me."

"Thanks, Charlie," I said and walked onto the street. The sun shone bright over the water. A few clouds floated here and there. Otherwise, the sky was a sheet of blue. Right across the road from Charlie's, the city pier stretched down to the bay. A small dock ran along the edge of the water, a tiny, skeletal structure that often reeked of seagull shit.

How had I seen Donnie Ray in the restaurant? A dream? Could you dream while you were wide awake? I pinched my nose and closed my eyes tight. The headache was returning.

I leaned against the side of the restaurant and lit a cigarette. My hand rested on a newspaper box—the *St. Vincent Sentinel*, a big name for such a small paper. I was fishing in my pocket for quarters when the door to Charlie's opened and she stepped out.

Dirty blonde hair hung down around her face in loose curls. A pale complexion. A small build—compact, lean. She held her arms across her chest, her lips drawn into a thin frown. Denise Miles. She had a sharp nose and thin, feline eyes. Like the rest of the Miles clan, she had a dusting of faded red freckles all over her face, but most prominent on her nose and cheeks. My breath caught in my throat. I'd not seen her in several years.

She'd graduated a year ahead of me, a quiet but fierce girl who wore black t-shirts emblazoned with heavy metal band logos. I nursed a heavy-duty crush on her for years. Back then, I was little more than shadow in the hallway at school. I thought that she'd gone off to college. I had no idea that she was in town.

"Well, hello," I said. "I haven't see you in a long time." I wanted say something about being sorry for her loss, but I'd heard that phrase so much myself, I'd grown to hate it. Plus, I didn't know if she knew about Donnie Ray.

"Are you guys following me or something?" she said. She stared at me.

"What?"

"I told that asshole Nuegent and that Yankee cop, what his name? Malone? I told them I wasn't even up there last night." Her mascara had run down from the corners of her eyes. She'd been crying. The black streaks had dried on her face, and tiny flecks of glitter shone there.

"I didn't—I wasn't," I said, looking for words.

"Well, I wasn't up there." She turned to walk across the road and I saw it: the green Mazda 626 that had been parked up at the landing not four hours ago.

"Your car was," I said. The words came before I could stop them.

She spun around. "If it's any of your damned business—and it's not, by the way—my boyfriend was driving my car last night."

"Who?"

"Are you an officer or detective? Because you ask a hell of lot of questions. My God, I can't even get a bite to eat. Some asshole wakes me up at five in the Goddamned morning . . ." she trailed off, muttering to herself.

"You don't remember me, do you?"

She gave me a once-over, flicking her eyes up and down my body. "Justin Everson, officer of the law and international man of mystery. Is that about right?"

"I'm sorry about your cousin," I said.

"Am I supposed to say 'thank you'?"

She opened the door to the car and looked back at me. "And Donnie Ray wasn't thrown out of the Army for dealing dope. You should get your facts straight before you start shooting your mouth off, even if you are a high-and-mighty 'officer of the law.'" I could hear the air quotes. "Everybody in this shitty little town is in everybody else's business."

"What was it, then?" I said. I didn't expect her to answer. But I wanted her to stay. I wanted to restart the conversation.

She slammed the door and rolled down the window. "You ask too many questions," she said and lit a cigarette. She put on a pair of over-sized dark sunglasses and backed out of the parking spot, drove slowly to the highway, and turned right, headed out toward Bay View.

I got in the cruiser and laid my head against the headrest. My heart was beating fast, and I smiled at my own crush, the first feelings I'd had for anyone in a long time. But this was stupid. Her boyfriend was undoubtedly Jimmy Danley. I couldn't see her with Tater. And no way would she hook up with Freddy Richards. A pang of jealousy shot through me and I laughed aloud. My chuckle sounded forced. I wanted to go home, turn on the History Channel, and do nothing. I hoped that there was some documentary on about ghosts or UFOs or demons.

I put the car in reverse and thought about Donnie Ray again. What had happened up there last night? Had he gotten so drunk he just fell in? And what did happen to him in the Army? Why was he gone only two years? The heat: it must have been so very different from the sopping humidity of North Florida. I tried to imagine waking up every morning in some hellish desert, so far away from here, so removed from St. Vincent Bay, from the stink of the paper mill, from the salt water, from these familiar streets and names and faces I thought I knew so well.

3

Leaving Charile's, I drove east on the highway, took a left on Bayou Boulevard, and headed down toward my neighborhood, a collection of 1960's-style homes with tiny front yards and chain link fences. When my father built our house back in early 1970s, St. Vincent had a population of 8,000. Now, it had grown to close to 12,000, mostly mill workers and fishermen. The town split along the railroad tracks, mostly white people living to the east, mostly black people living on the southwest side, right in the shadow of the mill, a tiny community everyone in town called the South Side.

A lot of folks worked for the railroad, too, and some worked in the various shops around St. Vincent. The town didn't have a police department, so the Apalachee County Sheriff's Department was in charge of all areas of law enforcement.

I parked the cruiser in the front yard, angling the bumper right up to the front door of my house, the same one I'd grown up in, the one Janey and I had shared two years of marriage in. She hated that we lived here, even though my mom had sold us the house for a song. She was moving to North Georgia to be closer to Aaron and the grandkids, so she let it go for next to nothing. Janey thought the house was another reason I'd never change, another tether to the past I couldn't let go,

Inside, I stripped of my clothes and turned on the shower and stood in the hot water for a long time, imagining the steam cleansing my lungs. I coughed and wondered if Chris was right. Smoking probably was killing me. It killed my dad, I assume. Heart disease. He never knew what hit him. The doctor called it a "violent myocardial rupture."

In the bedroom, I sat on the side of the bed and stared at a framed map of the Gulf Coast hanging on the south wall, one of Janey's decorations that I'd never taken down. Janey loved maps. When she moved in, she immediately began to make it hers. Mama's decorations were strictly religious, old-school protestant—crosses hanging on the walls and little plaques with Bible quotes inlaid in them.

Janey got rid of all that. She put up fancy picture frames with maps of places that she wanted to visit. She brought an old antique globe from a shop in Apalachicola and set it in the corner of the living room, right in the spot where Mama had kept a huge, oversized family Bible that traced our family tree back four generations. Janey threw away the plastic clips that held the living room curtains open and replaced them with this woven rope that looked like the kind of line you used to tie a ship to a dock. By the time she got done with the house, it didn't look much like the place I'd grown up. The nautical theme made the place feel like a houseboat. I'd once loved it. Now, I felt like a stranger here.

I lay back and closed my eyes knowing that I wouldn't sleep. I'd become used to this. I'd lie awake for a while and drift into a memory, maybe Janey, the wind in her auburn hair, the warmth of her hand in my palm. But somehow, the world stayed with me. I could never lose myself completely. The insomnia had started after Janey died.

After a while, I got up, put on some jeans and a t-shirt, and wandered into the living room. I turned on the TV and tried to find a show about the supernatural, a documentary about ghosts or Area 51 or Bigfoot. But all I could find was some celebrity waxing poetic about a medium who told her that her house was occupied by a demon. I snorted and turned off the TV and went into the backyard.

The shed was filled with boxes of old stuff, things that Mama had left behind. It was big shed, fifteen by fifteen. Beyond the old boxes, it held some fishing equipment that I'd once used regularly. I turned on the fluorescent light and waited as the two cylinders popped and glowed to life. I took down one of the fishing poles, an eight-foot surf rod I'd had since I was a teenager. I'd bought it as a combo pack, one of those cheap models that bait and tackle stores sell for weekend tourists. I'd replaced the factory reel with a Daiwa spinning reel. I hadn't wet a line in a long time. I cradled the rod in my hands and imagined casting a silver spoon jig into the wind.

Janey and I had been separated when she died. The divorce papers were likely in a manila envelope on the county solicitor's desk the morning that Cowboy stopped by the house, knocked on the storm door, and told me that Janey had been killed. He wanted to stay and talk. He wanted to see how I was doing. But I told him to leave. I went back into our bedroom and sat on the edge of the queen sized bed. The room smelled of her—the cucumber-melon soap she used, the lilac perfume. I laid back on the bed and wondered how to feel. I'd worked graveyard the night before. I needed rest. No one at the department would have blamed me if I'd taken the night off. But sleep wouldn't come. That had been three months ago. I'd hardly slept a wink since.

Now, standing in the sparse light of the shed, I wondered how much of my love for everything seemed to have died with Janey. I considered getting in the truck and driving down to the bay to spend the afternoon fishing. But it was too late in the day to catch anything. I felt bone-weary at the thought of loading the truck with tackle, poles, and an ice chest. Besides, I had to work graveyard. I put the rod back and went inside. The house was cold and dry, the dust motes in the air like insects, alive.

I liked graveyard. When I'd first been hired, working from 11:00 p.m. to seven in the morning had been a real challenge. I've never been a late-night guy. At first, those long, dead hours scared me. St. Vincent seemed like a different town. The houses and streets didn't look sinister as much as they looked different. Small things: An empty tire swing swaying in the breeze. A live oak tree by the court house looked unfamiliar, a skeletal, hoary hand reaching up out of the sandy soil. The first time I worked the late shift, those images haunted me. I couldn't drive down a familiar street without whipping my head back and forth, hunting the shadows for the thing that made this all seem so different.

After a few months, though, I began to think of graveyard as *my* shift. Particularly since Janey died, I felt changed, too. Maybe I was like this town: different at night, subtly changed, an aberration. When I got in my cruiser, I no longer worried about staying awake. I knew the night would be there, steady, waiting on me.

The night after Donnie Ray died, I went to work thinking of him and wondering if what Denise had said was right. I'd assumed he'd been kicked out of the Army for dealing dope. That story made sense, given his past. Denise probably didn't know the whole story. And even if she did, she'd have defended him. Denise was a Miles. Blood runs thick, particularly in places like Apalachee County.

Around midnight, my radio crackled, "Apalachee to One-twelve." Sheila Sanders was working dispatch. She'd been a dispatcher longer than I'd been a deputy, a fixture around the department with her frizzy blond hair and over-sized cat sweaters, woven, ugly patterned things that she wore even in the heat of summer.

"Go ahead," I said.

"Got a trespassing report out at Sandy Head Beach."

"Where at?"

More squelch.

"2401 Juniper Drive. It's an old house in Gulfaire. Being restored. Neighbor called and said he seen a flashlight."

"10-4. I'll check it out," I said and turned the car around. I was right across the street from the Swifty. As I pulled out onto the highway, the lights of the paper mill came into view. I drove toward them, edged the South Side, crested the overpass, passed through Bay View, and headed down a stretch of road crowded up to the shoulder with neat rows of pine trees, St. Vincent Papermaker's land.

Sandy Head was a small beach community just northwest of St. Vincent, about a three mile drive outside the city limits. All the roads looked the same, each one a pine-lined narrow drive that you can miss if you're not looking closely. I slowed to a crawl and used my side-light, trying to spot Juniper Drive. Many of the homes had been on Sandy Head since the early 1960s, when this land was still cheap. They were beach bungalows, mostly, small two- and three-bedroom shacks with tiny yards, all painted various pastel colors. In the 1990s, Clearwater Realty had built a few condos out here and had sold them quickly. The company bought a bunch of land along the beach, hoping to turn Sandy Head into another Panama City Beach or Seaside. When the national economy fell into the toilet after 9/11, all construction stopped. Sewer pipes stuck out of the sand here and there where home sites had been cordoned off. Plans had been drawn up, but no one had the money to complete the projects.

Juniper was a few miles past the bungalows, a street that drove into a subdivision called Gulfaire, a neighborhood of bloated mini-mansions built in the 1980s. The place was gated, a small office divided Juniper into two lanes. No one was in the office this time of night. The gate stood open. I drove through and crept along, reading the out-of-state license plates that lined the edge of the road: Tennessee, Georgia, Alabama, South Carolina. The homes hid behind sculpted laws and palm trees.

I parked and got out, shining my Maglite up at the address Sheila mentioned, a Cape Cod-style home trimmed in aqua and blue. Several stacks of new shingles and a few bags of beach sand sat in the yard. The flower bed out front had been dug up. Three boxes of Sears-brand shutters leaned against the wall by the front door. I kicked at a bag of cedar chips, sniffed, expecting a pleasant aroma. Instead, I gagged. The unmistakable tang of marijuana hung in the air.

I bounced the flashlight here and there, thinking that I might catch someone running, but hoping that I wouldn't find anyone at all. I clicked the radio on my right shoulder.

"One-twelve to Apalachee."

"Go ahead," Sheila said.

"I don't see anything." I walked around the side of the house. "Somebody was definitely out here. Probably teenagers, but they're gone now."

"You want Chris to drive down there?"

"No. I'm just gonna look around and head back to town."

I walked around the side of the house and looked up at the second floor. A large picture window stared out over the backyard. The inside was probably gorgeous, the kind of home that I'd never be able to afford, where the sun is your alarm clock and all's right with the world.

I was shining my flashlight in the front windows when something fell in the backyard.

I froze and crouched, right hand on the Beretta Px4 Storm .45 on my hip. I thumbed the holster's safety loose, listening. Something had fallen on concrete, maybe a shovel or a rake. I edged the east wall and looked around the corner. The marijuana smell was stronger back here. I realized that I had to pee and cursed under my breath.

I aimed the Maglite at the screened back porch and zipped the beam back and forth. A kidney-shaped pool sat enclosed in a screened cover. Natural stone edged it, not that hard stuff that cuts your feet when you walk on it. Somebody was spending a lot of money on this place: an outdoor kitchen with a gas grill, all stainless steel. A cooler. A firepit.

I tried the door to the screened porch and it opened. My pulse thumped like a cricket. Something was amiss. This place should have been locked. I let the door close with my hip. I strained, listening for breathing, anything. *Call backup* my mind said. *Call backup now. You don't know who's in here.*

"Nobody," I said in a whisper. I felt silly, freaking myself out over this. The lack of sleep was getting to me. Who did I expect to find, the Mob? I stood up straight and laughed. This was stupid. I turned around, went back in the yard, and peed beside one of the bushes by the house. I zipped up and walked back toward the back porch, shining the Maglite here and there. Nothing. I'd just about decided to leave when I heard the breathing.

Short, shallow breaths. I tried not to show that I'd heard. I studied the side of the house, as though I were looking at the décor, trying find the source of the sound.

Someone rushed me from my right, and I caught his arm, turned him around, and kicked him in the seat of his shorts. He stumbled forward, ripping the screen out of the storm door with his right hand, catching himself from falling with his left. His face hit the wall and he groaned.

The Beretta jumped in my hand on reflex—three point stance, safety thumbed back. I held the pistol leveled at him as he turned over. Blood ran freely from both nostrils. He'd hit the ground hard. A shadow to my right moved and I drew down on whoever it was.

"Hands," I yelled. "Let me see your Goddamned hands. Now!" My heart was a clenched fist, pulsing with pressure.

"Don't shoot me! Don't shoot me!" he shouted, holding up his hands. I squinted at him and lowered the pistol.

Teenagers. The one on the ground looked to be maybe fifteen or sixteen, thin, long hair combed down into his face. He wore a pair of shorts two sizes too big and a white t-shirt with the word "Loser" across his chest. His buddy wore a bowling shirt and his own pair of oversized shorts. Both wore Crocs. I hated Crocs.

"What the hell are you two doing out here? Does the word 'private property' mean anything to you?"

The kid with the bloody nose sneered. "That's two words, actually."

"Smart ass," I said. "I ought to shoot you on GP."

"Don't shoot me on GP," his friend said, holding his hands up high. "What's GP?"

"General principle," I said. I lowered my pistol. "Put your hands down, partner. Walk." Neither moved.

"Where are we going?" the one in the Loser shirt said.

"Around front. Let's go. Get up."

The one in the bowling shirt seemed scared to move. "Put your Goddamned hands down and go," I said. This was the last thing I wanted to deal with tonight: two morons. I thought about all the sleep I'd missed lately and felt bone-weary, tired.

The kid in the bowling shirt helped his friend up, and they shuffled ahead of me. We walked around the front of the house. I was half-worried that one of the little bastards would bolt, but I didn't have the energy to care. They looked harmless, and all they appeared to be doing was smoking some weed in an empty house. We walked back to my cruiser and I put one of them—the one with the bowling shirt—in the backseat of the car. He began wailing.

"I can't go to jail. Please don't take me to jail."

"Relax, kid," I said. "Just sit tight."

I took Mr. Bloody Nose back to the trunk.

Headlights flooded the cul-de-sac and an Apalachee County Crown Victoria cruiser pulled to a stop. Chris opened the door and got out and slammed his door. It echoed in the night.

"What's the word, hummingbird?" he said.

"Sheila radio you?"

"Yep."

"These two morons were trying to start a hippie commune."

"It's my dad's house," long hair said. "My stupid mom and her stupid new husband stole it from him. Plus, this guy pissed on it," he said and pointed at me. "You hear me? He *pissed* on my dad's house. That's a crime. Then he busted my nose. For no reason."

Chris cut his eyes at me and laughed. "Pissed on the house? Did he now?"

I sighed and nodded over my shoulder at the kid in my backseat. All three of us could hear his sobs.

"Talk to him," I said to Chris. "Get his story."

"They can't take us to jail," long hair said. "This is my dad's house. It's like private property." He wiped his nose and swallowed. His "Loser" shirt was streaked with dark red stains.

I grabbed him by the arm. "It's not *like* private property, nimrod. It *is* private property. Now what the hell were you two doing?"

"Exercising my freedom as an American," he said and held my eyes. I had to hand it to him: the kid had some balls.

"Well, Thomas Jefferson, I don't suppose you have any ID on you, then?"

He fumbled in the oversized cargo shorts and gave me a wallet. Inside, I found a condom that had obviously been there for a long, long time; an Apalachee County High lunch pass; a house key; a five dollar bill; and a learner's permit. Long hair's name was Chad Whitley. I looked from the ID to him. I knew the name. Joe Whitley was a lawyer who had an office in downtown St. Vincent, a fat cat. He had a reputation as a divorce lawyer. He was going through a nasty public divorce.

"You're Joe Whitley's kid, aren't you?"

"Maybe," he said.

"Your dad's a lawyer, right?"

"He sure is, and he's going to sue you."

"I'm sure that he is. Where'd you get the pot?"

"What pot?" Chad said. His eyes kept popping down to the left. I grabbed the pocket and he tried to stop my hand. "What are you doing?" he said, wrapping his tiny white hands over my wrists.

"Not a good idea, Mr. Whitley," I said. "You want a black eye to go with your bloody nose?" He stared at me for a fraction of a second and let go of my hand. I dug a sandwich bag half filled with marijuana from his hip pocket.

"It should be legalized," he said.

"You know what? I actually agree. But the bad news is that it ain't legalized. And you're not only trespassing, but you're also carrying."

I looked back at Chris. "He's carrying."

"This one's got paraphernalia," Chris said.

"You were peeing on my dad's house," Chad shouted.

"Shut up," I said.

We did our jobs. We got the stories. We listened to Chad Whitley's threat and listened to his friend, Paul Lee, cry and say that he was sorry time and time again. By the time we'd gotten finished, Frank Sutton had pulled up. He offered to drive the two back into town just as long as Chris and I did the paperwork after our shifts.

We watched Frank's car drive away and stood in silence. The humidity had broken just a bit, and the night felt cool.

"Do you think that was a good idea?" Chris said.

"What?"

"Busting that kid's nose like that? He wasn't lying. His dad might sue."

I laughed, a harsh bark. "Are you serious? For what? He fell. I didn't do it."

"I don't know, man. Your story. His story's probably different. Besides, what with what you've been going through lately."

"What? You think I can't do my job?"

"Calm down," Chris said, holding his palms up. "I didn't say that." I stared at the nubs of his missing fingers.

"Is that what they're saying about me?" I said. I could imagine all the deputies, talking in sad tones, saying that I had *once* been a great deputy, saying that one day I might have even been sheriff material, saying that Janey's death had ruined me. "I can't do my job? I'm a shitty deputy because Janey got killed? I'm coming unglued? Is that it?"

"Holy Christ, Justin," Chris said. "Calm down. I'm your friend, man. Remember? Your friend."

My eyes felt dry and I rubbed them with my palm. We didn't say anything for a moment. I studied the home, its massive front yard, its bay windows, and its half-finished driveway. It was already a mansion by any standard. When the remodel was completed, it would rival any home on Juniper. And all the homes were gorgeous.

"I'll never afford a place like that," I said.

Chris chuckled. He'd let my outburst go. "Not on this salary." He paused. "Beside, I wouldn't want it." He looked down at his hands, thumbing the nubs of his missing fingers.

"You wouldn't?"

"With the taxes out here? Hell no. You know what I want? I want a houseboat. I'd park it over in Apalach, right there at the mouth of the river."

I thought about Big Don's houseboat. Donnie Ray. Jimmy Danley.

"Guess who I ran into yesterday?" I said.

He shrugged. "Santa Claus? The Easter Bunny? No wait—the Tidy Bowl man?"

I smiled, thankful that Chris could always make me laugh, no matter what. I felt stupid and ashamed for blowing up at him.

"I'm sorry about snapping at you, man. I'm just—tired, I guess."

He shrugged again. "Whatever. I get it. So who'd you run into?"

"Denise Miles."

"Really now? What did she have to say?"

"Nothing. She was just eating up at Charlie's. I was, too. We just said *hi*. Nothing big."

He grinned, the edges of his teeth showing. "Wait a minute. You're not still carrying a torch for her, are you?"

"No," I shook my head. "No, not at all." I didn't know if I were telling the truth.

"Come on, man. You're better than that. You know she's been fucking Jimmy Danley for a while now."

I looked away. "Yeah, I know." I groped for words. "I just didn't know she was back in town. I was just surprised to see her."

"She's been back for about a year, I think." He leaned against the side of his car. "Jesus, you had a thing for her back in the day. Remember that time you were going to put a note in her locker? You chickened out. Be glad. She'd probably have laughed at you, you know. Made you feel like shit."

"Yeah," I said, remembering the note I'd scrawled on notebook paper while sitting in the back of Mrs. Patterson's English class. I'd asked her if she wanted to hang out. I'd written that I thought she was pretty and that I thought that we could be good together, all language from nighttime TV programs. This was eighth grade. "What's so wrong with Denise?"

"Nothing. Are you getting pissy again? Jesus, man, I'm just messing with you," Chris said. "Calm down."

"It was a long time ago. Forget it. Anyway, I think I pissed her off."

"What happened?"

"She overhead me and Charlie talking about how Donnie Ray was kicked out of the Army for dealing."

"I heard he decked a drill sergeant."

"No shit?"

"Lots of campfires in this town, man. Lots of campfires. And a lot of tales told around them."

We fell silent, and I turned to get into my car. Just as I opened the door, I turned back. "That was her car up at the landing," I said.

Chris nodded. "Yeah. Jimmy was driving it."

A pang of jealousy knotted my gut and I tried to dismiss it. But in the back of my mind, I was wondering what in the world Denise saw in a loser like Jimmy Danley.

Chris's lapel mic squelched. "Signal 38 in Stetson. Willey Road." A domestic. I'd worked plenty of them myself. Stetson was a little town just north of St. Vincent, the last town in Apalachee County before you hit Calhoun County.

"En route," Chris said. He looked at me. "Let her go. High school was a long time ago, and Denise Miles is one of them, now."

"One of who?"

"Jimmy's crew. Those folks. They're just as likely to buy you a beer as they are to cook up a batch of meth."

"That's not true," I said, waving my hand. I felt an odd need to defend Denise. "She's not like them. She never was."

Chris cocked an eyebrow. "Be careful. Don't piss on anything." He smiled and got in his car and pulled away. I watched his taillights fade into the night. I slid into my cruiser and turned on the radio and found some rock-n-roll. Guns N' Roses' "Estranged." The lead guitar was like some lone voice screaming above all the orchestration, completely alone.

Around 3:00 a.m., I drove down the old port. At one point in the 1930s, St. Vincent had been the only deep water port on this part of the Gulf of Mexico. The Apalachicola Northern Railroad had laid tracks all the way up to Atlanta. During that time, Port St. Vincent (as it had been known) was a boom town on the Gulf, a vacation spot for families from as far away as Tifton, Georgia. We'd learned in middle school about an 1845 Hurricane that had wiped Port St. Vincent off the map, not only destroying most of the town, but also creating a lot of the low-lying swamp lands and inlets along Apalachee County's ragged shoreline. The town of St. Vincent had been founded in 1866, right on top of the old town. The place thrived for a long time, but around 1940, another hurricane hit St. Vincent, this time sparing the town but ruining the port. The storm had washed in silt and sand, making the bay much shallower than it once had been. As such, St. Vincent's days as a growing shipping center stalled. Since then, the fishery and the mill had floated the local economy.

These days, the only thing that remained of that port was what people in town called the Docks, a long stretch of seawall a quarter mile east of the mill. People fished at the Docks, and I'd spent a lot of time down there, myself, casting a surf rod into the churning gray water.

I parked the cruiser and stepped out onto the mixture of sand and oyster shells that seemed to make up every parking lot in Apalachee County. I walked across the lot, the shells crunching beneath my boots. Near the water, I stepped on one of the old railroad crossties that edged the dock. A cool breeze blew. It stank of fish and brine and paper mill smoke. Out to the east, the mill's smoke stacks rose from the clouds like missiles.

The first year we were married, Janey used to ask me all the time, "What do you want out of life?" Looking out over St. Vincent Bay, the lights of the paper mill glowing softly in the west, I realized what I should have said. *I want St. Vincent to be the town it's always been. I want nothing to ever change.* I stepped over the railroad trestle guard and walked along the seawall, enjoying the smell of the bay air.

At the far edge of the Docks, what looked like an old stair case fed down into the water. I had no idea what it had been used for. It had been the same rusted skeleton reaching out into the gunmetal gray water all my life. Depending on the tide, it sometimes went right down into the sea. Though it was surrounded by a chain link fence the city had put up God knows when, a deep crease had formed where so many had peeled it back. I pulled the fence aside and stepped out onto the rusting stairway. The metal groaned.

If you stood long enough, you felt like you were moving. The water stilled, and the horizon rushed at you. If you blinked, the feeling went away. But I didn't blink. I just stood there, feeling the bay move beneath me, the dark steel gray water churning, moonlight glinting off it in sharp tinges. Salt stung my eyes. I held my gaze and felt the earth pass from beneath me.

gasket.

But Mack Weston was from around here. He knew this place and knew the people. He understood that certain things have to be done, and he understood that certain things *ought* to be done. I had no love for Donnie Ray Miles, but he was dead. This was about his daddy.

"I'll get it," I said. "Do you know where he keeps them?"

"Not really. Probably in the closet. Under the bed. Somewhere.."

It struck me then that I had no idea where Donnie Ray lived. "Where's his place? Bay View?"

"No. Bayard's Bayou. Single wide. It's at the end of Sixth Street, on the left. It's a kind of beige or tan color. You can't miss it. Sits way up off the road."

"You got a key to the place?"

"He keeps one—he kept one under the mailbox, wedged in there in a metal box. Just look where the mailbox is set on the post."

"So when I get them, just put them in your shed?"

"Yeah," he said. "Just—keep it discreet, you know?"

I nodded. Rules of decorum for Big Don Miles. What was the world coming to? "I'll take care of it."

"I was real sorry to hear about your wife. What was that, a few months back?"

"Ex. She was my ex. But thanks."

I thought he was going to shake my hand, but he reached into his shorts pocket and pulled out a red cigarette lighter and lit up. "I better run."

He walked across the lot, got in the truck and pulled out onto the highway. The 7:30 whistle blew at the mill, a long, shrill keen.

I went inside, bought a sausage biscuit and a cup of coffee. I warmed my breakfast in a food-splattered microwave and paid the clerk. Outside, I got in the cruiser and laid my head against the headrest for a moment, closed my eyes, and took a few deep breaths. I opened my eyes and looked in my rear view mirror and my blood froze.

Behind the bars separating the front and back of my police cruiser, Donnie Ray Miles sat, chewing a toothpick. His red hair and beard blazed in the morning sunlight.

I spun around in the seat, shouting, dropping the biscuit.

Nothing. The backseat was empty. My heart was beating in my chest, my breath coming in short, hollow gasps. I looked around, whipping my head back and forth. No one. I turned around in my seat and stared at the backseat. Nothing but black vinyl and barred windows. I rubbed my eyes.

The sausage biscuit was on the floorboard. I picked up the two biscuit halves and the overcooked sausage, flicked off some of the grains of sand, and took a bite. "You need sleep," I muttered and took another bite of the dirty biscuit.

I pulled out onto the road and turned east, out toward Bayard's Bayou. The bay was smooth as a pane of glass. The live oaks and palm trees that edges the shore line made me wish that I were somewhere with a fishing pole and cold beer.

As I passed the Methodist Church, Janey's parents' house came into view, a long yellow ranch home with a curved driveway. She'd been living there for a couple of months the day she was killed. I glanced out at the water. This would have been the route that she took that day. The bay was the last thing my ex-wife had ever seen.

Janey was driving to Panama City the morning that it happened. She had started taking classes at Gulf Coast toward a nursing degree. She worked as a receptionist for Dr. Anson in town, a job she'd had since she finished her two-year associates in business administration after high school. Half those credits she'd gotten in Apalachee County High's dual enrollment program. But working for Dr. Anson got her interested in being a nurse. She often talked about how much she wanted to help people, to be a calm presence. "You have no idea how freaked out people get when they come to the doctor," she told me once over lunch a few months before she moved out.

"About as freaked out as they get when they see a cop?" I said.

"I'm serious, Justin. If I become a nurse, I can be a soothing presence, somebody to help people calm down."

"Do you really want to do this?"

"Yes," she said. "I do."

She got some financial aid, so we paid little out of pocket. Plus, going to classes made her happy. Dr. Anson gladly gave her the days off. She went twice a week, every Tuesday and Thursday morning. When she left me, she kept attending classes. I knew because we still talked about once a week.

We'd been split up for three months the morning that it happened. She pulled off of 8th Street onto the highway, driving her little red Nissan Sentra, a car that I'd always hated because to me, driving it felt like driving a go-cart. She didn't see the log truck coming west.

I played that moment in my head time and again, turned into a movie I could watch, a crime scene I could analyze. I saw her, looking at the water, perhaps dreaming about a weekend sunbathing. She loved to go out to Sandy Head Beach and take her MP3 player. She'd lie there baking in the sun all day long, listening to Christian pop: Amy Grant, the Newsboys, DC Talk, all overproduced mess that I'd grown to tolerate because of her.

I pictured her reaching down to the radio in her car, perhaps scanning stations, maybe knocking up the volume a notch or two.

Her size 7 foot, tiny, barely more than a wedge of flesh.

Her foot pushing down on the gas pedal.

The pedal itself: grit and sand in the grooves.

I even smelled the inside of her car: an overly-sweet smell of fruit, a spray she kept in the glove box.

I saw the way the car inched forward.

At that point, the movie in my mind always stopped. Beyond that, all I could see was black and white photography:

The Nissan, the right side crunched and buckled, the fiberglass bumpers cracked, the paint flecked off, the frame bent nearly in two.

Glass on the pavement. I'd seen it so many times, working other wrecks. Something about it disturbed me: it was too much like salt, some seasoning poured on the ground.

Skid marks. I didn't work the wreck, so I had no way of knowing if she even slammed on breaks. Cowboy told me that there were no skid marks, but I couldn't shake the image from my mind: twin black scars on the faded asphalt.

I could never see her body. I tried to picture the way it must have been—a blood-stained white sheet covering her. Cowboy said I didn't want to know what it was really like, and I'd been tempted to just open the accident folder down at the department. It must have been bad. I hated to imagine her suffering, but if a tractor trailer carrying a load of timber hits a Nissan, then, I guess physics takes over. I hope that she went quickly, that she didn't even know what happened.

I hope that she looked down at the glowing LED of her radio station (always 98.5, The Message), and then knew nothing, only silence and darkness and not the scream of metal and glass and machine that I knew in my quietest moments she must have heard. She must have felt it all.

Donnie Ray, Jimmy, and Tater Wilson used to come to school on winter Mondays still stained with the blood of deer they killed the weekend before. They hung around St. Vincent for Friday night's football game, but Saturday morning, you'd see them headed out of town, all piled in Donnie Ray's truck, that same primered Chevy he drove until the day he died, headed east toward Apalachicola, where Big Don kept a hunting lease and a cabin. The three of them would hunt all weekend, stalking deer in the thick pine and cypress wood outside of Liberty County. They got up early on Monday mornings, hunted, and drove directly to school clad in their deep-wood camo, still smeared red from a deer they'd field dressed. The three of them sat in the courtyard before class Monday morning, stinking of sweat and blood. They looked like barbarians, fresh from sacking some foreign city.

They weren't the only hunters at school. Most of the boys hunted—and lot of the girls, too. But Donnie Ray and his crew hunted for the kill. Donnie Ray often said so in class, bragging about a deer he'd taken down, then describing the way he'd drug the knife down the deer's carcass and spilled its guts on the forest

I wasn't against hunting. I liked eating meat of all kinds, and I loved the gamey taste of venison. But Dad didn't hunt, so I never learned to hunt. We were fishermen. He showed me how to read the water, how to bait a line, and how to clean a fish. I knew how to run a trot line. I learned how to wade with my feet flat on the bay bottom to avoid stepping on a stingray. But I wasn't a hunter.

Dad had a few guns around the house—an old Remington .20 gauge and a .22 rifle. Aaron hunted off and on with his friends, rising early on cool Saturday mornings and not coming home until well after dark. But I never went. Though Dad showed me how to fire the rifle and shotgun when I was young, I never developed a real love for firearms. I bought my first pistol when I became a full-time deputy. Before I purchased it, I borrowed a Berretta .9 millimeter from Chris, who owned a huge collection of hand guns, shotguns, and rifles. I liked it so much that I bought one just like it.

I liked shooting, too, and I was good at it. I had to keep up my standards for the sheriff's department, so I went to the range a few times a month. But unlike Chris and some of the other deputies, I didn't spend my weekends driving to gun shows all over South Georgia and North Florida.

And unlike Donnie Ray Miles and Jimmy Danley, I could never take such pleasure from killing anything.

The military was a perfect place for him, I thought as I drove out toward Bayard's Bayou, a little collection of trailers and boathouses just ten minutes east of St. Vincent. I wasn't quite sure *what* Donnie Ray did in the army. Infantry, I imagined. Probably gave him a hard-on walking around, armed to the tooth.

People had been living at Bayard's Bayou since the 1930s. Supposedly, it had been named for a hunter who got lost in the mangrove and pine-crowded flood plains. Settled by fishermen, Bayard's Bayou was a collection of sloughs and inlets that made for easy access to St. Vincent Bay. Mullet fishermen, oystermen, and scallopers made a decent living off the water.

I turned onto 6th street, a limestone alley right across the road from Bayard's Boat Yard, where a few small boats sat moored at the graying dock.

A few pickup trucks sat in the lot.

Clumps of saw grass edged the ditches. Occasional trailers and one-family homes sat way back up off the road, yards mainly sand and scrub. Donnie Ray's trailer was the last one on the left, a tiny beige single-wide that sat a good forty yards off the road. I pulled the cruiser up slowly. A puff of white dust rose when I stepped out and I thought of how gravediggers used to put lime atop newly-dug graves to keep the odor down.

I walked out to the mailbox and found the key Big Don had told me about. Donnie Ray had pushed the key in the bottom of a curved M-4 clip, which he'd wedged beneath the rusting mailbox. I reached my index finger down inside the magazine and pushed the key until it came loose and dropped into my palm.

In the yard, small clumps of y-weeds and crabgrass clustered here and there. Two faded ice chests sat by the spindled metal stairs to the front door. An over-flowing coffee can filled with cigarette butts sat on a dry-rotted plastic table right next to the stairs. The storm door was crooked in the jamb. I pulled it gently, fearing that it might come off in my hand. The front door lock was rusted, and I had to jam to key in hard.

The place was cleaner than I expected. I'd pictured a mess—piles of fast food wrappers, empty cigarette packs, and beer cans everywhere. But the living room was spotless. The place smelled like some kind of air freshener, strong and pine-scented. A large, flat-panel television sat atop a coffee table against the sidewall, a DVD player and a PlayStation beneath it in a tangle of black wires.

In the kitchen, the countertops were clean and barren, save for a small wicker basket and a four-cup coffee maker. The carafe sat in a bright green dish drainer. The wicker basket held a couple of dollars in change, some old receipts, and few business cards. I thumbed through them: Harley's Bait & Tackle, Clawson's Fisheries, some doctor in Franklin County.

A phone and an answering machine sat on the bar that separated the kitchen from the living room. A red two flashed—the number of messages. I stared at the machine. It was a GE, the same model I had at home. Chris gave me hell all the time about keeping a land line. "An answering machine?" he often teased. "Get with the program, man. It's the 21st century. You ever heard of voice mail? Do you have a telegraph line, too, just in case?"

I pressed the button with a tiny triangle on it, the one that played messages.

"Donnie Ray," a voice said. "The meeting's Thursday night at 7:00. A bunch of people are coming. I talked to Cedric. He said he'd be there. Come if you can."

The voice sounded vaguely familiar, but I couldn't place it. I pressed the rewind button and then the play button twice. The message was now marked as *new*.

Down the hall, two bedroom doors were separated by the bathroom. I pushed one bedroom door open with my boot. Inside, a deflated air mattress lay crumpled on the floor. Otherwise, the room was empty.

The bathroom was clean, too, recently mopped. A bleach white shower curtain hung over the tub. A cup by the sink had a toothbrush and a tube of toothpaste in it. The tube was rolled tight from the bottom up. It was still half-way full.

An American flag hung on the wall behind the queen-sized bed that took up most of the master bedroom. But what drew my eyes were the rifles, three of them, laid out side by side neatly on the mattress ticking: a Browning 30.06, a Mossberg .12 gauge, and a Remington 4-10. They'd been recently cleaned, their barrels shining with oil. A few stained rags lay near the bed. Pushing them with my foot, I saw that they had originally been t-shirts.

I squatted down by a short bookshelf at the head of bed and studied its contents: *The Grapes of Wrath. For Whom the Bell Tolls. The Things They Carried.* I picked up a slim, sepia-colored volume and turned it over in my hands, a book of poems entitled *Papermill* by Joseph Kalar. I frowned. Donnie Ray reading poetry? It didn't make sense.

I flipped through the book and put it back on the shelf. In a black tackle box under the bed, I found three hundred rounds of bullets for the Browning mixed in with several shotgun shells. Behind the tackle box was a cigar box stuffed with rolling papers and two butane lighters. One lighter had a swastika one it. The other featured a nude blonde with her tongue out. I pushed it all back underneath the bed and stood up, wondering why I felt disappointed.

A mirror hung above a chest of drawers. Military issue, it looked like the kind my grandfather had from his time in the Navy: rectangular, edged in a white frame. My face stared back—gaunt, drawn. My eyes looked like raisins, shriveled and dry. I needed a shave. I brushed a free hand through my hair, which now seemed sparser than ever before, and studied the scar above my left eye, remembering that summer up in Georgia, when my grandfather had taken me and my brother camping at Lake Hiawasee. I'd fallen from the dock and hit my head on the edge. Granddaddy thought that I was dead. He'd jumped right in behind me and pulled me up with one arm. I'd needed sixteen stitches. I'd always meant to take Janey up there. She'd have loved the mountains.

On the chest of drawers was another cigar box. I opened it and found instead two Case pocketknives, a few dollars in change, and a photograph of a black-haired woman with deeply tanned skin standing in front of what might have been a lake or river, maybe even an ocean. She was thin and long. Her shape made me think of a canoe, all one graceful curve. She wore desert camouflage fatigue pants, standard-issue boots, and a black tank top. She leaned against what looked like a power pole or maybe a streetlight, her hands behind her back. The light in the photograph said summer—it was bright light, hard, the kind of thick sunshine that comes in late July and settles a fiery glaze over everything. I turned the photograph over. Someone had written in lower-case letters, "Lucy, KIA." *Killed in Action.*

I turned the photo back over and studied her face. She was young, no more than nineteen or twenty. She might have been Hispanic, maybe even black. A girlfriend? I doubted it. I couldn't see it, not Donnie Ray, who had a Rebel flag on his truck back in high school, who had no problem with the word "nigger." I put the photo back. Who on earth was she?

The box also had some foreign money, no doubt Iraqi. There were a few bills, folded and held together with a paper clip. I picked up the money and studied the artwork—four men on horseback, some kind of Arabic writing above their heads. I put the photo and the money back in the box and closed it and opened the top drawer: two rows of neatly-folded underwear and several pairs of socks, folded military style. I shut the drawer quickly, suddenly embarrassed. Why the hell was I going through this guy's stuff? Who the hell did I think I was? I looked around the room, half-expected to see Donnie Ray in there with me.

The box of videos was behind the hanging clothes in the closet. There were several DVDs, all featuring naked women and naked men staring at each other with dead eyes, fake plastic lust on their faces. Something in me wanted to look away. Certainly, I'd seen an adult movie a few times; but somehow, these things embarrassed me. Janey and I had watched an adult film once, on my suggestion. It was a few months before we got divorced. We'd been drifting apart, and I thought maybe a romantic night together would help. I'd thought it would have been sexy, the two of us making love while watching it. It turned out to be awkward, with Janey commenting on the size of the girls' breasts and the lack of interest they all seemed to have in the guys they were with.

"How in the world can you get turned on with a camera in your face?" she'd wondered aloud. We'd been sitting in our bedroom, sipping wine. She was wearing a negligee and looked absolutely stunning, her small breasts visible through the sheer fabric. I'd shrugged, feeling more and more stupid and more and more embarrassed the longer we sat together. When two sweaty actors started going at it on screen, I felt distinctly turned off. Janey sat and watched the movie out of morbid curiosity. We turned the movie off soon after. I told her that she was frigid. She called me a pervert.

That evening, I wound up smoking in the front yard alone while Janey went to bed early.

I shook the memory away, picked up the box, and left the trailer. Back outside, I shut the storm door walked across the yard to the cruiser, holding the box of movies under one arm. In the car, I lit a cigarette and stared at the trailer for a moment. I wasn't sure what I'd find in the place, but it wasn't this, not this neat, Spartan place. As I drove away, I watched the trailer in the rear view I half-expected to see Donnie Ray looking out he window, his eyes angry and red. Instead, the trailer slowly receded, blending into the brush, anonymous and forgotten.

, wondering what to do.
?" I said and looked at Chris. I hoped that he'd have something
Something to cut the tension.
, what?" he said. "I don't know about you, man. But I'm
tarting tomorrow. Okaloosa County is always hiring."
t place is full of meth heads," Frank said.
I'd be one employed meth-headed busting son of a bitch,"
left the room, his face drawn tight. I didn't like it. I didn't want
Chris looked worried. Chris never worried. Maybe nothing was
e, but I had a feeling somebody somewhere had a hammer and

sed up the cruiser at the pumps behind the department. How
t be before we had to pay for our own gas? Maybe Janey had
faybe the best thing to do was to get out of this town. I didn't
ed it all out of my head. I wanted to focus on something real
St. Vincent.
evening shift routine was repetitive and simple, a routine I'd
er time. I drove out to Sandy Head Beach and cruised through
uple of times so that the rich folks could see me looking after
Used to, before I was hired, night shift deputies started on the
t toward the cape, and worked their way west. But after a few
rom the Gulfaire residents requesting more police presence, the
d around, making the place a priority.
en I finished with the beach, I drove back east into town and
ugh the South Side, just to be seen. Some nights, I stopped in
for a cup of coffee and chat with the night clerk. Then, I'd
downtown St. Vincent, get back on Highway 98, and drive out
cape. There, I was supposed to check to see that none of the
had been crashed.
going was slow tonight. No one was out. Three hours passed.
lot about what I'd seen in Donnie Ray's trailer: the books, the
anliness of it all. Who was the girl in the photo? Lucy, killed
e might have been someone he'd hooked up with over there.
ol, Donnie Ray had dated a girl named Anne Waites. Though
in Franklin County, Anne enrolled at Apalachee County High
had a better college prep curriculum than Franklin County did.
ing girl with a long swimmer's body, Anne was too smart for
, but she stuck with him. I didn't know if they were together
ined the Army.

5.

Janey once told me, "I like you because you're like this town. You're quiet." She was right. I don't like to talk. My father once told me that God had given me two ears and one mouth. "Now which one do you think you ought to use more often?" he often asked. I liked to look and study. I liked the silence of a long drive, the only sound the hum of tires beneath my car.

Janey, though, was a social animal. She knew everyone and everyone knew her. Driving back into town after I left St. Vincent, I wondered why she married me at all. I'd had these thoughts before—that our marriage had been one big sham, that a year into it, she'd started making plans to leave. I didn't know if that were true. But one thing was certain: she wanted to leave St. Vincent. I didn't. I looked out over the bay. Thunderheads to the west. The water looked dark and muddy, the waves choppy with white foam. To the west, the mill sat on the horizon line, smoke stackss chugging white into a pewter sky.

I couldn't imagine a world beyond St. Vincent. When I became a deputy, I liked the idea I'd be a kind of protector for this town. I'd fallen in love with the bay and the river and the live oaks and longleaf pines. As a lawman, I could give back to this place. I could ensure that it would be here for a long, long time.

A white and blue pickup truck turned out ahead of me and took off like a channel cat. I was officially off-duty, but I pressed the gas to the floor, anyway. I flashed the lights and flipped the siren. The cruiser easily caught up with the truck. I recognized the stickers on the bumper: a "Save our Waters" seal by a black-and-white one that read "Yes, I Fish and Yes, I Vote." Hokey Lee, a foreman down at Clawson's. He was close to Charlie's age, a St. Vincent lifer who seemed to know everyone in town. You'd see him eating lunch at Charlie's every now and again. Where the hell was he going in such a hurry? He was making sixty in a forty zone.

He pulled to the shoulder, and I edged up behind him and got out. He studied me in the rear view and said, "Hey, Justin. Sorry. I just wasn't paying attention."

I walked up the truck and leaned against the door. "Where you headed in such a hurry, Hokey?"

"Down to work. Trying not to miss a meeting."

"I read you guys are downsizing. Is that what you're meeting about?"

"Yeah, something like that. We're trying to minimize it, you know. Holidays are coming. This is the first we've heard about it. They didn't even tell management. I don't know, Justin. What with the mill, feels like this whole damn town's falling apart."

"Tell me about it."

"What about y'all? Down at the sheriff's department?"

"I haven't heard anything, but you never know," I said.

He took an empty water bottle from between his legs and spit tobacco into it. "How are you doing, boy? I haven't seen you in a long time?"

"I'm doing okay."

"I hated to hear about your wife."

"She left me."

"I heard that, too. I'm working on the third wife right now, myself. Just the other night, she told me right where I could go. I dang near kicked her out right then. Figured I ought to before she kicks me out first."

We both laughed, but it felt forced. We stood in silence, and I patted my pocket, looking for the box of cigarettes I'd left on the dash in the cruiser.

"I was still sorry to hear about Janey."

I nodded. An orange SUV drove by, the wind throwing sand and grit all over me. I squinted, trying to make out the tags.

"Tourists," Hokey said.

"Yep," I said. "Listen, Hoke, do me a favor and slow down, okay? No meeting's worth wrapping your truck around a palm tree."

"Thanks, Justin." He turned the truck on, and the engine coughed and sputtered, the whole chassis vibrating. He shouted above the bad muffler. "You been fishing?"

"Not in a while."

"I heard they're tearing up the drum down toward Apalach."

"Me, too. Maybe I'll get out there."

He put the truck in gear. "Bull minnows. Remember that—bull minnows." With that, Hokey pulled back out onto the narrow stretch of highway. I watched him for a moment and turned back to the cruiser. A bolt of lightning flashed out over the water. A storm was coming.

Mack Weston called a mandatory department meeting the next afternoon. I was scheduled for graveyard. I'd been in and out of sleep since coming home from Donnie Ray's. During my shift, I planned to put the box of movies in Big Don's shed and forget about the whole thing. Being in Donnie Ray's trailer had spooked me. I spent a good part of the morning, clicking away on my ancient desktop, surfing the web, trying to find out why I'd seen Donnie Ray twice since he died. I'd convinced myself that they were waking dreams.

By the time four o'clock rolled around, I'd wasted the rest of the afternoon, dozing, watching TV, and thinking about Denise. She'd seemed

so angry at Charlie's. I wondered what s
she'd quit school. Maybe she'd graduated
of things, like what Mack was going to re
sense of dread.

We met in the squad room at th
jail, some of us sitting on swivel chairs, so
were fifteen deputies working for Apalac
Chris and Frank. Other like Hector Tejada
Some I knew only in passing: David Ga
others. I looked around the room, wonde
years in this place and know only four pe

We chatted for few minutes be
followed by Davis Malone and Cowboy, h
and I wondered for half a second if this v
Chris had been right. Maybe Mack was a
assault. The thought seemed ludicrous.

The truth was worse. The comi
not good. When the budget numbers ca
Christmas, we were switching to twelve ho
thought about the paper mill and Clawson'
drying up and blowing away.

"Listen," Mack said, surveying the
But budgets come and go. Nothing's etched
of it is this—we've got to begin cutting b
back the number of deputies on duty. We're
first shift, that means five deputies, not six. S
shift will have two deputies on duty, one on
end."

"Just two?" I said. "What if someth

"Sergeant Nuegent and I will be d
happens, one of us—both of us—will be t
than you."

"Are we losing our jobs?" Frank said
at home. If we're going to lose our jobs, I n
position. That's my position."

"Frank, this is why I called the me
loop. I don't know any more than what I've
getting fired." He put his hands on his hips a
I don't know what else to say. The sergeant
up tomorrow. You guys have a good night." I
Cowboy followed. Malone took a cell phone c

a few second

"W
funny to say

"W
looking. I'm

"T

"A
Chris said a
to worry, b
etched in st
a chisel.

I g
long would
been right.
know. I pu
and tangib

M
developed
Gulfaire a
their hom
east end,
phone cal
routine tu

cruised th
at the Sw
ride throu
toward th
gated hon

I though
guns, the
in action
In high
she resi
because
A good-
Donnie
before h

By 2:00 a.m., I wanted a Coca-Cola, so I drove to the Swifty and parked on the far edge of the front of the store, just beyond the reach of the fluorescent outside lights. The night clerk stood with his back to the window, filling the rack above his head with cartons of cigarettes. I felt for my wallet and got out. It was a hot night, though October was only a week or so away. A humid haze coated everything in a wet sheen. I went inside, bought a Coke and a pack of menthols, and came back outside, packing the box against my palm's heel.

A green Mazda pulled to a parking stop in front of the store and Denise Miles got out. She wore a long black coat that she held closed with her right hand. The coat covered her rear end, but she wore fishnet stockings, and I couldn't help admiring her legs.

Her eyes widened a fraction of a second when she saw me, and I wondered what I'd caught her doing. "Justin Everson, international man of mystery. Working late?" she said. She wore thick mascara. Her hair had been teased up, but it had fallen down. She smelled like sweat and perfume.

"Graveyard. Where are you coming from?"

"You are one curious soul, aren't you? Is that what international men of mystery do? Ask a lot of questions?"

"Just being friendly."

She pointed at my cigarette with her left hand, her right one keeping the black coat cinched. It was a man's jacket, a long faux-leather job you could get at Wal-Mart or Target. "I stopped for a pack of those, so, I suppose I better get them."

"Go ahead," I said.

"I don't need your permission."

"I didn't say you did."

She studied me for a moment and walked into the store. She stood at the counter and purchased the cigarettes and came back outside. I started to say something, opened my mouth, and gaped, silent. She looked at me, her eyes flicking up and down. She started to walk away but then turned back.

"I didn't mean to pop off at you at other day," she said.

"It's okay," I said. "Don't worry about it."

She opened a new pack of Dorals, shook one out, and lit it. Her jacket fell open. Beneath it, she wore only a golden lamé bikini top and a tight pair of matching shorts. She smirked as she pulled the jacket closed. "You like what you see?"

"No," I said on instinct. "I mean, yes, I mean." I trailed off and took a drag of my cigarette.

We didn't say anything for a minute. "Look," I said. "I'm sorry about your cousin. I shouldn't have been asking you questions the other morning, anyway."

"Whatever. It doesn't matter."

"And I don't know why Donnie Ray got kicked out of the Army, if he did at all. I mean, I just have always heard it had something to do with drugs."

"People talk. That's what people in St. Vincent do. They talk. Always have. Always will." She put a hand on her hip, opening the jacket and I tried to look away. Something like a smile touched the edge of her lips.

"So do you know what happened for real?"

She looked at me out of the corner of her eyes and blew a thin cloud of smoke. "To tell you the truth, no. I'm not sure I'd tell you if I did."

"You really don't know?"

She crossed her arms and looked out at the highway. "No, I don't. You're the cop. Why don't you find out?"

"Did he ever talk about being over there? Did he mention anyone he knew? Any friends he made?"

"Not really. He was quiet when he came back. Really quiet. He quit talking to everyone."

"Jimmy, too?"

She nodded. "Well, him and Jimmy weren't getting along all that good, anyway." Her voice fell off and she stared out at the road.

I thought of the picture of Lucy. "Was he still dating Anne?"

She blew smoke through her nose. "I don't know. He didn't tell me anything after he got back." A gust of wind came in off the bay, and her jacket flew open again, revealing her bikini top and fishnets. She closed the jacket, muttering, "Shit" and looked up at me.

"I dance, sometimes," she said. "Over at a place in Panama City. Beach Bunnies. I usually don't wear this home. I wanted to get out of there, quick. Some fat bastard really crossed the line."

"What happened?"

She flicked her eyebrows. "Lap dance. He got gropey. He got— excited."

"Disgusting."

She shrugged. "The money's good. A table dance is twenty dollars," she said. "I can't pass that up, even if I think the patron's ugly as sin. We don't all have government jobs," she said.

"I didn't mean you."

She held out a hand. "Forget it."

I'd been to Beach Bunnies once, the night I turned twenty-one. Chris and I and a couple of other guys had driven over to the beach and stopped at several bars along the way, the Beach Bunny included. The whole visit had been at once titillating and a bit embarrassing. On the one hand, I liked looking at topless women wearing thongs. On the other hand, I knew that every woman in the place saw nothing but dollar signs when they looked at me. I also suspected that every one of them had an ugly story about why they were dancing. I couldn't reconcile the fantasy of beautiful naked tan bodies with the reality of a rent check in my mind.

"You look terrible," she said. "Seriously, you need some sleep, man. Have you looked in a mirror lately?"

I laughed because I didn't know what to say. "I'm haven't been sleeping too good lately." I flicked ashes on the pavement. "Hey, do you remember that time you told Mike Sheehan he was born with a silver spoon up his ass?"

She chuckled. "What? I said that?"

"Tenth grade. Mrs. Dungy's typing class. You don't remember?"

"Lord, honey, no. That was a long time ago," she said and smiled, a lopsided grin. "Mike Sheehan. What an asshole. Whatever I said, he probably deserved it." She took a long drag. "I've got to get home. I'm tired. It's been a long night."

"Yeah," I said.

She took a step toward the Mazda and I said, "How long have you been with Jimmy?"

"A little while," she said. "Why?"

"I don't know. Just making conversation."

She studied me again, her brow a tight line above hooded green eyes. "You should work on your conversation skills," she said. She turned to walk away, and I followed the seam of her fishnets until they disappeared beneath the jacket. She didn't look at me when she got into the Mazda, cranked it, and squealed out onto the road.

Frank Sutton was working the north end, patrolling the tiny towns of Stetson, Honeyville, and Trasker, as well as all the back roads in between. I hated working the north end. There was nothing up there but a single convenience store in Stetson. Frank was a Stetson boy. He'd gone to high school up there and played football for the Stetson Bears, the Apalachee County Seminoles' cross-county rivals. He lived there with his wife and three kids. I hated to think that he might lose his job. I hated to think about losing mine. I pushed the thought away.

"Apalachee to One-twelve," Sheila said over the radio, her voice crackling with static.

"Go ahead."

"Noise complaint out on Deerborne Circle. Caller said it sounds like a live band."

"10-4. In route," I said, wondering who the hell would be playing live music at 2:00 a.m. Deerborne Circle was at the far end of Cape San Vincente, out toward the tip, near the ruins of the old Spanish fort. The cape was a popular vacation spot for middle-aged folks with kids. You could rent a cabin or park an RV at the campground. Some people kept residences, as the occasional lit porch light attested.

I slowed down at the end of Deerborne and got out of the car. Only one house stood at the end of the circle, a large, sea-washed gray home on stilts. A Dodge minivan with Michigan plates sat in the wheel ruts of a sand and oyster shell driveway. I turned on my Maglite and shined it toward the house. No one was around, but I heard the music: Big Band or swing, something with brass instruments. The music made me think of old movies, where the world was black and white.

"One-twelve to Apalachee," I said into my radio. "I'm at the house, I think. You said you had a music *complaint?*"

"Yes. Said they heard a live band. Sounded like a woman on the phone."

"There's only one house out here. I'll check it out. I'll report when I'm done."

"10-4."

I walked across the yard. A white placard by the steps to the front door read "Paradise East." I knocked with the side of my fist. "Apalachee County Sheriff."

A face appeared in one of the narrow windows flanking the door. An old woman with dark gray hair regarded me for a moment, her tiny eyes narrow, suspicious.

"Do you have any identification?" she said through the glass.

Have you been watching too many movies? I wondered. I pointed to the star on my chest. "You called us, lady," I said. "You said you heard music?"

The door cracked and her face appeared in the slit allowed by a door chain. The music got louder. It came from behind her. "Yes, music. From that club down the street."

I looked back toward the road. The only place of business out here was Stick's. Something in my mind began to itch. This felt wrong. "Ma'am," I said. "Are you okay?"

"Yes," she said and closed the door. I thought for a second she wasn't coming back until I heard chain unlatch. She opened the door. "You can come on in. I just get so tired of that music. It's those boys at the NCO club, I know. They just don't know when to quit." She walked across the living room, a huge area with a picture window that looked out over the water. The decor was white and peach, all brights.

"I'm Mildred, Mildred Thomas. My husband's Winchell Thomas." She looked at me with a knowing smile.

"I'm Justin Everson," I said, confused.

"*Commander* Winchell Thomas," she said. "The Commander."

"The Commander?"

"My husband has to be up early. Those enlisted men—they just don't understand." She paused and looked at me. What looked like recognition ran through her eyes. "Oh, don't be offended. I know that you MPs are enlisted, too. But I'm talking about those sailors down at the wharf. Those boys who just came back from sea."

Dementia I realized suddenly and it felt like someone had punched me. I'd never seen a case this close up. I'd only read about it. "Ma'am," I said. "Is your husband here now?"

"Oh, yes, of course. He's out on the porch." She stood and began to walk down the hallway toward the west end of the house but stopped and looked back at me. "You look terrible, son. You need to sit down. You know, I don't think that we'll be in this war very long. My husband says that President Johnson wants to bomb all of Southeast Asia."

"That would do it," I said. I didn't know if I should play along or not. She turned at the end of the hall and took two steps down into a large screened-in porch. Two huge papasan chairs sat looking out at the water. Somebody slumped in one of the chairs. I knew instinctively that the husband was dead.

"Mrs. Thomas," I said, thinking quickly. "Can you—do you mind giving me and your husband—I mean, can I speak privately with the Commander?"

She studied me, her eyes uncertain, a frown creasing her face.

I groped for words. "It's a matter of national security."

She smiled and crossed her arms. "Well, you sailors sure like your secrets. This happened once before, just last March. I'll bet I know what you're going to tell him. I'll bet he's headed out to sea again. My mother told me not to marry a sailor." She laughed, an airy, thin sound that put me on edge. "But I told her that he'd take care of me. Okay, young man. I'm going to go back to the kitchen and get you a glass of lemonade. You need some. You can drink it when you leave." She headed back up hallway.

I knelt down by the man. He looked to be in his 70s or 80s. Dressed in pastels from head to foot, he had a tattoo of a shark on his left forearm. His right arm was blurred with tattoos, all gone gray and green in old age. What little hair he had was still cut high and tight, military regulation. He'd been a sailor at some point, probably a career lifer. I pressed two fingers to his carotid artery, trying to find a pulse, and jerked my hand away. He felt waxy and cold. The skipper had seen better days.

"One-twelve to Apalachee," I whispered into my radio.

"Go ahead."

"I got a four one nine out here at Deerborne. Male, seventy or eighty years of age. Probably dead an hour or so. His wife's 10-50. Send an EMS."

"10-4. They'll be in route."

I walked back up to the front of the house. The woman was sitting in one of the recliners. She was sipping from a large, narrow glass. Another glass sat on the bar. I picked it up and smelled it—lemonade.

"Did the Commander set everything straight?" she said and smiled.

"Oh, yes ma'am," I said, hoping that Frank was hightailing it out here. I didn't know how long I could keep up this charade. My head felt woozy and groggy and I wanted to lie down. I rubbed my eyes and leaned against the bar.

"Why don't you sit down?"

I nodded and slid into one of the bar chairs. The lemonade was cool, but it tasted overly-sweet. I swallowed and my stomach churned.

"When we first came to Hilo three years ago, you'd have never guessed that so many people would be here," she said. Things began to fall into place in my head. She thought we were on a Hawaiian island.

"Yes ma'am. The war has a way of bringing lots of people to one place."

"But Winchell loves it out here, just loves it. He takes the boat out every time he has a day off. He usually catches some fish, too. I've become quite the seafood chef," said and laughed her dry, thin laugh.

I sat the glass down on the bar and leaned my head down, feeling nauseous. The lack of sleep was catching up with me. My eyes felt sandy and dry. When I looked up, my stomach tightened to a fist and breath froze in my throat

Donnie Ray Miles sat across from the woman in the chair opposite hers. He stared out the picture window at the darkness. He sipped from a glass of lemonade identical to mine. I wanted to say something, to shout, to scream. But my throat squeezed shut.

"Now who's that?" the woman said. I thought that she was talking about Donnie. Her voice sounded like it came from deep in a well.

I shook my head and looked at her. She was looking back toward the front door. Blue lights flickered through the shutters and screen. I saw a bald head peering through window. Frank was here. I looked back at the other chair, where Donnie Ray had just been sitting. He wasn't there. I closed my eyes and tried to focus.

Frank knocked on the door. "Apalachee County Sheriff's Department."

"That's my partner," I said. "He's with the MPs, too." The woman had sat back in the chair and thrown her arm over her eyes. "He wants the Commander's orders."

"Orders?"

"Yes ma'am," I said. I looked back at the chair where Donnie had been sitting, trying to see if he'd left any indention, but there was none.

I opened the front door and slid out, closing it behind me.

"How'd you get out here so quick?"

"I was coming down to find you. I was bored as hell. Nothing's happening on the north end tonight. Sheila radioed. Said you had a crazy out here." Frank was a few year older than I, a chubby guy with a gigantic caterpillar of a mustache crawling on his lip. He was bulky and bald. His head shone with sweat.

"Dementia," I said. "I think that she thinks we're in Hawaii."

"What? Really?" He craned his neck around me to look through the window. At that moment, an ambulance pulled up, its lights flickering silently. The side doors opened and two men in white got out, paramedics. I started down the steps.

"Yeah. She also thinks it 1968."

Frank whistled through his teeth. "No shit? What should we do?"

"Let's find out," I said and pointed at the ambulance

"Hey," one of the paramedics said, "ya'll okay out here?" I recognized him—a man named Gene Bishop. Close to my age, he was tall and had broad, thick arms that rippled with veins and muscles. I hadn't seen him in a long time. He'd been an auxiliary deputy for a while, but he hadn't done a ride along in a pretty good while. He was one of the elders at Zion Hope, a black church on Third Avenue on the South Side. A studded silver cross hung around his neck. He smelled like leather, the scent of a cologne he always wore.

"Yeah," I said and explained what I'd seen.

"Definitely dementia," Gene said. "Is there anyone we can call?

"The van's got Michigan plates," I said. "Snowbirds. This is probably a vacation home."

"Dammit," Frank said. "What are we going to do? We can't leave her out here."

"We can probably keep her overnight," Gene said. Pine View had once been a thriving hospital back in 70s, but since the late 1980s, it had been little more than a glorified drug store. They had emergency services, but they didn't keep regular patients.

"There might be a phone number inside somewhere," Frank said. "Maybe we can call their kids."

Gene nodded. "Good idea. We've got to take care of that body, though. Can one of you take her to the hospital? We can't leave her here. They'll sedate her. She can get some sleep."

Frank nodded. "I'll do it. I'm headed back to the north end, anyway."

Gene turned to the other paramedic, a white kid, pale and skinny. Couldn't have been a day over nineteen. "All right. Let's get the body loaded up." The kid nodded. Gene turned to me.

"Justin, you okay, man? I know I don't see you very often, but man, I been praying for you. The whole church has."

"I'm fine. Just tired. I'm not sleeping too well these days."

I turned to walk back toward the house, but he put a friendly hand on my shoulder. "I know you're still hurting, man. You ought to talk to a doctor if you can't sleep. After my ma-maw died, I couldn't sleep, either. It was terrible. I kept thinking about her. Kept seeing her everywhere I'd look."

I froze. "You did?"

He studied my face. "Are you seeing her? You seeing Janey everywhere?"

I didn't say anything.

"It's dreams, man. That's what's going on. Your mind makes this chemical that's released when you sleep. That's what causes dreams. If you don't sleep, you can't dream. Eventually, you'll just start having these waking dreams. That's what the doctor told me. I had some bad ones. Nearly ran off the road driving the bus one time." He gestured toward the ambulance. "I looked over and Ma-maw was just sitting there, pretty as you please. Scared the hell out of me. I thought I was seeing ghosts. Told the doctor about it and he got me on these pills. They helped."

"Thanks for the advice. And the prayers."

"I'll keep on praying, but you should talk to a doctor. You look horrible. You don't see a doctor, you're gonna keep seeing that ghost." I looked back up at the house. Mrs. Thomas looked down at us from the long rectangular windows that flanked the front door. I felt sorry for her. She really was seeing ghosts. Me—no ghosts. Just hallucinations. Just very insistent hallucinations. I wondered why I was seeing Donnie Ray and not Janey.

By the time my shift ended, I decided that Gene was right. I needed to talk to someone. I had insurance, so there was no reason that I shouldn't see a doctor. I could get some pills, something strong, something that would knock me out and not leave me feeling hollowed out the next day the way over-the-counter sleep aids did.

I went to the sheriff's department to do some paperwork on Winchell Thomas's death and went home and took a shower. I felt jittery and wired. Too much caffeine. I needed something to do, so I decided to drive that box of pornos back to Big Don's. With any luck, everybody would still be asleep. It was still before 8:00 a.m. I could creep in the back yard, put the box in the shed, and be gone.

A tan minivan with Alabama plates sat behind Big Don's truck, its back bumper plastered in "Roll Tide" stickers. Must have been Molly, Donnie Ray's sister, in town for the funeral. I wondered if I should go, wondered when exactly the funeral was.

I parked in front of the vacant lot next door and got the box of movies out the trunk and walked around the side of the house to the backyard. Big Don stood by the gate, smoking, his back to me. He wore a white t-shirt and a pair of camouflage shorts, the kind you wear around the house or sleep in.

"Morning," I said and opened the gate.

Big Don turned around and nodded his head toward the shed. "Just put them in there."

The shed had natural wood siding on it and a painted sign above the door frame: "Miles Taxidermy." I cracked the door and the smell of chemicals hit me. Smelled like a high school biology classroom. I felt thankful that I had never attended an autopsy in my five years as a deputy. I had no desire to do so. I set the box on the floor and closed the door.

"Thanks," Big Don said.

I nodded. I wanted to say something. I wanted to offer condolences again. But the words died on my tongue, useless, meaningless.

"When's the—"

"Funeral's tomorrow," he said.

The sky was still overcast, but a spot of blue had opened toward the west. Some seagulls flew above us, screaming and squawking. Out east, the paper mill's smoke stacks churned out black and gray.

"Where is it?"

"Church of Christ. Visitation tonight at Skipper's," he said, meaning the funeral home.

He stared at me. No emotions. Flat eyes. Mouth pressed tight. This was how he mourned. I wondered if he'd prepared himself for Donnie Ray's death before his son had headed off overseas. Every night, the news reported American soldiers' deaths. He had to have thought that Donnie Ray would have died over there. Not like this. Not at home

I wanted to ask about the girl in the photograph, Lucy.

"How long was he over there?"

Big Don looked me. "What?"

"Wasn't he in Iraq? I mean, before he," I paused, trying to form a sentence. "Before he came home."

He took a drag of his cigarette and pitched the butt to the ground and crushed with his foot. He was wearing a pair of leather work boots. They looked limp and ragged at the end of his narrow, hairy legs.

"Long enough," he said.

"I didn't mean to pry."

"Get out of my Goddamn yard," he said and went up the back steps. He didn't look back.

6

Before Janey died, I'd attended two funerals in my life: my father's and my grandfather's, my mom's dad, who died when I was a child. I didn't remember much about his funeral, but I could still picture the First Baptist packed with people when my father died. All of his friends came, all of his mill co-workers, all of them mourning the loss of their leader, the man who'd organized the strike that saved their jobs. Everyone spoke to me to tell me what a great man he'd been. Aaron and I sat near our mother, gulfs of silence and grief between us, choking us. In the sanctuary of the church, the stained glass turned all the light blue. It fell over the aisle like water, and that seemed appropriate somehow. Even my memory of that funeral seems submerged, all the voices muffled as though beneath the ocean.

Janey's funeral was different. If Dad's funeral was a solemn, somber occasion of communal mourning, Janey's funeral was a tight circle of grief, one I was kept out of, the ex-husband who had no place in the family's loss. No one would feel sympathy for me there. Still stung from her rejection, I didn't know how to feel. I didn't want to be surrounded by former in-laws who saw me as an interloper. I'd attended the funeral, though, an overcast, humid Thursday morning. I'd gone in late and left early during the singing of "How Great Thou Art."

The night before, at the visitation, a few people spoke to me, mainly the Reverend Bradley Greene and his wife, Pamela, a round, butterball of a woman who looked like a cross between a bowling ball and a kiwi fruit in the lime green dress she was wearing. They offered standard condolences. Since I didn't really attend church—I went a couple of times a year with Janey on Christmas and Easter— Bradley didn't know me very well. He kept offering to stop by the house to see me, just in case I ever needed someone to talk to.

Of Janey's family, only her sister, Meagan, spoke to me, muttering "Hello, Justin," before disappearing into a group of mourners. Janey's father stared at me from across the room. I left by a side door ten minutes after I'd arrived.

Visitations struck me as an odd ritual anyway, a combination of mourning and socializing often followed by a meal no one wanted to eat. I still had memories of my father's visitation, the way he'd been laid out in his coffin, made-up to look alive; the long line of acquaintances and distant family members who hugged me and tried to be friendly; the emptiness I felt growing in me like a widening pool. I had no intention of going to Donnie Ray's visitation, but Chris thought it was the right thing to do.

"I didn't even know that guy," I said to him over the phone that morning.

"Yes, you did. We did. We graduated with him. He was our age. And we both worked the scene. It would look bad if we didn't show up. You don't have to go to the funeral, but I think you ought to go to the visitation."

"Fine," I said. "But I'm not staying long."

"Ride with me. I won't make you stay too long. I'll pick you up this afternoon."

I met him out in the front yard. I was leaning against the side of my Dodge, smoking a cigarette, when a huge gray Chevy with over-sized mud tires rolled up in front of the house. The automatic window buzzed down and he looked at me over a pair of shades. "Put out that cancer stick, and let's go do some visitationing," he said.

We drove across town in silence. I kept thinking of Janey's funeral, and Chris stared straight ahead, tapping his finger in time the music from the radio.

Skipper Memorial was one of two funeral homes in town, the other being Grayson Brothers, a place that only African American families used. It was on Main Street on the South Side, a refurbished store front with cream decor and thick, plush carpet inside.

Skipper's funeral home was a block away from the bay, a large historic Victorian home that had once been a private residence, back when St. Vincent had been a boom town. Now, it sat aging among the live oaks and pines, a sprawling reminder of what used to be. Wesley Skipper had been the mortician there for as long as I could remember.

"Hello, gentlemen," said David Strickland, the preacher at Bay View Church of Christ, the moment we walked into the front door. A bald, chubby man with a neatly-trimmed goatee, he wore round-rimmed glasses. A thin sheen of sweat covered his head. He shook both of our hands a bit too long.

"Reverend Strickland," Chris said and nodded. "Lots of folks here."

"Call me Brother Strickland," the preacher said and smiled a toothy grin. "Yes, indeed. Mr. Miles' family is already here. They're back in viewing area. There's going to be a short memorial service. Donnie Ray was a military man. We want to celebrate our fallen brother's patriotic service."

Yeah, and he was kicked out for dope, I wanted to say, but I only nodded. My eyes felt dry in the sockets. I stifled a yawn.

"We'll go say hello," Chris said.

We passed through a giant room with a grand stairwell that disappeared up into the second floor. I tried not to picture Janey laid out on one of the steel gurneys up there, Mr. Skipper hunched over her, filling her body with formaldehyde.

Voices drifted down a long hallway leading to the back of the home. I stopped by a raised table holding a guest book. I signed "Justin K.

Everson," thinking, as I often did when I signed my name, that my life would be different if I'd gone by my middle name, Kyle. Kyle went to college and got the girl. Justin stayed home and his world fell apart.

"Come on," Chris said after he signed his name.

Donnie Ray's coffin sat on the far end of what had once been a spacious formal living room. Four rows of white fold-out chairs faced the coffin and an aluminum lectern. I wondered who was going to talk. The coffin was closed and covered with an American flag.

"Oh, what the hell?" I muttered.

"What?" Chris said.

"Like Donnie Ray was Patton or somebody."

Chris didn't say anything.

Small groups of people stood in various places around the room. I recognized Reverend Bradley Greene and a few others. Denise and Tater were chatting with a blonde I couldn't quite place.

It took me a second to realize that it was Anne Waites, Donnie Ray's girlfriend from high school. Freddy was nowhere to be seen. I looked around for Jimmy Danley, but he wasn't in attendance, either. Big Don and his wife sat in the front row by a red-head who had to be Donnie Ray's sister, Molly. She kept her head down, huddling close to a big man with a bushy black beard. Probably her husband. Big Don was nodding, speaking with the bearded man. I wanted to go over and say something.

Chris led us over to Denise, Anne, and Tater, who nodded at us and walked away. He sat by himself behind Big Don and the family.

"Hey," Denise said. She held her hand out formally and Chris shook it. I did, too. She wore a tight-fitting black dress that narrowed at her knees. Her hair was pulled back tight, the strawberry blonde strands shining in the florescent lighting. I smoothed the front of my shirt, wishing that I'd decided to wear a tie.

"Sorry about all this," Chris said, gesturing toward the coffin.

Denise waved off the condolences and put her hand on Anne's arm and said, "I'm sure you guys remember Anne."

"Of course. It's been a while," I said. I took her offered hand and lightly shook it.

"Haven't seen you in a long time," Chris said.

She smiled a sad smile. She'd been crying. "It's good to see you." She paused. "I need to step out for a second. Would y'all excuse me?"

We nodded and she walked away. Chris pointed at the lectern. "Who's giving a lecture?"

Denise sighed and shook her head. "The preacher is going to talk about why soldiers are so important. Something like that. Aunt Betty asked him to do it." She looked over her shoulder at Donnie Ray's parents.

I thought of Big Don's Navy tattoos. He took his military service record seriously, it seemed. "Where's Jimmy and Freddy?"

"Jimmy's working," she said. "I don't know where Freddy is."

"Jimmy still down at Clawson's?" Chris said, making conversation. He crossed his arms and flicked at the nubs of the missing fingers on his hand. "I read about the layoffs. Does he know anything yet?"

"I don't really know," she said, looking away from us. She hugged herself as though cold. An image of her came into my mind: beneath the stage lights, music pounding, wearing nothing but a thong and high heels, her tiny breasts glittering. I tried not to look at her.

"How are you doing, anyway? How long have you been back in town?" Chris said, the words coming easy to him, as they always had. He had an easy smile on his face, the kind he used for small talk. I'd seen him use it when he pulled somebody over for speeding. By the time he got done writing a ticket, you'd have thought that Chris was doing the speeder a favor. He had a way of putting people at ease, a confidence that emanated from his strong build, his easy stance, his mid-ranged voice. People liked Chris immediately. I envied him

Denise responded just as I'd seen others respond: friendly, open. "I got back about a year ago, actually."

"Really?" Chris said. He rubbed his jaw and arched his eyebrows. "How did I miss that?"

She cut her eyes at him. "We don't exactly run in the same circle, Chambers." She smiled, an uneven grin that revealed only the left side of her mouth. I wanted to say something kind, but I had nothing to say. So, I took a seat on the back row and waited.

Chris joined me after a second. More mourners arrived: Linda Danley (Jimmy's mama), Dwayne and Cindy Reece (Tater's aunt and uncle on his mama's side), Patty Fields, Michael and Lisa Winder, David Claiborne. I'd arrested their sons and daughters and nieces and nephews. I'd poured their beer out onto the white sand of Duna Blanco State Park, where I had drank so much beer myself back in high school; I'd driven the drunk and the high back to the holding cell at the sheriff's department; I'd even gone to some of these folks' houses in the middle of the night, waking them up and telling them that I'd found their precious son or daughter commode-hugging drunk or spaced out and high. But I'd only reported one death. I hoped that I'd never have to do it again.

By the time Brother Strickland waddled to the lectern and peered at us over the rims of his glasses, the crowd had swollen to twenty or thirty folks. Anne had come back inside. She was sitting near Donnie Ray's family, a few chairs down from Big Don. My head throbbed dully and my eyes itched. I wished I were at home, watching television. I kept staring at the back of Denise's head, simultaneously wondering if she'd be dancing later tonight and trying to chase the thought from my head.

"Brothers and sisters," Brother Strickland said, "we are a Christian nation, despite what some of those Hollywood liberals would like to tell us. And we know how important the soldier's sacrifice is. Our lost brother, Donald—Donnie Ray—joined the United States Army after the devil—in the guise of the Muslim religion—brought down our World Trade Center. Well, I can't tell you how proud I am of Donnie Ray Miles. He, like so many young men and women, knew that this is America. Like Jesus, America rose again." An approving murmur swept over the crowd. I peered over at Chris. As close as we were, we never talked about politics. His crossed arms and eyebrow-cocked, bemused expression told me that he could feel the bullshit piling around his boots, too.

"Yes, sir. America rose again," Brother Strickland continued. "God called me into the ministry. I can remember the night it happened. I was just a twelve-year-old boy terrified of the fires of a literal hell. God called Donnie Ray into the service just like He called me and others, like our special guest here tonight, a fellow minister of the word. He, too, felt the call of service. And when he was eighteen years old, he enlisted in the U.S. Air Force. He's come to talk a little about national service. He knows freedom isn't free. Help me welcome my brother in Christ, the pastor of St. Vincent First Baptist Church, Brother Bradley Greene."

I applauded politely and fought an urge to sneeze. The room had taken on a sweaty, stuffy scent, too much perfume, too much deodorant, too many bodies pressed into one another. I wondered if I could sneak out the back.

"Thank you, Brother Strickland," Bradley Greene said. He dropped a thick bible onto the lectern. Though I'd only been to church with Janey a few times, I knew the reverend's preaching voice. Pitched an octave low, the preaching voice had a mystic's rhythm. He'd chant out scripture as though it were a magical spell, reading only from the King James translation, not, in his words, "because it's the most accurate but because it's the most beautiful."

"Friends and neighbors," Bradley Green said, "how many soldiers are there in the Bible? How many soldiers are there in the Holy Word of God? Does anyone know?" He let the question hang. Somebody behind me stage whispered "a lot" and a nervous titter swept over the room.

"A lot," Bradley Greene repeated, smiling so wide his cheeks nearly hit his ear lobes. "A lot is right. We could count them off. We could. Soldiers in the Old Testament. Soldiers in the New Testament. Even the Roman centurion who was saved at the foot of the Cross. But I'm interested in only one soldier tonight. His name was King David, and he wrote the Psalms."

I tuned out, then, my mind floating back to Summer Bible Round-Up, a yearly tradition at First Baptist, where I'd attended as a child. Each year, the youth leaders would have a week-long celebration, all of it cowboy themed, which always struck me as odd. I didn't know anyone in St. Vincent who owned a horse. Nevertheless, every July, you'd see these western-themed signs all over town: "First Baptist Summer Bible Round-Up," followed by whatever slogan the church had decided on that year. One year, it was "Herding the souls to Jesus Christ."

The church split the kids into groups based on age. We separated into classrooms and learned Bible lessons. Afterward, we all herded into what First Baptist called the Fellowship Hall—a large brick building housing a kitchen and dining area—and ate hot dogs or pizza or tacos or some other kid-friendly fare. Then, we all went into the main sanctuary, sang songs, listened to a little sermon, and had an altar call. I think I got saved every year between the third grade and the sixth grade.

By the time I got into eigth grade, I quit going to Summer Bible Round-Up. Aaron I and went to church only when our parents made us go—nearly every Sunday morning and evening and every Wednesday night. Chris's mom didn't go to church, so he often went with me and my family. I tried, awkwardly, to share my faith with him, unsure of what I was talking about.

Once, he looked at me after I'd told him about the "literal burning fires of hell," and said, "We're friends, right?" I'd nodded. "Then, dude, please, shut up. The kind of stuff you talk about gives me nightmares." I never talked to him about church again. Now, looking over at him, I chuckled to myself. He'd turned out much better adjusted than I did.

"And if David can sin—this very man who was after God's own heart—don't you think, brothers and sisters, that we'll suffer, too? Don't you know that we're not immune from the effects of sin? Don't you think that our beloved brother, Donnie Ray, suffered over in the Iraqi desert, surrounded by Muslims who pervert our God? Donnie Ray did more than serve his country. He went into the Lion's den. Yea, though I walk through the Valley of the Shadow of Death, he swam into the great fish's mouth and he wandered the streets of Gehenna, brothers and sisters," Bradley Greene said, his voice turning into that chant I'd remembered. The image of Donnie Ray, some exiled Christian wandering around in Iraq handing out Bibles made me want to laugh. I took a deep breath and started to stand up, hoping I could find a path to the door.

"What he was, was a true American hero," a voice slurred from the back of the room. All eyes turned, and there stood Jimmy Danley, fresh from the boatyards. He wore a stained white t-shirt, ripped jeans, and a dirty pair of wading boots. A sweat-darkened Skoal baseball cap sat crooked on top of his head. He stank of sweat and fish. He hooked his thumbs in the front pockets of his jeans and nodded. "He was a hero," he said again. "An American hero."

A hushed murmur of voices spread over the room, and Denise stood up and started toward the back of the room.

"Well, Brother Danley," Bradley Greene said, a plastic smile on his face, "I agree with your assessment. I'm almost done here, and maybe we can all talk about Brother Miles' sacrifice. Why don't you find a seat?"

"Ya'll don't know," Jimmy said and glanced around the room. "He damn near died over there. Then the government—"

"As I was saying," Bradley Greene said, talking over Jimmy, who was muttering something about the government and something about communism.

Bradley Green tried to continue his sermon while three men got up and started toward the back of the room. Jimmy Danley walked between the rows of chairs toward the front of the room. People began whispering to each other. Big Don looked back, his red eyes pitted deep in a gaunt face. Donnie Ray's mama hung her head and wept loudly.

Chris hit my leg and stood up. "Come on," he said.

"What?"

He nodded his head at Jimmy. "Let's get him out of here."

"I got something to say about my friend," Jimmy said, running his words together. He'd made it to the front of the room.

"Jimmy, why don't you take a seat right up here," a large, balding man said. He motioned to where he'd just been sitting.

"No, no, no. I got to say something. People got to know the truth about my friend. He got poisoned. He was poisoned."

Chris grabbed Jimmy from behind, twisting his arm around back. "Come on, Jimmy," he said. "Let's go outside and talk."

"Get the fuck off me," he said, trying to twist away.

I pushed by the gathering crowd and grabbed for Jimmy's ankles, thinking we could carry him out.

"Son, don't," Linda Danley called out, her voice as frayed as a dishrag.

"Jimmy, Jimmy," Denise was hissing at him. "What is wrong with you?"

"Get him out of here," somebody shouted.

"Get off me, motherfucker," Jimmy said, ignoring Denise, ignoring Big Don's stony stare, ignoring the growing cacophony of voices in the room.

Thin and wiry, Jimmy twisted his body, kicking at me while wrenching away from Chris. His ankle slipped from my grip, and I stumbled into him, my knees coming down hard on the carpet. He tumbled sideways into the lectern and hit Reverend Greene, who twisted to avoid Jimmy. Greene bumped hard into David Strickland, who tripped, falling backwards. His shoulder caught the edge of Donnie Ray's coffin, and it fell sideways, its weight pulling down the stanchions arranged around it. For a horrifying moment, I thought that the coffin was going to open, spilling Donnie Ray's bloated, distended corpse out onto the cardinal-red carpet.

"No!" Anne shouted, her voice a wet sob. "No!" Big Don stood up, but Molly's husband wrapped his arms around his father-in-law, whispering something furiously into his ear. Big Don glowered with rage. Donnie Ray's mama began crying silently, dabbing at her eyes with a tissue.

The room erupted into a chorus of screams and shouts, some people hurrying out the back. Someone in the back of the room said, "He's as stupid as his daddy." I heard a few voices on cell phones, one-sided conversations to the Apalachee County Sheriff's Department.

"You are under arrest," Chris said. Two men had tackled Jimmy and were holding him face down. Chris had a knee on Jimmy's neck and had produced some handcuffs from somewhere.

I pulled myself up looked around for Denise, but she'd left the room. I felt dazed, as though none of this were really happening.

"Call the office," Chris said and I looked over at him. "Justin, call the office. Get a cruiser down here."

The world whirled around me, everything at angles. I reached in my pocked and pulled out my cell phone, but I'd landed on it with my hip bone. It wouldn't turn on.

"They're on the way," somebody said.

"Where did you get the handcuffs?" I said.

He stared at me. "You okay? Sit down. Rest your head. Take some breaths."

I sat down and held my broken cell phone in my hand, wondering vaguely if I could get a replacement for free. Didn't this fall under some clause in my insurance? Did I have cell phone insurance? My head felt heavy. My chin dipped.

The two preachers were talking, shaking their heads, scowls scoring their faces. From conversation, I gathered that the rest of the men gathered around were deacons and elders from First Baptist and the Bay View Church of Christ. They sat the coffin back up. It was bone white and shiny, trimmed in red, white, and blue. Two of the men re-spread the flag back over it, their faces still, their eyes solemn.

The world closed down to a muted roar for me. Two deputies arrived, pushing their way through the gathered crowd: Frank Sutton and Hector Tejada. They took Jimmy out the side door, his mama right behind, sobbing and threatening to sue if they laid a hand on him. She kept saying, "It's his way of grieving. Don't y'all understand?"

I put my head into my hands and massaged my temples. The dull headache had blossomed into a throbbing gong. My throat felt dry. I pushed my palms into my eyes, trying to shake the surreal feeling that the world was coming unstitched around me.

When I looked up, Donnie Ray Miles was standing beside his coffin, looking out a back window, the last remnants of sunlight casting a slatted shadow over him. He was dressed in service greens, a formal uniform trimmed with gold medals and multicolored badges. A green and gold corded rope hung over his right shoulder. I had no idea what any of the medals meant. Had Donnie Ray been a hero over in Iraq? The smell of pond water and swamp was everywhere. I raised my hand to point at him, but no one would look at me. Chris had fallen into a conversation with the two preachers and seemed to be deliberately avoiding my gaze. The deacons and elders stood in a circle, their arms crossed, faces lined and grim.

Donnie Ray looked at me. He opened his mouth, and a gout of river water exploded from his throat. I remember screaming, falling over the chair I was sitting on, and then darkness.

The rest of the night runs together in my head when I look back on everything. Chris and some of the deacons helped me up to a standing position. The visitation room had cleared out after the deputies had arrived. The two preachers were giving their statements. Soon, the deacons left, and only Chris and I remained—Chris and I and Donnie Ray Miles in his coffin.

Chris didn't say a word about my freak out. He just sat next to me, saying nothing, just like he did the night he came over after Janey's funeral. That night, we'd watched three movies back-to-back on cable, a Vietnam war marathon: *Full Metal Jacket*, *Platoon*, and *Hamburger Hill*. We drank two six-packs of Yuengling and ate fried shrimp he'd brought over.

We sat that way for a long time in the visitation room, listening to voices out in the hallway. Mr. Skipper, the funeral home director, came in after a while. "Everything okay back here?" he said. He was a tall man with graying curly hair hanging down the back of his neck, too long for his age. "I hate to rush you, but I need to lock up."

"Yeah," Chris said. "We're about to head out."

"Thanks for your help with the disturbance," Mr. Skipper said.

"No problem," Chris said. "We're leaving now."

We went back into the hallway and exited out a side door onto the lawn. A black hearse sat parked on a smooth gray driveway that curled around the back side of the building. The sun had set completely. The air smelled of pine and salt and paper mill fumes.

"You want to get something to eat?" he said.

I shook my head. "I want to go home." The word *home* felt strange my lips. Nothing felt like home any more. I had no idea what I'd just seen inside the funeral home: a ghost? A hallucination?

Chris rubbed his face and set his jaw in a straight line. "Look, man. I don't know how to talk to you about this. Something's wrong with you. You know it. I know it. You need to talk to someone. Get some pills. Something. You can't keep going on like this." He stopped. I could feel his eyes on me. "Janey wouldn't have wanted this for you."

"Janey's dead," I said. "She left me. She didn't give a shit about me."

"You know that's not true," he said and blew a sigh.

"Yes it is," I said. "Otherwise, she wouldn't have left."

"Say she hadn't. You'd be mourning your wife instead of you ex. It doesn't matter. You're in bad shape."

"Either way, she didn't give a shit about me. I was a mistake. Did you know that? She said that we shouldn't have gotten married. She said that I was a mistake."

"Look at me. Listen. You're not a mistake. You guys weren't a mistake. People grow apart. Shit happens. And you move on. That's how it is. Why do you think I'm in no hurry to get married? Christ, Justin. Look at my parents. I used to think my dad split because he hated me. Because he didn't want me. But now, I think he left because marriage is just too much. One person? Your whole life? Come on, Justin. Think about it. You and Janey worked for a while. And maybe that's enough."

"I don't care, anyway. I'm not even sure I ever loved her," I said. I wanted a cigarette.

"That's bullshit and you know it."

I stared at him. "What do you know? Huh? Yeah, I was upset at first. Upset she left. Then I got mad. And I'm still mad. And you know what? I think I'm just figuring this out, but I didn't love her, either. I don't know that I ever did. I'm over her. I'm done with her memory."

"You're not over her. You're not over anything. Your falling apart."

"That's not true. I'm not falling apart."

"Tell me that this isn't affecting your job, man. Tell me that you don't see what I see. You are a zombie. I don't even know if you know where you are right now."

"I know right where I am."

"Did you know where you were the other night? When you pulled that shit with those kids at Gulfaire? You know that's going to bite us both in the ass, right? That kid's daddy is a lawyer, Justin. You think he's not going to make something out of this?"

"I didn't do anything wrong," I shouted. "That little shit is lying."

"That little shit has a bloody nose and a friend who'll corroborate that you were pissing on the side of the house—on private property."

"So what?"

He held out his arms. "Are you kidding me right now? Are you serious?"

I turned around and walked around the west side of the building. Chris followed. There was a small gazebo with a little garden of azaleas around it on the side lawn. I walked to the gazebo and sat down. Opened up the menthols and lit one.

"Those things are killing you," Chris said. He didn't sit down.

"You know that driving a car can kill you, right?" I said.

"That's a stupid argument. Your dad died of a heart attack."

The wind came in off of the bay in whipping sheets. The cedar and pine trees rustled in hissed whispers. The humidity settled on my arms and in my hair, a thin sheen of sweat over my forehead. Chris crossed his arms and looked out toward the highway. His left thumb brushed at the edges of the nubs where his fingers had once been.

He looked over at me. "What are you not telling me?"

I wanted to say, "I've been seeing Donnie Ray Miles everywhere I look. I don't know if it's a ghost or a hallucination, but it's really freaking me out and I don't know what to do."

Instead, I said, "I think that Jimmy Danley had something to do with Donnie Ray Miles' death." The words surprised me. I didn't know I thought it until I said it.

"What? What in the hell are you talking about?"

"You saw what just happened in there," I said. "You saw Jimmy. He's feeling guilty. That's why he came here. He wanted to clear the air."

"Justin," he said, his words slow, careful. "I'm your friend. Listen to me: you can't run around making these kinds of accusations. Mack would shit a brick if he heard you. Hell, Davis Malone's head would explode. Beside, it doesn't make any sense. What evidence do you have?"

I didn't want to let it go. It made sense to me. In some strange way, I felt like the story gave Donnie Ray's death meaning. "Denise said that they weren't talking much these days. Big Don said they had some kind of a falling

"Over what?"

"I don't know. He didn't say, but think about it. Donnie Ray grew up around here. He knew how to swim. He didn't just drown up there. Jimmy did something."

"*Jimmy did something?* Will you listen to yourself, man?"

"No, you listen. Maybe Jimmy had something to do with Donnie Ray getting kicked out."

"No, that's not what happened. You know what people say. He was selling dope."

"Denise said—"

Chris shook head. "Denise is his cousin. Forget about what she said. Look, I get that you don't like Jimmy. You never have. He was an asshole back in high school. He's still an asshole. I get it. And despite what we just heard in there," he jerked a thumb over his shoulder back at Skipper's Funeral Home, "Donnie Ray Miles wasn't exactly a paragon of goodness. But the case is closed. The death was ruled accidental drowning. You can't go shooting your mouth off about this. I mean, with what you've been through—with what you're going through. Don't think Mack hasn't noticed."

"What?"

"You. You, man. You, insomnia boy. You, what else?" He stopped and studied me. "You need some time off. I really think that you might be coming unglued, man. I don't know how else to say it."

"I'm not coming unglued."

"You're going off half-cocked and pulling a gun on a couple of snot-nosed teenagers. You're dreaming up cockamamie movie plots about an open-and-shut drowning."

"Just think about it," I said. "Both Denise and Big Don said they had a falling out. Maybe they got in some kind of a fight up there on the river. Maybe Donnie Ray didn't like Jimmy seeing Denise, you know? I mean, she's better than Jimmy. She could do better. So maybe Jimmy just pushes Donnie Ray in the river when no one's looking. He knew Donnie Ray was too drunk to swim. And what did he say in there a minute ago? You heard him. He said that he was poisoned. He said Donnie Ray was poisoned."

"Jesus H. Christ, Justin. Jimmy was drunk. Lord knows what else he'd say if you asked him. And Tater and Freddy were on that houseboat, too. You think they're all complicit in this? You really think that—what? A conspiracy? They all covered it up? Stop watching all those shitty ghost documentaries. They're messing up your head."

I didn't want to admit that what Chris was saying made sense. We both fell silent, listening to the wind, smelling the damp trees and soil, the salt in the air. "Do you have to work tonight?" Chris said.

I shook my head.

"Look. I want you to go home and take it easy. Try to rest."

"I can't sleep. I haven't been able to since Janey died."

"Not at all?"

I shook my head and took a long drag of the cigarette, pitched on the ground, and crushed it on my boot. He glared at me.

"What?"

"Pick it up."

I did and rolled the filter into a little ball between my fingers.

"I want you to talk to Mack tomorrow. I want you to tell him you need some time off. Don't say shit about your murder plot, please. Just tell him you need some time off."

"I'll think about it. Take me to the house. I just want to go home."

7

The first letters signed "The Treadless" began showing up in *The Sentinel* a week after Donnie Ray's funeral. *The Sentinel* had two ways to get your opinion in the paper. You could write a letter or an editorial, or you could call in and leave a message anonymously. These appeared in a short column called Flotsam and Jetsam. Just after Clawson's announced downsizing, the column ran few comments: "Nice job, Clawson's. Twenty years pulling shrimp, and now I can't pay my bills" and "The employees of Clawson's Fishing deserve better."

Then, someone named Wayne Childress wrote a letter decrying Florida's Right to Work Status, arguing that if the workers at Clawson's unionized, if they had collective bargaining rights, then this wouldn't have happened. "That state has effectively neutered any power the dockworker's union may have had. No one is standing in the way of Fred Clawson, a man who values profit over people," Childress wrote. The name "Wayne" rung a bell, but I just couldn't place it.

I was sitting in Charlie's Café a a week after Donnie's funeral, reading the newest issue of *The Sentinel*. More talk about the shutdown. More talk about the layoffs. Rich Richards, Freddy's daddy had published a letter, a long, unbroken paragraph demonizing unions and those who supported them: "Fred Clawson is a self-made American businessman. Unions are Communists who extort money from hard-working American citizens." He signed his screed "Rich Richards, President, The Treadless." Beneath his signature, he'd written, "The tree of liberty must, from time to time, be watered with the blood of tyrants." *Christ almighty*, I thought and took a sip of the coffee.

Why a first-class loser like Rich Richards felt like had a dog in this hunt eluded me. For as long as I'd known Freddy, his daddy had been a bottom-feeder. A thin, wiry guy built who shared his son's build, Rich also shared Freddy's complexion—olive skinned and tanned year around, as though he worked outside in the sun. But Rich didn't work anywhere. Once, he'd had a job at the paper mill, but it didn't last too long. He had a habit of showing up an hour or so after his shift started. He'd come in late, have a shout-out with the foreman, and refuse to leave, even if he was sent home. After he was fired, he'd tell anyone who listened that the mill fired him unjustly..

I rarely saw him. Sometimes, he'd be in downtown St. Vincent, parked at The Crow's Nest. Inside, he sat on a barstool and talked about how much the world had mistreated him. Once, Chris pulled him over on Sandy Head Beach for weaving. Rich was drunk and ready to fight. Chris took him in, and Rich spent the entire ride to the sheriff's department calling Chris a "revenue generator" and a "police-state fascist."

I scanned the letter again and shook my head. Rich Richards, protector of the free world. What had Hokey said? Feels like the whole damn world's falling apart.

The clock above the cash register read quarter until ten a.m. I had a doctor's appointment at 10:30. I put a ten dollar bill on the able and left and drove to Dr. Bristol's office, a small brick building a block over from the main drag in town.

The night of Donnie Ray's visitation, I'd fired up my ancient desktop computer and gone online to research symptoms, trying to figure out why I'd be having visions of a dead man. I found all kinds of forums and discussions. Everyone had a theory, it seemed, but no one had answers. I resolved that I had to visit the doctor, despite my fear that he might deem me unfit for duty. I had to get some sleep. The next day, I made an appointment with Dr. Bristol, a general practitioner in Apalachee County. He'd given my required physical when I joined the sheriff's department, but I'd not seen him in several years.

The office smelled like old magazines and antiseptic. The walls were wood paneling, more suited for a hunting lodge than a doctor's office. A mounted big mouth bass hung above the door to the back, its beady glass eyes dark and silent. I sat on a slick, faux leather couch and watched a muted morning talk show and flipped through an old issue of *Field and Stream*. Soon, the door opened, and a nurse, a young woman who couldn't been much older than me, poked her head out.

"Mr. Everson?" she said, her voice high pitched and girlish.

I nodded and followed her in the back. She weighed me and took me into an exam room. I sat on the edge of a paper-covered cot, and she wrapped a blood pressure cuff around my right arm and began pumping the valve.

"It's a little high," she said as she scribbled on a chart.

"Is it bad?"

She popped her chewing gum and shrugged. "It's high. Do you smoke, Mr. Everson?"

I nodded.

"Drink?"

"Not to excess."

"It's not dangerously high, but you should probably think about quitting. You stay here. He'll be right in."

I studied the pictures on walls while I waited: a human body's respiratory system, cartoony and red. A diagram of a human brain. A picture of a wild turkey, framed in wood. Dr. Bristol came in a few minutes later. He smelled of leather and old shoes. He looked like an extra from some

1950s-era courtroom drama, a tall, bulky man with a thick black mustache and a steel gray flat top.

"Deputy Everson," he said and smiled tightly. He pulled over a rolling stool and sat down in front of me. He took my chin in his hands and adjusted my head while he shined a light in my eyes.

"Your blood pressure's high."

"I smoke. It's bad. I know."

"So did your father, I remember," he said.

I mumbled, "Yeah" and tried not to think about my father's heart attack.

"So you can't sleep?"

"Not at all."

"How long?"

"A couple of months."

"That might be part of the blood pressure problem," he said more to himself than to me.

He wrote me a prescription for some sleeping pills—Ambien—and recommended that I see a counselor. He thought that I was still mourning Janey's death. I didn't tell him that I was seeing Donnie Ray everywhere I looked. I didn't want him to think that I was crazy. I thanked him and told him that I'd think about seeing someone.

"I'm serious," he said. "I think it would benefit you." He peered at me over the rims of his round-frame glasses.

"Can I ask you a question?"

He nodded. "Of course."

"Is it possible to dream while you're awake?"

He frowned. "Well, technically, yes. I guess if you don't get enough sleep. We call them 'waking dreams.' Are you having them?"

I didn't say anything for a moment. "Maybe," I said. "I'm not sure."

Dr. Bristol rubbed his neck and sighed. "Take the Ambien. Get some sleep. We can schedule you for a sleep study, too."

"I think I just need some rest."

"All right. Choice is yours. But listen, you really need to talk to someone. See a counselor, okay?"

"I'll do it," I said, not sure if I were lying or not.

He gave me a card for a counselor in Apalachicola and I left, wondering if I should go, wondering if Chris had been right. Maybe I did need some time off.

Walking out of the office, I felt hopeful for the first time in a while.

Things were going to be all right. My sleeplessness was part of mourning. I missed Janey. I missed our marriage. But I wanted to move on. My mind drifted to Denise, and I pictured her in Jimmy's arms and pushed the image away, angry at myself.

I wondered if I believed what I'd said to Chris. Did Jimmy Danley have something to do with Bill Ray Miles' death? The idea had floated at the back of my mind, a seductive reason to make a play for Denise. If I could convince myself that her boyfriend had killed his best friend, then maybe I wouldn't feel like such a scumbag for wanting to be with her.

I drove down an alley to cut over toward the Swifty for some gas when I saw a familiar green Mazda parked in front of the The Crow's Nest. Jimmy Danley, Rich Richards and Freddy walked out of the front door. Rich gestured around, pointing here and there, his mouth moving quickly. Jimmy had crossed his arms. He nodded, his face a grim line. Freddy stood near them, head down, hands deep in his jeans pocket. After a minute, Jimmy got into Denise's car and peeled out onto the road. Rich leaned into Freddy, talking into his son's ear, one hand on Freddy's shoulder, the other patting his son's chest. Freddy nodded, his face glum, and got into a tan pickup truck, a sun-faded S-10. Rich watched him drive away and went back into the bar.

I pulled through the alley and crossed over the street into another alley that ran between a hardware store and an out-of-business furniture warehouse. At the highway, I turned left, headed to the Swifty for gas. Seeing Freddy, Jimmy, and Rich together shouldn't have been odd. They knew each other. But something about the way Rich talked to Freddy bothered me. Something about it all seemed off. I didn't know if I should trust my gut. Maybe I was just making things up. I idled down the highway and turned into the Swifty's pock-marked parking lot.

As I was leaned against the side of my truck, watching the numbers on the fuel gauge go by, Freddy drove into the lot. He got out and went inside. He went to the counter and bought something and came out with a small white bag.

I locked the gas handle and walked across the lot.

"Freddy?"

"Oh, hey." He opened his truck door and got in. He didn't look at me.

I put a hand on his windshield and leaned into the rolled-down window. "Man, it's just terrible what happened to Donnie Ray. I know that you guys were friends."

He was opening a beef jerky. "Yeah," he said, not meeting my eyes. A patchy two-day beard grew on his olive skin.

"Did you go to the funeral? I missed it. I was at the visitation. Did you hear about what happened with Jimmy? He caused quite a scene."

He cranked the truck. "No, I had to work. I was working. I heard you caused a scene, too. You all right?"

My face burned, but I tried not to show any emotion. "I'm not sure what you're talking about," I said.

"Look, I got to run. Did I do something wrong?"

"No," I said. I didn't want him to drive off. "I just wanted to offer my condolences. Bad enough that he died. But Jimmy showing up at the visitation like that? Raising hell? That's just disrespectful."

"Yeah. Jimmy can be—Jimmy's a live wire," he said, his hands on the steering wheel. The truck's motor coughed, shaking the vehicle. He needed some transmission work.

"Hey, man," I said and leaned in further, "what happened up there?"

"Up where?"

"The houseboat. The night Donnie Ray died. Was Jimmy a live wire that night? Was he cutting up with Donnie Ray? I mean, I heard they'd been arguing a lot."

"No, you got it wrong. They were arguing, but it wasn't like that. They weren't arguing that night." He finally met my gaze. His eyes were large, round. Liquid. "Donnie Ray drowned. It was an accident. He just drowned."

"What did they argue about?"

"Look, am I under arrest or something?"

"No. I just wondered. I didn't work the scene. I just didn't know."

His shoulder fell as he let out a breath. "We were listening to music. Having a good time. We were going stay up there for a couple of days. It was Donnie Ray's birthday. He was there one minute. Then he was gone. I don't know, man. It was like he just disappeared. He fell in."

"Did any of you see it?"

"See what?"

"See him fall in?"

"No. Like I said. He was there and then he wasn't. I was inside when it happened." He bit his lower lip in a frown. "Look, Justin, isn't all this stuff in the police report or whatever?"

I held my hands up. "I'm sure it is, man. I just wondered. I mean, I knew him, too."

"Yeah you did. Can I go?"

I nodded and he backed out, pulled out onto the road, and sputtered away, the truck backfiring and coughing, the faded "Don't Tread on Me" sticker on the back window glowing in the sunlight like a challenge Freddy didn't have the courage to make on his own. One thing was certain: he was hiding something. Someone knew the whole story about what happened the night Donnie Ray drowned. And I intended to hear it.

I drove to the sheriff's department to see if I could find the case report on the drowning. I wanted to see if Freddy told the same story the night of the Donnie Ray's drowning. I wanted to know what all of them had to say, Tater and Jimmy, too. Especially Jimmy.

I walked to the back of the department to a shared office we all used. It had three computers and two work desks sitting near three filing cabinets, where we kept everything from incident reports to applications. I opened one and starting going through the files, looking for the crime scene report of Donnie Ray's drowning. I flipped through a thick stack of manila folders, cursing our budget cuts. Since we didn't have a full-time secretary anymore, individual deputies were in charge of filing. As such, the files were a mess.

"How you doing today?"

I turned to see Cowboy standing in the doorway, a Styrofoam cup of coffee steaming in his right hand.

"Sergeant," I said. "Doing okay." I felt caught, liked I'd been doing something wrong.

He pursed his lips and rocked back on his heels. "That's good. I was a bit worried about you."

"Oh yeah?"

"The incident," he said, his tone even. "The other night. You know what I mean."

"Just haven't been sleeping too well. I went to see Dr. Bristol this morning. He gave me a prescription. Ambien. I should be able to sleep better."

"What are you looking for there?"

I glanced at the open drawer. "I wanted to look at the Winchell paperwork again. I think I made a mistake on it," I said, not sure why I was lying.

He looked at the mass of unorganized folders. "That's a mess. Who filed the report?"

"Frank," I said. That much was true.

"What kind of a mistake did you make?"

"I think I put the wrong time on there. It was late."

He narrowed his eyes and blew steam off the coffee. "I talked to Gene Bishop this morning. Told me you said you were seeing things."

I blew a short sigh. "Not really 'seeing things,' per se. Just having weird dreams. It's not a big deal."

"Look, I know you've been through a lot lately, but that freak out the other night—"

"I didn't exactly freak out."

He cocked an eyebrow. "Well, you didn't exactly play it cool, either, did you? Whooping and hollering like that? Jimmy Danley was bad enough."

"I'm sorry," I said. "I planned on going by the Miles' house to apologize."

He shook his head. "No, you won't. You leave them folks alone. They've been through enough. I don't know what you were doing out there at Donnie Ray Miles' trailer the other day, either, but—"

I wondered how on earth he knew I'd been to the trailer. "Big Don asked me to—"

"I don't care," he said. "You listen to me, Justin. I've always liked you. You're a good deputy and a good man. But lately, you've been messing up. Your paperwork is sloppy. You spend too much time at the Swifty when you're on duty. You need to focus. It's a good thing you saw that doctor. I think you need some time off, but that's for Mack to decide."

I tried to speak, but Cowboy said, "Let me finish. There's some stuff coming down the pipe you don't know about. You remember that kid you busted a couple of nights ago? The one out at Gulfaire?'

I nodded.

"Well, you know who is, then? You know who his daddy is?"

I nodded again. My stomach was a pit. I didn't like where this was going. "Yes."

"His daddy called a lawyer. They're coming over here tomorrow morning. Mack's going to call you later today about it."

"Why? We didn't do anything wrong."

"Nobody said you did, but that kid says you roughed him up. He also said you pissed on the side the house."

"Can't Mack tell Whitley to go to hell?"

Cowboy shrugged. "Whitley's kind of got Mack's ass in a sling. Whitley's big on the county commission. Next year's an election year. You do the math. But the sheriff's in your corner. This is politics, that simple."

"When's the meeting?"

"Mack'll call you, I'm sure. Somebody will."

"Okay. Okay." I paused. "I guess I better get going."

"Wait a minute. I know this hasn't been easy on you—any of it. What with her leaving you and then getting killed." He paused. "Wait. You weren't looking for her file, were you? The accident report?"

"No."

"Just don't. Nobody needs to see that, especially not you."

"Is Mack going to fire me?"

He chuckled without humor. "I doubt it. With these budget cuts, we can't replace you."

I smiled weakly. "Yeah," I said. "I guess so."

"I got to run. I go things to do. Look, don't worry about this. But you need to know, you've got a support system here. Mack might even give you a few days off."

"I don't want to do that. Who'd cover my shift?"

"He might *have* to give you a few days off, if you get what I'm saying. Don't worry. We can make it work," Cowboy said.

"Thanks for the heads up."

"Go home, Justin. Get some rest." He walked down the hall and I shut the filing cabinet drawer. There were answers, somewhere. I just doubted they were in here.

Cowboy was right. Mack called that afternoon and left a message saying that I needed to meet with him tomorrow morning at ten. His kept his voice even, but I sensed a weight. I sent Chris a text message asking him if he'd gotten a phone call. A few seconds later, my phone buzzed. "Yes," the message read. We hadn't spoken since the night of Donnie Ray's visitation.

That afternoon, thunderheads formed over the bay and let loose a good, soaking rain. I sat in the den most of the afternoon, flipping channels, listening to the rain, thinking about Jimmy Danley and Denise Miles. Especially Denise. I couldn't see what she saw in Jimmy. She could have done better. She'd gone to college, right? For a while, at least. I didn't know what had happened. I figured that the next time I saw her, I'd ask. I'd ask her about a lot of things, maybe.

Around 6:00, I called Charlie's and ordered a hamburger. He had the best burger in town, thick ground chuck cooked to a char on the outside, medium well on the inside. He used only Florida or Georgia produce, too, so the tomato and onion always tasted fresh. Though I ordered it to go, I thought I might eat at the restaurant, something I did from time to time if the church crowd was thin. He usually closed at 7:00 most nights, but on Wednesdays, he stayed open till 9:30 for anyone who wanted a bite to eat after service.

Charlie's was busy. I parked in the alley behind the restaurant and walked around the side, past the paper box where I'd had my encounter with Denise the morning after Donnie Ray died. The rain had a thinned a bit, but a mist fell steadily. Trucks and cars lined the road. Rust scars scabbed many fenders and hoods.

The noise inside surprised me. The side room was filled, and all of the tables were taken. The whole place was packed with shrimpers and dock workers, some bearded, some clean-shaven, some young, some old, some black, some white, some Hispanic, but all with those deep-sunken eyes and chorded forearms a lifetime of fishing gives you. Many wore Clawson's Fisheries ball caps. Some wore Clawson t-shirts and jackets. They clustered around small tables, sometimes five and six folks sitting at four-tops. I'd never seen so many commercial fishermen in one place before.

Charlie's wife, Luann, was working the register. "Charlie's getting your order," she said and smiled. She was blonde with sun-baked, freckled skin. I always thought that Charlie had married up. Luann carried herself with class and grace. Someone across the restaurant yelled, "Luann," and she held up a hand. "Charlie will ring you up. Good to see you, Justin." She picked up a sweat-beaded pitcher of sweet tea and cut through the crowd.

Charlie came out of the back and put a Styrofoam clamshell on the counter by the register. "That's five even," he said.

"The burger's seven bucks on the menu."

He smiled, his eyes crinkled. "Not for you, deputy."

I slid a five dollar out of my wallet. "What's going on here tonight?"

"Union organizing. Clawson employees," he said, his voice swollen, proud.

"I read about the downsizing."

"These folks won't take being laid off lightly."

I picked up the hamburger and nodded. The gathering made me happy. I liked that these guys were standing up for what was right. It would have made Dad happy, too.

"I better run," I said.

"Be safe," Charlie said.

As I opened the door, I heard a voice, its clean, even tone recognizable. "Hey, Charlie, can we get two more menus?"

I turned around to see the fisherman I'd seen the morning Donnie Ray died, the one with the voice like a teacher. He wore a Clawson's hat and a yellow rain slicker and white waders over his shoes. He was sitting at a table with a young black man wearing a suit. He was talking on a cellular phone, one finger jammed in his ear.

"Good to see you again, deputy," the fisherman said. A trace of a smile pulled at the edge of his lips.

"You, too, man." I stuck out my hand. "Justin Everson," I said.

He shook my hand once, and I was surprised at the roughness in his palms. Part of me had suspected younger hands, smoother hands.

"Wayne Childress," he said.

"You wrote the letter in the paper."

"I did."

"You guys having a meeting?"

He squinted his eyes. "That's okay, right?" I couldn't tell if he was serious.

"Of course," I said. "I just wondered. That's all."

He nodded his head, never blinking. We both fell into an awkward silence.

"I better go," I said. "Good luck to you guys. What with the mill shutting down, I didn't know if Clawson's was next."

The young man on the phone snapped it shut. "Not if I have anything to say about it." He half rose and stuck out a hand, which I shook. His palms were smooth and cool. "Cedric Baldwin."

"Justin Everson."

"It's good to have an attorney in your corner," Wayne said.

"I'm sure it is," I said. "Think Clawson has lawyers too?"

"None as good as Cedric," Wayne said. Cedric grinned.

"You guys have a good night," I said and walked out the door.

Outside, the rain had picked back up into a thick drizzle, long lines of water pouring from the sky. I half-jogged back to the truck, suddenly very hungry thanks to the smell of the burger.

In the Dodge, I turned the heat on low. I smiled to myself, thinking about the crowd at Charlie's. Dad would have been happy about these guys standing up to Fred Clawson.

I didn't know Cedric Baldwin. He must have been an out-of-towner. But Wayne Childress's name danced at the edge of my memory, at once familiar and completely foreign. Even before I'd read his letter, I'd heard it before, but I didn't know where or when. There weren't any Childresses in high school, and I didn't know anyone by that name in Apalachee County. Something about him bothered me, though, something incongruent about his rough hands and the too-educated way he talked. Even the way he held his body seemed different from the others at Clawson's, not stooped and bowed like so many fishermen and shrimpers, but straight, even as a crease in a new pair of jeans. He looked to me like he'd have been more comfortable in a library than he would have been in a seafood warehouse.

I didn't know who he was, but that didn't mean anything. If being a deputy had taught me anything, it was this: there were millions of tiny dramas unfolding around me at any given moment of the day, a world filled with folks I didn't know, had never seen, despite sharing the same space with them for a lifetime. As I put the truck in gear to go home, I'd decided to call my mom the next day and ask her if she knew the Childress family when it hit me. Wayne Childress was the voice on the answering machine at Donnie Ray's trailer.

8

In the dream, I am beneath the waves, my body suspended in a currentless no-place. Salt water stings my eyes as I try to focus on tiny motes of plankton and sea weed that float by like ghosts. My lungs burn, and my mouth opens on its own. The suffocating intake of water wracks my body in a back-breaking spasm. My head shakes back and forth in an eternal no. No Janey. No Donnie Ray Miles. No St. Vincent. No Denise. I try to focus on something in my mind, a familiar face, my father's deep baritone, the lone keen of the paper mill whistle, the softness of Janey's palms—anything to bring me back to the surface. But the sound is mute and far away. Janey's hands slip from my grasp. Every face turns into a watery wraith, distorting, dissipating, disappearing. I twist and whip my head around, trying to gain my bearings, trying to find the surface, but there is only darkness visible, only me caught in some still Sargasso, arms stuck out like clock hands, moving, going nowhere, stagnant motion like storm run off in clogged ditch. My lungs suck in more water, and I know I am drowning, know death is close out in this black nowhere. The salted world begins to shrink, closing in like a circle, like the the last star winking out in an apocalyptic sky. Inked blackness. Total darkness. No way to know up or down, just suspension, stillness, no motion, no diurnal tide, no riptide, no undertow. Just the sea covering me in a preserved grave.

I came awake slowly, light filling my vision like a slow tide. My head felt light, airy. My last memory was undressing and lying down. The night had passed and I'd not woken up. I sat up and stretched. The world refused to come into focus, all the hard edges softened, distant. My wood-grained dresser, the full-length mirror Janey used for make-up, the three-shelf bookshelf we'd gotten for a wedding gift: all the corners look fuzzy, as though the world hadn't completely formed. I rubbed my eyes and took a breath.

The clock read 9:15 a.m. I squinted and looked at it again. I couldn't believe that I'd slept so long and not woken up once. The drowning dream was breaking up into fragments, but the suffocating feeling of drowning made my chest feel heavy.

I showered and dressed and made some coffee, something I'd not done at home in God knew when. I toasted a piece of bread and drank the coffee black. I had no creamer and no sugar in the house and nearly gagged on the stuff it was so strong. All his life, my dad drank his black, and so did a lot of guys down at the department, but I was strictly a cream and sugar man. Walking out the front door, I wondered vaguely if that said anything about my manhood.

At the sheriff's office, Chris was sitting at one of the communal desks in the squad room. He had bags under his eyes, the skin tight around his mouth. He was looking at a computer screen, eyes narrowed. I figured he was reading about statutes, something to throw into Whitley's lawyer's face.

I sat down at the opposite desk. "What you learning?"

"That I suck at blackjack," he said. He didn't look up from the computer.

"I went to see the doctor yesterday. He gave me a prescription. That stuff knocked me flat out last night."

He clicked the mouse.

"You're chatty."

He looked up at me. "I'm worried about this meeting. I don't want to talk about it. I'm worried. Leave it at that."

"You know a guy named Wayne Childress?"

"I've heard of him. Works out Clawson's, I think."

"I ran into him last night, down at Charlie's."

"Ran into him?"

"He was up there. We talked for a minute. I'd just never heard of him."

"I think he's from Apalach."

We fell silent. The buzz of the computer monitor sounded over the air conditioner's white noise. Every so often, you'd hear squelch and muffled voices from the dispatcher's room in the back. After a while, I said, "So, what's this all about? Is Whitley claiming we harassed the kid or something?"

"I assume." He clicked the mouse.

"Is Mack here?" I said. We still had few minutes before the meeting, and I wondered if we ought to talk to Mack, maybe build some kind of a strategy.

"In the back, talking to Cowboy."

I walked out of the squad room and back out into reception. I thought I'd go outside, burn a cigarette, and then have a chat with Mack and Cowboy. See just how serious this thing was.

Whoever was working reception had stepped out, and the front room was empty. I stared out the glass doors, trying to imagine a worst-case scenario, mentally prepping myself for it. I didn't think we'd be fired. Both Chris and I were five-year veterans with no strikes against us. At worst, we'd get suspended for a week. But I didn't want that on my record: suspension for doing my job. If I ever looked for another job in law enforcement, it would be in my personnel file.

Surely, lots of cops had worse in their pasts. On TV, guys like me had a bad reputation as thugs with badges, small-town good old boys who wanted nothing more than to crack skulls and harass local teenagers. Add in a dose of racism, and you had the Hollywood recipe for any southern cop. I wanted to distance myself as far as I could from that picture.

The bulletin board by the front door was covered in local business cards and flyers for church bake sales and yard sales. One typed-up sign caught my eye. *Apalachee County Paranormal Society Meeting. Every Second Saturday, 4:30-5:30 p.m.. Apalachee County-St. Vincent Public Library.* A phone number and an email address were centered at the bottom. I'd never heard of the group. Spook chasers in St. Vincent? It made sense. The old cemetery on the edge of town was supposedly haunted by a ship captain who'd succumbed to Yellow Fever in the late 1800s. A few old homes around town rumored to have ghosts.

"How about it, Justin?" a rumbling voice said. Cowboy was walking down the tiled hallway.

"I'll tell you in a little while."

"It's not as bad as you probably think," he said. "Just go in there and tell the truth, okay?"

I nodded, hoping it was that easy.

The meeting didn't last long. Whitley and his lawyer wanted me and Chris suspended indefinitely, claiming harassment. They talked about a lawsuit against the entire Apalachee County Sheriff's Department. The lawyer, some jackass from Panama City who probably got his degree online, claimed that I'd used excessive force on Jason—that I'd used my power and my gun to intimidate him.

Chris sat quietly in the hearing, hands on his lap, his right thumb stroking the spot where his index and middle fingers had once been. I sat next to him, trying not to stare at Jason Whitley, who grinned at me. He wore a charcoal suit and a black tie, just like his father, Joe Whitley, who sat next to him. He was a big, fat man with a bald head. The bunched skin at his neck made him look like a melting candle.

At one point, Jason pursed his lips and winked at me. I imagined landing my Maglite right between his eyes.

After the meeting, Mack called us separately into his office, Chris first. I sat in the squad room, reading an online forum about haunted houses until Chris came out, shaking his head.

"I'm on dispatch for three weeks," he said. He didn't look at me.

The room smelled like old coffee and toner, and my stomach felt sour. I walked into Mack's office and sat down.

Mack's desk was like his office: uncluttered and clean. The top of the desk shone bright in the fluorescent lighting. On the wall over his desk hung several citations and certificates and diplomas.

He leaned forward, fingers laced in a fist in front of him. "Well, this is all a load of grade-a bullshit," he said. His voice was like the rest of him, sharp, neat—a southern accent evident only in the elongated vowels. He was what my father would have called ship-shape.

"That's how I'd put it," I said.

"But you didn't make this any easier on us. You realized that, right?"

I nodded. I wanted to defend myself, but I didn't want to argue with Mack.

"Did you really piss on the side of the house?"

I didn't say anything.

He cocked an eyebrow. "Well?"

"You know, when you're out, and you think no one's around?"

He held up his hand, cutting off the rest of my explanation. "Holy hell, son. I thought my deputies were potty trained. How did the that little shit's nose get busted?"

"He tried to run away from me. I grabbed his arm and turned him around. He fell down. I didn't hit him."

He sat back in his chair and crossed his arms. The hair on his forearms was thick as a dog's fur. "Tell me something, Everson. Are you okay?"

"What do you mean?" I said.

"I heard about the other night. At the visitation."

I didn't say anything. What could I say?

He blinked a couple of times and sighed through his nose. "Here's the deal. Without agreeing to any wrongdoing on your part—and I mean none. I agreed to *nothing*—I told Whitley that I'd put you on administrative leave for two weeks. No formal reprimand. Nothing in your personnel file. I want you to spend some time at home. Get you head together. Grieve properly." He sat back in his chair and studied me, his eyes searching.

I stood up. "That sounds good," I said. "That sounds all right to me, I guess." Nothing was going on my record. That was good. But I wasn't relishing any time off.

"Doesn't your mama live up in Atlanta?"

"Decatur."

"Why don't you take a road trip? Get out of town for a while? Might do you some good."

"That's not the worst idea," I said, but I had no intention of leaving St. Vincent.

Mack looked up at the ceiling. He might have been talking to himself. "I probably should have offered you some kind of a leave of absence after she died, shouldn't I?"

"I think the job's been good for me. I guess it helps me not think about things."

"I understand that. I had a friend, long time ago, when I was living in Georgia. He shot a guy. Killed him. Routine traffic stop and the driver pulls a piece. My friend, Jake, drew and fired. Had no choice." He shook his head back and forth. "Messed him up good. He couldn't sleep after it. He'd get nightmares. But he kept working. Like you, said the only thing keeping him going was being on the road. So I get it. But I don't want you like Jake. Jake didn't do too well. He never really got over it."

"What happened to him?" I said, expecting a gruesome story, maybe a suicide in some remote cabin in the Georgia mountains.

"He quit. And the hell of it is that he was a good cop, a really good cop. The kind of cop you don't see on TV. The kind of cop that newspapers don't write about. When he quit, the public lost a great servant. And here's the point. I think you're a pretty good deputy. And I think you've got a long future in law enforcement. But if you don't get past this, you don't. It's that simple."

I nodded and shifted in the chair. "I get it," I said. "Do I need to go home and get my badge?"

He shook his head. "This isn't TV. Keep your badge. Go home. Do something. Take a road trip. See your mama. Go fishing. Whatever is you like to do. Whatever gives you some order, some structure, do that. I do want you to drive the police car up here later, though. Might as well have the mechanics go over it while you're off."

"Can I ask you a question?"

He nodded. "Yep."

I didn't exactly know how to ask it. "Was Donnie Ray's death accidental?"

Mack frowned, brow furrowed in confusion. "Yes. Medical examiner ruled it that way. It was wet drowning. Lungs full of water. Boy had a B.A.C. twice the legal limit." He leaned forward. "Why are you asking?"

"It's just that Jimmy Danley was up there that night."

He didn't say anything for a moment, his forehead creased, eyebrows bunched. "What are you getting at?"

"I don't know," I said. "I just think that—I thought that Jimmy Danley might have—"

"Last time I checked," Mack said, "you were a deputy, not a detective."

"I know."

"I don't know where this is coming from, but I'm going to write it up to sleep deprivation. Because it feels like you're questioning an investigation.

And I know that's something you wouldn't do, right?"

I looked down at my balled fists. "No, of course not. I'm sorry. It's just that—"

"Jimmy's a lot of things," Mack said. "He's an asshole, first and foremost, but he's not a killer." He looked off, shaking his head. "Boy didn't have much of a chance with the daddy he had, anyway. He didn't kill anyone that night. You can't go around making that kind of accusation. This is a small town. Stuff gets around."

I nodded.

"I don't like him, either. I don't like any of them, Freddy Richards, Tater Wilson, that whole damn crew. But nothing happened out of sort up there. Donnie Ray Miles? He was drunk. He fell in. That's it. End of story. It's not sexy. It's not a dime store crime novel. But it's what happened. Malone went over that whole boat."

"Okay. I just thought. I had a hunch."

"Hunches," Mack said, "work great when they're right. Otherwise? Not so much. Go home. Don't worry about all of this. Get some rest."

He stood up and we shook hands like grown men. His palms were hard and rough like asphalt.

"You take it easy, Justin" he said. "And don't worry about this Whitley bullshit."

I walked out into the squad room, looking for Chris, but he was gone. I looked around at the being filing cabinets and old computers. I wished I could file away Janey in a manila envelope, close some mental cabinet, and forget about her. I wish I could do the same with Donnie Ray Miles. But they were both alive in my mind, just at the edge of thought like something on the tip of my tongue, a familiar word that I just couldn't recall.

When I got back to my house, a green Mazda was sitting in my front yard, right behind my cruiser. Denise's car, the one Jimmy Danley drove. Why had he come to my house? I pulled into the driveway and eased all the way into the covered carport, scanning the side yard. Nothing. I put the truck in park and reached beneath my seat and pulled out the Beretta. Maybe Jimmy had heard about me asking questions.

I opened the door silently and slid out, holding the gun down by my side and dged my way down the side of the house. Had Jimmy gotten inside somehow? I hopped over a small mud puddle and eased the back gate open, looking around the backyard. He could have been anywhere—inside, maybe in the shed. I went into the yard, pulling the gate shut behind me.

Denise was standing near the shed. I trained the gun on her, a reflex.

Her eyes widened when she saw me and her hands came up instinctively.
"Whoa," she said. "Hey, slow down. Don't point that thing at me."

I dropped the gun, uncertain. "Denise? What the hell are you doing
in my backyard?" I scanned around, wondering if Jimmy were back here, in
hiding. Him, Freddy, and Tater, ready to pounce. A light rain had begun to
fall.

"Now wait a minute, I came by here to check on you." She stared for
a moment, and her features softened. "After the visitation, I didn't know how
you were doing. Somebody said you had a nervous breakdown."

I held the pistol limp in my right hand and blew a long sigh. "I'm
fine. It was nothing."

"Let's go inside," I said.

We went in the back door, through the laundry room that opened
into the den. I hoped that the house didn't smell as much like dirty laundry
as I thought it did.

In the den, I gestured at the easy chair and stepped into the kitchen.
"You want something to drink?"

"Depends on what you got."

I stuck my head back into the den. "What do you mean?"

"You offering me a beer or a Coke?" She smiled a bit, that crooked
grin that showed only part of her teeth.

I gave her a Yuengling and opened one for myself and sat down on
the love seat, where I'd burned so many hours the past few weeks.

"Isn't this your parents' house?" she said. She looked around the
room.

"We bought it from my mom," I said. "She sold it to me and Janey
when we got married."

"It looks it," she said, and I couldn't tell if she meant to insult me.

"Where's Jimmy?" I said.

She took a pull of the beer. "He went with Tater went to Tallahassee."

"What's in Tallahassee?"

"Besides the capitol?"

"Hardy-har." I took a drink of the beer,

"They went to look at a boat."

"He's buying a boat."

"Maybe."

We sat in silence for a moment. I studied the way she held the beer
loosely in her hands. I tried not to think about her stripping.

"He still working out at Clawson's?"

"You are one inquisitive dude, inspector."

"I didn't mean to pry."

"Sometimes."

"Sometimes? Sometimes what?"

"He works at Clawson's sometimes. Part time. He wanted to be on a shrimp boat, but they've got him in the warehouse. He doesn't like it."

"Can't get on with an independent captain?"

She shrugged. "His business. Not mine."

I figured he was using Denise for money. It made sense. No wonder she was stripping over in Panama City. I just couldn't figure out what she got out of the deal. What did she see in him? We sat in silence for a few minutes.

"I don't know why I came over here," she said. She smiled a bit, looking at her beer bottle. Sheepish. "I just wanted to see if you were okay. I mean, I heard you were seeing things."

My hand clenched around the beer bottle neck. "Heard what? From who?"

"It's nothing. Just talk. Everybody talks in this town." She started to stand up. "I better go. I don't even know why I'm here."

"Wait a minute," I said. "Don't leave. It's fine. I'm fine. I just had some sleep problems. That's all. Insomnia."

"I get it sometimes too. But I'm a night person. I can't stand the morning. I like it at night."

I thought about working graveyard. "It's got its ups and downs."

She sat back in the chair and looked up at the ceiling. Her eyes bounced around the room, jumping from framed photographs of my parents to a wedding picture of me and Janey that I'd never taken down.

"How did it happen?"

"How did she die?"

She nodded. "I heard it was a car wreck."

"She was going to work, downtown. She worked for Dr. Anson."

"The dentist?"

"Him," I said. "She pulled out of her parent's house over there on Gulf Avenue and was waiting to turn right on the highway. I guess she didn't see the log truck. It pretty much destroyed the car."

Denise swirled the beer bottle and breathed through her nose. "I'm sorry about that. I didn't know how bad it was."

"It's okay. She left me."

"I heard," she said. She opened her mouth to speak but stopped herself.

"What?"

"It's none of my business. I was just wondering why. What happened?"

"Life, I guess. Stuff. She said we were going in different directions.

I guess we were. She wanted to move. I wanted to stay." I looked up at the tiled ceiling. "She didn't like this house. My dad built it. She wanted to—I don't know—have our own lives or something. She wanted to move away. She wanted to leave St. Vincent."

"This place is a sandpit," she said to herself. Then, she looked around and frowned. "I guess I could understand that. I'd want my own place, too. I think that's why Donnie Ray moved out to Bayard's Bayou when he got back."

"Did you talk to Donnie Ray a lot? Were you guys close?"

"When we were kids, we were closer, I guess. Before Mama and Daddy split up."

"Your daddy—he's Big Don's brother?"

She nodded. "Yeah. He moved to Fort Walton Beach. It was a long time ago. Donnie Ray used to come by my place a lot, after he got back from Iraq. Just to get drunk. Not a lot lately." Her voice had gone soft, reflective. She looked down at her beer bottle and began peeling the label from the side of it.

I didn't say anything for a long time. "Why did he stop coming? Him and Jimmy not getting along?"

"Kind of," she said, her voice far away. "They argued sometimes about the war."

"The war?"

"Donnie Ray used to say it was a mistake. All of it. He said we didn't have any business over there—in Iraq or Afghanistan. Jimmy would get mad. He'd say that Donnie Ray was a hero. Donnie Ray said he wasn't a hero, not at all." She looked at me. "You know, one time, he even said, 'I'm more a criminal than a hero.' Lord. That pissed off Jimmy. They got into a big fight that night. After that, Donnie Ray just quit talking about the war altogether. Then, he started hanging out with this guy, Wayne, and he just didn't come around anymore. It was like losing him all over again. The night he died, I hadn't seen him in probably three months." She looked down at her hands, her eyes glazed. "He used to be so different. Then, when came back, he was somebody else. A lot of stuff happened to him over there."

"Like what?"

"Stuff. I don't know. Talk to Wayne. He was the only person Donnie Ray talked to for a while there. Maybe he'll tell you."

"How pissed was Jimmy at Donnie Ray?" I said.

"What do you mean?"

"Did he ever threaten Donnie Ray?"

"What are you driving at?"

I took a sip of beer. "Nothing," I said, lying and hoping that she wasn't as smart as she seemed. I was running scenarios in my head—if Mack knew about this, he might change his tune about Donnie Ray's death.

She stood up. "Look, I need to go. I just wanted to see how you were doing. Jimmy wouldn't like it if he knew I was here."

"I don't care what Jimmy likes," I said before I could stop myself.

"Well, I don't think he cares what you like, either. I gotta go. I don't even know why I came here."

I followed her through the laundry room. "Hang on a sec. I didn't mean to piss you off. I'm sorry. I just don't get it. You and him."

She held the back door open and turned to me. "I've known Jimmy a long time. We go way back. Besides, you don't have to get it. It's none of your business." She stepped into the rain.

"But you're so much better than him."

Denise turned around. Her white t-shirt was soaked. Strawberry blonde hair hung in wet strings in front of her eyes. "I'm not better than nobody. And neither are you."

"I didn't say I was."

"I saw the way you looked at me the other night. When I saw you at the store. When I came home from the club. I'm no Janey Pridgeon, but I'm not some slut, either. I dance. I don't sell my body. I'm not a prostitute."

I followed her through the backyard, around the side and out the gate. "I didn't say you were, Denise. Wait a minute."

She stopped by my truck and turned around. "What?"

"Why do you do it? Does he make you do it?"

"Do what?"

"Dance. Strip. Does Jimmy make you do it?"

She put her hands on her hips. "Nobody makes me do anything." She shook her head and rolled her eyes. "You can be a real asshole, you know that? I was coming over to check on you, not sit through an interrogation. No wonder Janey left you."

The comment stung. I could feel heat rising in my face.

She got in her car and cranked it up. The engine took a second to turn over and I thought she'd be stuck in my yard. But then the it fired to life. I ran over and knocked on the window. She rolled it down and glared.

"I'm sorry. It's none of my business. I shouldn't have said anything. Thanks for coming by."

She stared at her steering wheel. "Forget it. Just forget it. I've got to go." She put the car in gear and looked at me. "You tell me a better place for money, and I'll take the job. I make three times what those girls at the grocery store make. Three times what waitresses make." Then, she drove off, her tires throwing sand and mud back at me. The rain had soaked me to the skin. She turned at the end of the street, and I went back inside. I sat down on the love seat and felt very cold. "What the hell just happened?" I said to no one. Outside, the rain kept falling like it might go on forever.

9

I never wanted to be a detective, though I'll admit, to a lot of people, that job seems much more interesting than being a sheriff's deputy. In the movies, deputies are morons. They bumble around a crime scene and get in the way. They say stupid, racist things. They harass locals and tourists alike, then push up their cowboy hats and sneer. "That's how we do things around here, boy," they say to some terrified perp. Detectives swoop in and get the names, get the clues, get the girl, and solve the crime. Then, they stroll off in the moonlight, a man alone, beyond the crime scene, above it all. Detectives need answers. They thrive on the end product.

I liked being a deputy—the process of it, I mean. I enjoyed radioing in, saying I was on shift. I'd grown to love the respect folks gave when I pulled up in the cruiser, my lights flashing, ready to do what I had to do to bring order. I loved driving around St. Vincent, the man who protects, the man who serves, the silent but helpful watcher.

In a way, I thought that I was doing what my dad did as the president of the union: he worked with the system to make lives better. That's what I wanted to do. And, because of his service, he had a brotherhood of men who'd do anything for him, from Charlie Mason to the faceless souls who inhabit my visions of the paper mill.

Deputies form a brotherhood, too. We know what happens out there. We know what it feels like to make a life-changing decision in a fraction of a second. And we know what it's like to live with the consequences of that decision. I trusted them all—Hector, Frank, Chris. Especially Chris. I couldn't remember a part of my life that didn't include him. Chris was the grounded roots of a cypress tree to my loose pine needles, scattering in the wind. He was a firm hand on a pistol, a calm voice on the radio. I thought that he was the only friend I needed in the world, the only one I could ever trust.

A few days after my suspension, I got up before dawn and drove down to the Docks. I walked the seawall to where it ended and cast my reel into the still water. The hook was baited with frozen shrimp, and in the aftermath of the week's rain, I didn't expect to catch much. The bay would be watery. The fish would have departed for saltier, deeper waters. Winter was two months away. I doubted I'd get a bite. But I needed to get out of the house. I needed to forget about my job and Janey and Denise and Donnie Ray.

I fished for a good hour and finished a Thermos of coffee. I smoked a few cigarettes and thought about driving to Charlie's for breakfast when I finished up here. The sun broke yellow and orange toward the east, the lights like slats of molten steel poking through the morning clouds. I jiggled the rod, testing to see if the pull I felt was the current or a fish nudging my shrimp.

I was reeling in the line when a vehicle pulled up behind me, the oyster shells cracking beneath the tires. I didn't look back—probably another early-morning fisherman dreaming of spring and a big haul. The crunch of footsteps carried down from the parking lot, quick but measured steps.

"Good morning, Everson."

I turned around. Davis Malone was making his way down the slope to the seawall. Beyond him, the stairway down to the bay looked cold and gray in the morning light. He carried a St. Croix over his shoulder, the narrow, solid white handle bright and crisp.

"That's a nice rod."

He walked down the seawall and held it out in front of him. "Yes, they're nice."

"What kind of a reel is that?"

"It's a Shimano Cronarch."

He took up a position some fifteen or so feet to my right and threw into the water. The jig plopped audibly. He reeled the line tight and glanced at his watch. "It's almost seven."

"Yeah," I said. I'd never socialized with Malone. Until now, I didn't even know that he fished.

"The mill whistle—does it scare off the fish?"

I reeled my Zebco's line tight and bounced it, picturing the frayed shrimp dancing around the bottom of the bay, not a fish for miles around. "I guess," I said. "I've never really thought of it."

Malone got a strike and he pulled the St. Croix. "Damn it," he said.

"Lose it?"

He nodded.

Something about his presence made me uncomfortable. He seemed too at ease. The calm unnerved me. I began reeling in my line. "I think I'm going to hang it up," I said.

"So soon?"

"I've been here for an hour. There's nothing biting. The rain drove them out to deep water."

He pulled his line hard then and began reeling something in. The water splashed as he drew it in closer. He knelt down and grabbed the whiting by its gills, turned it over once, and loosened the jig in a smooth, fluid motion. The fish was gone in seconds. I blinked. It may not have happened at all.

He stood back up. "Sometimes they bite. Sometimes they don't. But you know that, right, Everson?"

"Well," I said. "I'm headed. Good to see you." I felt my front pocked for my cigarettes and began walking up the bluff.

"Let me ask you something."

I stopped. "What?"

"What really happened the other night with that kid?"

"Who?"

"Joseph Whitley's son. The one you roughed up."

It should have been an easy conversation. I should have been able to say, "Talk to Mack. He knows the story." But a chill ran through me, something cold as a fresh water current in the warm Gulf. Malone pulled at his rod, reeling. His jig bounced off the surface of the water and he let it sink back in.

"I didn't rough anyone up. I've already told this story to a few people. The kid tried to run. I grabbed his arm. He twisted back around and fell. I was doing my job."

"Your job includes busting up teenagers?

"Where's this coming from? Why are you here?"

He pulled his line out of the water and zipped back with a quick slash of the road. The jig plopped into to the bay. "I'm an investigator. It's my job to ask questions."

"You ask a lot of questions."

"That's what they pay me to do. Look, if you're going to drop the hammer on some kids, the least you could do is square you story with the assist."

"What the hell does that mean?"

"It means that you and Chambers aren't telling the same story."

I took a deep breath and took the box of cigarettes from my front pocket. I opened the end with one hand and shook one out and took it between my lips. I put the box back in my pocket and fished my lighter from my jeans. I lit the cigarette. "I'm not sure what you mean."

"Lately, you don't seem sure of anything, deputy." He didn't look at me. Out beyond him, the sun was up now, a misty ball of fire burning away the night. I half-expected Malone to look back over his shoulder, wink, and let me know he was pulling my leg, having a go at me. But he wasn't that kind of guy. He kept his shoulders square, military tight. I wondered if he'd ever been in the service. I walked back up the hill, put my tackle in the bed of the truck, and got in. As I backed away, I wondered what Chris had told Mack. I intended to find out.

Chris lived in an apartment townhouse beyond Sandy Head Beach on a stretch of highway that was empty clear to Panama City. The unit had five dwellings, all of them two-story, facing the road and the hundred or so yards of sand dunes and sea oats leading up the Gulf of Mexico. This stretch of beach was beyond St. Vincent Bay. Except for Harley's Bait and Tackle a mile back toward town, this building was the only structure out here.

I parked at the edge of the lot, a few spaces down from Chris's over-sized gray Chevy truck. The mud tires held the vehicle a good four feet off the ground. His cruiser sat right next to it, the brown and gold and white glistening in the morning sun. He must have taken it through the wash before he came home. Most of the lot was empty. Chris lived in the last unit on the west side. The two units to his right were unoccupied. I looked at my watch. It was 10:30 a.m. I wondered if he'd be awake. He worked graveyard the night before, patrolling the south end, my shift when I was on duty.

I took out my phone and texted him. *You around?*

For a few moments, nothing happened. I thought he might be asleep. But I needed to wake him up. I needed to find out what he told Malone. I needed to know.

I'm alive. Sup?

I'm at your crib. Can I come in?

After a second, I could hear the him unlocking the door. He opened it. He was bare chested and wore a pair of plaid boxer shorts.

"What's up, man? What are you doing out here this time of day?" he said, grinning.

I walked in and was overwhelmed by the smell of cats. Chris had three of them. Right by the front door, a gray litter box sat, its stench palpable.

"Christ, you don't smell that?"

He shrugged. "Cats gotta piss, too. Come in the kitchen. I'll show you what I'm doing."

We walked through the living room. A TV sat on a black entertainment center, a selection of war movie and war documentary DVDs crowded on the shelves—*The Longest Day, Hamburger Hill, The Civil War*. A bookshelf sat by a gray recliner. Most of the books were military history and biography. One book lay spine-up on the chair's cushion, some book about tunnel rats in the Vietnam War. A gray cat with large blue eyes sat on a a brown couch. He studied me, his tail swishing back and forth. Chris reached down and ran a thumb down the cat's head. "What are you doing, Herc? Guarding the castle?"

"Where are the rest of them?"

"Hercules is the only one who ever shows himself to company.

Hank Junior is probably somewhere watching you right now. Delbert's in the kitchen with me."

What looked to be several pieces of different kinds of pistols lay on a large oil-stained sheet thrown over a round kitchen table. Chris sat and picked up a barrel.

"What are you doing?"

"Cleaning. You want to help?" He pushed a rag at me. It had once been a white cotton t-shirt.

I sat and picked up the barrel of a .32 and began rubbing it.

"You got any coffee?"

He frowned. "I don't drink that shit. It's been linked to heart disease."

"So what, then, you drink protein shakes when you wake up?"

"It's better than coffee and cigarettes."

We cleaned the pistols in silence for a few minutes. I laid down the cylinder of a revolver and said, "Hey, did Malone ask you about what happened with the Whitley kid the other night?"

He didn't say anything. He put down the barrel he'd been wiping. "Yeah, he did."

"What did you tell him?"

He took a breath. "The truth, man. I told him the truth."

"What does that mean?"

"What do you mean 'what does that mean?' It means I told him what happened."

"Well, he's under the impression that I roughed that kid up pretty bad."

"Justin, you sort of did."

"What the fuck are you talking about?" I stood up. "What did you tell him?" My voice had raised an octave. Cat urine and ammonia stung my nose. I hated cats. Delbert, an orange tabby, lay stretched on the table. He studied me with doleful eyes.

"Calm down, Justin. Come on, man. Don't holler at me in my house. That's not cool."

"I thought we were friends."

"Christ, what is this, tenth grade? We are friends. I am your friend. I didn't tell Malone anything other than what happened. When I showed up, that kid looked pretty bad. He looked like he'd been punched. The other kid was scared shitless."

"I tried to put the fear of God into them."

He cocked an eyebrow. "It looked like you put the fear of Smith and Wesson in them."

"I didn't do anything wrong. This is messed up." Heat had risen to my face. I felt like I'd been slapped.

"Settle down, dude. You need to bring it down to a simmer."

"Man, you sold me out. For a couple of teenage dickbags. I thought I could trust you." I dropped the rag on the table and turned toward the door.

"Wait a minute, man. Calm down. All I told him was that I didn't know exactly what happened. That's all I said."

"That's it?"

"What else was there to say? I told him the truth. You scared the shit out of those two kids. And I told him that, if I was in your situation, I'd be the same way."

I frowned. "What does that mean?"

"What with Janey and everything."

I needed a cigarette. "I don't want to talk about Janey anymore. I'm tired of people talking about her."

"Then quit mourning her."

"So long, partner," I said. I turned to leave. "I don't need a lecture from you this morning. I came over her because Davis Malone pretty much interrogated me at the docks this morning. He said you were telling a different story than me."

He followed me through the cat-piss-smelling living room and into the parking lot. "Hang on, man. Just hang on a second. What did he say?"

"He said I lied."

"Lied about what?" He held the cylinder of a .38 in lift hand. The morning light shone bright off the gun oil.

"About what happened that night. About those kids?"

"He's feeling us out, Justin. You've got to see that, right?"

"What are you talking about?"

"I'd bet my last bullet that Mack told him to talk to me and you both, separately. He wants to find out what happened."

"I *told* him what happened," I said.

"Calm down," Chris said. "Cut the theatrics. There's lawyers involved. Mack's got to cover his own ass."

I patted my front pocket and took out a box of smokes. I shook one out, lit it, and shook my head. "Christ almighty, if only Malone had been as thorough with Donnie Ray's death," I said and trailed off.

"You still beating that drum?" He turned the gun cylinder over and began to wipe it

"We don't know the whole story. I can't prove a thing yet, but I can feel it Something's off.."

"Just 'feel it?' So, what's your theory, Columbo?"

I smirked. "Don't be an ass."

"I'm serious. What do you think happened?"

"I think that Danley and Donnie Ray got into over politics."

"Politics?"

"Donnie Ray had apparently been saying that the war was a mistake. He told people he never should have joined up—that's what Denise said. They'd been going back and forth about it for a while. My guess is the night Donnie Ray drowned, they got into a fight. Donnie Ray wound up in the water. He was so drunk he couldn't have swam. Probably sank like a lead shot. Jimmy was drunk, too. Before they knew what was going on, Donnie Ray's dead."

"Why didn't Malone and Mack work this angle?"

"They did. But Jimmy and Tater and Freddy got their stories straight up on the houseboat before they called us. Remember—they had to come back to the landing to get a cell signal. That's plenty of time to get a story straight," I said. Laying it out, I'd never been more convinced I was right then. The whole night played out in my mind like a movie. The boat, moored in a hidden dogleg, vines and branches hanging low above it. Jimmy and Donnie on the deck, shouting at each other. The splash as Donnie hit the water. The smell of river water, dank, strong.

"What's your evidence?"

"I know what I've been told. Both Big Don and Denise said that Jimmy and Donnie had some kind of a rift in their friendship. Something happened. And whoever this Wayne Childress character is, he's involved."

"Wayne Childress?"

"The guy writing letters to the *Sentinel* about that shit down at Clawson's."

"Oh. That guy."

"What do you mean, 'Oh, that guy,'" I said.

Chris shrugged. "I just think he's doing more harm than good. Clawson's closing that place. He's the only line those guys have to another job. You think he's going to give them good recommendations if they're all raising hell about some union?"

"Look, man, my dad was in a union. He's the guy who saved this town, if you'll think back. The strike in '83? Without him, St. Vincent would be a very different place."

Silence hung in the air between us. He wanted to say something, but I wasn't sure what it might be. I didn't know Chris's politics. I'd always assumed we were on the same page, but a pit had opened between us, something large and tangible. I wanted to press the issue, but I didn't want to lose him as a friend. It surprised me that I thought our disagreement would come to such, but something told me it would. Is that what happened to Donnie Ray and

Jimmy?

"Look," Chris said. "I know that your dad was big in the union at the mill."

"Forget it," I said.

"Man, I'm not trying to denigrate your dad. I've got reasons I feel the way I do, you know. Childress is not like your dad. He's out there making trouble. He's out there stirring up shit for no other reason than personal glory. You know what I heard? I heard that he is a student at some college. I heard that the union thing? It's a big senior project or something."

"That sounds like bullshit. How do you know what he's up to, anyway?"

"I've lived in St. Vincent as long as you have, buddy. I know just as many folks, and I talk to them."

I waved my hand. "Just—skip it. You don't like unions. You don't like Childress."

"Don't dismiss me like a five-year-old."

I stared at him. His steel gray eyes were staid, intense. "I don't want to talk about it," I said.

Another silence settled over us. We faced each other, our shadows like pylons sticking out of a sea of asphalt. After a few moments, Chris spoke. "Well, did you think about just asking him?"

"Who, Mack?"

"Jimmy Danley."

"What? Just go ask him if he killed Donnie Ray?"

"Why not?"

"Because Mack would kill me."

"Why?"

"He told me to stay away from it. Said the case was open and shut. Said it was none of my business."

"Does Mack have to know?"

"Danley would tell him. Just to spite me, Danley would tell him."

He crossed his arms and studied me. "You remember when we were kids and that spider dropped on your head that night at the park?"

I did. We'd been hanging down at the park near the city pier, drinking beer, and talking about whatever we that was important when we were sixteen. There were several of us—me, Chris, a few guys we knew. We were all parked beneath a copse of live oak trees near the shore line. The Spanish moss swung above us in silver and gray strands. I'd been in the middle of telling a story about something when I felt a tickling on my head. I reached up to swipe it and all the guys began yelling. A spider the size of a baseball mitt came running down my arm. You could have heard my scream in Stetson.

"Yeah. Of course. Why?"

"You hate spiders to this day."

I nodded. I did.

"Danley's that way with LEOs. He wouldn't go running to a cop any more than you'd have a pet spider."

It made sense. Chris turned the gun cylinder over in his hands. A log truck drove by, leaving a pine-scented wake. I took a drag of my cigarette. The smoke filled my lungs, and my head cleared.

"I'm going."

"You're going to talk to Danley?"

"I don't know."

"You know this is stupid, right?"

I ignored him. He followed me to the truck. I opened the door and slid in.

"Your truck smells like an ashtray."

"You house smells like cat piss."

"I don't smell it."

"You never do when you live in it, do you?"

I turned the key and the ignition fired to life, the rumble shaking me deep to my core. "Later," I said, shifting into gear.

Chris held up his hand. "Yeah. Stay out of trouble."

"Like I know how."

"Are we cool?" he said.

I studied him for a long moment. "I don't know." And I didn't. I didn't know if I trusted him anymore.

He nodded. "Yeah. I guess that's fair."

I backed out and pulled out on the familiar highway. The same scrub palm and oyster shell path-ways lined the road. The same graying, weathered mailboxes. The same soft, sandy shoulders. I'd driven the roads so often at night that now, it all seemed like another place. All of it seemed different in the day time.

10

Clawson's Fishery occupied a three-hundred foot swath on the shore of a canal cut from a tributary of the Apalachicola River down to St. Vincent Bay. A fleet of shrimp trawlers moored along the waterfront, the warehouse rising up on the bluff above. Every morning, you could see several boats cutting white wakes into the bay as they headed out for the peninsula at Duna Blanca State Park. There, they'd make the turn at the point and head out into the Gulf of Mexico to spend their day fishing. Some boats went out farther, but day trippers were the regular here, leaving early and returning late, boats full of darkly-tanned men with thick, tattooed forearms, many who'd known nothing other than shrimping their entire lives. I'd arrested my fair share of them. Some I knew. Some were transients, seasonal workers who seemed to come and go like the tide.

I parked my truck in a public fishing area beneath Marten Bridge, a newer structure that had been built right at the end of the 1990s. Back then, the county still had plenty of money. Marten Bridge replaced an old drawbridge that once connected Bay View to St. Vincent. It got stuck often, the old rusty motor refusing to lower the road halves. Throughout my school years, it was a regular occurrence for Bay View and Sandy Head Beach kids to be late. Some days, they didn't arrive until nearly noon. The bus drivers would take a back road up to Stetson and come to St. Vincent down Highway 71. All of that was alleviated with Marten Bridge, named for Benjamin Marten, a Florida congressman who'd grown up in St. Vincent. I slammed the door of my truck and looked up at the bridge. It was already starting to age, the once-whitened sidewalls now fading to a dirty gray, the undergirding home to seagull nests and dirt dauber hives.

The warehouse sat some sixty yards or so above the waterfront, a monstrous structured painted in dirty white and faded aqua blue stripes. You could have fit two football fields inside of it. Men and women were coming and going, workers in faded jeans and t-shirts. Some wore hats. Some wore hair nets. Inside, they worked the conveyor belt, picking through shrimp the trawlers brought in.

It was twenty until noon. With any luck, Tater would leave soon. I'd called the warehouse that morning and asked if he was working. The woman on the line told me that he was on from nine to six. She didn't even ask why I was calling. I planned to follow him when he left for lunch and "accidentally" run into him wherever he ate, as long as he didn't go home.

I wanted to ask about Donnie Ray and Jimmy and Wayne Childress. Then, I could talk to Jimmy, armed with Tater's story and Freddy's story.

Then, I could go to Mack and prove to him that I was right. He and Malone had missed something.

Tater came out and got in his truck right before noon. I followed him out onto the highway and back into town. He turned left down a street that led to the South Side, and I made a block around, wondering where he was going. I turned down an alleyway and pulled back onto the street, going the opposite direction. His blue Toyota pickup sat parked at Mama's Kitchen, a soul food place. I frowned, surprised that Tater would even go into a place like this, black-owned and on the wrong side of town. I sat in the truck for a few minutes, drumming my fingers on the wheel.

I opened my cell phone and called the number of the side of the building and ordered a barbecue sandwich and a side of baked beans. I listened to talk radio for a few minutes while I waited. Two guys were arguing about the national economy, which was sinking further and further into the toilet.

After a few minutes, I got out and crossed the broken pavement and went inside. Mama's Kitchen wasn't much bigger than a single-wide trailer, but the place was packed with small tables. It was loud with conversation punctuated with loud laughs or shouts. Music played in the background, something old, a 1970s soul tune. Two steel ceiling fans spun above, stirring the hot air. Most of the customers were black, as were all of the employees. An old woman with white streaks in her dark hair sat behind a cash register on a stool held together with duct tape. I wondered if this were the Mama of Mama's Kitchen.

"Help you?" she said. She looked at me from behind a pair of black framed glasses.

"I called in an order. Sandwich and baked beans. It's under Everson."

"Hang on," she said and shouted "Everson, pork combo" through a window into the kitchen. I moved off to the side and leaned against the wall and spotted Tater, sitting at a two-top by a window eating a place of food. He kept his head down and took frequent drinks from a large Styrofoam cup.

I'd known Tater as long as I'd known Chris. He'd been in my kindergarten class. His real name was Douglas Tate Wilson, but he'd been called "Tater" for as long I could remember. Built broad like his father, Tater had played linebacker in high school. He was a likable enough guy, and I never could quite parse his friendship with Donnie Ray and Jimmy. Tater's family lived east of town, in a nice area of St. Vincent. His father was a foreman at the mill. The family was solidly upper-middle class. But Tater always hung out with the backwoods bunch. In high school, he wore a lot of camouflage and drove an over-sized Chevy truck with a Hank Williams Junior logo painted on its back window. Since then, he'd worked at Clawson's off and on.

The woman behind the register handed me a white paper bag with my food and changed the ten dollar bill I gave her. I thanked her and turned around, trying to figure out how I was going to snake over toward Tater without *looking* like that's what I was doing. Then, he looked up and saw me. Waved.

I cut through the tables to stand next to him. "What's up, Tate?"

He took a long swallow from his drink. "You see it."

"Good cooking out here."

"Yep," he said.

I stood for a moment while he continued eating. "Heard about Clawson's closing. Damn shame."

"Yeah, it is. What with the mill and everything."

"There's talk of lay-offs down the sheriff's department." I was surprised at my small talk. I'd expected a confrontation.

"Whole damn world's falling apart. You can blame the Democrats, you ask me," he said and pointed to the open chair. "You want to sit down?"

I sat and tore open the bag and took out the sandwich (wrapped in white paper) and a small cup of baked beans. I went to a self-serve drink station at the other end of the place and for some sweet tea. When I sat back down, Tater was busy gobbling down coleslaw.

I forked at the beans for a minute, trying to figure out how ask him about the night Donnie Ray died. "You seen this week's paper?" I said. "There's a bunch of stuff in there about Clawson's."

"That's Wayne the Brain for you. Always trying to cause trouble," Tater said.

"Wayne the Brain?"

"Wayne Childress, works in the warehouse. He's the one that got everybody stirred up out there. You wouldn't even believe it."

I took a mouthful of the beans and enjoyed the maple and barbecue taste. "I don't know him. Saw his name in the paper, though. He's the one behind all this?"

"You ask me, yes."

"You ever hang out with him?"

Tater chuckled without humor. His broad shoulder shook once. "Hell no. Donnie Ray used to bring that communist around sometimes."

"They were friends?" I said, trying to sound incredulous.

"Yeah. I guess. They hung out a lot. Used to drive Jimmy crazy." He swallowed a mouthful of food. "You guys got a union?"

"Huh?"

"Sheriff's deputies. You guys got a union?"

"No. There's a Florida sheriff's union, but I'm not a part of it. I guess I could be. They send me stuff in the mail sometimes."

"You never joined?" He seemed to be feeling me out. I needed to say the right things if I wanted this conversation to continue.

"A lot of paperwork," I said and ate some beans. Took a swig of tea.

"I just wondered, what with your daddy and everything."

"Hero of the union," I said, my words flat. I wasn't sure if I believed of if I'd just heard it my whole life.

"That's what they say," Tater said. "My daddy's still in the one at the mill. It ain't doing him no good. That place is closing, union or no."

"So Wayne's trying to start a union out at Clawson's?"

"We've got one. Fat lot of good it's doing us. Wayne the Brain wants everyone to join it. Keeps scheduling meetings, but really, what does it matter now? Clawson's going to close that place, union or no. Doesn't matter, any how. Florida's a right to work state. Fred Clawson could saunter up in that place tomorrow and fire all of us. Not a damn thing any of us could do about it."

"That's messed up," I said, wondering how the paper makers' union had any power at all.

"It's law. But the Brain thinks the law is wrong." Tater gnawed at a rib bone.

"Why do you guys call him that?"

He laughed again, this time with genuine humor. "Because he's full of shit. He thinks that just because he's read a few books, he's smarter than everyone else. He's the reason the place is closing down. His union idea? That didn't help things. It hurt things. We heard a few months back that the dock was going to cut back. Then, Wayne started in on all his union stuff. Next thing we all know, the place is shutting down. I don't know why he doesn't get his ass back to Apalachicola, where he belongs."

"I heard that he doesn't even want a union," I said. "I heard he was a college student or something. Working on a project. The whole thing is some kind of a senior project."

Tater shrugged. "Sounds about right."

"How long's he been working out there?"

"Wayne? A little over a year. He started working there not long after Donnie Ray started."

"Donnie Ray and Wayne, they were friends?"

"Oh, yeah. They'd show up some nights. We'd be gathered up somewhere, drinking cold beers, trying to have a good time, and that motor-mouthed egghead would talk non-stop. What you said makes sense, about him being a student. He talked about books all the time. Kind of shit that makes my head hurt."

I thought about the books I'd seen in Donnie Ray's trailer. So Wayne had him reading, too.

"Wayne was all gung-ho about all this union stuff. Used to piss all of us off. He wouldn't shut up, though. Sometimes, he got Donnie Ray to talking about it, too," Tater said.

"Donnie Ray talked about the union? I mean, was he into that?"

He sighed. "Just about the only thing he'd talk about when he got back."

"From Iraq?"

He nodded. "Before Wayne, Donnie Ray didn't say too much about anything. Then, he started talking about our rights as workers and about how Clawson was exploiting us and all kind of nonsense. You ask me, Wayne was preying on Donnie Ray. That's bad."

"Preying?"

"Yeah. That's what Jimmy and Freddy started saying. It pissed off Donnie Ray."

"Jimmy didn't like Childress?"

He looked off from the corners of his eyes, reflective. "No, not really. He really monkeyed everything up. Donnie Ray started hanging around him and it was like none of us existed. I've known that boy since I was a kid. And all of a sudden, he's reading books and talking about how the war's wrong and all this crazy shit."

"Did he ever say what happened over there?"

Tater shook his head. "He never said a damn thing about it. Just said that we had no business in the Middle East."

"So Jimmy and Donnie Ray didn't get along?"

"Not when he Donnie Ray started talking about the war. I never understood why he'd say what he did—that the whole thing was a mistake. Tell you what, I'd love to shoot me a few those camel fuckers."

"What was he like after he came home?" I studied Tater's face, the rounded baby-like cheeks, the stubble on his jaw line. He looked like a little boy dressed up in man costume.

"Different. Quieter. He didn't raise as much hell. It probably made his mama happy."

I thought back to those days after the attacks in New York, how angry I felt. Angry and helpless. I'd driven to Panama City one night and sat in my truck across the road from the Army recruiter's office and driven home an hour later, feeling like a coward. "Did you ever think about joining? After Donnie Ray did?"

He sucked at his lower lip for a second. "For a few days. I wanted to pop me a rag head so bad. Those motherfuckers. I didn't, though. I didn't want to get blowed up. Hell, knowing me, clumsy as I am, that's the first thing that would happen." He laughed without humor at his joke.

I looked at my watch and feigned surprised. "Man, it's nearly 12:30." I pushed my chair back and stood up. "I got to get going," I said. "Good talking to you."

"Freddy told me you talked to him," Tater said.

I tried not to look surprised. "Did he?"

"He said you was giving him the third degree day before yesterday, asking all these questions about the night Donnie Ray died." I expected his expression to sour, his jaw to jut out, anger to creep into his voice. But nothing changed. "Here's the truth, Justin. I've known you my whole life, and I'm telling you the truth—one St. Vincent native to another. We don't know what happened to Donnie Ray," he said and looked down at his food. "Nobody does. One minute, he was there. The next, he was gone. He just fell in, I guess."

"Yeah, but did you see it?" I said, studying him, looking for a lie.

He didn't anything for a moment. Then: "No."

"Where were you when he fell in?"

"Probably inside, I guess. I don't know. Freddy and me were doing shots. Jimmy started yelling up on the deck—" He stopped and stared at me. "Are you guys still investigating this?"

"No," I said. "Not at all. I was just talking to Freddy. If he thought I was grilling him, man, he was wrong. You know how Freddy is."

He stared at me for a long time and finally smiled. "Yeah. Guy jumps a mile every time a truck backfires. I'd be just like him if I was raised by Rich Richards," he said. "Freddy's daddy is as crazy as a shit house rat."

"He's in charge of that group in the paper, right? The Treadless?"

Tater nodded and swallowed. "Sort of. No one's really in charge. But I'll tell you what, but just because Rich is involved doesn't mean the ideas are crazy. You know, man, you ought to come out for a meeting sometime."

"Who's all involved in that group? Where do you guys meet?"

"Down at the Crow's Nest once a month. I go. My daddy goes. Jimmy shows up sometimes. Freddy. Rich. A few others guys. It's a good group, Justin. We're just fed up with the government. Nobody wants to work. It's like those fools in Washington want everybody to be on welfare. You ought to come down one night."

I studied him. "I just might do that. Look, man. I got to run. I'm sorry about Clawson's closing down."

"Yeah," he said. "Feels like this whole town's shutting down."

I knew how he felt. And I agreed.

Chris might have been right about Jimmy Danley. I couldn't picture him running to the sheriff's department if I tried to talk to him about Donnie Ray's death. But he might run his mouth. And in St. Vincent, word gets around. Which meant that, eventually, Malone would know that I'd been talking to him, something Mack had forbidden. No, I couldn't talk to Jimmy, at least not as a cop. But if I approached him as a guy fed up with the federal government and fed up with all this union talk, he might be willing to share a beer with me and let me know exactly what happened.

Jimmy's trailer was on the final street before Bay View turned into a floodplain forest of twisted pine trees, sand spur nettles, and palm scrub. The roads out here were old, the asphalt cracked and broken. The driveways crushed oyster and clam shells. For every three single-wide trailers, you'd see a weather-beaten bungalow with mildewed vinyl siding and a storm door half hanging on the hinges. The lots were huge, though, and mainly not mowed, the grass calf-high in some places. It was a Thursday afternoon. The sun shone white in the sky, the air heavy with humidity. The sky was the color of melted nickle.

I parked in front of a vacant lot a few houses down from Jimmy's trailer. I had a six pack of beer and new box of cigarettes and a story I wanted to tell Jimmy. He'd be home. It was the middle of the day, and he wasn't working. I'd hoped that Denise wouldn't be home. I was wrong. Her green Mazda was parked in the driveway.

I rapped on the door and Denise peered out. She studied me. "What do you want? I can't talk to you right now," she said, her voice a whisper.

"I'm actually here to see Jimmy," I said. I fought the urge to say something more. I wanted to talk to her. I wanted to pick up where we'd left off at my house.

She frowned. "Are you on duty or something?"

"No. Just wanted to talk."

She bit her lip, her eyes searching me. Then, she spoke. "I don't know what you're up to, but it's something. He's around back," she said and pulled the door closed.

The backyard was overgrown with crabgrass and sun-scorched Bermuda. A single oak tree grew at the edge of the property line, where a bowed chain link fence separated Jimmy's yard from his neighbor's, a virtual clone of this one. A rusted Ford F-150 the color of coral sat in the center of Jimmy's backyard. It was buried to the rims in sand. The hood was open, and Jimmy had half of his body stuck inside.

"You got a mess," I said.

He jerked out and looked at me, eyes narrowed. "The fuck you want, law dog?"

"I just wanted to talk," I said.

"You want to talk? Talk to one of your revenue-generating buddies."

"Look," I said. "I just want to talk. I brought a peace offering." I held up the six pack of beer.

He sniffed and spat. "Peace offering?"

I pulled a long neck Budweiser from the carton. "About the funeral. About Donnie Ray's visitation. I know he was your friend. I'm sorry he died."

He walked over. Bare chested, he was bathed in sweat. He wore a University of Florida baseball cap backwards. He ran his tongue over his front teeth, bulging out his top lip. He had a thin mustache and a two-day beard. He took the offered beer, twisted off the cap, and drank half of it, never taking his eyes off of mine.

"I ought to kick your ass," he said and burped. "Next time you think about handcuffing me, you better rethink it, son. The only reason I'm not stomping a mud hole in you right now is that I don't want no trouble. What the hell do you want?"

I opened a beer and sipped it. "I'm serious, man. It's a peace offering."

"You serious?"

I nodded. "Serious up."

His eyes traveled up and down me, looking, searching. He seemed ready to bolt off across the yard at any moment. Then, he relaxed. The muscles in his forearms loosened. His shoulders fell. "Yeah. It was a Goddamn shame. I've known that boy my whole life." He wandered back to the buried F-150 and put one hand on the hood to support his weight.

"What happened?" I said and tilted my beer at the vehicle.

"Weather."

"Weather?"

"Transmission was leaking. I couldn't get to it from the top with hood open. So, me and Tater dug a big pit and drove the truck over it. We thought we could get to it easier that way. Then, fucking rain. That night, the whole thing collapses. Buried the truck."

The idea seemed profoundly stupid to me, but I said, "That sucks."

"Tell me about it. I tried to crank it up, but it won't turn over. That fatass Tater says he's going to tow me out. I don't even know if he can with that rice-powered piece of shit he drives. Probably bog down. Goddamn sand. Give me another beer."

I handed one to him and reached in my front pocket for a box of cigarettes. I ripped off the cellophane and offered him one. He took it. I lit one myself and handed him the lighter. He sat down on a bleached plastic chair and I leaned against the truck.

"What do you want?" he said. "I'm not stupid. You can't just roll up at my house and expect me to be your best friend."

"I really just wanted to tell you I was sorry about Donnie Ray drowning. I know what that sounds like. People keep telling me they were sorry about Janey dying. It sounds fake. But I'm serious."

He exhaled a white cloud of smoke that hung in the air like blown glass and then dissipated in the breeze. "I heard about that. Log truck, somebody said."

· I nodded. "Yeah. It was ugly."

"Denise said y'all was split up."

"We were." I took a sip of beer. "And that's the hell of it, I guess. I don't know how to feel about her. Does that make any sense? I was so pissed when she took off. Then, she dies. I'm in this weird space between being sad that she's gone and mad that she left. Does that make any sense?" I'd come here to play a role, to pump Jimmy for information. But something had happened. We were talking for real. We could have been two old friends.

"Fucking A." He pulled at a strand of thread hanging on his jeans shorts. The cigarette stuck out of the side of his mouth. Smoke obscured his features. "Same shit with Donnie. Same shit." He took a swig of beer.

"Yeah?"

"I didn't even know that boy when he got back."

"Iraq?"

"Yep. The god-almighty U.S. government fucked him up good. And then, he's back here."

"What happened to him over there?"

"Fuck if I know. All I know is he left one person and came back another."

I thought about what Tater had said. "Was it Wayne?"

"Wayne the Brain?"

"Yeah. Did he change him? Was it Wayne's fault."

"No, but that commie motherfucker didn't help."

"This whole union thing."

"What about it?" he said. He'd tensed up again, his arms tight. He leaned forward in the chair, his knees locked, ready to spring.

"Like you said. It didn't help. I'm bothered by how it's hurting the town," I said. It sounded like bullshit, but he didn't seem to mind.

"It's fucking everything up."

"I heard that old Wayne the Brain is behind all of this."

He studied me from the corner of his eye and took a swig of beer. He put the cigarette between his lips and squinted behind the smoke. "That's what you heard, deputy?"

"Yeah," I said, pretending not to notice his suspicion. "I heard that things were cool at Clawson's until Wayne started up. I've read his letters in the paper. He's clearly the one causing all of this shit. Seems that Clawson's and St. Vincent were a lot better off before Childress showed up. Who is he, anyway?"

Jimmy chugged the rest of the beer. "Fuck me if I know. He's some radical. He's always talking shit about worker's rights this and strike that. He needs to get his ass back to Franklin County, where he belongs. I don't get why Donnie Ray listened to a word he said." He looked pointedly at me. "If you're serious, you ought to come down to the Crow's Nest on Tuesday evening."

"For what?"

"Treadless meeting." He studied my face, jaw working. "You wouldn't be the first cop who came."

"Really?" I wondered who on earth would fall in with these low lives. I tried to keep my gaze steady, easy. I swirled the remaining beer in the bottom of my bottle. A cloud passed over the sun, and a darkness settled over the yard. You could feel fall behind the breeze, the chill that was to come. "Childress—he turned Donnie Ray against you?"

He eyed me sideways and took the cigarette out of his mouth. "He turned Donnie Ray against the whole country."

"The whole country?"

"Yeah. He told us that the war was a mistake. Said the U.S. was run by imperialists or some shit."

"Do you think that's why it happened?"

"What?"

"Why he died."

"The fuck are you saying, law dog? You saying something?" He stood up, his left fits a tight ball of flesh and bone. He held the Budweiser bottle in his right hand like a club.

I fought to remain calm, though my heart beat like a hummingbird. "I'm saying that somehow, this place turned against him, since he turned against it, you know? Like, maybe he fell in and drowned. Or maybe, somehow, the river knew. It took him because he betrayed this place."

"What kind of voodoo bullshit are you conjuring, man?" He'd relaxed, but he still gripped the beer bottle. I flicked my eyes from it to him. The burnt nub of the cigarette looked like a fuse in his mouth.

"I'm just saying that, maybe he kind of . . .had it coming, you know?"

He blew a long steady breath and shook his head. He chuckled, a deep, throaty laugh, and looked up at the sky. "You know, Everson, if you weren't a deputy. I'd land this bottle right between your beady eyes."

I stood up. This was over. The air felt charged here. Sunlight broke through the clouds like a white blade. "I'm sorry, man. I didn't mean to suggest."

"Yes you did." He flipped the beer bottle over several times as though it were a knife. "I don't know what you wanted when you came here. I don't know what you expected to find. But you can go straight to hell. You and every one of your government buddies."

"Look, man," I said, but he cut me off.

"Look, man," he said, his voice high, mocking me. "Look, man. Look, man. Shut up. Let me tell you something. Your time's coming. You, that fat-ass sheriff, that Yankee detective. The criminal mayor. All the way up the pipe. You don't get it because you're stupid and because you're a shill. I'm telling you this just because I know you. Things are going to change."

"Change?"

He looked down at the sand, his eyes far away. "This country's going to hell. Niggers and wetbacks everywhere. Illegal immigrants taking American jobs. Used to be, things were different. But everything's gone to hell. Things are coming. Things are changing." His gaze cleared and he locked eyes with me. "Now, get the fuck off of my property."

A heat ran through me then and I wanted to charge him, slam into the trailer, and kick his ribs until I heard a crack. An image of him, there on the ground, bloody and broken, came into my mind. I tensed my arms and took a breath, fighting for control. "Fine," I said. "I'm leaving. I was only trying to offer my condolences about your friend."

"My friend. Not yours. Donnie Ray had no use for you government motherfuckers, either."

I started to tell him he'd contradicted himself, that he'd just told me that Wayne Childress had brainwashed Donnie Ray into someone Jimmy hardly knew, but I picked up the beer carton and walked away. I didn't want to turn my back to him, but I didn't want to back away from him.

"Get the fuck out of here," Jimmy said, his voice low, dangerous.

I hurried around the side of the house. I peered over my shoulder, but he wasn't there. I took a long breath as I walked toward the truck, trying to work through what I'd learned. If Jimmy was willing to beat me—a sheriff's deputy—to a bloody pulp in his back yard in the broad daylight (and stone sober, at that), then did it make sense that he'd killed Donnie Ray? Yes, I decided as I opened the Dodge and slide in, it made perfect sense.

The ignition fired to life, and I turned the radio dial, hunting a song I could recognize, something familiar, but all the songs seemed new, things I'd never heard. I looked back the trailer. The curtains had parted in one of the window and Denise looked out, her mouth drawn tight. She might have known that I could see her. She pulled the curtains closed and disappeared.

Mack threatened to fire me. And I could tell that he meant it. After I finished talking to Jimmy, I'd driven right to the sheriff's department, certain that I'd found an angle that Cowboy and Malone had missed. I figured it was better that I talk to him first before he heard about my visit with Jimmy second hand. Mack was sitting his office on the phone, so I waited, constructing the narrative in my head. I wanted him to see what I saw, how it all fit together. I wanted him to understand this union back-story, the thing the investigators had missed about Donnie Ray.

"The key to all this," I said, "is this Wayne Childress character. Has Malone talked to him?"

"I don't even know what to say about this. You say you talked to Tate Wilson and Jimmy Danley?" Mack said. He sat behind his desk, arms crossed, looking at me as though I'd just told him I saw a UFO.

"What about Wayne Childress? Did you or Malone talk to him?"

"And this Treadless situation is getting out of hand," I said

"Out of hand?" Mack said, his words echoing mind. "Out of hand? Would you listen to yourself?"

I tried to say something more, but he laid into me about running my own investigation and ignoring departmental policy. He reminded me that I was a deputy and not a detective and that I didn't have any business or authority questioning anyone. He told me that he thought that he'd made it clear: leave the Miles family alone. I tried to remind him that I wasn't talking to Big Don or Betty, but he cut me off.

"Even after that Richards boy complained, you're still on this?"

"Freddy complained?"

"Yes," Mack said. He'd calmed a bit. His voice had lowered to a simmer. "Yes. Him and his daddy both. Rich wanted to swear a complaint against you. And that was after I talked him out of trying to sue this entire department. What the hell is in your head, son? You're already on suspension."

"Come on, Sheriff. Rich isn't going to sue anyone. He's full of shit and you know it."

"What the hell do you think he's going to do when you start accusing his son of murder?"

"I didn't accuse him of anything." I dug my fingers into my palms and tried to remain cool.

"Rich Richards is looking to blame the government for all of his problems. And make no mistake. The government has royally screwed all of us—time and again. That's nothing new. But for Rich? He's looking for a fight."

"With who?"

"With the government. And guess who he sees as representatives?"

"Us? We work for the county. We're not feds," I said.

"Do you think that matters to Rich Richards? Damn it, Justin. After that mess with the Whitley kid and now this?" He looked at me, his wolf-gray mustache and beard pointed down his chin. "If I could, I'd fire you. I want you to know that. I really would. But I can't afford to replace you." He shook his head and exhaled. "But I will if you keep this kind of nonsense up. Listen to me. You will not run around town undermining what we do out here. I hear any more of this from you, and I don't care if I can't replace you. You'll be fired." He punctuated the last three words by tapping his finger on his desk. "This is important. You listen to me. You go home. You stay the hell away from anybody who was on that houseboat that night. And you keep away from the Miles family."

"But what about—"

"I don't give a damn," he said. "There is no 'what about?' There is no 'what if?' Do you understand me, Deputy Everson? Tell me that you understand me."

I did. I went home and spent the afternoon in the den, flipping channels. It amazed me that he didn't even want to talk about what I'd learned. Why was Mack turning a blind eye to this whole thing? Maybe it was me. Was I making up stories? What if I just wanted a bad guy and Jimmy fit the narrative? I dismissed it. If he could have gotten away with it, he'd have buried that Budweiser bottle in my forehead. No doubt about it—he'd made sure Donnie Ray fell into the river.

By that evening, I'd grown stiff and bored from being home all day. I ate a frozen pizza close to dinner time and tried to watch a movie, a gangster flick about four guys trying to rob a diner in a small southern town. But it had been edited for TV, and the censors had muted the curse words. The result was a strange staccato effect, each character speaking in what appeared to be halting bursts, their mouths moving in silence. It was as though whatever they had to say turned inward, their external dialog becoming interior monologue. By ten o'clock, I'd taken Ambien, and the world muted to a grainy haze. I fell asleep on the couch thinking about the night Donnie Ray drowned. Just as I slipped into sleep, I imagined the world through his eyes, the way the flood lights on the houseboat would have slowly darkened as he sank lower into the water, the world above little more than a memory just slipping from the edge of consciousness, a rumor that rings false, a dream slowly dissipating in the cold light of dawn.

11

When Aaron and I were kids, my dad used to tell us a story about a family of ghosts on the farm where he grew up in south Alabama. He said that behind the family's house was a large barn, a long, low building that held a tiller and the few meager agricultural tools that my father and his father used to tend the land the family sharecropped. He said that barn—or, the area around it, at least—was haunted. "Full of haints," he'd say. "Just full of them."

Granddaddy grew cotton and peanuts on three four-acre fields on U.S. Highway 84, right on the edge of the Georgia line. The land had been in its owner's family for generations, and supposedly, nearby, there had once stood an old black primitive Baptist church. Some of the whites in the area had torched the place in the 1960's, killing the preacher, his wife, and their two baby daughters in the process. Dad said that the county had covered up the crime to the point of bulldozing the land and flattening it out for use as farm land. No one knew where the church had actually been. But everyone knew it was in some proximity to the fields the Eversons sharecropped.

"Some nights, especially when it was cold," Dad would say when he told the story, "you could hear what sounded like the popping of a fire." He'd stop and study me and Aaron, his face flat, eyes wide, mouth partially open. "And I'm not talking about one these little piddling boy scout fires. I'm talking about a big one. I'd be lying in bed just about shake out my skin from the cold, and I'd hear it, snapping and popping. You know how a big fire will roar? Well, you'd hear this big whoosh of wind and popping and crackling. Your granddaddy would grab his rifle and run out back to the barn, and I'd head out behind him. We'd get right to the edge of the barn. You could hear that fire just burning, and we'd creep along the edge. Then, we'd jump out to where it should have been. And do you know what we saw?"

Aaron and I shook our heads, knowing exactly what he was going to say. But we wanted him to say it again, to paint the picture for us.

"Nothing," he said and spread his hands out wide, like a magician revealing a trick. "I mean dark-thirty nothing. And quiet. Just dead quiet. A wrong kind of quiet. Out there at night, you could hear all kinds of things, insects and birds screeching. Dogs barking. Trucks out on the highway. But after we'd hear that fire, that place would be so quiet, you could hear your own heart beating in your chest."

Sometimes, we'd pump him for information, asking him if he ever saw anything else. He said he'd once heard a little girl laughing in the barn when no one was home. He also said that the dogs they had wouldn't sleep in the barn, even in the rain, and that sometimes, they'd bark at the building randomly. The older we got, the more Aaron lost interest. He'd cut off Dad during the story and say something like, "Could it have been wind blowing dirt against the side of the barn?"

But not me. I believed. Or, I wanted to believe. I tried to picture it, the dark Alabama night, the moon like a bone charm in the sky, the popping and hissing of the ghost fire. I ate it all up. All though those years, I read book after book about ghosts and watched more horror movies than I could remember. I raided the local video store on weekends and forced Chris to watch the kind of horror I liked: not gore, but suspense. I was a sucker for a haunted house. My favorite movie was *The Changeling*, a George C. Scott flick about a writer living in a haunted mansion. Chris wanted to watch slasher stuff like *Friday the 13th* and *Nightmare on Elmstreet*. Me? I didn't want spectacle. I didn't need some monster distracting me from the dead. I wanted to be scared so much that I questioned the world around me. I wanted, just for a moment, to believe.

In the years after his death, I found myself wishing for his ghost to appear. I'd jump at every groan the old house made. I'd wander through it after dark, squinting, hoping that maybe, just maybe, my father would reach out to me from beyond the grave. He never did. Neither did Janey. The only thing close to a ghost that I'd ever seen were those waking dreams of Donnie Ray. But after the sleeping medication made those go away, I found myself missing him from time to time. He'd been the only real evidence that I'd see my father again. He'd been the only assurance that one day, I could tell Janey that I was sorry, that I'd been wrong, that I should have left St. Vincent with her, not chosen this town over our marriage.

But Donnie Ray's ghost, like the ghost on my father's childhood farm, had been nothing more than a story, a kind of lie that brought me comfort and hope, but a lie nonetheless.

The St. Vincent Public Library sat about five blocks off from the waterfront, right down 2nd street, a few streets over from Skipper's Funeral Home. Saturday afternoon, the wind came off the bay in a long wet exhale. Though the weather was humid, you could feel a hint of autumn behind the breeze.

I parked my truck on the side of the street and walked across the road. Inside, the air conditioning hummed at a low roar, white noise. I took off my hat and ran a hand through my hair and looked around. The library was one of the few modern buildings in St. Vincent, constructed in the early 1990s thanks to a state grant. I followed the signs down a long beige and brown hallway, enjoying the smell of books, a musty odor I associated with school. I'd spent a lot of time here when I was a teenager. I read my way through every Stephen King, Ray Bradbury, and Richard Matheson book they had on the shelf.

The members of the Apalachee County Paranormal Society sat around a large rectangular table, a few chatting quietly, a few thumbing through books. No one looked up when I entered the room. I wondered if anyone I knew would be here and felt embarrassed and stupid. I was considering leaving when I saw Denise. She sat away from everyone else, with an empty chair on either side. She was reading a paperback book.

I walked over and took a seat to her left.

She looked at me and squinted, as though she couldn't quite believe what she saw. "What are you doing here?"

"I saw a flier the other day. Thought I'd check it out."

She pushed buttons on her phone and didn't say anything.

"You still pissed at me?" I said.

"I'm not pissed at anyone." Her voice was tight.

"Look," I said, "I'm sorry about grilling you. I just ask a lot of questions, I guess."

"Yeah. You do. About stuff that's none of your business."

I held up my hands. "Truce. I'm sorry." I waited a moment but she didn't respond. "I really did see a flier for this meeting the other day. Somebody put one up on the bulletin board at the sheriff's department. I've always been interested in this kind of stuff. What are you reading?" I wanted to change the subject.

She held up the spine: *Unconquered People: Florida's Seminole and Miccosukee Indains.* "What in the hell were you doing at my place the other day?" she said.

I started to speak, but a woman at the head of the table stood up and smiled at everyone. "Well, it's about time," she said and glanced at her watch. "I think we should get started." She was a stocky woman. Early 40s. Gray-streaked curly black hair. "If this is your first time here, I'm Marie Butler, president of the society. If you're interested in joining us, just talk to me after the meeting." She was talking to me. Everyone else looked as though they belonged.

I'd read about the group on their website. They met once a month and organized ghost hunts around the area. Once a year, they tried to go big, visiting a famous supposedly-haunted site. They'd just posted pictures of last year's trip to Savannah, Georgia. I'd flipped through the online photo album, unimpressed with the grainy photos of "orbs" and shadowy lights. I had no intention of paying the $50.00 a year membership fee, but I did want to see what the meetings were all about.

The meeting started with the dues-paying members voting on using some of the club's money to travel to Atlanta to see some psychic give a lecture. "He can communicate with spirits," a teenaged girl said. She had dyed black hair and a silver ring in her lip. She looked around the room, seeking approval. No one said anything. She looked down at the table and murmured,"I think we should go."

"Bullshit," an old man with a military-style haircut said. "Guy's a Goddamn fraud."

"Language, Mr. Flanders," Marie said.

Flanders scowled. "Well, I'm not going, and I'll rescind my membership if we spend any money on that fraud." He pulled at his white mustache and crossed his arms.

The meeting lasted around forty minutes or so, the highlight a story that an overly-excited young man in a black t-shirt told about "thermal readings" he got at different stores during a recent trip to St. Augustine. I sat back, my arms crossed, wondering what on earth I was doing here. I felt convinced that the sleeping meds Dr. Bristol had me on were messing with my decision-making. I'd come here out of curiosity, but this was the same mess I saw on television documentaries: half-formed opinions masquerading as facts and excited gullible people telling stories. After the meeting adjourned, I slipped out while Denise was talking to Marie and the girl with the lip ring.

I browsed through books for a few minutes and checked out a copy of James Lee Burke's *Neon Rain* and went outside to smoke. I stood at the edge of the steps and looked out at the road. With a week of administrative leave left, I needed to find something more to do with my time besides watch TV. The meds helped me sleep, and they kept me from seeing Donnie Ray Miles everywhere. But I spent most days in half a fog, driving around town, reading and watching movies at home, and wishing that I were working. Donnie Ray Mile stayed at the edge of my thoughts, though, and I kept wondering about Wayne Childress: who he was, what he wanted. But Mack had warned me off the case. And as much as my curiosity and sense of justice niggled at me, I decided to let it lay. For now.

"Did you follow me here? Be honest," Denise said behind me.

I spun around, coughing smoke. "What? No. Of course not."

She put her hands on her hips and squinted, her head slightly cocked, studying me. "So, you're into all this paranormal stuff, too?"

"I don't know. Sort of. I've always been kind of interested in things like this." I felt sheepish, immature, like she'd caught me stealing in a baseball card shop.

"Yeah," she said. "Me, too. Look. What the hell were you doing at my house the other day?"

"I came by the see Jimmy. I wanted to express my condolences about Donnie Ray."

"Are you serious?"

"Yes," I said. "I am." I hoped she believed me.

She squinted. "I think you're full of shit. You're lucky Jimmy didn't start something."

"I'm not worried about Jimmy Danley."

Her eyebrows arched. "Maybe you ought to be. He said you tried to interrogate him. You didn't make him happy."

I started to say, "He killed Donnie Ray. I don't care how he feels." But, I didn't want her to leave. So, I said, "How's Big Don and Betty doing?"

She held out her hand. "Give me one of those," she said, and I fished the box of cigarettes from my pocket. She lit it with my lighter.

"Good as can be, I guess. I was over there this morning. Aunt Betty's in a funk. She doesn't even leave the house. Uncle Don? He's sort of on autopilot. My shithead daddy didn't even come to visit. I hate him. He could have made Uncle Don feel better. Taken him out to eat, something. Gotten him away from the house. Somebody from Panama City's got him mounting three huge swordfish. He spends a lot of time in the shed, working, I guess. Anything not to think about it."

We fell silent. A couple of cars drove by. The breeze had died down, and the afternoon sun burned, bright and hot. Soon, the temperature would drop. One morning, I'd wake up to frost on the ground, even this close to the bay. The cedars and pines in the library's lawn drooped, lethargic. Though the recent rain had everything looking bright green, the ground still looked old, tired.

"You know what sucks the most?" she said after she'd smoked half the cigarette.

"What?"

"They'd already lot him once."

"What do you mean?" I said.

"After he came home, he just wasn't the same. It's not like he was sad all the time. That's what everyone thinks. He wasn't sad. He just wasn't himself. Do you know the only reason he was even up at the houseboat that night?"

"Yeah. I heard it was his birthday."

"It had been a couple of weeks before. Used to, we'd all get together and go out. But the only person he talked to was Wayne."

"Wayne Childress?"

"You know him?"

"I've heard of him," I said.

"Jimmy calls him Wayne the Brain. He came over with Donnie Ray a couple of times."

"You don't like him?"

She blew a thin jet of smoke. "He's intense."

"What do you mean?"

"He's just got a lot of ideas," she said and looked away. "But Donnie Ray would talk to him. He hardly talked to anyone else, so I guess Wayne isn't all bad."

"Did Donnie Ray quit talking to Big Don?"

"He quit talking to everyone." Denise looked down at the ground and rubbed her arm. I studied the sprinkle of cinnamon freckles on her nose and cheeks. She pitched the cigarette butt down and ground it with one pink-sandaled toe. "I got to get going," she said.

"Did he ever talk about being over there?"

"Not really. Said it was hot. He hated it, I think. Donnie Ray never was any good at doing what people told him. I can't imagine he liked that part. He mentioned another soldier one time. Sherrill, I think."

"Were they friends?"

"I don't know."

"Why did he come home?" I said.

"I told you already. I don't know."

"I'm serious. Everyone in town says he was thrown out for drugs. You say it's not true."

"That's because it's not."

"Then what happened?"

"Why do you want to know so bad? What business is it of yours anyway? A year ago, he was just some redneck to you."

I stopped. I wasn't sure how to answer. "I don't know. It seems important. If it's not true, about the drugs, then maybe people will stop saying that. I'll stop saying it."

She leaned her head back and looked up at the sky. I studied her face, the slight curve of her jaw, the tiny sharp V of her chin, the light down on her thin arms. "You know what? I don't even know what happened. He never talked about it, so I never asked. I don't know if anyone knows, not even his parents."

"What are you doing right now?" I said.

She frowned. "What? Besides wasting my time talking to you?"

"Let's go somewhere. Let's have a beer."

She thought for a second. "I can't. I have to go to work later."

"Just a beer," I said.

"I have a boyfriend."

"Just a beer," I said again.

"Just a beer. Are you driving?"

We picked up a six pack of Yuengling at the Swifty and drove out east on Highway 98, the same road that took us back to Bayard's Bayou, and beyond that, Duna Blanca State Park and Cape San Vincente. I turned the radio on to a classic rock station and beat my fingers on the steering wheel in time to the song. The tide was high, the gray water flooding the shoreline and filling the sawgrass-crowded inlets along both sides of the road. From the top of a small bridge we crested, you could see a man up to his waist in the bay, his cast net open like a black cloud above him.

We passed through the nicer homes on the far end of Gulf Drive and curved out southeast, toward Bayard's Bayou. I felt good for the first time in a long time, a beer open between my legs, the road ahead clear, Denise beside me. She leaned against the door of the truck, not looking at me, her chin resting on her hand. Every now and again, she took a sip of beer.

After a while, we came to the entrance of Duna Blanca, the stretch of land that formed St. Vincent Bay. You could stand on the west end of the cape and see the lights of St. Vincent at night. Duna Blanca had been a state-funded park. Back then, regulations kept anyone from building out here. But over the years, environmental restrictions had been eased, and a few houses and condos appeared.

The only other thing on the cape were the ruins of a Spanish fort. It had been excavated in the 1970s but nothing notable had been found. The state had tried to turn it into a tourist spot in the 1980, but few would drive this far off the highway. These days, a locked-up and deserted admissions hut the size of an outhouse was the only relic of that time. Behind a rusting, chain-locked gate, the crumbling remains of the fort still stood, half-sunk into the sand. It was supposedly haunted. The place was still popular with local teenagers, who'd hope the fence and wander around at night, drinking beer and trying scare each other. I'd done the same thing, tagging along with Aaron and his friends.

When I was a kid, you had to pay five dollars a car load to drive on the peninsula. These days, the cashier station was empty, its windows frosted with age. We drove down the two-lane road and came to a cut-off that led to a bluff overlooking the Gulf of Mexico. The tiny road was sandy, and I worried that I might get stuck, but the recent rain had packed the sand hard. I drove slow, sliding by long leaf pines and palm scrubs. After a minute, we came to the overlook and I put the truck in park.

I pointed at the old fort. "You ever visit that place?"

"Yeah. Sixth grade, I think. A field trip."

"I heard it was haunted."

She looked out at the Gulf. "This whole town's haunted."

I drank another beer in silence. Denise hadn't finished the one she'd opened back in town. She reached back and played with her hair. I wanted to reach over and take her hand, but I knew that I couldn't. I stared at her leg and wondered what her skin felt like. The crush I'd nursed in high school smoldered in my chest.

"How long have you been with him?"

She breathed as sigh. "Off an on for a while. Why do you care?"

"Just wondering."

"More questions."

"That's what I do."

She laughed. "Yes, it is. The truth is that right now, we're on the outs."

I ignored the boyish swell of hope in my chest. "Oh yeah?"

"Yeah. Not that it's any of your business, but it's just not working. He's gone all the time. And I'm working nights."

"Dancing."

" Dancing. Yes. But I wanted to be an archaeologist," she said. "A long time ago."

I laughed. "Indiana Miles? You'd need a whip and hat."

She scowled. "Fuck you if you're going to make fun of me."

I shook my head. "Sorry. It was stupid." She didn't say anything. I took a swig of beer. "Is that what you majored in when you went to college? Archeology?"

A brief nod. She took a sip of the beer. "Yeah. The University of West Florida in Pensacola? They've got this big program for archeology. They're always digging up pirate wrecks up and down the coast."

I tried to picture Denise as a professional archaeologist. A tan safari suit. A crumpled hat. "Really?"

She looked at me. "Yes, really." She studied me, frowning. "Are you making fun of me again?"

"No, not at all. I just never pictured you quite like that, I guess." An image of her dancing, nearly naked, came into my mind and I tried to push it away.

"Like what?"

"An archaeologist."

"Well, how exactly did you picture me?"

A vision of her small, tight body wrapped around a pole on a stage came through the haze in my mind. I tried to ignore it. My heart beat hard in my chest, and I felt myself growing aroused. "I don't know," I said. "I guess I thought you'd stay here."

"Get a job? Get married? Have kids?"

I shrugged and stared out the the Gulf of Mexico. The water churned gray and foamy.

"I didn't finish."

"Didn't finish?"

"My degree. I didn't finish it."

"What happened?"

"I don't know. I didn't really fit in, I guess."

I thought back to her in high school, the grungy black t-shirts, the black mascara, her curly hair straightened, parted down the middle. "You didn't like school?"

"I thought we'd be out doing things, you know? Going to digs, that kind of thing. All I ever did was go to math or English or history. I hated it. I finished that first semester, but I didn't want to go back. So I came back to St. Vincent. But I got my mind made up that spring that I was going to go back, so I applied for a loan, and they gave it to me. It paid my tuition and then some. So, I went back the next fall and I did okay. I made some Cs. I took another loan for the next year because I couldn't find a job." She stopped and bit her lip. "Well, that's not really true. I guess I couldn't find a job I wanted. Plus, they offered me the loan, right? So I look it. I lived in this little studio apartment right close to campus. It was great for a while. I made some new friends, theater types, a lot of English majors, wanna-be poets and writers. Everybody seemed to be in a band of some kind. Then the next semester came and I took another loan. Only this time, the classes were harder. I was repeating classes that I'd failed. I hated math. I couldn't even pass remedial algebra." She sighed and shook her head. "By the next spring, it was easier not to go back. So I came back here to this shit hole. To St. Vincent."

I shook a cigarette from a nearly-empty box and put it between my lips. "You don't like St. Vincent?"

"This place is a sand pit. The harder you try leave, the more it just sucks you down."

"Really?"

"Yes. Do you know how many people I know who've tried to leave this place? They just wind up back here again, every time. It's creepy how often it happens. I tried to leave. Donnie Ray tried to leave. I know some other people, too. They just keep winding up back here."

I thought about Chris, how he'd tried to join the service. And Janey, how she wanted more than anything else to leave. I lit my cigarette and rolled down the window. We watched the white-capped waves roll in, the water gray, churning. Just that morning, the news had reported a tropical depression south of Cuba. Late October. Hurricane season. St. Vincent had been spared for many years. The peninsula shielded us. But everyone figured that one day, a storm would come through at the right angle, get in the bay, and bury this place.

A thought struck me. "Is that why you do it? Is that why you dance?"

She wouldn't look at me. "Yes. When I first got back from Pensacola, I got a job at the Pelican," she said, meaning a small motel out on Sandy Head Beach. "I worked there for a while, about a year actually. Then I started getting bills. At first, I just didn't pay them. I know that's stupid, but I couldn't afford to give them any money. Then a friend of mine told me about forbearance. Do you know what that is?"

I didn't. I shook my head.

"It means you don't have make payments on your loans if the government accepts the forbearance. You just have to give them a reason. I said financial hardship. I did that for a few months, nearly a year. I kept going on the federal student aid website and filling out this form. Then, about a year ago, they went me a letter saying that I couldn't forebear the loans any more. I had to start paying them. They started garnishing my wages at the Pelican, so I quit. I didn't know what I was going to do. I have a friend who lives over in Panama City, girl I knew from my Pensacola days. She danced. She told me about all the money she was making, and I figured, 'Hey, what the hell?'" She took a cigarette from the box I'd left resting the dashboard. I lit it for her.

"What's it like?"

"About what you'd expect. It's not glamorous at all. I walk out there, dance, get money. It's about as unsexy as you can imagine."

"So how long—"

"Am I going to do it?"

I nodded.

"Until I make around ten thousand dollars, I guess. It's good money."

I didn't know what to say, but I needed to say something. "I'm sorry. I didn't know about that. I thought that he made you do it for some reason."

She laughed, a bitter snort. "Like Jimmy has any control over what I do." She looked at me. "You really don't like him, do you? What's he ever done to you?"

"He's a bully," I said before I could stop myself. "He always used to just push everyone around in high school, did whatever the hell he wanted." I thought back to the things I'd seen him do in high school, harassing freshmen, mouthing off to teachers, dominating his group of friends. I thought about the look in his eyes the other day, the beer bottle he gripped like a club in his right hand.

"A bully?"

"Yes. You remember that one guy, Chad Andrews? When I was in the tenth—no, I think it was ninth—grade, Jimmy and Donnie Ray beat the shit out him in the locker room after PE. You know why they did it? Because Chad kept calling Donnie Ray the 'Ginger Bread Man' when we were playing basketball. I remember standing there. Jimmy grabbed Chad from behind and Donnie Ray started punching him, just wailing on him. I was stunned. I don't even know how long it lasted. The coaches pulled it apart. But for me? That's your boyfriend—jumping people, being an asshole." Anger had built up inside of me and I was breathing heavy. "We had to walk on tiptoes around him."

"We?"

"Me, whoever else knew him."

She shook her head and flicked ashes out the window. "That was a long time ago. Ancient history. Chad Andrews was—and as far as I know still is—one of the biggest pricks in North Florida."

"Maybe, but did he deserve to be beaten that way?"

"Did Joe Whitley's kid deserve what you did to him?"

I glared at her, surprised that she knew about what happened. "I didn't bully that kid. He was breaking the law," I said. "I was doing my job."

"Yep," Denise said, her voice a clip, "I'm sure that you were."

"I'm not anything like Jimmy Danley."

"No," she said, not looking at me, "you're not." After a few moments, she spoke again. "You don't know a damn thing about him, do you? You've already written the story in your head. Jimmy's the bad guy. You're the good guy. And I'm the girl who needs saving. Is that it?"

"No," I said. "Just wait a minute."

"No, you wait a minute. Your life is a cherry compared to Jimmy's. Did you know his dad used to beat the shit out of him when he was a kid? Did you know he still has scars on his back from where his dad put out cigarettes on him?"

"Did you know my dad dropped dead of a heart attack when I was seventeen? Did you know that my wife left me and then was killed my a log truck? Shit happens to everyone, Denise. Am I supposed to feel sorry for him?"

"No, but you are supposed to have a little empathy. You said it yourself. Shit happens to everyone. That should be enough reason for you to be aware of who you are. You act like you're this big and bad deputy from some cowboy movie, patrolling this town, looking out for all the good citizens. But the truth is that you're just another one of us. Another kid who never left."

"I didn't want to leave," I said, my face flushed.

"Is that what you tell yourself?" she said. She stared at me for a long time and then turned away. I had the distinct feeling that I'd just missed some kind of an opportunity. For what, I didn't know.

We sat in silence in the truck for a while, and then, I drove her back to town, both of us quiet. The sun had fallen in the west, and the sky glowed orange and pink. I slowed down near the library and she got out.

"Thanks for the beer," she said.

"Wait," I said. "Can we do this again?"

Her eyes flicked up and down my face. "I don't think so."

"Wait," I said.

She turned around. "What?"

"Why not?"

She looked into my eyes. "Because I'm not sure I want to."

"What if you weren't with Jimmy? You said you guys were—what? On the outs?"

"It doesn't matter. I've got to go."

She got in her Mazda and drove away. Within an hour, she'd probably be on stage. I wanted to be aroused by that thought. I wanted to do something crazy like raid my bank account and go to Beach Bunnies tonight. I'd use all of that money on Denise, keep her from having to dance for anyone else. Keep all those losers away from her. They didn't know her story. They didn't know that the only reason she was dancing was economic. They took advantage of her. They were using her. The whole world was using her. I reached back for my wallet and dug out my ATM card and pulled out onto the road. But just as I turned into the bank, it struck me. If I kept her from dancing for anyone else, she'd still be dancing for me. I'd be no better than the customers I thought I hated. Maybe I was no better than them, anyway. I pulled through the bank parking lot and cut down and alley back toward the main road. There, I turned out toward the old Apalachee Cemetery, where the paranormal society wanted to have a ghost hunt.

Aaron and I had gone there as kids. Every kid in St. Vincent did at some point or another, usually on a dare. You ran between the faded gravestones and told each other that you'd seen a spirit. You'd say you saw a man's ghost, vomiting blackness, a sure sign that he'd died from the infection that nearly wiped St. Vincent off the map.

We learned in eighth-grade Florida history that around 1850, a Spanish ship had moored in St. Vincent. The sailors aboard carried Yellow Fever, a disease that quickly took and spread through the population. Many at the time thought that it was a Biblical plague, God's judgment brought upon a sinful people. Since the disease came on the heels of the 1845 hurricane that had destroyed the original settlement of Port St. Vincent, many agreed, fleeing north to escape, never to return. Those who remained buried the bodies in the cemetery, then just an empty, deforested spot on the edge of town. After the plague passed, St. Vincent never fully recovered. But the city fathers turned the spot into a historic cemetery, a place that succeeding generations continued to honor and restore, maybe as a reminder of what once was, of what could come again.

No new bodies had been buried here since the 1960s. I drove along the edge of the cemetery and eased the truck to a stop and got out. I walked down the river stone pathway and through the gate. Most of the graves were so old that you couldn't make out the names. I stood for a moment, feeling the cold air, smelling the cypress and live oak, and willing myself to believe. I wanted to see something—anything. But the only sound was the wind cutting through the trees. This place was empty. It always had been.

I'd never driven to Janey's graveside to leave a bouquet of flowers or say my final piece to her, and now, standing among the dead I never knew, guilt rose in me like a slow tide. But standing in the silence of the graves, I knew why I'd never gone. I knew why I never liked visiting my father's grave in Ashford, Alabama, where he'd been buried next to his mother and father. It wasn't the sight of a plot already bought and paid for by my father's grave, a spot for my mother. I accepted death. I had to. It came for you, despite your beliefs or religious affiliation. No, it wasn't fear that kept me from Janey's graveside. Instead, it was this: the silence that pressed in around me, as tangible as water, the one real, true thing I could know.

12

Cool weather came to St. Vincent early that year. Some years, it never seemed to come at all. The heat would stick around until after Christmas, bathing everything in a humid sweat. But after a rainy summer, the dip in the temperatures came in late October, the last week of my suspension, the weekend before Halloween. One morning, I went out to get the newspaper and felt frost beneath my feet. So many people think that we never cool down here in Northwest Florida. It snowed the year I turned two. I didn't remember it, but I'd seen pictures: me and Aaron in our backyard, wet snow surrounding us in dirty, grayish clumps. I had just as many pictures of us in shorts on Christmas Day, though. Hot as hell and cold as hell: the only two seasons we ever seemed to have in Apalachee County.

Fall is football weather, too, and St. Vincent loved the Chiefs, the county high school's football team. Hometown pride was a big thing, and the locals were fervent supporters, making posters with player's names, leading chants, and having cookouts before the home games. In high school, I went to the games, too, but not to play, of course. I hung around the field with Chris and a few other guys, slowly wandering around the stadium as the night stretched on, trying to talk to girls. I wasn't a fan of the game, then, and I didn't grow to be one, either.

Chris liked college football, and when Janey and I were married, he'd come over some fall Saturdays with whatever girl he was dating. We'd cook on the grill and watch Florida State, his team. Usually, I dozed off while they yelled and screamed. Janey thought I was being anti-social. The truth is that I felt embarrassed about my lack of knowledge. Chris could tell you every player's stats. He knew which pro teams were scouting Florida State players. I barely knew the difference between a quarterback and a half-back.

Donnie Ray had played for the Chiefs, as had Tater, a big kid the coaches loved to put on the offensive line. On Fridays, they wore their jerseys to class, brown and gold passports to popularity and acclaim. Everyone fawned over them—girls, guys, teachers, administrators. I'd seen it all before. My brother Aaron was an Apalachee High celebrity.

I was no fan of Friday night football games in St. Vincent. But when Mack Weston called Thursday morning to say that my suspension was over and that I could come back to work early and that I'd be working the Friday night game, I said that I'd be happy to do it and thanked him for letting me come back to work.

"But let me tell you something," Mack said. "You're not coming back to work to play detective. You're a deputy. I expect you to act like one."

135   A Stairway to the Sea

I promised that I would.

I enjoyed almost every aspect of my job as a sheriff's deputy, even the tiny things, like writing reports. But I hated football duty. Standing in the road, directing incoming traffic, breaking up fights between pimpled teenagers, keeping an eye on any drunks who were out to ruin everyone's night: thankless work, usually reserved for newbie deputies. I'd worked a lot of games my first couple of years, but I'd not done so in a pretty good while. Since budge cuts kept the department from hiring new deputies, Mack decided that we'd all rotate the game shifts. I'd be working the game with Hector Tejada, who'd been on the force a little over a year. He was still fresh from his law enforcement standards. A St. Vincent native who'd played baseball in high school, he was tall and well-built with a deep, radio DJ voice. He talked like actors on TV, his accent flat.

"So, you're back on full time, then, man?" he said and ran a hand through his thick black hair, combed back on both sides. It glistened from oil or sweat or both. We'd been at the game for about an hour.

"Yes. For the time being."

We were on our fourth or fifth circuit around the field. Deputies circled the field during games so that we remained visible. Most people won't step out of line if an officer is right in front of them.

"So what did happen with those kids? The ones out at Gulfaire?" Hector said. He stopped walking and leaned against the chain link fence surrounding the football field. We were just behind the visitor's goal posts. On the other end of the field, the scoreboard showed Apalachee County ahead by two touchdowns.

"Nothing," I said. "I don't think that the kid liked me telling him what to do."

"Whose house was it? Frank said it some rich guy's house."

"Joe Whitley. Local asshole."

"Lawyer guy? The one with the commercials, the with that big fat head?"

I nodded.

Hector crossed his arms and watched the teams slam into each other. "Want a drink? Let's get a Coke. I'm thirsty."

"Sure," I said. My stomach rolled. I'd not eaten much that day. My head throbbed dully, the screams from the stands and the noises of the game and the cheers had all blending into a hissing white noise. I missed being in my cruiser, driving around town, alone.

I'd not talked to Denise since dropping her off at the library a few days before. I replayed our conversation over and over. I wondered if I should have said something different. A part of me thought that I should have taken her into my arms and kissed her. Another part of me knew that she'd have pushed me away. Had she been telling the truth? Were she and Jimmy broken up?

"Are you married, Hector?" I said as we approached the concession stand, a converted single-wide trailer with a plywood awning. It was painted with school colors, brown and gold.

He laughed. "Hell, no, man. Look at this," he said and held out his arms, presenting his body. "This is the American dream. I can't rob the females of North Florida this pleasure, can I?" He pursed his lips in a mock kiss.

I laughed while he flexed his arms. Like Chris, he frequented the gym downtown, and his lean, tone body showed it. He had thick forearms and wide shoulders. He turned back to the cashier at the window, dug out his wallet and ordered two large drinks. He handed me one.

"I ordered diet. I hope that's okay."

"That's cool. Here. Let me give you some money for mine."

He held up his palm. "Keep it, man. Get me next time. He took a drink from the straw. "How long were you married?"

"Two years," I said and took a long drink. I hoped the caffeine would do something to stop my head from hurting.

"I don't know if I ever told you, man, but I'm so sorry about what happened to her," Hector said.

"Don't worry about it. I'm fine. We were not really together when she died."

"I'd heard. Were you guys working on it?"

I bit my lip and looked down, thinking back to her refusal to take my calls. My refusal to seek counseling when she still lived with me. "Not really. Maybe. Hell, I don't know, man. It's so complicated. She left and then she died. Tell you the truth, most days, I'm still confused about all of it."

"You ever think about seeing somebody else?"

"Not really." I thought about Denise.

"*Mijo*, you're young. There's plenty of women who love a man in uniform."

I laughed. "Yeah. You're right." I studied the crowd. So young, all fresh faces, new haircuts. I felt much older than I actually was.

"Hector, man, I'm going to sneak out and have a smoke. You got this?"

"Smoke? Come on, Justin. You need to quit those things."

"I do," I said and began slapping a pack of cigarettes into my palm.

"So do you got this or what?"

"They kill you. They're called cancer sticks for a reason."

"Do you got this or not?"

"Yeah," he said. "Go ahead. Just hurry. Halftime's soon. I'll need you back then."

The football field had been smoke-free for about six years. You had to be at least twenty-five feet from any entrance, so I walked down the sidewalk back toward the high school. I stopped and lit up, studying a water tower that rose above the tree line. Someone had painted "Fuck you" right beneath the high school's logo, the profile of a Seminole warrior, basically the same logo used by Florida State in Tallahassee.

"Same to you," I muttered and wondered who I was talking to: the water tower, the town, or myself.

"Well, if it ain't deputy dog," a familiar voice sounded behind me. I glanced over my shoulder to see Jimmy Danley a few yards down the sidewalk. He wore a denim jacket and a camouflage baseball cap advertising some feed store in Stetson. He hung his thumbs from the pockets of his jeans and stared at me, his head titled back. A cigarette hung from his lips, smoke unfurling in a gray curlicue.

"What do you want, Danley?" I said. I was in no mood for him tonight.

"You think you're a real smart guy, don't you? Coming by my house, talking about peace offerings and shit. You think you're real smart."

"What you are talking about?"

"You think you're a real bad ass, too?" He stayed down the sidewalk. The lights of the stadium and the noise of the crowd suddenly seemed very far away.

I blew a cloud of smoke out of my nose and turned to face him. "I think a lot of things. What's on your mind? What do you want?"

He rubbed his chin. "I'm just saying. You got a right to think you're a bad ass. You drive around in that car. You got that pistol strapped to your waist like some fucking cowboy. What's that? A forty-five?"

"Go beat up a tenth-grader," I said. "I don't have time for this." Hector would be wondering where I was. I didn't want to deal with Jimmy Danley. Not tonight. Not on my first night back.

"I should have beat your ass the other day, coming by my house, sticking your nose in my business. Thing is, if it wasn't for that pistol, I'd whip your ass right here."

I studied him. He hadn't moved. He stood, shoulders relaxed, body slouched like the yew of a cypress tree. "You got a problem, Danley? Is that why you're threatening an officer?"

He rolled the cigarette from one side of his mouth to the other. "Yeah, go ahead and throw those bona fides in my face. They're the only things keeping me off your right now."

"What is your problem?"

He took two steps toward me, his fists balled at his side. Sweat glistened on his forehead. "You stay the fuck away from her. I don't know where you get off, you privileged motherfucker, but you stay away from Denise."

I wondered who'd told him. Had someone seen us together? Had Denise told him?

"Look, man," I said, "I'm not messing with your girlfriend, okay? Just back off before you do something stupid."

He looked at me as though I'd just said the stupidest thing imaginable. "Jesus Christ, Everson. You think I'm stupid? This is a small town, man. Shit gets around."

"I don't know what you heard. And I don't care." I fought to keep my voice even, calm. "You've got a lot of secrets yourself, you know. Things do get around." I looked him in the eyes and didn't blink. I wanted him to know that I knew what he'd done.

He shook his head and looked up at the sky, holding his arms out wide, as though he were pleading his case before a silent judge. "Can you believe this shit? You were always a little shit back in the day, and you're a little shit now. I don't give a fuck if your wife just died. You stay the fuck away from Denise, or let me tell you something, Mister 'Officer of the Law,' your ass will come up missing."

Anger flared through me, white and hot and electrical. Dangerous anger. The kind of rage that makes you stupid things. I took a step toward him. "You need to back off before I lock your ass up. You got that? You don't come at me making threats. Do you understand me?"

"Fuck you," he said. "You stay away from what's mine, town boy. I'll bury your ass."

My lapel mic squelched. "Twelve, get back in here. It's halftime." Hector. Halftime was nuts. Kids everywhere. Lots of traffic problems.

Danley glared at me, his gray eyes narrowed, his fists tiny balls of knuckled flesh. I stared back, unsure of what was about to happen.

"Twelve?" Hector's voice came through the mic tinny with static. "You read me? What's your twenty?"

I pinched the talk button. "Coming. Be there in a second."

Danley took the cigarette from his mouth and blew a cloud of smoke at me. He pointed at me. "You remember what I said."

"You remember I've got a badge."

"Yeah," he said. "And that makes you a real bad ass, don't it?"

"I'm the one with the gun," I said.

He grinned. "Right now you are," he said. Then, he turned and went back to the stadium.

An hour or so after midnight, I was parked right behind the worm-eaten, weather-worn "Welcome to Historic St. Vincent, Florida" sign on the edge of town, between Bay View and Sandy Head Beach. Since the football game ended, I'd broken up a fight at the Swifty, busted up a beer bash at the old Spanish fort, and pulled over a drunk driver, a twenty-something stoner from Franklin County who kept calling me "chief." He was now sleeping it off in the Apalachee County jail, his beige Del Sol impounded. Hector stayed in St. Vincent to work the south end with me because of all the extra traffic.

I was smoking a cigarette and staring at the highway, thinking about Jimmy Danley and Denise.

Just then, a tiny pickup drove by, one headlight out. I pulled out behind it and squinted at the rust-pocked rear bumper—no tags. A hand-lettered sign behind the driver's said read "Tag Applied For." It was an old Datsun, run-down and pocked with rust, probably someone's old work truck.

I flashed the lights and the truck pulled the side of the road just outside of Bay View. In the distance, Marten Bridge rose, its light hazy yellow. I pinched the talk button on my lapel CB.

"Apalachee, this is One-Twelve."

"Go ahead," Sheila said.

"I've got a tan Datsun pickup pulled over just east of Bay View. No tag. Ring a bell?"

"Not really." The radio squelched. "Local?"

"Probably," I said. "I'll check it out. I'll let you know."

"You want me to radio One-Fifteen?" she said.

"Yeah, go ahead," I said, thinking that me and Hector could drive up to the Swifty afterward and get a cup of coffee. I didn't want to do any paperwork and planned on letting the driver go with a warning. "One-Twelve, out."

I studied the back of the truck—one driver. A chain held the tailgate closed. I tapped my finger on the steering wheel. Something felt off. The driver wasn't moving. No cars drove by on the highway.

I turned the floodlight on the truck and opened my cruiser door. I shined my Maglite at the driver's side mirror, trying to catch a glimpse of a face. I edged toward the truck.

"Hey, buddy," I said. "Can you put your hands outside the vehicle, please?"

The driver didn't move.

"Driver," I said. "Please put your hands outside of the vehicle."

Nothing. I reached for my pistol, unbuttoned the holster, and drew it. Thumbed back the safety.

"Driver, please get out of the car," I said.

The driver's side door opened and he slid out, a thin, familiar form. Rich Richardson.

"Did I do something wrong?" he said. He stood, facing me straight-on, his arms at his side. Usually, at this point, suspects put up their hands. Rich didn't. He looked like a man facing a firing squad.

"Mr. Richards," I said and eased the gun back into the holster.

He squinted. "Oh, it's you. You here to harass me, too? My son not enough for you?"

A spark of anger began to smolder in my chest. "Can you come back here for a minute, please?"

"You know I spoke to your high sheriff," Rich said. "I told him about you following Freddy."

"I didn't follow anyone," I said and stopped myself. This asshole didn't deserve any explanation. "Could you please step to the rear of your truck?"

"Did I do anything wrong?"

"I said, please come back here. Just lean against the back of the truck."

He didn't move. "I'm on my way to get cigarettes. Is that still a legal action these days?"

"Look, I just wanted to let you know that you've got a headlight out—"

He spoke over me. "You're a revenue generator. You know that, right? You're nothing but a tool of the state. Do you enjoy harassing citizens?"

"Damn it," I said to the night. The bay churned, the waves rushing, and I wished that I were on a fishing boat somewhere deep in the Gulf of Mexico.

"I am going to get in my truck, and I'm going to drive to the store, and I'm going to purchase a pack of cigarettes. I have done nothing illegal. You are harassing me."

"No, I'm not. And you're not going anywhere. You're going to stand there and shut up, and I'm going to write you a citation for that busted headlight."

"I don't recognize your authority," he said and crossed his arms. "I'm a sovereign citizen of the United States of America. The Constitution gives me my rights, and you can't take them away." His face glowed in the light, eyes and mouth reduced to black holes.

The anger in me welled up. "It doesn't matter what you recognize." I took three steps toward him, but he didn't move. I stopped, unsure. I didn't want another hearing with Mack and a lawyer. I didn't want to lose my job.

He flicked his eyes up and down, studying me. A smile hinted at the edge of his lips. He was stone sober.

Headlights flooded the side of the road. Hector. Rich and I stood, staring at each other. Hector's footsteps crunched behind me.

"What's going on, m'ijo?" he said.

"He has a broken headlight," I said. "I wanted to give him a warning. He's not cooperating."

"Get back in your car," Hector said. "Mr. Richards, please get back in your truck. Don't go anywhere."

"I'm doing so on my own free will," Rich said. "Not because you told me to."

"I don't give a shit," I said. "Get in the car."

"Thank you, sir," Hector said, talking over me.

Rich eyed the two of us and then took a step backwards and got in. He sat still.

"What are you doing?" I said. "That piece of shit is going to jail."

Hector sighed through his nose. "Listen to me, man. Don't give him this."

"What are you talking about?"

"That's Freddy's dad, right?"

I looked at him. "You're from St. Vincent. You know good and damned well he is. You know what he told me? He said he was a 'sovereign citizen.' You ever heard of such bullshit?"

He put a hand on my shoulder. "Listen to me. This is what he wants. He's already gone to Mack about you. You're on thin ice at the department. You know that."

I shook my head. "No, you listen. I was just going to give him a warning about the headlight. I didn't even know it was Rich until I pulled him over."

"So says you."

"Well, yeah, so says me. And you."

Hector nodded. "Yes, but that's the story he wants. Two cops team up to bully him. That's his thing, right? The Treadless? Don't give him what he wants. You run him in, imagine what he'll tell Mack."

"I don't know, Hector, man. He ignored my commands. You can just ignore an officer like that."

"You need to think this through, *amigo*."

"So we just let him go?"

Hector shrugged. "It's that or deal with the shit storm he'll rain on you."

"It's worth it," I said.

"Maybe to you, *mejo*. Maybe to you."

"What?"

He squeezed my shoulder. "Listen, man. You know about the budget. You know where this is headed. I don't want to get laid off. I don't want to get fired. And if I do, I don't want some kind of a harassment charge—warranted or no—in my file, *comprende*?"

I stood for a moment anger surged through me, shaking my shoulders. I bit my lip and dug my fingers in my palms. "Goddamn it, Hector. Just Goddamn it. This is bullshit."

"The world's bullshit, *mejo*."

I didn't say anything. I walked back to the cruiser, got in, and slammed the door.

Hector went to the side of Rich's Datsun and leaned in the window on his elbows. They talked, but the waves from the bay muted their voices. After a minute, Rich's headlight turned on, and the truck rumbled to life. He turned out onto the highway and drove slowly past. We locked eyes and he smiled. I fought the urge to lift a middle finger to him.

Hector walked back to my cruiser, and I let the window down.

"Did you at least write him citation?" I said.

He shook his head. "Verbal warning."

"Just a verbal warning? He ignored an officer. If you hadn't driven up, he'd have probably started something. I'll bet he had a weapon in the car."

"He probably did."

"Why are you so calm about this, Hector? Jesus Christ. Don't guys like him piss you off?"

He rubbed his jaw. "Yeah, they do. But losing my job would piss me off even more. If you think that Rich Richards is driving around with a busted headlight in the middle of the night without a reason, you're crazy. He was trolling. And you bit. I'm willing to bet he was recording us, somehow."

"A camera?" I said and began going over the altercation in my head.

"Maybe. A recorder. Something. He's looking to cause trouble. I went to one of those Treadless meetings one time."

"What? Really?"

He shook his head. "Yeah. Look around the country. It's in bad shape. These guys were talking about personal responsibility. Less government interference. I like that. Sounds like the stuff my pops used to say to me. But whenever Rich spoke up, he was talking about a war between people and the government. Spooky stuff. I got out of there. Didn't go back."

I took a breath and looked out at the mill. "You think they have a point? All this government stuff?"

"Look, *mejo*, I don't know. I just know what I've seen on this job. The future isn't pretty."

I punched my right fist into my left palm. "Rich Richards is a piece of crap," I said.

"He is," Hector said. "But you know what they say about turds like him, right?"

"What's that?"

"You play with shit, you get your hands dirty."

I had to agree. Lately, my hands had begun to stink.

13

The South Side of St. Vincent had its own main street, Hamilton Avenue, and its own school, J.B. Coolidge, a place that had been closed since integration. Now, the citizens on that side of town used it as a community center. Every February, J.B. Coolidge hosted a big Black History Month rally, featuring kids' games and presentations and capped by a speech from a prominent African American Floridian. Meanwhile, the white side of town carried on relatively unaware that just across town, an entirely different St. Vincent existed within the confines of the city limits.

The South Side had its own cultural traditions, too, including a Christmas parade that always took place the Saturday after St. Vincent's Christmas parade and a Halloween/Harvest Festival that everyone called All Saint's Night, or, usually, just Saint's Night. Some of the more conservative churches like First Pentecostal (a white church) had been calling Saint's Night "Satan's Night" for years. First Pentecostal even partnered with a small fringe black church, Divine Sword of Prophecy, to hold a rally against the festivities a few years back. Nothing came of it, though. Saint's Night carried on, a local tradition that turned Hamilton Avenue into a street fair with vendors and food and games for the kids.

At the sheriff's department, we always worked All Saint's Night, usually parking at both ends of Hamilton Avenue and generally just trying to be seen. I'd worked it every year that I'd been on the force, spending the hours between 7:00 p.m. and 2:00 a.m. in my cruiser and walking up and down Hamilton. I smiled at folks. I chit-chatted. I broke up fights between drunks or teenagers. The department made a few arrests each year, nothing major. The town had a lot of held-over racial tension from the late 1980s, when a racist sheriff named Rodney Motley had made it a practice to shake down black citizens whenever he could. I tried to distance myself from any conversations about race. The black community in St. Vincent didn't exactly trust the sheriff's department and probably for good reason. Rodney Motley wasn't the first racist to work for Apalachee County, and he certainly wouldn't be the last.

Of course, a lot of us at the department didn't trust the South Side, either, a place that had its share of drug dealers, drunks, welfare louses, and general low-lives. We'd busted up cocaine deals and prostitution rings over here. It was easy to get lost in the racial politics of it all, and some deputies did. With its low-income housing and low property values, the place seemed to breed crime. You could say the same thing about pockets of Bay View. We'd busted up a meth lab there not a year back. But on Saint's Night, the place looked like a carnival.

I was on duty with Chris, Cowboy, and Hector, two of us on either end of Hamilton Avenue. Chris and I parked driver's-side window to driver's-side window at the east end of the street. Hector and Cowboy were on the other end. The night was loud with the sound of partying: several kinds of music blended to a rhythmic cacophony that floated above the steady hum of voices. The air stank of the paper mill. Off in the distance, the tower lights showed yellow and green.

Chris and I hadn't spoken since that afternoon at his house. I'd worked hard to give him the benefit of the doubt, trying to deduce what I'd do if I felt my job were on the line and Malone came to me, demanding answers. But there was nothing to tell—I'd done nothing wrong.

In the week since my run-in with Rich, I'd done nothing but think about Rich and Jimmy and Donnie Ray. Jimmy and Rich were friends. They went to Treadless meetings together. That much I knew. Which meant that Jimmy was as anti-government as Rich was—and that he hated cops as much as Rich did. Given Rich's angry anti-union stance and given Donnie Ray's and Wayne Childress's friendship (however unlikely it may have seemed), then my guess was that Jimmy must have done something to Donnie Ray that night on the houseboat. Maybe he pushed him in the water. Maybe he threw him. Whatever the case, Jimmy Danley knew more than he was letting on.

But I couldn't tell anyone. The incident with Joe Whitley's kid still hung over me at work, a cloud of suspicion that I couldn't quite shake. I had to keep my suspicions to myself. I couldn't even tell Chris.

I scanned the crowd and my eyes landed on a trailer selling barbecue. "Richardson's Barbecue" was painted on the side in bold, red letters. You could smell the sweet, smoky scent in the air. I wanted some, but I didn't like the idea of eating ribs in the cruiser. I'd get sauce everywhere. Instead, I picked up the new issue of *The Sentinel.* I'd picked it up just before my shift started. I flipped through, scanning the articles and letters. The stuff at Clawson's had blown up big-time. The pro-union group was planning a rally to raise awareness. I smiled. Maybe they'd stick it to old Fred Clawson.

"Did you see this?"

Chris flicked eyes at me. "What?"

"The union guys are planning a rally down at Clawson's."

"Hmmm," Chris said, noncommittally. He studied his hand, flicking the nubs of his missing fingers.

I put the paper down and felt for the cigarette box in my front pocket. I shook out one and lit it, cupping my hand over the flame.

"How many of those do you smoke every day?" he said.

"I don't know. Less than a pack."

"How often do you buy a pack?"

"I don't know. A couple of times a week."

"Didn't your dad die of a heart attack?"

Didn't your dad run off and abandon you and your mom? The sentence formed in my mind. Only biting the cigarette filter kept my from speaking. A wave of shame hit me then. No one talked about Chris's dad. I knew the story only because he'd told me in confidence when we were teenagers. Now, here, ten years later, I'd been primed to deliver the lowest insult I knew, the one that would get past my best friend's cool exterior, the one that would finally break his calm facade. It was the one that would have torn our friendship apart. I looked down at the newspaper. This thing at Clawson's was tearing us all apart.

I held the cigarette in my fingers and rolled it back and forth. We sat in silence and watched the crowd. I opened my mouth to say something several times, but no words came out. I didn't know what to say.

"What do you think about Denise Miles?" I said after while.

"I don't know. Can't figure out why she's with Jimmy Danley, but hell, I've dated psychos, myself. Remember that girl from Stetson? Addie?" He looked at me from the corner of his eyes. "Why?"

"I don't know," I said. "I just was thinking about her. I saw her at the library the other day."

"You still have a thing for her, don't you?"

"I don't know. Maybe. She's with Jimmy. Lord knows why, but she's with him."

He studied me. I could feel his eyes on the side of my face. "You know, Jimmy might not be that bad a guy, right?"

I cocked an eyebrow at him. "What?"

He shrugged. "He's an asshole, sure. But in his world, you're an asshole, probably. Everyone's an asshole to somebody."

"Yeah, but we're talking about Jimmy Danley here."

"Denise sees something in him."

"So? And?"

"Think about it. Don't you think that somewhere in this town, there was a dude who looked at you and Janey and thought 'What the hell is *she* doing with *him*?' That's how people, think. Don't set yourself above everyone. Don't make yourself into some white knight. None of us are. You know better than that."

I blew a cloud of smoke out of my nose and said nothing. We watched the party on Hamilton Avenue. The night wasn't a Halloween Party, per se, but many revelers dressed up, some as movie characters, some as ghosts and monsters. A few of the children ran around dressed like wizards, their tiny hats bouncing as they chased each other in the street. Music played and bass hits shook the ground. The smell of barbecue was cut with acrid stench of the paper mill.

"He threatened to kill me the other night at the football game."

Chris frowned. "What are you talking about?"

I filled him in on Jimmy's threat and he shook his head. "I'd ignore it, man."

"What?"

"What were you doing with Denise, anyway? Did you guys—did you hook up with her?" He turned in his seat and looked at me.

"No, we just drove. That's all. She told me about stuff."

"Stuff?"

"We just talked, okay? Besides, it doesn't matter. Jimmy Danley threatened to kill me."

"He's a jackass. I'll admit that. He loves to shoot his mouth off. He always has. Somebody probably saw you and Denise together in your truck. Freddy. Tater. Somebody. You'd have been pissed if you'd seen Janey riding around with some other guy, right?"

"Janey's dead."

He rolled his eyes. "You know what I mean."

"You don't think I should tell Mack?"

"I wouldn't say anything to anyone, not with your track record lately. I'd let this go if I was you."

"So you don't think it's serious that Jimmy Danley threatened an officer?"

"He didn't threaten an officer. He threatened a guy who's running around with his girlfriend."

"I'm not running around with his girlfriend. They're on the outs, anyway," I said.

Then, my lapel radio crackled. "Twelve?" Cowboy's voice, deep and gravelly.

"Go ahead."

"Signal twenty-two. Corner of Easton and Fifth."

"En route."

"What's up?" Chris said.

"A fight. Over at the liquor store. Let's go. I'll follow you."

"But wait a minute," I said.

"What?"

"We're not done talking about this."

He nodded put the car in gear and pulled out. He turned off of Hamilton to cut down an alley. Easton Avenue was two streets south. Fifth

Street cut down the edge of the South Side and dead-ended into Highway 98.
We pulled into the parking lot of a small cinder block building known only
as The Liquor Store or sometimes just "The Store." In the local phonebook,
you could find a listing for "Richmond's Package Store," but I didn't know
anyone named Richmond attached to the store. Two police cruisers sat in
the lot, their lights flickering soundlessly. Cowboy stood at the front of
his cruiser, a tablet of paper open in his hand. Hector Tejada was near the
building's entrance, talking to a couple of teenagers, both dressed in over-
sized t-shirts and baggy jeans. I parked behind Chris and followed him across
the dark parking lot. He walked with an easy, relaxed stride, and I tried to
mimic that gait.

"What's going on?" I said as we approached the front of the store.

Cowboy had a young black teenager cuffed. He sat on the concrete,
his back against the bumper of Cowboy's cruiser. He kept his head down.
Another teenager sat in the backseat of the car. He, too, kept his head down.

"Don't know, really," Cowboy said. "Some kind of an altercation
inside."

"Motherfucker tried to mug me," the teenager on the ground said.
"I told you."

"You heard it," Cowboy said, nodding down at him. "Clerk says that
three of came in together. There were five involved in the fight out here a
minute ago." He nodded his head toward Hector. "Those two say they saw
the whole thing."

"You break it up?" Chris said.

Cowboy nodded. "Me and Hector."

"Don't lie, *viejo*," Hector shouted over at us, his white teeth flashing
in the darkness. He grinned like a jackal. "I did all the heavy lifting, right,
Sergeant?"

"You're full of shit, Tejada," Cowboy said.

At that moment, one of the boys Hector was interviewing bolted
for the alley beside the store. "Hey!" Hector shouted and took off after him.

I did, too, Chris right behind me. I shined my Maglite ahead as I
ran, illuminating Hector's back. He looked over his shoulder and pointed at
the building. "The other side," he shouted. "Cut him off." His voice came in
huffs and puffs.

"Go," Chris said, breathing heavily. "I'm with Hector."

I turned toward the small parking lot at the back of the store. I could
circle back around to Easton and catch the guy if Hector hadn't caught him
by then. Even though the night was chilly, sweat ran down my back, soaking
through my t-shirt. My vest would be wet, soon. A coughing fit hit me, and I
stopped to catch my breath. I leaned over, hands on my knees, and hacked. I

spit on the street and thought that Chris was right. I needed to quit smoking.

"Thirteen, you got him?" I said into my lapel mic.

Squelch. "Yep. What's your twenty?" Chris said.

"About a block down."

"Get back up here."

"Where?"

"Back at the store," he said.

"10-4." I turned to head back to the front of the store, my mind spinning around Denise and St. Vincent and Janey and Donnie Ray Miles and Jimmy Danley. This damn place. I took a deep breath and started coughing again, my chest heaving, my throat stinging. I spit out a mouthful of phlegm that tasted like nicotine, nearly gagging.

At the end of the block, a truck made a quick turn, its wheels squealing. In the cruiser, I'd have flashed my lights at him. But now, I squinted, willing my eyes to see clearer in the dark. A faded "Don't Tread on Me" logo with a winding snake was visible, even in the sparse streetlight. A tan Chevy S-10. Freddy's truck. He had only one reason to be on the South Side tonight: purchasing—pot, likely. A plan took shape in my mind. If I could catch him in the act, he'd be terrified. I could talk to him, then, find out what really happened on the house boat that night. I could find out if Jimmy really did kill Donnie Ray.

I turned and jogged back toward the liquor store, pushing my legs, ignoring the burning in my chest. The streets were empty. Up ahead, Hamilton Avenue glowed through the trees. The barbecue scent still hung in the air, though I was a good two blocks away. A sudden memory of an 8th-grade health book surfaced in my mind, then, a picture of a smoker's lung. The teacher, Mrs. Williams, had said, "It looks like smoked piece of meat." My mouth soured and I fought the urge to puke.

At the liquor store, only Hector remained, sitting his cruiser, writing on a clipboard. I walked over and leaned against his car. "Where did everybody go?"

"Chambers went back to Hamilton. *Vaquero* took the perps to the department. Damn, *m'ijo*. You don't look so good."

I nodded. "Thanks. You're a perfect gentleman."

"It's cigarettes. Those things are killing you."

"So's life," I said over my shoulder as I walked toward my cruiser. I got in and put it in gear and backed away. Hector waved, his black-gloved hand like a blade.

I saluted him, two fingers to my brow, something I'd seen Cowboy do when he drove away, and turned back out onto the street. Freddy had turned on Fifth Street, headed south, away from the highway and toward the mill. He must have been headed to Stink Town, the oldest area of the South Side. Stink Town was little more than a few city blocks of old, run-down shotgun houses. It was the original South Side, back when the only land African American could buy was here, in the shadow of the mill. Stink Town was the worst of the worst. We'd busted crack dealers there, taken in prostitutes. I'd responded to domestic there my second year. A man had beat his wife to death with a baseball bat. Stink Town was a valley of pain and poverty and suffering, the kind of place you hope exists only on TV. But it was real. If Freddy was headed back there, he was looking for something more than the pot he could have purchased in Bay View.

The further south you drove, the more the houses thinned out. Up ahead, the mill loomed before me, its towers reaching into the smoky night sky. Here, the air smelled of turpentine and pine and ammonia, the stink that settled over St. Vincent when wind shifted east. But here, the smell was always present, something as tangible and real as the weather-beaten, dilapidated shacks that appeared the further you drove.

My lapel radio squelched. "Twelve? What's your twenty?"

Cowboy. "I got a ten-thirteen. Road out to Stink Town."

"Ten-four. Need back-up?"

"Negative. It's not bad. I'm issuing a verbal warning."

"Ten-four. Head back up to Hamilton when you're done."

"Ten-four." I wondered if I should have lied. In the back of my mind, a little alarm went off. This didn't feel right.

Stink Town was deserted for the most part. Everyone was up on Hamilton, celebrating Saint's Night. Most of the windows were dark. Only every other streetlight seemed to work. The ever-present smoke gave the place an unnatural darkness. Freddy's truck was nowhere to be seen. I slowed the cruiser to an idle and shined the side-mounted halogen lamp into the streets. A few people sat on what passed for porches, their faces obscured in shadows.

I stopped in front of a shotgun house that ran up to the edge of the cracked asphalt. An old woman sat on the porch, fanning herself. Above her, a naked light bulb swayed back and forth. A steel fan sat in the open door, its blades whirring, stirring dust.

"Evening officer," he said. She didn't move.

"Hello," I said, fighting the urge to exchange pleasantries. I wanted to find Freddy before he got out of here. "Did you see a truck drive by earlier? A Chevy S-10?"

"I don't see too good," she said, her voice guarded, suspicious. I didn't blame her.

"It would have been just a minute ago," I said, pressing. "It might have been driving very slow. A white guy driving it."

"White boy, huh?" she said, still fanning. The sparse light from the window behind her framed her head, obscuring her features. I realized that even if I could see her clearly, I likely didn't know who she was. Stink Town might well have been an entirely different planet. I wondered if the black residents of the South Side felt the same way about Bay View.

I nodded. "Yes ma'am."

"Well, there's one road out here and one road in. If he was driving on it, he'd have gone down that way," she said, gesturing toward the mill with her fan. "And if he was leaving, he'd come out over yonder," she said, tilting her head back up toward Hamilton Avenue.

"So you haven't seen a truck, then?"

"I don't see too good, like I said." She fanned herself and rocked a bit in her chair. He words sounded final, like a church door closing.

I nodded. She'd told me in her own way all that I needed to know. I got back in the cruiser and drove down the unnamed road. It came to a dead end, an overgrown, sandy lot that lead up to a ten-foot chain link fence surrounding the paper mill. If you looked back east, you could see the old deep water port, the place I'd gone the night Janey died. I looked both ways and spotted Freddy's truck parked a quarter mile down the road to the west. I killed the headlights and idled the cruiser down the road, squinting in the dark. I didn't want him bolting if he saw me. If I was lucky, I could catch him getting back into his truck.

Freddy's truck sat near an abandoned, boarded-up store, a place that might have one been a feed and seed or a neighborhood grocery. The free-standing building faced the paper mill. A wooden fence with missing slats divided the store from a weathered single-wide trailer sitting parallel to it. I pulled in on the east side of the old store and got out.

I edged the side of the building and went to the fence to peer through one of the missing slats. Around the corner of the single wide, voices murmured, one deeper, lower, the other higher, younger, possibly female. I crouched and listened, making out fragments, pieces of sentences:

You said three.

Lucky I don't . . .

Who told you?

Not now.

You've got the money?

Can I shoot it?

Here? Fuck no, dog. Shoot on your own peckerwood time.

A coldness ran through me, as though my blood had chilled. A gun. Freddy was buying a gun. No wonder he came out here. This was bigger than

I'd thought. I sat still, wondering what to do. If I called this in, there was no way I could interrogate Freddy about Jimmy and Donnie Ray. Chris wouldn't let me. Cowboy was working tonight. He'd shut it down. If I tried to take him on my own, he might do something crazy, open fire on me. And what about the person (girl?) he was buying from? He or she might decide that a dead cop is better than a trip to the state pen for the illegal sale of unregistered firearms.

I was out here, in the darkness, alone. And I didn't know what to do.

Take it or get the fuck out here.

I'm going.

. . .up to Hamilton.

The sale sounded complete. I'd watch Freddy come around the corner and follow him to his truck. There, I'd pull my piece, aim down on him, scare him a little. But I'd keep it quiet. No, I wasn't calling this in. He could tell me what happened on that houseboat. He could tell me that Jimmy Danley killed Donnie Ray Miles.

Freddy came around the side of the building, a brown paper back in his hand. I eased along the wall toward the edge. Before he got in the car, I'd come out behind him, gun drawn, and get him against the car. This was too perfect. I had him lined up. My heart beat in my chest, blood pulsing in my ears. Behind the trailer, a car cranked, something loud—glass packs, a muscle car, a throaty rumble. Gearhead that he was, Chris could have told me the make and model from the sound alone. I ignored it and leaned forward, ready to spring.

Freddy passed my hiding spot, head low, taking quick steps. I pulled my Baretta and ran into the street. "Against the car, Richards. You're under arrest."

He dropped the bag and turned around, his eyes white, bulging in his skull. He held his hands up in front of his face.

"Against the hood of your truck!" I shouted. "Now!" I dropped one hand to my belt, searching for handcuffs. I inched toward him, feeling the belt, hunting the button. In just a moment, I'd whip them out and lock him up in one smooth motion. I'd done it countless times.

He bolted across the street, and I took off after him, unthinking, not seeing the headlights to my right, hearing the brakes squeal too late. I tried to dodge and something exploded in my hip. Air rushed by me, cold as river water, and I realized with a kind of removed curiosity that I was flying through the air. The asphalt rushed up at me, impossibly fast, and I closed my eyes, wondering if this is what Janey saw, too.

14

The hospital room was white, antiseptic, a double that should have stuck me with a roommate. But the other bed lay empty across the room, the vinyl blue mattress little more than a reminder of what I felt inside: I was alone, alone, alone.

I had no clear memory of what happened after the car hit me on Saint's Night—just impressions. The taste of my own blood. A sharp, hot pain in my right hip. Streetlights. Cold, freezing temperatures. Shaking all over, my body one big quake.

Then, the ambulance: Chris looking down at me, Hector asking me if I knew what happened, Gene Bishop checking my vitals. My neck was in a brace, and my hip felt twisted in my pelvis, painful and uncomfortable, like a loose tooth with an exposed nerve. I could taste blood. I kept blacking in and out on the way to the hospital in Panama City, where they admitted me at Bay Medical Center, the same place I'd been born.

I'd been there two days. The X-Rays had been done the night I came in. I had a hairline fracture in my right femur, but the doctors wanted to keep me for observation. They were worried about nerve damage. Nurses came and went out of my room. Time meant nothing. I spent a lot of time in and out of sleep, the morphine pulling me deep into a gray and black sleep, the dreams little more than fragments of images.

The second day I'd been there, Malone called to ask me a bunch of questions about the accident. No, I didn't know who hit me. No, I lied, I didn't know the person I was trailing for reckless driving. Why was my car parked off the road? What was I doing? I lied over and over again. I told him I didn't remember. And partly, that was the truth. I had no idea who hit me. I assumed that it was the person Freddy had seen, the gun dealer. Part of me wanted to believe that the hit and run had been a real hit—an attempt on my life. Jimmy knew I was close to finding out what happened to Donnie Ray. But I knew better. I was in the wrong place at the wrong time. Malone promised me that we'd have a longer talk when I got back to town. "I have a feeling, deputy," he said, "that your memory might clear up by then." I had zero intention of telling him anything.

It was Wednesday afternoon. I stretched and groaned and reached out for my phone. A text from Chris, checking on me. Four missed calls. Two from Chris, one from a sheriff's office number. One number I didn't recognize. Two voice mail messages. I put the phone down. Whoever it was could wait. I didn't want to see anyone.

I flipped on the TV. A religious program. A gigantic balloon of a man with slicked-back black hair and a complexion like cottage cheese made a pyramid with his fingers and leaned into the camera, his bulk threatening to tumble him forward. "The question, then, brethren, is this: where will you spend eternity? Heaven or hell? There are only two paths. There is no purgatory. There is no antechamber to hell." The camera swept over an auditorium full of worshipers, three quarters nodding in agreement. I turned the program off and sat back, trying to ignore the dull throb in my hip.

I must have drifted off to sleep because the next thing I knew, Charlie and Luann Mason were in the room. Charlie sat on the couch by the window, flipping through a newspaper. Luann sat on the beige chair by my bed. She was smiling at me when I opened my eyes.

"Well, hey darling," she said. "How are you doing?"

I yawned. "Good." I wasn't sure if I was lying. I rubbed my hip and a dull pain throbbed there, muted by the pain meds running through my IV.

"Boy, you had me scared," Charlie said. He put the paper down and came to the bedside. He patted my thigh once, a hard tap, and crossed his arms over his chest. "I called your mama and talked to her. She said she called."

"I didn't call her back," I said. I looked over at my cell. "I should have. Is she okay? What did she say?"

"She was worried," Luann said. "But we calmed her down." She pulled her sun-bleached hair back and reattached her pony tail. I studied the constellation of dark freckles over her skin, baked dark by years laying out on the beach.

"What did she say?"

"Said to make sure you were okay," Charlie said. He leveled me with his gaze. "You are okay, right?"

"I think so. I'm going to be. How long have you been in here?"

"Walked in just before you woke up," Luann said.

"Do you know who hit you?" Charlie said.

"No," I said, lying again. "They'll find whoever it was."

"I reckon so. I hope so."

"So," I said, trying to change the subject. "What's the news in St. Vincent? I read about the worker rally out at Clawson's."

Charlie's eyes darkened. "The Treadless—they've announced a counter-rally."

"A counter-rally?"

"In support of Frederick Clawson. Some of the workers were saying that folks down at the docks are drawing lines. You're with Clawson or you're against him. People see Wayne Childress as an agitator. They're saying things were fine before he came along. It's ugly talk, son. Ugly. People are throwing around words like 'scab' and 'traitor.'"

"Who the hell is this dude, Wayne Childress?" I said. "Denise said that Donnie Ray and him got tight right there at the end."

Charlie shook his head. "Yeah. They used to come into eat sometimes. But I've got no clue. I've never heard of him. Somebody said he was from Apalachicola. He's pissed off a lot of folks. He's the one driving this train. I don't know much about him. I think he's trying to do the right thing, but that's not a popular opinion in town."

"Why don't they just walk out?" I said.

"Who?"

"The dock workers. Just walk out. Show Clawson he can't treat workers that way."

"Strike?" Charlie said.

"Yes," I said. "You guys down at the mill did it back in the eighties. I remember it. You and my dad and all the men down at the mill. I know what you did. I grew up hearing about it."

He arched his eyebrows. "Then you don't know much. You don't know the whole story."

"What do you mean?" I said.

Luann's cell phone rang. The ring tone was a electronic warble that played "Fur Elise." She flipped the phone open and said to Charlie, "I'm going down to the waiting room to take this."

"Is it the restaurant?"

She shook her head. "It's my mama."

Charlie nodded and she left the room.

"What do you mean I don't know the whole story?"

He sighed and sat in the chair by my bed. "You've never worked in a factory, so you don't know what it's like. Someone mentions 'strike,' and the whole tone of the place changes. Sure, maybe yesterday, you were all grumbling about pay, cursing about your bosses, pissing and moaning. But when someone says 'strike,' the gloves come off. It's serious then. People you thought were on your side—they change. Friendships end. It's ugly, Justin. Very ugly."

"What happened with the mill strike?"

"It lasted damn near three months. St. Vincent came to a standstill. I'd never seen a thing like it. Haven't seen a thing like it since. The thing I remember the most? Not seeing lumber trucks. You see them all the time on the highway, but all the pine stopped coming to town. I remember the air not stinking. One morning, I went out to get the paper and I looked out over the bay from my porch. The mill's smoke stacks were just concrete tubes—no chugs of white smoke. No rotten egg stink."

"It must have been something, though," I said. "You guys got your way, right? I mean, the place opened back up." Then, Dad was still alive. I would have been in kindergarten, Aaron in the third grade. Mama would have been working part time at the Pentecostal church. I could dredge up only fragments of images from that time. High grass in the backyard. A toy soldier I loved and kept beneath my pillow. Aaron dressed in pee-wee football gear.

Charlie shook his head. "Yes and no. We got our way. But things afterward weren't the same. I lost friends during that time. Your daddy and me had a falling out about the whole thing. He didn't want the strike."

"But Dad was the president. He was the architect of the strike," I said, using language I'd heard my entire life.

"He was the best union president we ever had," Charlie said. "But he didn't agree with the strike. He thought it was the wrong thing to do."

"Why?"

"He was right. It shut the town down. A lot of the part-timers at the mill never got hired back on. The economic slow down caused by the strike really cut into Clawson's. This was in October, peak of shrimp season. People quit buying. Businesses all over the Gulf Coast quit buying. Timber was big business. They were scared the strike would lead to a big economic slump. We got our way, but we hurt the town in the long run. Your daddy saw all that coming.

"He wanted to sit down with management one more time. We'd been in negotiations for over two years. We wanted insurance. Well, we wanted better insurance. We already had some, but it was just a pittance. We also wanted better pay for hazardous duty, for those men who worked the paper machines. We'd seen three fellas killed in two years. We needed safety upgrades. But the management kept pleading money, money, money. If we wanted all this stuff, they were going to cut our pay. Your daddy thought we needed to talk more.

"I didn't. Me and bunch of other guys pushed for a walk out. We met one night, all of us crowded into the Beach Baptist Chapel. We voted. And we decided to strike. In the end, your daddy voted with us. It was unanimous. But Vince Everson and a few others saw the problems before the rest of us did. No, your daddy didn't want to strike, but he did."

I frowned. I didn't remember any of this. Dad had never mentioned any of it to me. "And you guys stopped talking?"

He shook his head. "No, nothing like that. We just—we weren't as close." He frowned and pulled at his mustache. "Look, you're missing the point, Justin. I'm trying to tell you that even without the Treadless, a walk-out may not be the best thing those workers can do."

"What can they do, then? Clawson is going to lay them off. Without them, there is no Clawson's Fishery. They deserve better."

"They likely do, son. But at what cost? If they walk out now, with layoffs on the horizon, Clawson's likely to pull the plug on the whole place."

"But the St. Vincent fishery in the biggest one he's got."

"It won't make a never mind to him."

I lay back in the bed, exhausted from talking. Charlie got up and walked over the window. He stared out at the afternoon sun. I flipped channels for a moment.

Luann came back in. "Mama said that since we're in town, we need to stop by," she said.

Charlie rolled his eyes and looked at me. "She's damn near a hundred years old and still thinks she can run Luann's life."

"Don't listen to that old coot. If your mama's in the nursing home one day, you stop by and see her. You've only got one mama." Luann looked at Charlie, "Come on, your old cuss. Let's let the boy get some rest."

"You call us if you need anything," Charlie said.

"I will."

Luann said, "When are they letting you out?"

"Soon, I hope."

We said our good-byes and they left. I flipped the channels and thought about what Charlie had said. I'd always seen my father as a hero for those men out at the mill. He was their union president. He fought for what was right. Now, Charlie had told me he wasn't even sure that the strike should have happened. I stared up at the ceiling, and the world seem to shift, as though all the pieces I'd put together fractured. I thought I understood him. I'd made my peace with his death. Now, I wasn't so sure. The world seemed stitched together with secrets.

I called my mom after I'd eaten my hospital supper, a tasteless pork chop and some dry and tasteless green beans. The nurse didn't even laugh when I told her how much I enjoyed the first-class cuisine at Bay Medical. She did, however, tell me that I'd be going home soon. A doctor was supposed to come evaluate me later.

At first, Mama wanted to drive down to St. Vincent, but I told her that I was going to be fine. There was no reason for her to come. Besides, I explained, I was okay.

She was silent for a long time on the other end of the line. She was trying to make a decision. "Are you sure you're okay?"

"Yes. Don't worry about me. I'm okay."

"Do they know who did it? Who hit you?"

"It was a hit and run. It was during Saint's Night. You know how that goes. Probably a drunk driver."

"Well are they looking for whoever did it?"

"Yes."

"Son," she said, "are you sure that you're doing okay? Why don't you let me come down? I'll stay with you while you recover. You're not going right back to work, are you?"

She had come down after Janey's funeral and stayed for two weeks. We spent those long, hollow days tiptoeing around each other. I was sure that the house reminded her too much of Dad because it certainly reminded me of Janey. We didn't talk much those two weeks. She cooked for me and tried to be happy.

The morning she left for home, she hugged me tight and whispered in my ear, "Please let me know what I can do to make you better."

Now, on the phone, she said, "What can I do to help?"

"I'm fine," I said. "It's a hairline fracture. It's not that big of a deal. Really. I got to go. The doctor's stopping by later to talk about my release. I'll call you soon. I love you."

"I love you, too, Justin."

"Let me ask you a question."

"Okay."

"Do you remember the strike? Back in 1982?"

She fell silent. And then, after a moment: "Sure I do."

"What do you remember about it?"

I pictured her brown narrowing, could feel her mind journeying back there, probing the details, trying to dredge up an old memory. "I guess I remember everybody was worried. We didn't know what would happen. We didn't know how long it would last."

"Do you remember how Dad felt about it?"

"He was worried, like the rest of us. Why are you asking about all of this?"

"Charlie Mason came by to see me this morning," I said. "He told me something I didn't know. He told me that Dad didn't want the strike."

Again, she fell silent. "Nobody wants a strike, son."

"Were him and Charlie close back then?"

"Yes. They were. They used to fish together. You and Aaron went with them a few times. You remember? What did Charlie tell you?"

"He said that Dad didn't want the strike. He said that after it, they were never quite the same. Is that true?"

"Might be. I don't know. Your daddy was a private man."

"You lived with him for thirty years."

"And you lived with him for nearly twenty, yourself. Vince Everson was a lot of things, but he wasn't what you'd call forthcoming. Sometimes I felt like I had a roommate, not a husband. Why are you thinking about all of this?"

"The workers at Clawson's are threatening a walk out."

"Listen—son. You're getting all het up over this. This isn't your problem. You need to let this go."

"You're probably right," I said, half-believing my own words. "Mom, I'm sorry I brought all this up."

"Do you want me to come down there? Can I come down there?"

"No. I'm fine. I just—needed to talk, I guess."

"Justin, I love you. Let me be your mama."

"You are. I've got to go."

"Call me if you need anything," she said. "I love you, son." She hung up.

Her voice was satiny and smooth. It made me think of freshly washed sheets. It always soothed me. In the weeks after Janey's death, she'd called a few times, trying to convince me to move up to the Atlanta area to be closer to her and Aaron and Kristen and the kids. Aaron even called once. We had an awkward conversation about my feelings, which neither of us wanted to talk about. In the end, I convinced him that I'd think about looking for a job in Georgia one day soon. None of us had mentioned my moving since.

I listened to my voice messages. Two from Chris. One from Cowboy. They wanted me to know they were looking for the hit and run driver. No one had seen a thing. Chris said he planned on coming to the hospital when he got off shift. I sent him a message and told him not to worry about it and that I'd call him when I knew I was being released. I needed a ride home.

Then, the doctor came in with a whiff of rubbing alcohol. He looked to be my age, a short, boyish-looking man with rounded cheeks and a pointy chin. His light brown hair was trimmed short, two thin sideburns coming down his cheeks. He stood by the side of the bed and flipped through my chart.

"How are you, Mr. Everson? I'm Dr. Leiby."

I shook his offered hand. "Thanks for taking care of me."

"Well, deputy, looks like that hairline fracture will be okay if you stay off of the leg. You've also got some significant bruising on your hip. I'll prescribe some pain killers. You're not on any medication now, are you?"

"Ambien. Sleep aid." My right hand was wrapped in a thick bandage. I'd torn my palm open when I tried to catch myself as I fell on the pavement after the car hit me.

He nodded. "That shouldn't be too much of a problem. Do you stick with the prescribed dose?"

"Usually."

He flipped the pages on my chart. "Do you drink alcohol?"

"Not to excess." Part of me wished that I did. Maybe then I wouldn't worry about things so much.

"Smoke?"

"Yes."

"A lot?"

"Define a lot."

He frowned. "How many do you smoke a day?"

"I don't know. Half a pack, maybe. A whole pack some days."

He flipped through the chart. "Says here you have a family history of heart disease?"

"My father. He died of a heart attack."

"How old was he?"

"Fifty-three."

Dr. Leiby whistled through his teeth. "I probably don't have to tell you this, but smoking is a really bad idea. Especially with your family history."

I nodded and stared out the window. The morning light was bright, too bright. It hurt my eyes. "Yeah. I've been meaning to quit for a while."

"No time like the present. Your blood pressure's high."

"How high?"

He squinted at the chart. "One-thirty-six over eighty-seven."

"Is that really high?"

"It's not low. It's pre-hypertension. You've got a family history. Do you exercise?"

I thought about all the times Chris had urged me to join the gym. All the lectures about smoking. "No. Not really. I don't have a lot of time. I work a lot."

"How's your diet?"

"Truthfully?" I said. "A lot of hamburgers. Junk food. It's bad. I know it."

He nodded, not looking at me. "Here's the deal, deputy. You've got to do something. You're not going to die tomorrow, probably. But you've got some problems coming down the road. I can refer you to a dietician, but I don't know if you'd go. What it comes down to is this—you've got to decide if you care enough to do anything." He didn't sound angry or sharp, just matter-of-fact. I understood. He had a whole hospital full of patients who needed him.

"Thank you," I said. "I'll consider the advice."

He shook my hand. "You should."

I nodded. He told me that he recommended I take a week off of work and keep any weight off my right leg. He said that I should stay home and rest. He prescribed some pain meds and a cane. I didn't relish the idea of more time off. I needed the schedule of my job. It kept my days focused and arranged. During my suspension, I'd done little more than lay on the love seat watching television. I had no intention of taking a whole week off. Maybe a few days, but not a whole week. Dr. Leiby also asked if I had a way home. Then, he shook my hand one last time. "Be good to yourself, deputy," he said. "No one else will."

I was released the next day. Chris picked me up at the hospital that afternoon. A nurse pushed me to the lobby in a wheelchair, despite my protests. "It's policy," she said. At the front desk, I signed a few papers and met Chris out by the curve. He wore street clothes, loose jeans and an Atlanta Braves t-shirt. When I came out of the automatic sliding doors leaning on the cane, he laughed. "You got a top hat to go with that that thing?"

"Hardy-har," I said. "Thanks for coming to get me. I was one step away from asking mom to come down."

"How is she?" he said. We walked across the drive-through to where he'd parked his gray Chevy. It sat high up off the ground, the tires caked with mud.

"She's good," I said. "Enjoying life. How about your mom? How is she?" Chris's mom worked as a night nurse at an old folks' home on the other side of Panama City Beach, in a tiny town called Laguna Beach. She'd been there for a long time.

"She's good. Keeping on keeping on," he said and climbed up into the truck. I opened the door on the passenger side, unsure if I'd be able to get up with my hip. Right now, the pain was dulled with medication. But I dreaded what was to come. I threw the cane up on the seat, and tested my weight on my good leg. Chris reached across, his palm open.

"I'm good," I said, pulling myself up on the chrome handle just inside the truck's door. My left arm felt weak then, and I slid back down. I didn't have the strength to push off my bad leg again. My hip throbbed.

"Give me your hand," he said, and I reached out. He pulled me up into the cab.

"I'm hungry. Let's get some food."

We drove to a place called The Captain's Table in St. Andrew's, the historic district close to the old downtown. Inside, we ordered fried shrimp and raw oysters and a pitcher of beer. I scanned the walls, studying the old black and white photos of historic Panama City.

As we ate, Chris and I talked about the night I'd been hit. He told me that Saint's Night was relatively quiet. A couple of arrests for fighting. Some noise complaints. Nothing out of the ordinary. The teenager we'd been chasing had run from us because he thought he had warrants for an unpaid speeding ticket. He didn't, it turned out. His mom had paid the tickets off.

Chris drained the dregs from a glass of beer. "Let me ask you something, and and I want you to be honest with me."

"Go ahead."

"What happened out at Stink Town?"

I played with my fork, pushing an empty oyster shell around on the tray. "I got hit by a car. You know that."

"Why were you out of the car?"

"Why this third degree?" I said.

He cocked an eye brow. "Because this time, I think you might have gotten yourself into some deep water, kimosabe. Mack is asking some pretty hard questions about that night. Why were out there? Who were you tailing? Why did you get out of the car?"

I studied him for a moment, this boy who'd been my friend for as long as I could remember, with his easy way and his missing fingers, with his steady gait and his always-there-ness, this boy who'd become a man I thought I could trust, a man who, despite our differences, I'd follow into the gates of hell if he told me he needed me. I needed to tell him the truth. He deserved that much. "It was Freddy."

"Freddy? Why?

"I thought he could tell me what happened to Donnie Ray Miles. I thought if I pulled him over and talked to him, just the two of us, he'd tell me what really happened on that houseboat."

"Justin, Mack told you to let this lie."

"I don't want to let this lie," I said. "I want to know the truth."

"You know the truth—he drowned. He fell. His BAC was twice the legal limit. He was blitzed out of his mind, man. There's no conspiracy here."

"How do you know that, Chris? How do you know?" I said, my voice raised. Some of the other patrons looked at us. "With those urban terrorist assholes the Treadless involved, God only knows what happened."

"Lower your voice, man. Calm down," Chris said.

Our waitress came over, a teenager with honey blond hair. She wore a t-shirt advertising the restaurant. "Can I get you gentleman anything else," she asked, her voice hesitant.

"We're good," Chris said and she nodded. "Just the check. One bill."

"I'll pay my share," I said.

"Calm down. Let me get this," he said and smiled at the waitress. As usual, he'd managed to calm the situation. I felt more at ease, more in control. She left us alone.

"Let me tell you something about the Treadless," Chris said. "They're not who you think they are. They're not all as crazy as Rich Richards."

I waved my hand. "How would you know, dude?"

He brought his hands together, clasping his left hand over his right, hiding the missing fingers and the smooth skin where they'd once been. "I know because I've been to a couple of their meetings."

My mind reeled, trying to make sense of what he'd said. "What? Are you working undercover?" I lowered my voice and glanced around the place to be sure that no one was listening to us. "Does Malone have you working undercover?"

He grinned. "No, look. Calm down. It's just that I think that some of their ideas might now be so bad, you know? Government overreach is a big thing. Did you know that the majority of the city salary budget goes to administrators? Not guys like me and you. No folks actually doing the work. But administrators. Bureaucrats. Pencil pushers. The country's going broke, Justin. The Treadless are just calling attention to it."

Something clicked in my head. "Jimmy said a cop had been coming to the meetings." I'd thought it was Hector. Now I felt like I was sitting across from a stranger. Where was the Chris I'd always known? Who was this guy?

"The downsizing at Clawson's is just part of the story. The overreach. The feds in control of everything. You know that there's legislation about firearms right now in D.C., right?"

"Are you turning into one of these 'they're coming for our guns' people, man? Tell me you're not," I said. "Doesn't Rich Richards go to those meetings? Doesn't Jimmy Danley?"

He pulled his lips tight and nodded, a gesture that seemed less about me and more about him. "Just because Jimmy Danley is an asshole doesn't mean the Treadless aren't making some important points," he said. He sighed. "I thought you might react this way, what with your dad and everything."

"Leave my dad out of this," I said.

The waitress came over and Chris gave her his debit card. I looked up at the fluorescent light and tried not to think about what he'd just said. How did I feel? Betrayed? That wasn't quite right. Rather, I felt like something had shifted when I wasn't looking, as though the world had somehow come off of its tracks and I was the only person who noticed.

"So, are you and Jimmy big buddies, then?" I said.

"Christ, man, would you settle down? Worry about what matters. Look, if I were you, I'd tell Mack that you got out of the car because you thought you heard a gunshot or something, after you gave the verbal warning to whoever you pulled over. Say you stopped the car and got out to investigate. Tell him that you didn't see who hit you—and that's true. Tell him it was your mistake, that you just weren't looking where you were going."

I picked up my beer mug and saw that it was empty. "That sounds good, I guess," I said.

"Unless you want to tell him you were following Freddy."

I shook my head. "No. I'll tell him what you said."

If my father were alive, this was exactly the kind of thing I'd asked him about. But he was dead. And I didn't who to talk to. I didn't know what I'd say even if I could seek someone's counsel. I looked down at the table and studied the cracked lacquer. I pulled at a loose piece with my fingernail. It flaked off with ease.

Chris and I chatted on the way home. He ribbed me about Denise and said that he'd heard that she and Jimmy were nothing more than roommates at this point. He told me about Deanna Branch, a girl he'd been seeing. She worked at the bank in St. Vincent and had been out of high school only a year. I wanted to give him hell about how young she was, but my mind was elsewhere. I thought about my father and the paper mill union. I'd lived my life believing him to be a union hero, the man who saved the mill. The man who saved local jobs. The man who saved St. Vincent. But Charlie said he didn't even want the strike. The man I'd built in my mind, my father, now seemed distant and hazy—not quite a ghost, not quite a memory. More like a story. More like an old song I'd been forgetting all along.

15

All my life, I've heard all these stories about small towns. That in a small town, everyone knows everyone else. Everyone stays, as folks say, in everyone else's business. That small towns are safer than big cities. That small town people are more earthy and real than city people That people in small towns are kinder and nicer than big city folks. That there are no secrets in small towns. I don't know if I believe any of it, particularly that last one. If there were no secrets, you wouldn't need people like Davis Malone to ferret out the facts after a crime is committed. If there were no secrets, I'd know what happened on that houseboat the night Donnie Ray died. If there were no secrets, I'd have known that Chris was going to Treadless meetings. If there were no secrets, I'd know why Donnie Ray came home from Iraq so early. If there were no secrets, I'd understand what Denise saw in Jimmy and what she didn't see in me. If there were no secrets, I'd know for certain why Janey left me and why she had to die. The truth is that secrets are everywhere. Life, to a large extent, is deciding who you share those secrets with.

The day Chris dropped me off, I took two sleeping pills and went to bed, trying to forget everything that happened. I woke up the next day, convinced that my hospital stay had been a dream, but when I put my feet on floor, the pain in my hip doubled me over and I fell back into the bed, a cold sweat breaking out over me. My hip throbbed, each pulse a tiny swell of fire that made grind my teeth. I managed to get up, take some pain pills, and get a shower. The rest of the day, I ignored phone calls and watched paranormal documentaries on TV. Ghosts. Bigfoot. The Bermuda Triangle. All those secrets. All those lies, some might say. I was a paranormal agnostic, I'd always said. Belief and doubt a bullet and a shell. Only together do they work.

I spent a week at home, hiding from the world, my head in a fog of Ambien and muscle relaxers. My mother called to check on me every day. Frank Sutton dropped by one night on patrol to say hi and check up on me. Tuesday at noon, Charlie dropped by with a hamburger from the cafe. He made me eat it while we talked about the upcoming union rally at Clawson's. I had so many questions about my father, but I didn't even know where to begin. I put the burger down and said, "Tell me something, Charlie."

He nodded. "Anything."

"Did you and my dad lose your friendship over the strike? Over politics?"

He wiped his mouth, as though he were drying the white mustache that had been on his lip for as long as I'd known him. "I don't know if we lost our friendship. I wouldn't put it that way."

"Then how would you put it?"

He took a breath. "I'd say that we saw the world in different ways. I'd say that we realized that we didn't have to be just alike to be good friends. Hell, the week he died, we were supposed to go fishing."

I nodded. The hamburger lay on the plate, half-eaten. I thought of Chris and the years we'd spent together. We were closer than Aaron and I had ever been. A pain ran up my hip and I bent forward, my stomach rumbling.

"Are you okay?" Charlie said and half-stood.

I held up my hand. "I'm fine. It's this medicine. I can't eat a lot when I'm taking it." I looked at him. "Listen, there's something I need to tell you."

He sat back down. "What?"

"The night I got hit by a car, I was following Freddy Richards. He drove out toward Stink Town. He was at this trailer—I don't know who lives there. I parked at an old store and tried to creep around to see what he was doing. At first, I thought he might have been buying drugs, but I think I overheard him buying a gun."

Charlie frowned and rubbed his hand over his face. "Did you tell the sheriff?"

I shook my head. "I can't. He told me to leave Freddy alone. Rich threatened a lawsuit. Said I was harassing his son. The city's budget's in the crosshairs. Mack can't risk any trouble right now. He might or might not actually sue, but Rich threatened. After that stuff at Gulfaire, Joe Whitely threatened to sue the city, too. I've stirred up a lot of shit as of late."

"If you stir it," Charlie said, "it always stinks." He took a deep breath and folded his hands beneath his chin as though he were about to pray. "So who hit you, then?"

"I think it might have been the gun dealer."

"Sounds right."

"I know it's right." I sat back in the chair and shook my head. "This whole town has gone crazy, Charlie. I don't even recognize it anymore. Everybody mad all the time."

"Everybody's always been mad. So what are you going to do?" he said.

"I don't know. I don't know why Freddy would be buying a gun. Jimmy Danley's probably got fifty of them. I don't know why he'd be down in Stink Town doing it anyway. Whatever is going on, it's not good. I know that much."

I stood up and we walked to the front door. Charlie studied me, the gray in his eyes like the slate skies before a storm. "You remember one thing, Justin. Politics changes everything."

"What does that mean?"

"Just what it sounds like," he said. He smiled and we shook hands. I promised to call him if I needed anything. Then, he walked across the front yard, kicking up magnolia leaves. He got in his truck, a two-tone Ford, and pulled out onto the road, waving one last time before driving away, leaving me in the house, a question on my face, my stomach queasy, unsettled.

Tuesday evening, my house phone rang. It was a chilly night. I had the front windows open, and a cool breeze blew through the house. The last remnants of summer were gone. Autumn had arrived, full-throated and seemingly angry that it always got short-shifted in Apalachee County's humid environment. The air felt dry, crisp as sheet from the dryer. I'd been in the kitchen, scrounging around for food. I had a box of Cheerios in my hand when the jangling ring cut through the muffled voices from television. It had been on most of the evening, though I'd not been watching it. I'd been lying in bed, half-heartedly reading a detective novel and wondering why I couldn't be more two-fisted, more badass like the character in the book, who called everybody "partner" and wasn't above landing a two-by-four upside a perp's head. It was 11:15 p.m.

"Hello?"

"Hey." Denise. Her voice was low. Music pulsed in the background. Something techno. Dance. "Are you at work?"

"I don't have much time. I just wanted to check on you. Are you okay?"

I massaged my hip and winced. The pain murmured beneath the surface, a tide always on the verge of breaking. "I'm okay," I said. "I'm fine."

"Who hit you?"

"I don't know," I said.

She didn't speak for a second. "You're being weird."

"How?"

"You're answering me with words. Talk to me. I'm checking on you."

I started to hang up, but a part of me wanted to keep talking. "I'm okay. I'm sorry. It's late. I'm tired. I need sleep."

"Look," she said. "I don't have much time. You need to know something."

"What?"

"First, I'm not with Jimmy any more. I'm living with him," she said and trailed off. I could pictured her eyes, wandering, trying to figure out the best way to proceed. "Or, he's living with me. We're both paying rent. I've got nowhere else to go."

"Okay," I said, still stung by her first rejection, still wondering why she'd ever been with Jimmy in the first place. "I'm sorry it didn't work out."

"I'll bet you are. Listen, there's more. The other night, Freddy came by the house. He and Jimmy were in the backyard for a long time, talking. I could hear them from my window. You need to watch out. Jimmy's up to something. I don't know what, but I heard him say something like 'Deputy dog's gonna get his, whether he likes it or not.'"

My mind reeled, spinning, building stories, constructing narratives and conspiracy theories. Jimmy and Freddy killing Donnie Ray. The sheriff somehow in bed with all of them, working hard to keep me off the scent. But then, a kind of clarity took my mind. It was as if someone had poured a glass of ice water into a boiling pan. For a moment, the bubbles continued. But then, everything went smooth, calm.

"I don't care what he says," I said. "I don't care. I don't have the energy to care."

"I'm serious," she said. "I think he blames you for me and him. For us breaking up."

I paused. "Is that the case?"

She didn't say anything for a long moment. "No. Yes. I don't know. Because—look, I get the feeling that I've pissed you off, somehow."

A cold wind blew through the house and the front curtains whipped, knocking something off the coffee table, probably a glass or a cup. "I'm not mad at anybody," I said. "I'm tired of all this. That's all. Just tired. Thanks for calling. I'll keep my eyes peeled."

She said goodbye and I hung up the phone. Blue light flickered from the television, ghostly and distant.

One night, I dreamed of a treasure chest buried in the sand just off the tip of Cape San Vicente. Far beneath the emerald waters, down deep where the sun above is little more than a flicker of globular light, past the curious fish that dart away when you reach out for them, a valley runs, the sand cresting down into the Gulf of Mexico. Somewhere in this valley is a barnacle-encrusted treasure chest. Above, I have motored out into the shimmering water in a twelve-foot boat with a console and a canvass top. I am dressed in a wet suit. A single air tank it on my back, and even as I navigate the clear water, I hold the respirator hard between my teeth, as though the air here is dangerous, unpalatable. I wear the rusted key on a knotted black cord around my neck. In the treasure chest is a single item: a huge, leather-bound tome, the cover encrusted with glyphs and undecipherable markings. I could dive down and find this chest and bring it up the surface. I could use the key around my neck, open it, and pull this book out. I could open it. But in the dream, one thing is certain: the book's pages are all blank.

On Thursday morning, my phone buzzed and I picked it up. A department phone. I didn't recognize the extension.

"Hello?"

"Deputy?"

"This is Justin Everson," I said. "Who's this?"

"Davis Malone," he said, and my heart sped up. "How are you doing, deputy?" I was lying on the couch in in the den. I sat up a bit and muted the TV—another ghost documentary.

"Well, I lost a fight with a car, so I've been better," I said. I didn't laugh.

Malone chuckled, but the laugh sounded rehearsed, perfunctory. "Well, I'm glad to hear that you're in good humor. I was calling to ask you a few questions about the night you were hit."

"I don't know. I'm not feeling my best. These pain meds—they've got me pretty washed out." I fought to keep my voice even. I'd called into the department Tuesday morning and given Frank Sutton my statement, the lie Chris had crafted. I told him I pulled over a speeder, issued a verbal warning, and heard what sounded like a gunshot. I pulled the cruiser to the side of an old building to hide it and then went back to cross the road so that I could search for the shooter. There, I'd been hit by a car. No, I couldn't tell the make or model. No, I didn't get a tag number. I remembered only a flash of blue.

He clicked his tongue, the sound like a static snap in my phone. "I hate to hear that, deputy. I understand that you've got a week off, yes? Maybe you need more time?"

The threat was obvious. He knew I wanted to work. "Can we talk in the morning?" I said.

"Sure thing, deputy," he said. "You take care."

I closed the phone and started at the TV. A ghost hunter was explaining how a lighthouse in St. Augustine, Florida, had been the site of many paranormal happenings over the years. "So many people have told stories about this place that it's hard to separate fact from fiction," he said.

"You got that right," I said and turned off the TV.

The next morning, I woke up early, showered, dressed in street clothes, and took two pain pills. I needed to look like I was in no pain whatsoever. I was headed to the sheriff's department, and Mack Weston didn't need to see me limping across the parking lot like some geriatric lawman come home to roost. I ate three pieces of peanut butter toast and shotgunned a cup of black coffee. The pills would numb me. The protein and caffeine to fortify me and ward off any fogginess from the pills. The prospect of talking to Malone made me feel the way I did back in school when they sent me to the guidance counselor to talk about the nebulous concept of "my future."

The counselor—Mrs. Gibbs, a large woman shaped like a navel orange—seemed to have access to secret information about my future. She'd say things like, "In five years, you'll be finishing your bachelor's," and I'd sit there, dumbstruck, wondering how on earth she knew where I'd be in five minutes, much less five years. I knew she was speculating, but her confidence threw me. How could she be so certain? My limited interactions with Davis Malone were the same. He had a way of convincing you that he was right, even if you knew he was wrong.

I parked my Dodge by a fountain at the edge of the parking lot closest to the road. A waist-high concrete structure, the fountain had a metal State of Florida seal on it and held two flag poles, one flying the stars and stripes, and a little lower beneath it, the state flag of Florida. The fountain was off. I wondered if it had ever frozen over. Wind whipped from the north, cold like water. I pulled my jacket tight as I walked across the lot, trying to ignore the dull ache that was not quite pain in my hip.

At ten a.m., the department was quiet. A radio squelched from dispatch. The central heating hummed. The place smelled like scorched coffee and burned lint. I blinked, trying to fight off the fog gathering in my peripheral vision. I looked around for Mack or Cowboy, but the place was empty. Mack could have been anywhere—on call, in a meeting. Cowboy might have been off.

I passed a few doors on my way to Davis Malone's office. His door was open. I stuck my head in. He sat hunched over a laptop computer, his fingers tapping each key in quick succession. He wore a starched white shirt and a black tie. He didn't look up when he spoke.

"Thanks for coming in, Deputy Everson. Why don't you have a seat there?"

I eased into the wooden chair. The faux leather was cold, and I fought an involuntary wince. "No problem," I said. "I'm feeling a lot better."

He turned in the chair and faced me, a brisk, curt motion. "I wanted to talk to you about the night you were hit," he said. He picked up a cream-colored file folder. "Everson" was printed on the tab in neat, blocky print, each letter capitalized. He opened the folder and studied a piece of paper for a moment. "Says here you pulled over a speeder, issued a verbal warning, and then went to investigate what sounded like a gunshot. Is that what you told

Deputy Sutton?"

"Yes." I tried to raise my foot to cross my legs and a sharp pain ran up my hip. I winced and coughed.

He studied me, his eyes dark and sharp as the beak of his hawk-like nose. "Are you okay?"

"I'm fine." I tried to smile and hoped it didn't look pained.

He put the paper down. "Look, deputy, I'm going to be straight with you here. I think you're lying. I don't know why, and I have no idea what you'd be hiding. But this story simply doesn't add up." I started to speak, but he held up his hand. "Let me finish, please. For all intents and purposes, I am internal affairs here in Apalachee County. I'm the one who decides who's telling the truth. And I don't think you are. I think something else happened that night." He stopped and studied me. He had a sharp widow's peak. His hair was short, high and tight, military-style.

"I'm not sure what to tell you. I'm telling the truth," I said, wondering if I should call him "Davis" or "Mr. Malone" or just "Malone."

"Why don't you take me through it, step by step, so that I can understand? Maybe I'm not fully understanding Deputy Sutton's report— your report, which he filled out."

"As I was leaving the liquor store after the altercation, I saw a tan pickup truck headed south, out toward Stink Town. The driver was speeding. I didn't put a radar on him, but I'd guess he was going fifty in a thirty. I figured he was coming home from Saint's Night, not paying attention. Just got in a hurry. I was going to pull him over. See if he was drinking. I did pull him over and issued a verbal warning."

"Who was the driver?" Malone said. He flicked his eyes from me to the report.

"I didn't know him."

"You didn't check his license?"

"I was lazy. I know it's protocol. But he was sober. It was late. He said he had to get home, had to get to bed. Had to get up early the next morning. I let him off with a warning." The lie sounded so much like bullshit I wondered why the office didn't smell.

"Was the driver African American?"

I nodded.

"So what's this business with the gunshot you heard?"

I took a breath. I was walking into dangerous territory here. The more info he wanted, the more I had to lie. If the truth came out, I'd look very bad. "I don't remember much. My head hit the pavement pretty hard. I just remember hearing a gunshot and deciding to investigate. I thought I could sneak up on whoever was playing with guns."

He looked at the papers in his hand for a long time and then back at me. "I think you're lying."

"Prove it," I said, surprised by my bravery. Around me, the world had sharpened. My heart raced, and I fought to remain calm.

He leaned forward. "Here's the deal. According to your own backup, you lied about the night at Gulfaire when you beat up Fred Whitley's son. You've continually lied about running your own investigation on the Miles drowning. Everybody in this department knows you've been running all over town, asking questions, undercutting the authority of this department. You're an insomniac who has admitted to having visions."

"How do you," I began.

He held up his hand and continued talking. "You are not fit for duty, not in my estimation. You are on the verge of a mental breakdown brought on by the untimely death of your ex-wife, and your work has suffered. I don't know what went down in what you all around here call Stink Town, but I can guarantee that it was more than the story you just told me. No, I can't prove it. But the truth is funny, deputy. It's a bit like a cancer. You can ignore it as long as you want. You can spend your days pretending that you don't have it. But no matter what, those cells are attacking your own. Soon, they'll all metastasize. And then it won't matter. You'll die. And everyone will know."

I stood up. "Are we done here?"

He stood up, as well. "You're, what? Twenty three?"

"Twenty-six."

He nodded. "You're just a kid. You think you know something. You don't. The world is divided into two types of people—the good and the bad. You need to remember that, and here's why. Good, deputy, is a choice. Any nonsensical idealistic idea that your generation carries around about the inherent goodness of humanity is nothing more than a fool's dream. Truth is, we're all pretty rotten. Good is a choice because the default? That's bad. That's evil. That's where you get your Ted Bundies. That's where you get your Saddam Husseins. That's where you get your Hitlers. Your Stalins. Your Richard M. Nixons. These are people who didn't make that choice. You need to think about the kinds of choices that you're making."

"I don't appreciate being called a liar," I said.

"I don't appreciate being lied to. Keep in mind, too, budget cuts are coming. And layoffs? They're not outside the realm of possibility."

"Are you threatening to have me fired?"

He looked at me in the eyes the way you might patiently stare at a child who said something rude during dinner. "No, that's not what I'm saying."

"Then what are you saying?"

"I'm saying," he said, his dark eyes flat as the bay on a moonless night, "that when the truth comes out, you'll have to live with its consequences, whether you're employed or unemployed."

He stood and held out his hand and I shook it on instinct. His palms were smooth but hard. They reminded me of a varnished piece of marble, cool, solid. He pumped my hand twice and dropped it. "Have a good day, deputy," he said. "Get off that leg. It's obvious that you're in pain."

I went out into the hall, wondering what I'd done, wondering if the truth were eating away at the ground beneath me, threatening to open a pit that would swallow me forever.

16

The week leading up to the union rally at Clawson's, the temperature dropped and the bay turned to a slate color, the waves rolling in with foamy caps the color of storm clouds. Mornings broke clear and bright, not a drop of humidity in the air. By the end of the day, the sun sank into the bay, the long golden rays knifing across the salt surface, the light glistening on the water, scintillating. You'd see shrimp trawlers early in the morning, making final runs before the season closed in mid-November. I went back to work that Monday morning on day shift, my belly sloshing with coffee, my head light from the pain meds, my hip numb but tender, a constant reminder of that night.

I still had a lot of questions about what exactly I'd overheard. From what I could put together from my fractured memory of the night, it seemed as though Freddy was buying a gun. But that didn't make a lick of sense. Even if he wanted a piece with the numbers shaved off, he could have found it in Bay View. And who'd run me over? I suspected whoever had sold him the gun, but I couldn't pursue it without telling the sheriff I'd been out there that night, tailing Freddy, doing exactly what Mack had told me not to do.

Part of me thought that Mack already knew. At the sheriff's department, I half expected him to call me into the office the first day and fire me. But it began to dawn on me that Freddy was in the same situation I was in: he couldn't say a word. If he came forward, he'd have to admit that he'd left the scene of a hit and run. He'd be interrogated about why he'd been in Stink Town that night. Maybe my job was safe for the time being.

Around town, people lined up, taking sides on the union issue. Some of the older men who'd been in the papermakers union when my father was alive gathered in Charlie's Cafe each morning, their old, salt-scoured trucks lining the road. These were old-school Democrats who believed in worker's rights and couldn't understand the opposition. They talked about wages and benefits. They remembered the paper mill strike and spoke to me whenever they saw me. Some of the younger people around town supported the union, too, mainly single people and couples whose livelihoods depended on the waters around St. Vincent.

Another element existed in town, however. Many of them were stoked by talking heads on cable news who constantly warned of fascism taking over America, never seeing the irony that unions were the absolute opposite of fascism. A lot belonged to churches and believed that Democrats were all bound for hell. They spoke to each other in huddled groups and shook their heads sadly at any open statement supporting the union. These people would have judged my father an evil man. They saw Fred Clawson as a self-made businessman beleaguered by a radical faction of anti-American scum. As much as I wanted to fault them for their thick-headedness, I found it harder and harder to take a side. I believed in the workers' right to organize, but I knew that not every person who opposed the organization was like Rich Richards, an angry anti-government loon. Chris Chambers was a number of things, but he wasn't crazy.

These two groups sparred online at the *St. Vincent Sentinel's* message board, posting long screeds about their side, belittling other opinions, and getting downright nasty at times. Wednesday after work, I went home for dinner, trying to avoid Charlie's hamburger and fries. I'd been thinking a lot about Dad's heart attack and about my high blood pressure. I'd promised myself that I'd cut back on smoking, too. I was on the third day of smoking only five cigarettes a day: two in the morning, one after lunch, one mid-afternoon, and one in the evening. I'd cheated only once, smoking an additional cigarette in the afternoon on Monday.

In my kitchen, I sliced a tomato I'd picked up at the Piggly Wiggly and salted and peppered the slices. It would be tasteless but healthy. I sliced a big hunk of hoop cheese off of a wedge and wrapped a piece of white bread around it. I made a glass of iced water, turned on the radio for some noise, and sat at the dining room table, remembering the time I'd watched my father come home from the mill for a quick lunch. It had been a hot summer day, the kind that boils everything around you and makes the magnolia leaves droop. The air smelled like pine sap and ammonia. He stood over the kitchen sink and ate a tomato like an apple, peppering it after every bite with a shaker he'd taken from the shelf above the stove. I'd never since seen someone enjoy something so thoroughly.

When I finished eating, I took a bottle of Yuengling from the refrigerator and went into the backyard. The weather was dry and cold, the light in the west marbling through lines of cirrus clouds. I had a small fire pit surrounded by cement blocks, and I gathered a few pine cones from the yard and threw them in the pit. I didn't have any wood save a few pine limbs, so I put them in, too, and covered it all with pine straw. I lit the pine straw with my lighter and watched the fire take life. It burned quick, the blue-green flames igniting the pine cones. The pine sap inside the cones boiled, and they flamed out with a hiss. The wood burned fast, too, and I threw what sticks I had on top. Then, I pulled up a plastic chair, opened the beer, and took out my final cigarette for the day.

I ran it beneath my nose and inhaled. The tobacco smelled sweet and my mouth watered. I lit the cigarette and sat back, enjoying the taste and the feel of smoke on my throat. I blew a smoke ring and stared up at the sky, where the Evening Star glowed, a single pin prick in a clear spot of sky.

A car door slammed from the front yard, and I sat forward, wondering who'd be coming by. Chris came around the side of the house. He was dressed in street clothes—a denim jacket, a pair of jeans. He wore a black baseball cap with an Army Special Forces logo on it.

"Pull up a seat," I said. "There's beer in the fridge."

He shook his head. "Can't stay long. Thanks, though." He stood opposite the fire from me, his hands in his jeans pocket. The light flickered on his face.

I took another drag and blew a cloud of smoke. "Don't worry," I said. "This is my final one today. I'm quitting."

"How are you doing?"

"Good. My hip still hurts, but it's better. I had that week to recuperate. I'm getting there."

He nodded. "Look, I'm sorry that I didn't come by last week to check on you. I know you were laid up. It would have been the right thing to do. But, I thought you needed some space."

"Space for what?"

"You know what I'm talking about, Justin. This whole politics thing."

"The Treadless?" I said. "You've got your politics. I've got mine. That's America."

He nodded. "Yeah, I guess it is. But I don't think we're cool."

I studied him, trying to figure out how I felt. "We're cool, man. We're cool."

"Cowboy and me were talking earlier today. What he said made sense. I didn't have a dad like yours. My dad took off. He didn't want me. Your dad wanted you. Of course, you'd share his opinions. Your dad is important to you."

"Look, man, I can think for myself. My politics are my politics, not his. He was important to this whole town, not just me."

"Let me finish." He shifted. The wood in the fire popped. A pine cone fell from a nearby tree, landing softly in the grass. "I think you're seeing this as some kind of a betrayal. I'm not pissing on your dad's memory. I need you to understand that."

I leaned forward in the chair. "I don't think that," I said, unsure if I were lying. "I just don't get it—you, the Treadless. You're throwing in with Rich Richards?"

"He nodded, a gesture that seemed more for him than me. "This is not about the Treadless. I don't care if the workers walk out. This is about the country. Think about how much money we're spending on that war in the Middle East. Think about how much money we've borrowed. Have you ever looked at the national debt? At the deficit? Do your realize how royally screwed our kids are? I mean, we're a generation from saluting a Chinese flag, man."

I chuckled. "I doubt that, man. You're overreacting."

"And how would you know?"

I stopped, searching for something to say. I had nothing. The cigarette burned between my fingers, the filter hot. I pitched it into the fire. "I don't know. I just don't think the answer is to hate the government. Hell, man, we work for the government."

"I don't think so, either. I think you've got me wrong. We need a government, but it needs to be smaller and cheaper. And it needs to stay out of people's lives."

I stood up. "Listen to yourself, Chris. You sound like one of those nuts who orders shit from survival catalogs. You go to these meeting with Rich and Jimmy Danley and Freddy—"

"Freddy quit coming from what I hear."

I waved my hand. "Look, it doesn't matter. Whatever. You believe what you need to believe, friend."

"Look, man," he said. "I don't even go to the Treadless meetings anymore. I went to two of them—two of them. You're acting like I'm Judas. No one's crucifying you, partner. I don't have any silver pieces on me. We just disagree about this. And that's got to be cool. We have to be able to disagree."

We both fell silent. Wind blew, rustling the pine needles. The night had grown dark as a new moon. My fire flickered. Only the embers glowed. I squatted down, ran my right hand over the cold ground, and scooped up a fist full of pine needles, which I dropped on top of the embers. They glowed for a second and were consumed.

"I got to get going," he said after a moment.

I didn't look at him. "Where you headed?"

"Date. Deanna Branch. We're going Panama City."

"Deanna?"

"She's young."

"Yes," he said. "She is."

I started to tease him about how young she was but stopped. It didn't feel right. I didn't know what to say to him. I could have said, "I accept your view," but that would have sounded magnanimous, arrogant, as though he'd passed some test I'd given him.

"Are you really quitting smoking?"

I nodded.

"Well, good luck with that. I hear it's the hardest thing in the world to do.. Later." He turned and walked across the yard and disappeared into the darkness on the side of the house.

I went inside and spent the evening half-watching television while I tried to figure out what had just happened. It looked like politics were on the verge of destroying my friendship with Chris, my oldest, most trusted ally. I never trusted people easily. I preferred to be alone. I liked silence and solitude. But Chris had been a part of my life for as long as I could remember. Losing his friendship would be like losing a finger. I thought of his missing fingers. Did he have ghost pain? Did he ever catch a glimpse of his open hand and wince as he realized, once again, he'd never have a whole fist again? It was like losing Janey. She should have been here, at my side, helping me work though all of this. All that remained was an empty home that felt more and more like a memory.

Later that night, lying in bed, I remembered the day I'd seen Rich and Jimmy and Freddy come out of the bar. He'd been so nervous when I talked to him at the Swifty. What the hell was he hiding? The world felt cut off from me, then, like a TV program on mute. I could see all the moves, but I had no idea what anyone was saying.

The rally at Clawson's was Friday evening. *The Sentinel* reported that it was to begin at 7:00 p.m., billing it a "Meeting of All Concerned about Coming Layoffs." Flyers around town promised "Information for Concerned Workers." Scuttlebutt at the department said it would be the Wayne Childress show. Word had gotten around that this whole project was indeed a school thing. Some people said he was a high school teacher trying to put together some object lesson. Someone else said that he was some leftist grad student from Florida State filming a documentary about the death of the fishing industry on the Gulf Coast. Whatever the case, most people felt the same: we didn't like being someone's spectator sport. I liked that Childress was organizing the workers. I didn't like that St. Vincent was some living experiment for him.

For their part, the Treadless didn't advertise their counter-rally. But around town, you'd hear about it, folks saying they were coming out to support Clawson. The gossip about Childress helped them. More and more, the name Wayne Childress was linked with "communism" or "pinko." He'd been scarce the past few weeks. Even Charlie said he hadn't been in the café in nearly a month.

Friday evening found me and Chris sitting in the same cruiser, parked at Clawson's, watching the growing crowd. Pickup trucks and old beaters crowded the parking lot, their paint all faded after years in the salt air. The rally was going to be inside of the main warehouse. It was set to begin at 6:00. Over the bay, the sun dipped into the horizon, the light glowing pink, orange, and purple. Men and women arrived in thick jackets and flannel shirts, baseball caps and toboggan caps pulled low over their eyes. The weather report last night had forecast an early freeze. We were a week into November.

Officially, Mack had sent out deputies to direct traffic, though we'd really come to watch for trouble, and we all knew it. Frank and Hector stood at the parking lot gates right now, waving in slow-moving vehicles. Cowboy sat in his cruiser across the lot, close to the huge metal doors that led into the warehouse. Chris and I were supposed to man the gate after the meeting, standing out in the night air, waving flashlights to keep the traffic moving steadily.

The Treadless had been gathering in the front parking lot, the one that ran along Scallop Street on the west edge of the warehouse. They held up signs with slogans like, "God Bless the USA" and "Capitalism Not Communism." I'd expected a platform, some kind of make-shift podium, Rich Richards shouting at the crowd with a bullhorn. But so far, the Treadless gathered together near their vehicles, all of them huddled together to ward off the cold wind. I wondered if Chris would have rather been with them than with me.

The inside of my cruiser smelled of cigarettes and coffee, despite the pine-scented tree I'd hung from the rearview mirror. The radio was tuned to a rock station. Grungy guitars. Angry vocals. Seemed appropriate.

A Channel 7 news van out of Panama City coasted into the lot and slowed to a stop. The doors opened and several people got out, including a blond woman in a tight-fitting skirt.

"That Jenna Farrar?" Chris said.

I nodded. "Looks like St. Vincent's made the eleven o'clock news." Farrar was the lead anchor. She read the news in a stilted monotone.

"First on the coast," Chris said, quoting Channel 7 news's motto and Farrar's robotic delivery.

"We'll be—right back—and now—the weather," I said.

"She's hoping for a fight," Chris said. "That'll make for some entertaining news."

"If it bleeds, it leads," I said and shifted in the seat. My hip throbbed with a dull pain.

Jenna Farrar and her news crew had set up in one of the limestone pathways through the parking lot. She faced the camera, holding a microphone with an over-sized number seven attached to it at just beneath the mic's head. I hoped to make it home in time to see the report. St. Vincent rarely made the news. Even when a hurricane blew through here, forecasters identified us as "an area between Panama City and Apalachicola."

Cowboy's voice sounded through my lapel mic. "Twelve?"

"Go ahead."

"Y'all drive over to the parking lot. Go inside. Keep an eye on things."

"Ten-four," I said. "Twelve out."

We drove through the crowded lot, edging between closely-parked vehicles and packs of people. I coasted the cruiser to a stop near the side door, about thirty yards from where the Treadless had set up. Jimmy Danley leaned against the side of a rusty Dodge truck. He was talking to Tater, who stood still, his arms crossed. The group consisted of some twenty or so men, some young. Most of them looked to be in their forties, all white guys. Some wore black t-shirts with a "Don't Tread on Me" flag on the front. Rich stood in the center of them, a grim look on his face.

"Somebody's looking to stir up shit," I said.

"He might be. But that's why we're here," Chris said.

We got out and I winced at the pain in my hip. I'd used the doctor-prescribed cane for all of one day before I felt stupid and abandoned it. It leaned against the nightstand by my bed. Part of me wished I had it with me now.

"How's the hip?"

"Still there," I said.

I leaned against the car and scanned the crowd, hunting any sign of trouble. More and more people showed up, but the Treadless stayed by themselves, their numbers swelling. They stayed quiet, chatting with each other, leaving people alone. They seemed peaceful, but I didn't buy it.

There was something in the air, a thickness as tangible as the frost we breathed in the cold night. Men walked with their fists balled in their pockets, as though they'd sheathed them like weapons. Everyone seemed hunched over as though tension pushed them down, bending their spines. Even the air felt close, thick as humidity, even though the weather was dry.

My lapel mic squelched. "Twelve?" Cowboy again.

I pinched the button. "Go ahead."

"Patrol the side of the building. Keep an eye out."

"10-4. What are we looking for?"

"Trouble."

"10-4."

We got out of the cruiser walked around the backside of the warehouse. The air stank of fish and ammonia and salt, all smothered in the chemical stench of the paper mill. The wind cut my ears.

We went inside through a small door that fed into a narrow hallway. It was dark and cold. The place stank of fish. The rumble of the meeting carried through the walls. Someone was already talking. I hurried my steps, worried that we'd miss something. The door at the end of the hallway opened into the warehouse proper. Large shelves of scaffolding lined the walls. The high ceilings echoed the sound. Someone was talking through a bullhorn above the crowd.

We emerged into a large open area where someone had erected a makeshift platform out of wooden pallets and sheets of plywood. The dock workers crowded around it. On the platform stood Wayne Childress. His doe-colored goatee had grown long. A beard covered his face. He scanned the crowd, his eyes jumping here and there. Four other men stood on the platform, as well. One was Hokey Lee. He wore a dark blue toboggan. He had his arms crossed and said a few words to Wayne, who nodded. Their faces were grim. There were others on the platform, too, including Cedric Baldwin, the lawyer I'd met at Charlie's.

Wayne took up a bullhorn and spoke. "It's wonderful to see you all out here tonight." His voice echoed through the high ceilings. A rumbled of approval came from the gathered crowd. "It's an American tradition to organize in this way. We're kicking ass for the working class!" he yelled, and a roar went through the crowd.

"We're not here to make trouble," Childress continued. "We're here because we believe in our rights as human beings. Many of you have given your working lives to Clawson's. You deserve better. We've approached management. We've made offers to talk. They don't want to talk. They want us to shut up. They want us to keep quiet. Well, we're not keeping quiet any more!"

A cheer erupted from the gathered crowd. Some held signs, poster board with slogans like "No Talk, We Walk" and "Clawson is a Grinch."

"There was no negotiation. No discussion," Childress said, his voice nearly chanting. "This company used us up. And when the economy got tough, who suffers? Does Fred Clawson suffer?"

"No!" the crowd roared, the voices blending into one.

"Does Fred Clawson have to worry about a mortgage? Does Fred Clawson have to tell his children that there will be no Christmas this year?"

"No!" The crowd was getting fired up. Some smiled at each other. Others looked on, their mouths drawn and tight.

"Tonight," Childress said, "is about us. Tonight, we're putting Clawson's on warning."

I scanned the crowd, hunting Jimmy and the Treadless. They all stood near the double doors at the front of the warehouse. Jimmy was shouting something at Tater, who laughed.

"Without us, there is now Clawsons!" Childress shouted and a roar went up from the crowd.

"You are Clawson's. We are Clawson's. I am Clawson! I am Clawson! I am Clawson!" Childress said, trying to start a chant. A few took up the words, but many just yelled, their voices blending to a tapestry of rage.

Hokey took the bullhorn from Childress. Before he spoke, the workers began cheering and applauding and whistling.

"Y'all know me," Hokey said, trying to speak above the crowd, but they continued on yelling, anyway.

"I've been working for Clawson for thirty years," he said. The crowd began again, some shouting "Me too." Hokey held out his hands, trying to quiet the men and women down.

"Clawson's has been good to me. This place put both my sons through college. This place paid for my house. And in return, I've given this place my life. I've gone home smelling like shrimp for nearly three decades." More yelling and screaming. More shouts of assent. "I hear you. I hear you all. Let me tell you, I know what you're feeling because I feel it, too. I've never been one to complain. Y'all know that. When the downsizing started earlier this year, thanks to this man, we tried to do something about it." He stopped and cuffed Childress on the shoulder. Wayne smiled and nodded. He mouthed something to Hokey. "Thanks to Wayne and Mr. Baldwin. We called management. We set up meetings. We made overtures. We didn't get a single response. Then, they started talking layoffs. They didn't even have a conversation with us.

"And now, we're asking you all. We're pleading with you who work here. Join us. There's a bunch of us. Because Clawson's not listening to us. And that means he's not listening you, the workers, the folks who go out on that water every day and bring in the catch, the folks who pack up these boxes and ship it out. The very people who keep this place afloat." The crowd cheered, some clapping, some shouting.

"Unions are communist," a voice shouted out over the crowd. I thought it was Jimmy, but he stood leaned against the wall, his arms crossed over his chest, a smirk on his face.

"Florida's a right to work state," someone yelled.

A few other shouts arose from the gathered workers, some agreeing with the unnamed voice, others trying to shout him down.

Childress had taken back the bullhorn. "Florida is a right to work state. All we want is our right to be heard! You've got a right to—"

His voice was drowned out as the crowd grew louder. Some of the workers had noticed me and Chris and were pointing our way, talking. I worried that we might be sending the wrong message. What if they thought we were here the break up the meeting? I looked over at Chris, but he was inscrutable, silent. He leaned against one of the empty shelves, arms crossed.

Cedric Baldwin took the bullhorn from Wayne. "Good evening," he said, his voice smooth as pressed leather. He had sharp, angular features and looked like a teenager ready for church. The wide starched color of his dress shirt pressed against his cheeks. He wore a blue and red tie, the Windsor knot wide as a child's fist. "My name is Cedric Baldwin," he said. "I am a lawyer with Proctor, Hoeffer, and Bender out of Tallahassee. Wayne approached me a few weeks ago. I want to represent you, the workers. I want to fight what Clawson is doing." A cheer went up and a wave of applause spread across the room.

Baldwin reached into the inside pocket of his jacket and withdrew a folded sheet of paper. "I want to share with you an excerpt from a letter sent to me and Wayne Childress by the management at Clawson's: 'Mr. Clawson would like to thank the workers for their years of service. Truly, without the efforts of the St. Vincent shrimpers and dock workers, the success of Clawson Industries would not have been possible. However, as the country continues to be mired in recession and as the future economic prospects of our great nation continue to dim and as more and more environmental regulations are foisted upon the fishing industry, our company is forced to make hard decisions. As such, Clawson Industries has made the difficult choice of closing the St. Vincent, Florida, fishery and warehouse, effective December 31st of this year. Mr. Clawson and the entire Clawson family extend their sympathies and well wishes to the workers during these trying times.'" Baldwin paused and looked at the crowd. "I want you all to understand that this letter comes in response to my request for meeting, a meeting in which I wanted to discuss severance for those of you who the company laid off."

Baldwin stopped reading and looked out at the crowd. Angry voices churned and the warehouse took on a textured feel, as though the air were tangible. I felt jumpy, the fingers of both hands popping. I scanned the crowd. Jimmy weaved through the gathered men and women, bound for the platform. I pointed.

"I see him," Chris said. He pressed his lapel mic.

"Sergeant?" Chris's voice came clear through my radio.

"Go ahead," Cowboy said.

"Something might be happening in here. Signal five," Chris said, indicating caution.

"Ten-four."

"This," Baldwin said, "is unacceptable. We want severance. It's the only right thing to do. This fishery has been one of the top employers in Aplachee County for nearly fifty years. The men and women who work here deserve more than a brush-off." He held up the letter by its corner, as though it were stained and contaminated. "You want to know what he's offering?

One month of severance. One month. That's unconscionable. Three months would be a place to begin negotiations. Six months is the least you deserve. And that's what you're going to get. I've read the papers. I see the Treadless here tonight. Some people say, 'Oh, go get a job somewhere else. Clawson has a warehouse in Pensacola.' Well answer me this: how on God's green earth is a man who can barely get by on the sorry salary Clawson's pays going to be able to afford picking up sticks and moving two hundred miles east? Who's going to pay first month and last month rent in a new home? Clawson? Who's going to pay deposits on utilities? Clawson? Somehow I doubt it."

"He's a crook," a deep male voice rang out. Other rose in assent. "Tell Clawson to go to hell!" Other voices went up, too, some in assent, some crying foul, all of them angry, angry, angry. The lights from the warehouse above spun. I felt unsteady on my feet. I'd taken two of the pain pills that morning because it felt like someone was jabbing an icepick into my hip when I woke up. I was regretting my decision.

Childress took the bullhorn from Baldwin. "You want to know what you can do? Let your voices be heard. Write to Clawson. Write to the newspapers. Post on forums online. Start a blog. This is happening all over the United States. It's us—the least of the least—we're the one's suffering. But we've got to be Tom Joad. We've got be there. No one else will."

"Communist," someone yelled. I couldn't have proved it in a court of law, but I would have sworn it was Jimmy. I'd lost him in the crowd. I looked for him in the sea of flannel and jackets, but he'd disappeared.

"No," Childress said, "you go to hell. You might as well say 'The kids can go to hell,' too, buddy, whoever you are."

The mood changed, then, something subtle about the air, about the heat in the room, about the quality of the voices. Frustration had become rage. The fuse on the powder keg had burned.

And then, as though in slow motion, a single green beer bottle came out of the crowd, tumbling end over end. It flew above the gathered men and women, turning, casting light, a slow bomb that found its mark, hitting Cedric Baldwin in the side of the face. He spun around, falling into Childress, who stumbled backwards.

"Goddamned nigger," someone shouted.

Then: pure chaos. The room exploded. Everyone began fighting, jostling against each other. Fists flew. Faces flickered in the crowd, some vague but familiar, their eyes shut tight, their teeth gritted. The shouting and screamed blurred to a white nose of rage. My hand went to my pistol, and I began backing up, looking for the best way out. My stomach flipped, nausea threating to swoon me.

"Let's go," Chris said and broke for the crowd. He held his pistol high and started yelling, "Apalachee County Sheriff's Department! Get on the ground!"

I took off behind him, my right hand flicking loose my holster safety, my left hand pinching my lapel mic. "Cowboy," I yelled. "This is going south quick. Signal twenty-eight." I'd never called the riot signal before. The noise swirled around the dim warehouse, a cacophony of angry screams and shouts. Everything felt like a nightmare I'd wandered into. Surely, this wasn't St. Vincent, Florida.

"Ten-four," Cowboy responded. "We're coming in now."

In the middle of the crowd, I fought for equilibrium, tried to keep my footing. I grabbed people by the shoulder and pointed to the back, "Get out," I yelled. "Get out of here before you're arrested." Many of the workers towered above me, and through the lattice of raised arms and crowded torsos, I could see flashes of Jimmy Danley fighting someone. I elbowed and pushed my way through the bodies, trying to get to him. I had to push my way to him, shouting "Apalachee County" and "law enforcement."

Jimmy stood a few feet from the platform. He held what appeared to be a four-legged stool and swung it like a baseball bat, breaking it over the back of man who had to be in his late fifties. I ran straight for him, my pistol drawn.

I ducked between two dock workers and Jimmy ran, twisting his body left and right, his shirt tail flowing behind him. "Stop," I shouted. "Sheriff's Department." He didn't miss a step, and I took off after him through the crowd, stumbling and half falling every few steps. A voice began yelling in my lapel mic, but I ignored it. The pain in my hip had amped up to a white hot glow. I wanted to stop and catch my breath, which came in raspy gasps. My lungs felt heavy, filled with phlegm. Something wet rattled in my cough.

Jimmy made his way to the rear of the warehouse, where Chris and I had come in. He took off down the dark hallway and I chased him, my Maglite out in front of my like a lance. "Jimmy Danley, stop," I shouted, hoping that the first and last name together sounded official.

He turned down a hallway to the left, one that I thought snaked back around to the east side of the warehouse, the side on the waterfront. If I didn't hurry, he'd make out a side door and disappear. He could claim that he'd never been here. He'd get away with everything.

The hallway turned out to be a dead end. As I came down the end of it, he stood at what must have been a locked door, pulling at the handle.

"Hands up," I said, shining the light on him. The noise of the crowd had filtered back here, a stead roar. I leaned against the metal wall, trying hard to ignore the pain from my hip. It now shot up my back in waves. I needed to draw my Beretta, but I didn't want to take the light off him.

"Piss off," he said, his voice as edged as a scallop shell. He squinted in the light, tilting his head left and right. He grinned and held out his hands. "Come on, man. I thought we had a peace offering?"

"Seriously, Jimmy," I said. "On the ground. Now."

He held his hands palms out, smiling. "You're doing it again, coward. Hiding behind that badge and that gun."

I coughed and stumbled forward.

"You don't look too good, Everson," he said. He took a hesitant step toward me, just the lightest movement of his right foot.

"Seriously, Jimmy," I said, fighting to control my voice. "Turn around. Get on the ground."

"You going to shoot somebody?" he said, again, his voice taunting, teasing. In the flashlight's thin beam, his eyes narrowed to thin slits. "Think you're man enough to put a bullet in somebody, deputy dog?"

"Twelve, what's your twenty?" my lapel mic squelched out. Chris sounded panicked. He never sounded panicked.

I reached to press the button so that I could talk back, taking my hand off the wall. The Maglite lowered for just a fraction of a second. Jimmy rushed me before I had time to think, his hands on my chest, slamming me into the wall as he ran by. I hit the concrete hard, my forehead bashing into the wall. Pain erupted in my head and my vision went white.

I groaned and rolled over and spoke into my radio. "Back of the warehouse," I said. "Where do you need me?"

"Up here," he said. "Now. Are you okay?"

"Yeah," I said. "I'm coming. Over."

I pulled myself up and half-hobbled, half-ran back toward the center of the warehouse, my head throbbing in pain. The wall had opened a gash in my forehead, and blood oozed down my face. I wiped it away, my mind reeling, wondering where this was headed. Every cop in St. Vincent would b here by now. Mack would probably call in Bay or Franklin County, but both were over thirty miles away, an eternity of driving in a situation like this. And Jimmy—I should have just shot him.

Just as I rounded the corner back into the main area of the warehouse, a lone voice began to cut through the noise. Up on the platform, holding the bullhorn, Cedric Baldwin shouted. He held a white rag to his face, where the beer bottle had hit him. It was soaked with blood. "We need to calm down," he said. "We can do this in court."

He looked around, his eyes wild and wide. Childress had been standing off the left, shouting down someone at the edge of the platform. He came over and took the bullhorn. "Let him speak," he said. "Let him speak." The shout echoed above the fighting.

Nearly every deputy on the force had arrived, some leading handcuffed men away, some in the middle of scuffles. Cowboy had a man against the wall, slapping cuffs on him. Mack had his knee in someone's back. Hector and Chris were handcuffing a guy the size of a two-door refrigerator.

Childress yelled into the bullhorn again, his voice angry and gruff, "Stop!" Then, the fight drained from the room for a miraculous moment. Curious faces peered at the man on the platform. It was though everyone stopped to catch their breath at one time.

Childress handed the bullhorn Baldwin, who spoke. "I told you that I am a lawyer and that I am representing the dock workers of Clawson Industries. I told you I'd fight for you, but you didn't let me finish." He took the rag from his head and held it up. "Somebody didn't let me finish. But that's not stopping me. That's not stopping us." He turned to Wayne. "Mr. Childress here has something to announce to you."

A wave of applause swept through the warehouse. The worst seemed to be over. I leaned against the wall, trying to catch my breath. I wiped blood from my vision and looked at my palm. There wasn't as much as I'd thought. The cut on my head was smaller. I probed the gash with my fingers and winced.

Wayne said through the bullhorn. "We are going to sue Clawson for wrongful termination." More cheering. More applause. Childress turned to Baldwin. "And Mr. Baldwin here assures me that he won't see a dime unless we win. That's how strong he thinks our case is."

"What if we lose?" someone asked.

Childress stood, thoughtful for a second, stroking his beard. "We won't," he said, finally. He looked out at the gathered workers. "We can't."

I heard the gun, three impossibly loud pops, the sound echoing in the warehouse's high ceilings, and Childress fell. The world narrowed for a long, slow second. Then: chaos. Screams. People running in every direction. Fighting. More screaming. I scanned the crowd focused on Cowboy, his right arm extended, pointing at the plywood platform.

My breath caught in my throat and a pit the size of the Gulf opened in my stomach. Everything went hazy and white. I thought I'd throw up. I ran toward the platform, limping, my teeth grinding at the pain in my hip and my forehead. There, at the edge of platform, stood Freddy Richards, frozen, eyes wide and white, both hands closed around a revolver, the barrel still smoking. Wayne Childress lay still, covered in blood, his eyes staring up at the lights, words on his lips little more than shapes his mouth took.

17

In the days following the shooting, St. Vincent took on a strange air that reminded me of an empty church. The streets were deserted. People seemed to go home earlier, closing their homes up behind them. The entire town was quieter. Even the ever-present mill whistle took on a kind of muted quality. I lived those days in a dream. In my memory, they are hazy and sepia, distorted as though seen through a fishbowl. I went to work and came home. I drove the same routes. But something about the town I'd always loved seemed off. It was familiar, yes, but it was changed. It reminded me of the final days in my marriage with Janey. Rather than live *with* each other, we existed around each other. We spoke with calm tones. We treated the other as you might a polite stranger. Now, St. Vincent felt the same, less like my hometown and more like the house of an acquaintance, a place where you're scared to touch anything because it might break.

The people who lived in the city limits of St. Vincent had always regarded the residents of Bay View with a kind of suspicion and haughtiness. It wasn't the scorn they heaped on those who lived up in Stetson, whom St. Vincent folks thought were backwards and countrified in the worst way. It wasn't the outright hostility and racism they dished up for the denizens of the South Side. Rather, St. Vincent looked at Bay View the way you might look at a cousin who lived deep in the woods, a backwards individual who clung to outmoded ideas, someone who hunted with a black powder rifle and cooked his meat in a wood burning stove. You'd hear the word "redneck" applied to Bay View people. I knew; I'd used it myself, plenty of times. I'd thought of Donnie Ray as a redneck. I'd more than once referred to Jimmy Danley as a redneck. For me—and, I suspect, for the people of St. Vincent proper—that word meant nothing more than someone you're better than, someone who you'd never be. Deep in our collective subconscious, I wondered if we all feared the same thing: that we were rednecks, too, separated from what we saw as backwards and hardscrabble living only by Marten Bridge.

In the days after Freddy Richards shot Wayne Childress, I heard plenty of talk about the people of Bay View, how they were violent and angry, the kind of folks who'd shoot you over anything, from a card game to a claimed fishing spot. I suppose I believed a lot of it because I said it all, too. I told Chris, "I'm not surprised about Freddy at all. Where he grew up? Who he grew up with? No wonder." But deep inside me, I had a niggling suspicion that maybe, just maybe, I wasn't so different from Freddy Richards.

After Freddy was arrested without incident, he was taken to the sheriff's department jail, where he refused to talk to anyone. But as he was led away in handcuffs, he looked toward Rich and said, "I'm no coward." Those words would come up again at his trial a year later, when we learned that Freddy had quit the Treadless after Rich called him a coward during a meeting. The reason? Rich had wanted Freddy to shoot me for harassing them both. But I didn't know any of this until much later. In the immediate aftermath of the shooting, they seemed just another part of the nightmare that had become my hometown.

I helped clean up the scene. I interviewed witnesses. I gave my statement to Davis Malone, who moved about the crime scene with military precision, snapping photos with a digital camera and writing notes on a legal pad enclosed in a leather binder. He didn't mention our meeting, didn't question my story. He focused on the problem at hand.

The week after the shooting, I walked around in a stupor, trying to wrap my mind around what had happened. This was St. Vincent, Florida, not New Orleans, not New York, not Las Angeles. Things like this weren't supposed to happen here. The Tuesday after the shooting, I came home from day shift, opened a Yuengling, and sat at the dining room table. I'd not turned on the light, and the house was dark. The walls, the furniture, the television, the china hutch that had once held plates and bowls Janey and I had received for our wedding: all of it was soft and fuzzy, all of it removed from me, all of it less like reality and more like memory, more like a story I told myself that I no longer believed.

I woke up early the next Saturday and stared at the clock, wondering what had jolted me awake at 6:45 a.m. I put my arm over my eyes and lay on my back, trying to drift back to sleep. It wasn't often that I had a Saturday off, and I wanted to sleep in. But it was no use. Before long, I'd risen and made coffee and sat out back in my lawn chair to drink it. Then, I went inside, took a pain pill, turned on my old stereo, and put a Blackfoot CD in. I cleaned the entire house. I did laundry. I dusted. I wiped own all the counters in the kitchen. When the house smelled like bleach, I went out back, got the lawn mower out, and mowed the winter-faded grass. When I finished, it was half past ten. I stood out in the sunlight, still feeling that I had to get away. I went inside, took a long shower, and grabbed my keys.

The city of Apalachicola sits thirty or so miles east of St. Vincent. A small fishing village, the town is about half the size of my town. The local economy is almost entirely driven by fishing. The place is known for its oysters. The oyster beds are passed down generation to generation, and nothing can get you in as much trouble as harvesting from a bed that doesn't belong to you. The oysters from Apalachicola Bay are known far and wide. Nothing in the world tastes quite like an Apalachicola oyster: salty and cold like the bay itself.

My father loved the place. He'd often load me and Aaron us in the car on a Saturday morning, and we'd drive toward what most of us called "Apalach," find a secluded fishing spot on Apalachicola Bay, and fish all morning. Then, we drove into town and eat at a seafood restaurant, usually a place called The Seafood Grill right in the middle of down town.

Janey didn't like the town. She claimed it smelled like rotting fish. Said she could taste fish even in the tap water. I didn't buy it, but I didn't say a word. As such, I didn't visit the little town for a number of years.

Rows of slash pines and long leaf pines crowded the side of the road between St. Vincent and Apalchicola. While the mill leased a bunch of land in Apalachee County from the county, a lot the land between Apalachicola and St. Vincent belonged to St. Vincent Papermakers. What would happen to it after the mill closed? Would someone buy the land, build condominiums? Speculation was rampant around town. Frank Sutton said that he'd heard they were going to build a planned community out here. "They did it over there on the other side of Panama City," he said one night as we were talking at the sheriff's department. "Just built a whole damn town. Folks will move in later." I squinted at the undeveloped forest and tried to picture rows of homes. This place had always been paper mill land. I couldn't imagine anything different.

As I left Apalachee County and passed into Franklin County, I had the odd feeling that I was leaving fantasy and passing into reality. The dilapidated old homes on the outskirts of town were the same as they'd been when I was a kid. The oyster-shell cut offs to the bay were the same. Apalachicola hadn't changed. Thirty miles behind me, St. Vincent had changed into something I didn't recognize.

More and more, St. Vincent had started feeling like a myth. But Apalachicola had always been here, always real, always waiting, a town that I'd never really loved but a town that I cared for just the same. I didn't love it because I didn't know it—not the way that I knew St. Vincent. But driving into town, passing the giant old river houses and southern mansions, I felt a stirring in my chest. I could see myself here in thirty or so years, retired, fishing the days away, haunting the local library.

I slowed near a convenience store and pulled in. I eased around the back of the store and parked beneath a China berry tree. The town was packed for the Seafood Festival, an annual event that had been going on as long as I could remember. We went a few times when I was a kid, but my parents didn't like fighting the traffic. I grew up with that same prejudice. But after the past few weeks, I wanted to get away. I needed some down time. I wanted to find an oyster bar near the river and eat until I couldn't move. It was nearly noon.

The town smelled like fried food. Country music filtered down the streets, piped in from some speakers set up on the sidewalk. People milled about up and down the streets, some in shorts, most in long pants. The temperature hovered right at fifty degrees. I wore a pair of faded jeans and a denim jacket. I'd put on an Atlanta Braves ball cap. I dug my hands deep into my pockets and walked east, heading for the river. I could already taste the oysters.

I crossed the highway and bent down to adjust my shoe. When I stood up, I was facing a small home with an overgrown yard. Palm fronds hung low, obscuring the tiny front porch of the sea-bleached home. A sign out front read *Alvin Gillies, M.S. Family and Individual Counseling.* I squinted at the sign, trying to figure out why it seemed familiar. Had one of the doctors I'd seen in the past few months directed me here? I couldn't place the name, and I walked away.

At Market Street, I turned right and ducked through the craft fair. Tent after tent of handmade items lined the street, which the Apalachicola Police Department had closed. I studied two police cruisers parked at the edge of the street, admiring them. Dodge Chargers, older models. No way they'd purchased them recently, not with the economy in the toilet. But they were clean and shiny, the black and white glowing in the morning sunlight. I thought of my own cruiser, with its balding tires and a dry-rotted back bumper.

I stopped in front of a storefront where an old woman with faded sandy hair and sun-darkened skin was selling driftwood crosses. I picked one up and felt it in my hands.

"The tide does that," she said.

I looked up. "Does what?"

"Carves them smooth. I do very little work to them. I find them on the beach like that."

"Already shaped like a cross?"

She nodded and smiled. "It's a mysterious world."

I smiled at her. "I guess it is."

I put the cross back and thought about how much Janey would have loved something like this. She liked knick-knacks, little things to set around the house to give it character.

As I turned to leave, a familiar person passed. Swimmer's body. Long blonde hair. She was with a group of people, some guys and some girls. They milled about in the craft fair, browsing the tents, having a good time. Anne Waites, Donnie Ray's old girlfriend. I studied her for a long time, trying to decide if I should talk to her. The last time I'd seen her was Donnie Ray's visitation, the night Jimmy showed his ass at got thrown in jail. Talking to her would only stir up bad memories for both of us. But I took my hat off and smoothed my hair, determined. I felt like the least I could do was say hello.

She saw me as I walked over, and she smiled. "Hey," she said. "How are you doing? What are you up to? "

"I'm good. Just seeing the sights. I haven't been to the Seafood Festival in a long time."

She nodded. "It's big money around here. I don't think I've missed once since I was a girl."

"Anne?" one of her friend said. She was a short girl with a round face. Her hair curled around her face, framing it. She looked kind of like a bear cub, but in a cute way.

"This is Justin Everson," Anne said. "We went to high school together. He knew Donnie Ray."

Bear cub girl looked at me and smiled. "Hey. I'm Marla."

"Hi, Marla," I said. I shook her hand lightly and felt awkward, like I'd stumbled into someone's private residence. "I was just going, actually."

"Where are you headed?" Anne said. "We're going to grab lunch over at Boss Oyster if you want to join us. You're certainly invited."

"I don't know. I don't want to crash y'all's party."

"No, really. You're not. Come one. It'll be fun. We can catch up. The last time we saw each other, we didn't exactly get a chance to talk." Her eyes fell just slightly then, and I knew she was thinking of Donnie Ray.

"Okay," I said. "As long as the invite's open. That's where I was headed, anyway."

We all made our way to the restaurant and got a seat on the deck, right on the Apalachicola River. Marla and Anne were only two of a much bigger party of eight, five girls and three guys. I was introduced to everyone and promptly forgot everyone's name. Everyone ordered raw oysters, and we split several pitchers of beer. We talked a lot about high school. Anne told stories about seeing me and Chris and some other friends hanging out at lunch, all of us deep in conversation about the latest horror movie. "They were so weird!" Anne said and squealed with laughter. The three guys in the group laughed, too, each one confessing their own geekiness. Marla hung onto a big, burly, bearded man named Mark. "He's my sci-fi guy," she said and confessed that she'd never seen *Star Wars* until they started dating a year ago.

"What?" I said with mock-horror. "Are you now or have you ever been a member of the Communist party?" We all laughed, and I felt relaxed for the first time in ages.

Anne talked a little about Donnie Ray, and the laughter in the group began to feel forced. It was clear that she didn't talk about him much. The conversation moved on, though, and three dozen oysters in, I'd told all the funny cop stories I knew, including the one about Chris pulling over a naked old man on Sandy Head Beach two years ago.

"Like stark naked?" Mark said. He beat the table and laughed, his great belly shaking with his guffaws.

I drained the last of a mug of beer and nodded. "He had to be sixty if he was a day. Dude was driving an old ragtop. Rusted to hell. Chris said the car smelled like weed. Guy was clearly burned. Completely high. And naked as the day he was born."

The table doubled over in laughter, and I ordered another pitcher of beer. Two of Anne's friends (a couple who looked like they could have been brother and sister with their identical tan skin and dark brown hair) said that they had to leave. Then, three of the girls went to the bathroom, leaving me, Anne, Mark and Marla alone.

An awkward silence settled. My face ached from laughing so hard. I looked out at the river and smelled the air and loved the way the salt and brine mixed with the scent of seafood and alcohol. I wondered if the Franklin County Sheriff's Department had any openings.

"It was really good to run into you," Anne said.

"Yeah, I feel the same way. This was great. I've not laughed this much in a long time. And the food, man."

"Don't get me started," Mark said. "This is the best restaurant on the Gulf Coast." He looked at me. "So you knew Donnie Ray?"

I couldn't say what I wanted to say: that I thought Donnie Ray had been an asshole back in school. That I thought that most of his friends were shit-headed bullies. That I thought maybe, just maybe, his best friend had something to do with his death. Instead, I said, "Yes. I knew him. Not too good, but I knew him. I guess you and Marla knew him?"

"Anne used to bring him around some in high school," Mark said. "I only met him a few times."

"How do you guys all know each other?" I said.

"We've been friends since I was little," Anne said. "Mark grew up two houses down from me. And Marla and I've been best friends since, what?"

"Preschool," Marla said. She looked around. "Can you smoke in here?"

"Out front, baby," Mark said. He looked at me and rolled his eyes. "Addict."

"I just quit, myself," I said, feeling proud of that fact for the very first time. It was a white lie. I still smoked one a day. A single cigarette sealed in a sandwich bag was in the glove box of my truck. I wanted it. Bad.

"Congrats, man," Mark said. "Hear that, baby? If he can quit, so can you."

"I can quit a lot of things, mister," she said and fake punched Mark in the arm. The both stood up. "I can't let her catch cancer alone," Mark said and they left, leaving me and Anne by ourselves.

Anne and I sat and didn't speak. I played with a leftover oyster shell, still pushing away the thought of a cigarette. Anne sipped at the last of her beer.

"So that's a mess you've got over there in St. Vincent," she said. "What with the shooting and all."

"Yeah. It's bad. Childress is still in the hospital in Panama City, laid up."

"Did you see it? Were you working that night?"

I nodded. "The shooting? Yeah, I did. The whole town's at each other's throats. I don't even recognize the place any more. It's weird, you know? I've lived there all my life. It's all I know, and I don't even feel like I belong there." I shrugged. "I don't know. It's just not the place it used to be."

She looked down at the table. "Donnie Ray said something like that once, not long after he got back from overseas."

"Was he different?"

She sighed through her nose. She looked tired, then, the skin around her eyes pinched, the soft beginning of wrinkles creasing the edge of her mouth. "He didn't even talk to me. Not at first."

"Were you guys still together when he joined up?"

"Sort of, I guess. After I graduated, I moved to Tallahassee for a little while. Went to college for two semesters."

"Florida State?"

She shook her head. "No. Tallahassee Community College. My parents helped me pay for a place right close to campus. Donnie Ray used to come up sometimes. I guess we were together. Then, you know, 9/11. He joined up and it all just happened so quickly. I dropped out." She paused and looked out at the river. "I don't even remember why. I'm going back, though. I'm signed up for a couple of online courses this spring."

I played with an empty beer glass. A long beige center console boat eased by the deck, the engine humming loudly. The boat's bow sent waves breaking up the edge of the dock.

"I tried to talk him out of joining," Anne said. "He wanted to go. He wanted to do something. I had a cousin who drove all the way to New York to help with the clean up at Ground Zero. He was even on the news in Tallahassee. Donnie Ray wanted to help like that. So, he joined. And I was not happy with that at all. It kind of drove us apart. I didn't know if I'd ever see him again after he shipped out."

"And then he came back."

She nodded.

"What happened?" I said. "Why was his tour cut short?"

"I have no idea. He wouldn't even talk to me any more. I called him a few times. One time, I called his parents. His dad hung up on me." Anne looked at me, her eyes brimmed with tears. "I didn't do anything wrong. I don't understand what happened."

"So he cut off all communication with you?"

"We talked a few times. He didn't tell me much. I thought he might have been seeing someone else. He mentioned a girl he knew there, another solider named Lucy. He said they were friends. I assumed they were seeing each other. I figured that's why he didn't want to talk to me anymore. I didn't know he wasn't going back. I thought he was on leave. When he never let, I had to put two and two together."

Lucy. The girl in the picture in Donnie Ray's trailer. They must have hooked up when he was in Iraq. "Everybody in St. Vincent thinks he was kicked out for dope."

"Dope?"

"I heard he was selling marijuana over there."

She laughed. "No, that can't be right. That's not true. He liked to drink. But he didn't smoke pot." She studied my face for a moment. "I mean, he smoked it before, I guess. He tried to get me to do it with him one time, but I didn't want to."

"So you don't know why he got kicked out?"

She blinked. "I think he might have quit."

"Quit?"

"My daddy told me he'd read about stress cards or something. He said you could plead mental stress and get out. That's what I figured happened. It makes sense. What with the psychiatrist and all."

Some blocks fell together in my head. Dr. Gillies. "He was seeing a counselor?"

A nod. "Yeah."

"But you guys weren't talking by then?"

"Not really. I didn't see him very much. I did see him once. Well, I saw his truck. It was parked downtown. He was probably here hanging out with Wayne. Yeah. I didn't get their friendship at all."

"No one did," I said. "You know Wayne?"

"For a long time. He grew up here. Wayne's Dad is a professor."

My mind reeled. "What? Really?"

She looked at me and smiled at the look on my face. "Oh, yeah. He keeps it hidden pretty good. But Wayne's daddy teaches at Florida State.

History or something. I don't know. I've known Wayne a long time. We went to school together. He was in my class." She glanced out at the water. "I supposed I should go visit him in the hospital. Do you know if he's gong to be okay?"

I sat back and folded my fingers behind my head. "He's alive," I said. "Last I heard he was in intensive care. I met him once. I suspected something was different about him. He wanted everybody in St. Vincent to think he was just another fisherman."

She shook her head and laughed. "Wayne wants everyone to think that."

"What do you mean?"

"Oh, he's always been a kind of Bruce Springsteen wannabe. When he was in high school, he used to play guitar at a little bar down the marina there," she said, pointing. "He'd play Woody Guthrie songs, stuff like that. He took himself so seriously. I think most people laughed at him. He's not a bad dude, but he's one of these guys who wants to change the world on his own terms, if that makes any sense. I mean, why else would he be working at Clawson's?"

"What are you saying?"

"Don't look so shocked, deputy," she said. "He's a graduate student. That whole thing at the docks is his master's thesis. Everybody knows that."

Bay Medical Center is on the banks of Watson Bayou, an inlet from St. Andrew's Bay, close to downtown Panama City. After budget cuts and downsizing forced Pine View Hospital in St. Vincent to close its maternity unit in the early 1970s, Apalachee County babies were born in Panama City, either at the newly-opened Gulf Coast Regional or Bay Memorial (which was later christened Bay Medical Center). The year my brother Aaron was born was the last year of Pine View's maternity ward. When I came on the scene three years later, my mother delivered me at Bay Memorial.

By the 2000s, Bay Medical was a state-of-the-art care center, boasting some of the finest doctors in the Southeast. It was where Wayne Childress spent a week in intensive care, his body torn from the three bullets Freddy hard fired from a Saturday Night Special, a snub-nosed .38 pistol. Freddy had rushed the platform, firing randomly. Wayne took one bullet to his left thigh just above his knee, one in left flank (that somehow missed any internal organs), and one in his left shoulder. That was the bad one. It had shattered bone and torn cartilage and muscle. Wayne nearly bled out in the ambulance ride to Bay County.

I parked my Dodge in the shadow of a live oak tree at the edge of the parking lot in front of Bay Memorial. It was just past six o'clock, and traffic crowded the highway, bumper to bumper. Holiday traffic. Despite the national recession, people were flooding the stores, putting items on credit. I didn't know whether to pity them for going into debt or to feel impressed that they'd go into debt for others. The sun had already sunk into the west, and the sky was the color of a plum.

Inside, I stopped at the reception desk. I wore my sheriff's department uniform. No one knew that I'd left St. Vincent an hour ago. No one knew that I wasn't officially on duty. "What room is Wayne Childress in?"

The receptionist was a redhead with freckles on her face. She wore her hair pulled back from her face, but the bangs that hung on her forehead made her look like a teenager. She smiled. "Let me check, officer." She clicked some keys and read from a screen. "Let's see. He's on the third floor. Room 321."

"Thank you," I said and smiled in a way that I hoped look official.

"Wait," she said, and I stopped, expecting some question about my visit. I prepared a lie, something about Wayne and I knowing each other back in high school. "He was just moved from trauma this morning. I'm not sure if he's settled in the room yet. Would you like to call up?"

I shook my head. "No. Thank you, though. I'll just see if he's there. I'll wait if he's not. Wayne and I go way back."

She smiled again and I walked away. I didn't have to lie to her. My uniform did it for me

The third floor was all patient rooms, the long, carpeted hallways broken up by the occasional nurses' station or drink and snack machine alcove. A few people sat in small waiting rooms, watching muted television news or flipping through magazines. I walked past a dining cart and hoped that Wayne was alone. I'd waited most of the day after my chat with Anne. I'd worn my uniform tonight just in case anyone was around. I'd say something about official business. Something about questioning him.

I didn't have to worry. Wayne was in a private room. The hospital bed was inclined, and he laid his head back on a couple of pillows. His left shoulder was bare only in one area, and a railroad track of stitches disappeared beneath the bandages. He held the nurse call/remote control in his right hand. His left arm lay next to him, palm up. An IV ran from the crook of his right elbow down his arm and snaked up to a pole holding four bags of fluid. A covered brown dinner tray sat on a rolling table next to the bed. The room smelled salty, like fried chicken or bacon. The scent was tinged with an antiseptic hospital odor.

His doe-brown beard had grown out long and shaggy. Hair hung down his forehead in long, untamed strings. I thought he was asleep. But his eyes moved to mine and what might have been a smile touched the corners of his lips.

"Deputy," he said. "Come on in. You'll forgive me if I don't get up."

I didn't know how to take the joke, so I just nodded. "It's Justin. You can call me Justin."

"Justin," he said. His tone suggested he was turning the name over and over in his mind, looking at it from different perspectives. "Justin the historian?"

"No. I'm a cop."

He laughed and gestured at a rolling recliner chair by the bed. "Sit down. I'm joking. You've never heard of Justin the Historian?"

I shook my head and sat. The chair felt stiff, industrial. How on earth did some people sleep in these things?

"First century historian. He lived during the Roman Empire. I like him, but a lot of historians don't. You know why? It's because he loved digression. He'd report on a certain civic action, but then he'd write a few paragraphs about his own thoughts on the law. I like that. It's honest." His voice was slow but determined. He sounded tired and drugged. He look long breaths every few words.

I nodded again, unsure of what to say. "I never was much for history. I like to read, though. I like horror stuff. Mysteries."

"History is a horror story, and I guess, it's a kind of mystery, too," he said. "So what's with the house call? Business or personal?"

I studied his beard. A few gray hairs had begun in his sideburns. It was easy to picture the old man he'd one day be. "Are you okay?"

He shrugged, but the movement pained him. He winced. "I'm going to live." He looked at his shoulder as though it were something removed, an object in the room. "Do you need another statement? I talked to the investigator already."

"No. I'm not here officially." I followed his eyes to my badge and looked down at my uniform. "I came here from work."

"What is it that you need from me?"

"I wanted to ask you about Donnie Ray Miles."

He licked his lips. "What about him?"

"From what I hear, you were the only one he'd talk to. I need to know something. It's been bothering me for a long time. Do you think that Jimmy Danley had anything to do with what happened to Donnie Ray?"

He breathed in and exhaled. "Do you?"

"I don't know. Maybe. Yes. I'm not sure. Jimmy is a bad guy. A really bad guy. I think he thinks the world owes him something. That's why he feels like he can do whatever he wants. I know that he and Donnie Ray had been fighting about politics, at least that's what I hear."

"Donnie Ray didn't fit in with them anymore. I don't think your friend Jimmy liked that."

"He's not my friend," I said. "What do you mean?"

He shifted in the bed and his eyes squinted in pain. I stood up, unsure.

"Can I help you?"

He nodded at the cabinet beside the television. "Get a pillow. Put it behind my back. I need to sit up."

I did, and he sat up and stretched his shoulders, his face tight with pain. "Thanks," he said. He reached to his side table and picked up an over-sized beige cup and sipped from the straw. "I met Donnie Ray at Clawson's. I'd been there maybe two months when he started. He was quiet, removed. We worked on the conveyor belt together, sorting shrimp. One day, I asked him about something I'd seen on the news—civilian deaths in Iraq. The first words he ever said to me were 'The U.S. government is run by crooks and liars.' We started talking about stuff. About politics. About the war. He was—angry. Let's say angry—about a lot of things."

"I heard you were running some kind of a school project. Was Donnie Ray a part of it?"

He smiled as though I'd caught him cheating at cards. "You heard that? Well, no use lying about it. It's true. The job was a part of my thesis. It's for my master's degree. And no, Donnie Ray didn't have a thing to do with it." I didn't like his tone. He sounded like he was lecturing me. I crossed my arms.

"A thesis? Are you serious?" I said. I tried to gauge my response. I felt something akin to insult, but that wasn't quite it. The feeling reminded me of the way I felt whenever I saw tourists taking pictures of the paper mill. I didn't like the idea that St. Vincent, where so many made their homes and built their lives, was merely a backdrop for someone's vacation.

"Yes." He didn't look away.

"Why?"

"Why? Why not? The south used to be a place where unions mattered. Did you know that? The right wing drove them out of here. Right to work? How about 'right to organize?' How about that? After the Taft-Hartley Act, labor in the south was crippled, big time. Then, Arkansas passes this 'right-to-work' nonsense in the 1940s. God, you add to all this a big dose or racism, and you get absolute dearth of worker representation in the South." He was leaning forward now, his tone of voice rising. But as soon as he got excited, he sat back, spent by the outburst. "Why would I not want to start a worker's movement?" He fell back, breathing heavy.

I thought about my father and Charlie and the mill and the union and the strike. I thought about the war and Donnie Ray and Jimmy Danley and Denise. I thought about how little I understood about anything. "I don't know," I said after a moment. "I don't know if I know anything anymore." I sat down in the chair by his bed and a feeling of loss tangible as a tide washed over me. I felt tired and stupid. I had no idea what I'd expected to find out here.

"What is it, deputy?" he said. "You disagree? You think that Clawson's right?"

"I thought maybe you knew," I said.

"Knew what?"

"What happened to Donnie Ray in Iraq. Why he came home so early. I thought maybe he told you."

He tilted his head at me. "Is that why you came here?"

"Yeah. I don't even know why anymore. I just need to know what happened to him."

"I'd tell you if I knew, deputy. I would. He never told me. He just said that he made a mistake. He said the Army didn't agree with him. I figured he'd blown up on a superior, maybe blew a gasket, hit somebody. One night, he went off on this big tirade about how he'd been completely screwed by the Army. He said it blamed his mistakes on him. But I don't know the details."

"I don't think anyone does," I said and remembered something. "Did he ever mention a girl named Lucy?"

He arched his eyebrows. "Yes. A few times. Lucy Sherrill. She was a truck driver, I think he said. They were stationed in the same place. I knew they were friends. I asked him once if they were more than that, and he told me no. He said he thought of her like a sister. How do you know about her?"

"Listen, Wayne. This is important. What did he say about her?"

"Nothing specific. He'd mention her every now and again. He's say, 'Lucy thought that was funny' or 'Lucy used to talk about that.' That kind of thing." He shrugged. "I think he might have had a thing for her. I told him one time he ought to drive up and see her."

"Drive up and see her?"

"Yeah," Wayne said. "She's from south Georgia. I think he said the name of the town was Donalsonville. It's not too far from Tallahassee. I went with him once to Tallahassee to look at a truck. We saw a sign for the place. He said that Lucy lived there."

"Did he ever go?"

"I don't know. Not that I know of. I saw him nearly every day up until the night he died."

I stood up. "Thanks, Wayne. I'm sorry to bother you."

He shook his head. "You're not bothering me. I thought you were here to arrest me."

"I'm not, but I've got to get going."

He squinted. "Are you really on duty?"

"I don't know."

I left the hospital room and hurried down the hallway. I had to get home. I was making a trip to Georgia in the morning.

18

We left St. Vincent around 7:00 a.m. I picked up Denise at the Swifty. She'd parked her Mazda at the public library and walked to meet me. She wore a pair of black jeans, a pink shirt, and a light jacket. She had a purse and the same book I'd seen her with that day at the library, a history of Native Americans in North Florida. When she got in the truck, she smelled of cigarette smoke and perfume, an odor I'd come to associate with her and one that, despite my attempt at quitting smoking, I didn't find off-putting. There was something comforting about it, a whiff of the past, a remembrance of my father.

I'd called her the night before as I drove home from my chat with Wayne Childress. She agreed to go with me and didn't ask me any question, something I felt glad about because I didn't have any answers. I wanted to know what happened to Donnie Ray. Denise wanted to know. I felt that somehow, I owed it to him to find out. I had an address and a genuine hope that I could be honest and open enough to get Lucy Sherrill to talk to me.

I'd gotten on my old desktop briefly when I got home and searched out Lucy Sherrill in Donalsonville, but nothing popped up. I tried just Sherrill, but that didn't tell me much, either. My only plan was to go into town and ask. With hope, the place would be the kind of small town where everyone knew everyone else. All I'd have to do would was be friendly and ask.

Not long after we got on the road, Denise said, "Jimmy's gone."

I didn't look at her. "What do you mean 'gone'?"

"He took off the night after the rally at Clawson's. He hasn't been around since."

"So you're living alone?"

"For the time being. I don't know if I can swing rent and utilities by myself for long."

I didn't respond, and we didn't talk much as we drove on. I'd tuned to radio to NPR, but Denise flipped it over to a classic country station, and as steel guitars whined and old men sang of the last love and last bottle, the flat, sandy shoals of North Florida gradually changed to a more ridged and rugged landscape broken by untamed forests of longleaf pine and pecan orchards. As we drove further into Georgia, we passed huge fields, all barren and fallow, the dirty faded brown and left to lay for the winter season.

"How do you know she lives here?" Denise said, looking out the window, studying a big, weather-gray barn with a collapsed roof.

"I talked to Wayne Childress last night," I said and adjusted the thermostat. It was getting chillier. Tonight, the wind off the bay would be freezing cold. I had to get back to St. Vincent before 11:00 p.m. for night shift.

"Is he okay?"

"He's going to be."

"What's going to happen to Freddy?"

I shook my head. "I don't know. Depends on what the county prosecutor wants to do. They could go manslaughter or attempted homicide. Depends."

"On what?"

"The political winds."

I studied her. Her face had taken on a pinched worried look. She chewed her bottom lip.

"Why are you so worried?"

"He's never had much of a life, Justin. He palled around with Jimmy and Donnie Ray and Tater because they didn't treat him like shit. They just ignored him. That was more of a courtesy than his crazy ass dad every showed him."

"I guess," I said. "I thought I knew him. Heck, I thought I knew everybody in town. I'm starting to think I don't know thing one about St. Vincent."

She didn't answer and stared out the window as if the answers to all of our questions were buried in some barren cotton field. She might have been right. I pulled off the highway into a Shell station—a rectangular building and old-timey analog pumps. You couldn't swipe your card. I squinted at the front door, hunting a Visa sign, worried that we'd need cash.

"They'll take my card," I said, spotting a credit card sticker. "I'll take care of it."

"Bathroom's probably around back," she said and opened the door. A cold, dry wind blew in, the kind that stings your skin and makes you squint.

I shivered and pulled my jacket tight. The black Aplachee County Sheriff's Department baseball cap on my head didn't do much to warm me. I wished I'd worn a toboggan. "See if they have any fresh coffee," I said. I handed her my bank card and she took it and looked me, her eyes narrowed, studying me.

"Just pay for it," I said. "Get whatever you want. On me."

"You don't have to."

I waved my hand. "Just go," I said as she walked away. "Get cream and sugar."

She went inside and I tried not to watch her as she walked away. I leaned back against the truck and waited for the attendant to turn on the pump.. Just beyond the station, a barren field stretched out toward a row of tiny shotgun houses. A blackbird flew over, its shadow a dark dart in the sunlight. The pump clicked on, and I watched the numbers roll by and wondered about Lucy Sherrill—what would she tell us? Wasn't there some regulation in the Army about romantic relationships in a combat zone? Maybe that was why Donnie Ray came home. If that was the case, then she'd be home, too.

I finished pumping and was getting in the truck when Denise came out, holding a small bag and a cup of coffee. She got in, handed me the coffee, and took a banana and a bottle of water out of the bag. It was paper. I couldn't remember the last time I'd seen a paper bag.

I sipped the coffee. It was hot and fresh. "This is good," I said. I turned the heat up and was sat in silence for a moment.

She opened the bag, took out a granola bar, and opened it. "He'd just brewed the pot."

"There's probably some kind of cafe downtown," I said. "We can stop in there and ask if anyone knows the Sherrills."

"No need," Denise said and took a swig from a bottle of water.

"What do you mean?"

"I asked the old guy inside. He knows the family. They run a garage in Iron City, this little town about ten minutes from here," she said, her voice nonchalant.

"Well, look at you, Detective Miles," I said, excited. "Let's go see Lucy." I put the truck in gear and pulled out onto the highway.

"We can't see her, Justin."

"Why not?"

"She's dead."

Iron City, Georgia, was little more than a crossroads and a railroad track. I slowed the truck to a crawl as we came into town off the highway. We passed a shuttered cafe and a gas station that had seen better days. A lone Ford pick-up truck sat out front, its sun-faded blue paint job nearly gray.

"It's on the other end of town," Denise said. She sipped from her bottle of water.

"What did the attendant tell you?"

"He just said that he heard Lucy died in the war," Denis said for the fifth time. I couldn't wrap my head around it. Dead? The possibility hadn't even occurred to me. I had no idea what I was going to say when we got to the garage. I wasn't even sure anymore why we were going.

I pressed the brake and pulled over to the side of the road.

"What are you doing?"

"I don't know," I said. "I mean, why are we doing this? If she's dead, let's go home. Her parents probably feel just like Big Don. They probably want to be left alone."

She sat back in the seat and nodded a few times, as though she were looking at the idea from different directions in her mind. "Yeah," she said after a moment. "We could do that. But I don't want to."

"Why?"

"Because Lucy was the last person who knew the Donnie Ray I knew, before the war messed his head up. That's why. And I'm not going home until we know something."

I pulled back on the road and we drove in silence until a placard sign for "Sherrill Automotive" came into view. The lot was small and a tow-truck sat backwards in front of the cinderblock office, which was connected to a two-car garage. An RC Cola drink machine sat by the front door. I got out and looked up that the sky, which had gone iron gray.

"What do we say?" I said.

"I don't know," she said.

As we walked up toward the office, the door opened and a man in blue coveralls came out. His skin was sepia and dark freckles covered his nose and cheeks. He smiled, and his features crinkled, his eyes disappearing into folds of skin. "How y'all folks doing?"

"Good," I said. "Is Mr. Sherrill around?"

"That would be me," he said. "You having trouble with the Dodge? What is that, a '98? '99?"

I stopped and Denise and I shared a sideways look. "You're Mr. Sherrill? Lucy Sherrill's father?"

His eyes narrowed and he took off his hat, revealing a bald head. "Who's asking?" he said, his voice guarded and suspicious.

I nodded toward the office. "Can we go inside and talk?"

He looked from me to Denise and back again. "You're not reporters are you?"

"No, sir," I said. "Truth is, I don't know why I'm here. Maybe it's better if we just talk. My name is Justin. This is Denise."

He frowned for a second and then nodded his head. "All right, let's go."

We followed him through the front office, a tiny, square room that smelled of scorched coffee and motor oil. Mopar and Ford calendars on the walls. A coffee maker with half a pot, the brew black and thick. He sat down in an ancient rolling chair behind a desk and nodded at an industrial couch by the front door. "Have a seat," he said, his voice pinched. He kept eyeing both of us. He pursed his lips a few times and steepled his fingers and rested his chin on his thumbs.

"What do you all want to know about Lucy? You serve with her or something?"

I shook my head. "No. A friend of mine did. Look, here's the truth. I didn't even know she was dead until half an hour ago. A guy at a gas station told us when we asked if he knew her. A friend of mine died. He served with her. I thought I could talk to her about my friend. He knew her. They were deployed together in Iraq."

He took a long breath. "She was killed two years ago. What happened to your friend?"

"He died at home. I'm—we're from Florida. I'm a deputy sheriff," I said and watched him wince. I held up my hands. "I'm not here in any kind of official capacity. Donnie Ray, my friend, he came home different from Iraq. He left the Army early, I think. I don't really know. It's just that I thought maybe Lucy knew what happened."

He opened his mouth to speak, but nothing came out. He sat back in the chair, his hands clasped in front of him. "You said your friend came home early?"

"Yes," I said.

"He was my cousin," Denise said. "He came back after just two years of service. He never left again." Then, she told him the whole story. About how different he seemed. About the union. About his falling out with Jimmy. About Wayne Childress. About everything. The more she spoke, the slower and more hesitant her words. It was as though she were just learning about Donnie Ray for herself, as though she'd never really considered everything. When she finished talking, her eyes were damp. She pinched the bridge of her nose. "The only thing we really know about him is that he knew your daughter. He was private. His family doesn't even know what happened over there."

Mr. Sherrill leaned forward and studied us, chewing his jaw. He didn't speak for a long time. I looked around the office. Its dark wood paneling. The framed business license. The family photograph of him, a white woman with dark hair, and what must have been a teenaged Lucy, her smile wide, two dimples marking her cheeks. She had her mother's almond eyes, her father's freckles. She could have passed for Hispanic with her long black hair.

I pictured her spending a lot of time here, probably, growing up with a dad who was a mechanic. No wonder she wound up driving trucks when she joined the Army.

"Friendly fire," Mr. Sherrill said. "One of her own killed her. They told us that it happened at night, during a fire fight. They said it was confusing. Couldn't have been avoided. I've seen it movies, how they come to your house and notify you when someone dies. They came to our door, two boys from Fort Bragg. One of them was a black fella. When Jamie—my wife, she's white—answered the door, I think they thought they had the wrong house. When I cae out, we all sat in the living room. Real formal. They said the U.S. Army regretted to inform us that our daughter, Specialist Emma Lucille Sherrill had been killed in combat in Iraq. They didn't tell us about the friendly fire thing until later. I don't know why. Maybe they thought we'd sue. I don't know. We didn't. Money won't bring her back."

"I'm sorry," I said, my mind reeling, trying to wrap my mind around what I'd just realized. "I'm sorry."

He looked at me over his fingers. His hands looked hardened with age, his fingers knicked and scarred. "No sorrys needed."

"I think," Denise said, her voice quiet, as though she were asleep, "that Donnie Ray might have shot Lucy."

He breathed through his nose. "What did you say? What was the name?"

"Donnie Ray," Denise said. "Donnie Ray Miles."

Mr. Sherrill took a long breath, and it seemed as though he deflated inside of his blue coveralls. "He wrote us a letter about six months ago. I'd show to you, but it's at the house."

"A letter?" I said.

"Yeah. He said he was sorry. He said he didn't mean for it to happen. He said he'd changed so much that he kind of thought he'd died too, that his old self was dead or something. It was weird letter." He studied us, his dark eyes moving from Denise to me and back again.

It made sense. Him being home early. His change in politics. PTSD. All the tumblers fell together in my mind, and I felt stupid for not seeing this all before. No wonder he kept her picture. No wonder he distanced himself from everyone. How do you live with it, knowing you shot and killed one of your own? I thought of Freddy, sitting in his cell back in Apalachee County, his wide eyes filled with images of the night at Clawsons, things he'd never be able to forget.

"I'm sorry. I had—we had no idea," I said.

He held up a palm. "No need, son. No need. Please don't apologize anymore. Tell you the truth, I've heard enough sorrys to last me a lifetime."

"I'm sorry he shot her, Mr. Sherrill," Denise said, her voice still small, as though she were talking to herself. "I'm sorry that he did that." She started crying, and I put my arm around her, and she leaned into me.

"That letter probably didn't help things," I said, wondering what it would have been like if someone had written me a letter, apologizing for Janey's death. I never knew the truck driver's name. Some out-of-towner. I rubbed Denise's back.

"He might have needed to write it," Mr. Sherrill said and opened his hands wide in a "who knows" gesture.

Denise sat up and wiped her eyes with her palms. "I know you said not to apologize," Denise said, "but I don't know what to say."

"Sweetheart," Mr. Sherrill said. His voice was kind. "He didn't do it on purpose. Look, my name is Abe. You can call me Abe. Everyone does."

The phone rang on his desk, and I jumped. He grinned at me and held up a finger. "Let me see who this is."

I nodded and looked at Denise. I took her hand. Her palm felt cold and wet. I wanted to pull her to me and assure her this would be okay, but I couldn't. I didn't know if that were true.

"Sherrill's," he said. "Oh, hey babe. Yes. Half gallon of milk. No ma'am. I won't forget this time." He smiled as someone spoke on the other end. "All right, hon. Love you." He hung up. "My wife," he said. "You forget to stop by the store one time, and they call you a thousand times. You don't treat him that way, do you?" he said to Denise.

She snapped to and blinked. "No. What I mean is, we're not together. We're not married."

"Oh," he said and arched his eyebrows. "I'm sorry. I made it awkward, didn't I? Sarah says that's my specialty. Awkwardness. That's my wife, Sarah. There, I did it again, didn't I?"

I couldn't help chuckling. "No, sir, Mr. Abe. Not at all." I stood up. "I'm sorry that we bothered you here."

"You didn't bother us. Have a seat. You ought to come back to the house. Sarah's making a roast for dinner."

I shook my head and pulled Denise to a standing position. She seemed to have gone back into some catatonic cave, her eyes vacant. "We need to get going. I've got to work tonight."

"Night shift?"

I nodded.

"I used to that, a long time ago. I worked security at a warehouse in Atlanta. Those are long hours."

"They are," I said and extended my hand. He took it and shook. His palms were like asphalt, hard and pocked. "It was nice to meet you, Mr. Abe. I'm sorry that we just busted in here like this on you."

He shook his head. "Cut that Mr. stuff out. And don't even have a second thought about coming here. It's not an imposition at all. I'm sorry about your friend. It's a terrible thing to survive that war and come home to die in your own hometown."

"Yeah," I said. "I know you said no more apologies, but I apologize on his behalf. I'm sure he didn't mean to do it."

"I never once thought he did. The only people I blame for my Lucy's death live in a huge white house in Washington, D.C."

We walked out into the cold. The sun had come from behind the clouds, its rays sharp and bright, the kind of light that comes in the clarity of winter air. Without the haze, everything looked crisp, clean. Our shadows stretched out in front of us, black pools on the cracked concrete parking lot. He followed us to my truck.

"It was nice to meet you," Denise said and walked around the side of the truck and got in.

"She was close to him," I said, keeping my voice low. "She doesn't mean to be rude."

He shook his head. "When I found out what happened to Lucy, I didn't speak to anyone for a month. No my pastor. Not my friends. Not even Sarah. It took me a long time to wrap my head around the whole thing. I imagine she's processing all this. I can't believe y'all didn't know. His parents don't know, either?"

"I don't know, but I don't think so." I said. "They're a clannish bunch, the Miles. It's hard to say."

We looked at each other. He stood a good head and shoulders above me. I noticed a number tattooed on the back of his right hand—twenty-seven. He followed my eyes. "That? My college football number. All of us got them. Thirty-five years ago, I thought it was a good idea." He grinned.

"My brother played a few years back. At Georgia Southern."

"Well, I'll be damned. That's where I played. You all got a long drive back to Florida?"

"A couple of hours. St. Vincent, Apalachee County. Ever heard of it?"

He shook his head. "Not sure. I don't think so."

"I don't think it exists," I said, thinking of Wayne and Freddy and Rich and Donnie Ray and all the secrets that had been revealed. The St. Vincent I thought I knew didn't seem to exist at all.

He looked at me, brow knit in confusion. "What do you mean by that?"

"Nothing," I said. "It's nothing. We've got to go," I said. "Thank you."

He waved as we pulled out and I watched him in the rear view as we drove away. The road beneath the truck hummed, and I pressed down the gas. We had to get home. Next to me, Denise gazed out at the empty fields.

The live oak in front of the First Baptist Church where Janey's funeral was held had been growing since I was a child. I remembered seeing it when I was a boy, its trunk just smaller than a fire plug, its branches stretching out like wide open arms, its deep green tea teardrop leaves the size of my palm. Now, it had grown large, its truck fat and round, the bark thick, laced through with shades of gray and white. It stretched up into the sky, its branched still filled with leaves. By early winter, they'd begin to fall. Sitting beneath it in my cruiser, I realized how little it resembled the tree I'd known as a boy. It had changed, yet it remained familiar. Maybe St. Vincent was the same way. Denise certainly was. I'd dropped her at her car after we got back town. She'd said little in the journey home, answering my questions with single words and head shakes. The news had shaken her, badly. The news had shaken me, too. I'd thought I knew Donnie Ray Miles, thought I understood him. I hadn't at all. Maybe that was Denise's problem, too. Maybe Donnie Ray was her tree, a thing that grew so subtly in front of her that she never noticed the change.

It was just past three in the morning. I was drinking a cup of coffee and trying to stay warm. A low pressure system had pushed south, bringing cold weather. A frost advisory had been issued. I wore my bullet-proof vest under my uniform and a black jacket. The heater ran full-blast, but I still felt chilled. Something about wet air seeped right through any protective layer. My hip ached dully, stove up from a long day of driving. Chris was working the north end tonight, away from the coast, probably doing the same thing I was doing, huddled in his car, trying to stay warm and trying to stay awake. I yawned and rubbed my eyes.

I kept thinking of Abe Sherrill's words, "This is nobody's fault." On the drive home, I'd been astounded that he hadn't been angry with us. We were the link to Donnie Ray. Donnie Ray had killed his daughter. I never knew the identity of the truck driver who hit Janey. It wasn't hidden from me. I just never wanted to know.

The radio erupted in static. "One-twelve?"

I pinched my lapel mic. "Go ahead."

"We've got a Signal 22 at Bay View. 220 Periwinkle. Caller said it sounded like a domestic."

"Ten-four," I said.

Noise complaint. A domestic. I imagined a white trash couple going at it after a twelve pack of Natural Light—not the kind of thing I wanted to deal with.

I was worried about a phone call I'd gotten. When Denise and I got back into Apalachee County, a voice mail popped up on my cell. We'd driven through a dead area. Malone wanted to talk to me in the morning. I knew what it had to be about—following Freddy out to Stink Town the night he bought the pistol. Probably some trick his lawyer was going to try to use. My stomach knotted.

I turned out on the highway and passed Charlie's Cafe and wished that I was sitting in there, eating a plate of fried mullet. The road unspooled in front of me, and I crested the overpass. The mill spread out beneath me, all shadows and dark scaffolding. A few lights burned. No smoke from the smokestacks. A mile later, beneath Marten Bridge, Clawson's Fishery sat silent and empty by the waterfront. Wayne's shooting seemed like a lifetime ago.

I took the first right off the highway, Redfish Street, and followed it back toward Periwinkle, one of the last streets in Bay View. Beyond it were sand flats that turned into thick, untamed woods. The trailers and tiny bungalows on Periwinkle were quiet and dark, save for the occasional porch light. I rolled the window down and winced at the sudden blast of cool air. I scanned the yards with my dash light and listened for raised voices, any sign of a disturbance.

At the end of the road, I turned around on an oyster shell cul-de-sac and rolled the window down and shivered as cold air flooded the cruiser. I stuck my head out the window, my teeth gritted, and tried to listen. Nothing. I nearly drove away, but then, beneath the rustle of palm fronds and the engine's hum, a man's voice: "You'll Goddamn do what I'll say you'll do." Rich Richards. It had to be. I didn't want to deal with this loon tonight, especially not after what happened at Clawson's.

I leaned farther out of the window, trying to pinpoint the sound. Then, a woman's voice, clear as the mill's whistle: "Rich. Rich. Please calm down." Gina Richards, Rich's wife. How and why they stayed together eluded me.

I pulled off the edge of the road and got out. The wind blew hard, a cold, hard wind that stung my cheeks and made me wish for the ninety-degree temperatures of summer.

The Rich's trailer was a single-wide sitting in a narrow, overgrown lot. Dead gray weeds poked out of the cracked driveway. Rich's rust-eaten Toyota pickup sat out front, its windows rimed with frost. There was no porch light. I took out my flashlight and turned it on and took three steps across the small yard to the porch, which looked like little more than a plywood plank sitting on cinder blocks. The voices continued from the back (or maybe from inside) the trailer, him yelling about her doing what he said, her trying to reason with him, telling him that she had to work tomorrow.

I knocked on the door with the heel of my hand, trying to make a lot of noise. "Hello? Apalachee County Sheriff's Department. Please open the door."

Shuffling from inside. Muffled voices. "Hello?" I said and hit the door again.

The door cracked and Gina Richards stood there, her face streaked with tears, strings of black hair hanging down over her face. She had a bruise on her neck. Her red blouse was torn, exposing a dingy and worn-out bra strap. She crossed her arms. "I want to press charges. That's the last time he lays a hand on me."

"Come on outside," I said. I needed to get some distance between her and Rich. Just as I pulled the door to, someone stopped it—a kid who looked a lot like Freddy, thin with a narrow face and a dark complexion.

"What's going on?" he said and yawned. He wore a t-shirt and a pair of boxer shorts. "It's cold." I shined the flashlight at him and he squinted.

"Go back to bed, Jonathan," Gina said. "Just go to bed."

"It's all right, kiddo," I said. He'd probably been through a lot lately. "Just go on back inside. We'll sort this out."

"Mama, what's," Jonathan began, but Rich cut him off, his voice slurred.

"Get your Goddamn ass back in the bed," Rich said. He stumbled out onto the front porch. He wore a pair of bright orange hunting coveralls and a matching hat.

"Let me tell you something, Mr. Revenue Generator. You are wasting your time," he said, leaning into me, pointing. His breath smelled like a mixture of alcohol and road kill. "That woman? She's a Goddamn crazy case. What you call it? Fifty-one fifty."

"Go back inside," I said and pushed him through the door. I kept a tight grip on the flashlight.

Something changed in his eyes. The moment I touched his shoulder, he grew stiff, and his face took on a crumpled, feral look, his jaw drawn tight, his eyes narrowed to slits. "Get your hand off me. Don't you *ever* touch me. You have no authority here." He was drunk. Calm drunk. Dangerous drunk.

"Sir, you need to calm down."

"I'm a sovereign citizen of the United States of America. That's what I am. I don't recognize your state-sanctioned laws. So get off of my property."

I tensed and tried to remain calm. "Go back inside, Mr. Richards. I need to talk to your wife." I'd be taking him to jail. In Florida, if a deputy sees evidence of a domestic dispute, we don't have a choice. Rich Richards was going to join his son down at the county hoosegow.

"Mama, what's going on?" Jonathan said from inside the trailer.

"Go to bed, son," Gina called. She stood down at the edge of the steps, her arms crossed. Her voice sounded tired and weepy.

"Is there someone I can call to be with your son?" I said.

"I'm his daddy. I'll staying with him," Rich said. He puffed out his chest and stared at me. "The state's not going to take this son, to."

I said, "Mr. Richards, please go inside."

"Isn't it enough you threw Freddy in jail for defending his country?"

"Oh for the love of God, shut up," I said. For the first time in my half decade on the force, I wanted to quit. "Your son tried to murder someone."

"Fuck you," he said. "He was defending us all from that communist bastard."

"Rich," Gina said. "Please."

I wished I were at home. I looked over at Gina, "Ma'am, are you okay?"

In the moment I'd looked away from him, Rich Richards threw himself into me, his shoulder slamming into my gut. We fell back off the porch onto the hard, cold ground, and the breath went out of my lungs. I'd landed flat of my back. Rich was small but wiry, his legs wrapped around my waist. I tried to twist, but he dug his chin into my chest, and my back arched. Pain shot through my hip, fresh and angry. Then, I felt his hands on my gun belt.

He was going for my pistol.

I grabbed the holster with both hands. If I let go, he'd get the pistol and kill me. I had no doubt about it. My mind reeled. I couldn't let go to call for backup.

"Call 911," I yelled, my voice gone high, the scream of a trapped animal. Rich head-butted me, and blood flowed in my mouth, sick and salty.

I tried to gulp breath, but the fall had knocked the wind out of me. I gritted my teeth and tried to turn my body, but Rich's weight kept me on the ground. He'd put his shoulder into my face and was pushing with his legs for leverage.

Rich grunted and mumbled into my chest, his voice a throaty growl. "Government's going to leave me alone."

Jonathan and Gina screamed and yelled, and their voices swirled around me, and I lost them. I didn't know who was saying what. I had one mission: to keep Rich from getting the pistol out of my holster. It was loaded with hollow points. If he got it, I didn't have a chance, not at this close a range. He wouldn't shoot me in the chest. He'd shoot me in my face. An image jumped into my mind, then, of my body lying still, blood pooling around my head. I tried to push it away. But it stayed right at the white edge of my vision, a threatening prophecy. I couldn't see beyond Rich, couldn't hear anything more than his grunting threats, couldn't feel anything but his clawed fingers on my hands, his shoulder grinding into my chin, his knees on my body. I couldn't focus. My head throbbed. My hands had pricks and needles in them. My hip hurt, waves of pain radiating up my side. The whiteness at the edge of my eyes grew brighter. I was going to die. I thought of Janey and then Denise. I couldn't let this happen. Fight, Everson, fight. Stop it. Fight. Fight. I pushed my knee up and we turned sideways on the ground, trapping the pistol between my hip and the hard ground. I tried to head butt down at Rich, but it was no use. He was too far away. He kept muttering, "Going to kill you."

I don't how long we wrestled. My shoulder began to ache. My lungs felt deflated, useless. I couldn't catch a breath. Time lost meaning. I knew only that I couldn't let go of the holster. The dark night sky reeled above me, the stars all leaving white tracers, writing in some language I could never understand. Gina kept screaming, yelling at Rich, saying his name over and over again. Jonathan was crying, saying "No, no, no," over and over again. Rich dug his fingernails into my hand, drawing blood, and the pain shot up my arm. My fingers loosened. Sweat had slicked my palms (and his, too). I tried to shout for someone to call 911, but I still had no breath, and my head felt heavy, like it was full of cement. I must have cried out. I must have yelled. Cursed. I don't know. I knew only the Beretta. I had to focus on the pistol. I thought of my father's stone, gray and etched and granite. I squeezed my eyes shut and tried to push the images away. I focused on the gun.

Then, it happened.

My hands slipped off the holster, and the gun came loose and Rich Richards pulled the pistol free and I kicked at him and he stood over me and a shot fired and he fell, blood blossoming on his coveralls. He dropped my nine millimeter and staggered back, his mouth working wordlessly. I twisted my head up to see Chris Chambers in a three-point stance, his gun pointed at Rich. He looked down at me and nodded, just the slightest tip of his head. Then, I closed my eyes and the world narrowed to darkness.

19

That first week after Rich nearly killed me, I thought I was okay. I tried to keep working like nothing had changed. But each time I closed my eyes, my body shook, and I was right there in his front yard again, fighting for my life. I could see him rise above me. I looked down the black hole barrel of my own pistol. But this time, Chris Chambers didn't save the day. The bullet exploded from the gun, tiny fragments spinning behind it. It tore through my neck, opening my throat up in a red spray. I bled to death while everyone watched. Wednesday morning after a sleepless night, I called Mack and told him I needed some time off.

I didn't make my meeting with Malone the next morning, and to his credit, he didn't call. I overslept. Mack Weston called instead. He told me that Rich had sworn out a complaint against me for harassing his family. But when he tried to kill me, Mack and Malone had back-burnered the complaint. Rich was a few cells down from Freddy. The department had charged him with attempted manslaughter.

Mack told me that he knew I wasn't doing well. He told me to take some time off. I took a week of vacation, and I knew by the third day that I wouldn't be going back to work for the Apalachee County Sheriff's Department. Whatever that part of my life had been—and it had been a lot of things—was over. At first, I thought that the town I'd chosen over Janey had changed, but as the days stretched on, cold and dark, I began to suspect that perhaps the change lay with me.

That week, I spent a lot of time sitting on a lawn chair in the backyard. I built a fire almost every night, and I'd sit, wrapped in a blue quilt, staring at the flames as the sun went down over the bay. My backyard looked gray and dead in the cold weather. Daily, the temperatures got up to sixty or so. By night, they plunged into the low twenties. The cold seeped through my thick covering, and I'd shiver, thinking of the look in Rich's eyes as he stood, the canopy of night behind him, the gun's barrel open like a surprised mouth.

People checked on me throughout the week. Jimmy Greene from the First Baptist Church called and left a message, wanting to take me to lunch. I didn't return the call. Charlie and Luann brought me dinner on Tuesday night, and we sat in the den and talked about the old days, back when my dad and Charlie were friends. I hadn't called my mom to tell her what happened yet, and Luann urged me to. "If you was my son, I'd want to know," she explained, but I knew that Mama would just want to get in the car and come down to St. Vincent. I didn't much feel like dealing with her.

One night, Chris stopped by with a six-pack of Yuengling and we watched a haunted house movie and didn't say much. Hector stopped by with his girlfriend a day later, and we sat in the backyard around the fire pit, talking about Freddy's coming arraignment, talking about the looming budget cuts, talking about the coming mill shut down. Frank came by one evening during his shift, and we stood in the front yard and talked for a while. None of us talked about what seemed to me a given: I wasn't going back to work for the department. I'd made my peace. My days as a sheriff's deputy were over.

Saturday evening, the temperature had risen back to the mid-60s, and I'd decided to get out of the house. I thought I'd drive out to the cape, sit in my truck, and watch the Gulf of Mexico. Something about the coming and going of the tide relaxed me. It said that no matter what, the world would keep spinning. I'd gotten in the truck and cranked up when Denise's green Mazda pulled into my front yard. She got out, and I opened the truck door.

"Hey," she said.

"Hey," I said.

"You okay?"

I nodded. "Good. I guess. What about you?"

"I don't know." She looked up at my barren magnolia tree. "I'm tired. I spent last weekend moving."

"Where are you living?"

"With a girlfriend in Parker," she said, meaning a little subdivision just east of Panama City. "Where you going?"

"I was just going to drive around. I don't really know."

"You want me to come with you?"

I didn't say anything at first. Then, she said, "I haven't heard from Jimmy."

"Let's go," I said.

We drove out toward the bay, hung a left on the highway, and took the same route we'd taken that day after I'd ran into her at the library. She played with the radio as I drove, scanning stations, until she settled on some 90s alternative rock." We listened to the guitar wailing above the orchestra, and I drove us to the same bluff overlooking the Gulf.

After a moment, I reached over and took her hand and pulled her to me and our lips met. Her mouth was hot, and she tasted like cigarettes and Sprite. I ran my hands down her back, feeling the muscle and bone there, and enjoyed how real she felt, how here, how corporeal. She climbed into my lap and pulled me closer, and as she moved against me, I felt a part of me let go of St. Vincent, let go of the mill, let go of Clawson's, and let go of Janey. For once, there were no ghosts and no shadows. It was just the world in all its bright glory.

Later, we drove to my house and sat on the couch. I flipped channels and rubbed her arm, enjoying the warm smoothness of her skin. On her right bicep was a tiny tattoo of a butterfly, intricately inked in blues and pinks and yellows.

"When did you get this?"

She turned to look at it. "In Pensacola, when I was in college."

"It's nice," I said and pushed my face into her hair. It smelled like shampoo, some floral scent that made me think of a rain forest. "Why'd you get it?"

"It's stupid," she said. "Don't make fun of me if I tell you."

"I won't," I said, and I meant it.

She shifted to look at me, and I studied the sea green of her eyes and the constellation of cinnamon freckles on her nose and cheeks. "It was symbolic," she said. "I thought that Pensacola was a kind of rebirth for me. I thought that I'd once been a worm, here in St. Vincent. In Pensacola, I wasn't just Denise Miles anymore. I could be anyone."

"So, a butterfly from a cocoon," I said.

She squinted. "Yes."

"I promise you. I'm not making fun." I run my fingers of her arms and massaged the tattoo with my thumb. "I think it's cool. I like it."

"Do you?" She nearly smiled, the edges of her lips turning up slightly.

"I do," I said. "And lots of people get tattoos that a symbolic. Think about Mr. Sherrill. He got that tattoo with his college football numbers on it. And you uncle, Big Don, has a bunch of tattoos. He's got that anchor from his time in the Navy."

Something clicked in my head, and I sat up straight, pushing Denise off of me.

"What?" she said. "What is it?"

"The tattoo," I said. "Cowboy has the same tattoo."

"A butterfly?"

"No," I said, shaking my head. "An anchor."

"So what?" she said.

"I need to go talk to him," I said. It was fifteen after eight. He'd still be up.

"Tonight?" Denise sat forward, resting her elbows on her knees. "Are you serious? Can't you talk to him tomorrow?"

"You can stay here," I said. "I don't care. I'll be back in an hour."

Her mouth fell open just a bit as though she were going to speak, and then, she closed it and smiled a sad little smile. "It's okay. Go."

"I don't want you mad at me."

"I'm not mad," she said. "I promise. Go. I need to head back to Parker, anyway. I've got to work in the morning."

"Are you sure?"

She nodded, and I pulled her up off the couch and kissed her. "I'll call you," I said. "Tomorrow. I'll call you tomorrow."

Cowboy lived north of town, just off Highway 71. The house sat on small hill in a copse of pine and sweet gum trees. I turned up the gravel driveway and eased along, letting my truck idle its way. The two-story home came into view, its blue siding glowing in the bright light mounted to a pole at the edge of the yard. Cowboy's cruiser was parked facing the highway. A red and black two-tone Chevy truck sat halfway in the garage. A border collie stood barking on the front porch when I got out of the truck. The front door opened, and Cowboy's silhouette filled the frame.

"Shut up, Shorty," he yelled at the dog. He squinted in the darkness, trying to focus. "Justin?" he said, his voice echoing out over the yard.

I waved. "Hey, Sergeant. Sorry to bother you at home." I walked over to the porch with my hands in my pockets. My jacket was still in the truck.

He shook my hand and smiled. "Not a problem. Come in. What's going on? Everything okay?" Shorty sniffed at my heels and wagged his tail. I reached down and ran a hand over his hand.

"Good boy," Cowboy said. He patted the dog's side.

We went inside and stood in the foyer. Shorty stared in at us through the storm door, wagging his tail, tongue hanging from his mouth. The house smelled like cinnamon. Blue light flickered from a TV in a room somewhere down the hallway. A Christmas tree that stretched all the way to the home's vaulted ceiling sat in a bay window that looked out over the backyard. The tree glowed yellow and green and red.

"Martie gets a bigger tree every couple of years," he said.

"It's beautiful."

"Come on in," he said and walked down the hallway toward the tree. The floor looked like natural stone. "You want a drink? I was about to pour me one."

"Cal," a woman's voice called from somewhere in the house. "Who is it?"

"Just Justin," he said, as though I were a regular visitor here. "Everything's okay. I'll be back there in a minute."

We went into the kitchen, a huge wood-framed affair right out of *Better Homes and Gardens*. He opened a cabinet beneath a spacious bar and took out an oversized bottle of Bacardi dark rum. He got two highball glasses from the cabinet and filled them with ice.

"Coke?"

I nodded and he mixed our drinks. He slid mine over to me. We drank in silence. The drink tasted sweet and strong. I put it down and studied the bar. It was granite, the same color as the floor.

"What's on your mind?"

I didn't really know where to begin. I didn't want to outright accuse him of lying because he didn't lie. I didn't want to demand that he tell me anything. He didn't owe me an explanation for anything. Two or three sentences formed in my mind, but didn't say anything. I opened my mouth.

"I just want to see what you think about all this stuff. The department shutting down. I don't know. I was just worried about my future, I guess."

He swirled his glass around and looked at me, his eyes telling me that he didn't believe this was the reason I'd come to his house at nearly 9:00 p.m. on a Saturday night. "Well, it's complicated. I don't think anyone really knows what's going to happen." He leveled his eyes at me. "Do you even want to come back to work?"

"I don't know," I said.

"That's kind of what I thought. You know if you do, Mack's going to let Malone at you. He knows what happened that night out at Stink Town. Freddy Richards was buying a gun, same pistol he used at Clawson's. If you'd told us, we might could have been on the lookout for him."

"I'm sorry. I didn't realize."

"No, you didn't. The sheriff's got a meeting with the city manager next week about the budget. We'll get our marching orders after that, I'm sure. But folks are leaving, Justin. Chris got a job in Bay County."

"He did?" I had no idea.

"Sure did. It's like rats in a sinking ship out there. Truth is, Justin, this place is drying up and blowing away." He took a long sip of his drink and leaned forward on the counter. "I've been here twenty years. I've never seen anything like it. When my daughter was young, I used to read to her every night. She loved fairy tales. And every night, when I closed the book, she'd always ask me what happened to the people."

"The people?"

"In the book. She wanted to know what happened to the people when I closed the book. I used to laugh about that, a little girl's fantasy. I used to tell her that they'd wait between the covers there on us. They'd be there tomorrow night when we read again." He looked down at the granite countertop. "Now, I'm not so sure. Kind of feels like that here in St. Vincent. Like somebody's closed the book."

The tattoo on his right forearm had faded over the years to a dull purple. Still, it remained clear—the outline of an anchor wrapped in a thick rope, both sides flanked by stars. *USS Davidson* was written in script beneath the anchor. The same tattoo Big Don had. I'd missed it. I'd not been observant enough.

"I got that when I was nineteen years old," Cowboy said. "I was a stupid kid back then. I probably wouldn't get one now. I wouldn't let my daughter get one and she's in college, same age I was when I got this." He shook his head. "I guess she probably went ahead and done it, anyway. That's what I would have done."

"Big Don Miles has one just like it," I said.

"Yeah," he said and looked me in the eye. I wanted to look away. I couldn't. "He does. We served together. But you knew that, probably. We went through a lot together. We were only on the *Davidson* for a year. But a lot happened." He nodded, and that slight tilt of his head revealed a story that I would have loved to hear, but a story that would probably remain buried in Cowboy's past. That head nod was the closest thing to an emotional outburst that I'd ever seen from Cowboy. "I've known Don Miles a long time."

"Is that why you did it?"

He frowned and pulled at the edges of his mustache. "Did what?"

"Covered it up. What happened to Donnie Ray Miles."

"Justin, I don't know what you think you know." His demeanor changed. He stood up straight. "Why'd you come out here?"

"What happened with Donnie Ray Miles?"

"He drowned. And I wanted to pin it on Jimmy Danley and that crew, but there was no way that we could have. We tried."

"I'm not talking about that, Sergeant."

"Then what are you talking about, deputy?" he said, emphasizing the last word.

I crossed my arms, fighting a dull blade of anger that cut my gut. "I know he shot somebody in Iraq. I thought Jimmy Danley killed him. Every time I got close, you and Mack and Malone worked hard to keep me away from the truth."

Cowboy's eyes narrowed. "This is none of your business. I'm not sure why you came out here tonight. I don't know where this is coming from. Maybe you just ought to go home."

"Sergeant," I said. "I know he shot somebody. Why were you sitting on this?"

"Why do you want to know so bad? What does this have to do with you?"

"Everything," I shouted. "It has everything to do with me. Donnie

Ray Miles, he was my age. He was one of us. He graduated with me. He joined the Army and I was too much of a coward to join. After 9/11, I wanted to join. I wanted to go. And you know what? When I heard that Donnie Ray joined, I laughed. The *Sentinel* called him a hero. Remember that article? And I laughed. I said he'd be a bullet catcher. That's what I said. A bullet catcher. What kind of a person says that, Sergeant? I said it because I hated Donnie Ray Miles. He was such an asshole back in high school, him and his Goddamned buddy, Jimmy Danley. You have no idea. They strutted around St. Vincent like they were bullet proof. Like they just didn't give a shit about anything. Cocks of the walk. Me? I was nothing back then. Nobody even knew I was alive. Danely and that crew made me sick back then. You should have seen the way girls swooned over them. I was amazed. I don't get it. Seemed like the more disgusting Donnie Ray made himself, the more people liked him.

"And then, he joins the Army and he's a hero? What am I? I'll tell you what I am. I'm a coward. I didn't join and I'm a coward. And Janey's dead. And Donnie Ray's dead. And damn it, I want to know what happened to him in Iraq, and I want to know if Jimmy Danley killed him up at that houseboat." My breath came in short gasps, and my chest was heaving. I had no idea why. I wanted to cry, but I willed the tears out of my eyes. After they'd welled up out of me, the words left a huge hole in my gut where I'd been carrying them for so long. Right then, I felt so exhausted that I thought I might fall over.

Cowboy held out his hand. "Wait a minute. Calm down."

I shook my head. "I can't calm down. This town's dying. Everything is dying, Sergeant. Everything is dying." My head was spinning. Words seemed to fill up in my throat. I wanted to say it over and over again, "Everything is dying." I wanted to punch something. I wanted to scream or run. It was as if high pressure system in my head had suddenly broken. I wanted a cigarette.

"Is everything okay?" Cowboy's wife said from the living room.

"Yes," he said, more to me than to her. "We're just talking, Martie. We're going to go out on the porch."

"You want me to pause this?"

"No, go ahead." He looked at me. "*Dances with Wolves.* I watch it about every other day."

I played with the still-filled glass of rum and Coke. My hip ached. I wanted to go home and collapse in bed. I wished I'd stayed with Denise.

"Come on," Cowboy said, and we went through a door out into the backyard.

The night's chill shook me and I crossed my arms.

"I'm going to go get my jacket," I said.

"You're not leaving are you?" Cowboy said. "Come back."

"Just getting my jacket," I said and got it out of the truck. I opened the glove box and took out the sandwich bag with the one cigarette in it. I found a lighter beneath the seat. When I got back around to the yard, Cowboy had piled some wood in a fire pit at the center of a cedar deck. He squatted by the pit and used a long lighter to set some pine cones ablaze. He sat down in a plastic lawn chair and folded his legs, his big body bowing out the chair's sides. He took a cigar from his inside pocket and put it in his mouth, unlit.

I took the cigarette out of the sandwich bag and smelled it. The tobacco's scent was stale, but my mouth watered anyway. I lit in the cigarette and took a deep drag. Immediately, my head felt light and my heart rate sped up. The smoke tickled my throat and a coughing fit seized me. I couldn't stop. The spasms wracked my body and tears squeezed out of the edges of my eyes. After a few moments, the coughing stopped, and I spit out onto the yard.

"You going to be okay?"

"Yeah," I said. "Just been a while since I smoked. I've been trying to quit."

He chewed at the cigar. "I quit a long time ago. I don't light these anymore. I just chew at them. Martie hates them. But that's not what I was talking about. Are you going to be okay?"

I didn't know what to say. I wanted to say "Yes." But that might have been a lie.

"You ever thought about talking to someone? A counselor?"

I took a drag of the cigarette but didn't inhale.

"No shame in it," Cowboy said. "I had to see one a long time ago."

"I probably ought to."

"After what happened with Rich Richards, I think you ought to."

We sat in silence. Then, he leaned forward in the chair. "Jimmy Danley didn't kill Donnie Ray Miles."

"Then what happened on that boat? Why did somebody hide the crime scene report at the department?"

"No one hid it," Cowboy said. "Davis Malone moved it in his office. He knew you were sniffing around, asking questions. So he moved it. It was none of your business, Justin. But you made it your business." He sat back. "The truth is that no one knows what happened to Donnie Ray. Me and Malone interviewed Tater Wilson and Freddy Richards and Jimmy Danley over and over again. Their story was always the same. One minute, he was there on the bow of the boat. The next minute, he was gone."

"They could have been lying," I said. "They could have gotten their stories straight. Donnie Ray and Jimmy had a big falling out because of the union at Clawson's. Did you guys know? Did Malone know?"

"Of course. Malone's a good investigator. We worked that angle. We kept asking them the same questions in different ways. We separated them. If any of them was going to break, it would have been Freddy Richards. But he didn't."

"Freddy. That's a whole different story."

"Tell me about it. I never would have guessed that little shit would shoot anybody." He chewed at his cigar and stared into the fire. It cracked and the woods around the house answered in an echo.

"Do you think it was suicide?" I said.

"Maybe. It's possible. Donnie Ray had a bad case of PTSD. But I doubt it."

The cigarette had started to taste sour and old. I took it out of my mouth and crushed it on the bottom of my boot and threw the butt into the fire. "So he just—died? No one knows what happened?"

"No. Nobody knows for certain. But you ask me? It was an accident. You should have seen his BAC. Way off the charts. I knew he'd been struggling with some things, but there was no note. There was nothing that led us to believe he'd killed himself. Suicides follow a pattern. You know that."

"Yeah, but sometimes they don't."

"That's true. But you got to look, Justin. You've got to observe. And we did. Malone and I worked every possible angle there. We made a promise. We turned that case inside out. There's nothing there. He's just dead."

"Why?"

He took the cigar out of his mouth and cocked his head. "Why? Why did he die?"

"Why'd you guys work the case so hard?"

"We work every case hard, Justin. You ought to know that by now."

"No," I said and leaned forward. "What promise are you talking about? Why did Malone move that case file?"

His face fell and he sighed, resigned. "That's a long story, but I suppose by now, it doesn't matter who knows."

What he told me changed everything I thought I knew about Donnie Ray Miles.

"Donnie Ray was deployed in Northern Iraq after he finished boot camp. He was first infantry. Apparently, he'd distinguished himself as being one hell of a shot. Don said that he'd thought about applying to sniper school, but he just wanted to get over there. Wanted to blow some terrorists' heads off. His battalion was on the ground maybe a month before it happened.

Donnie Ray was a part of a squad sweeping a village southeast of Baghdad, in the Al-Kut province. They'd been doing the same thing since he'd been there—sweeping. They swept village after village. This was back when we were still looking for weapons of mass destruction. The U.S. brass thought that Saddam might been hiding weapons in these tiny villages. So, the Army moved in, usually at night. Element of surprise, you know.

"So, Donnie Ray's squad is sweeping this village, going house to house. They're looking for a bomb manufacturer on top of looking for weapons. They had intel that this place was hiding a man who built bombs for Al-Qaeda.

"He wrote Don one letter. It arrived the day after all this went down. Donnie Ray said the whole squad was tight. Frosty. They'd not had much sleep because they'd been working at night. Donnie Ray was in bad shape, real bad shape.

"He'd shot a guy a few days before when he was on patrol. You wouldn't think that would bother him. But it did. Told Don it shook him up really bad. The guy he killed? Just a kid—about Donnie Ray's age. About your age. And it wasn't from a distance. It happened up close. They'd surprised him hiding in a house in some tiny village. Kid came out of the closet with a pistol and Donnie Ray opened fire. I imagine with an M-4, he sprayed the fella's guts all over the wall. Couldn't have been an easy thing to see.

"Anyway, that night—the night this happened—Donnie Ray's squad had moved down a street and circled the block back to the rear of the convoy, right where they'd come in, putting him and four other soldiers behind the truck that brought them to the village in the first place. I don't know what exactly happened. I imagine it's written down in some briefing somewhere. Donnie Ray saw somebody with a rifle. You've got to understand. It was dark. Very dark. They were tired. Donnie Ray was a mess after shooting that kid a few nights earlier. He looks up, sees a rifle, and fires. Hits his target in the neck.

"But the target wasn't an Iraqi soldier. Wasn't a civilian, either. He shot one of his own. A truck driver. Girl named Lucy Sherrill. The hell of it is that he knew her. He told Don that he liked her and thought she was a decent person. They might have even had a thing. I don't know.

"She died that night. Killed by friendly fire. The Army investigated it and found Donnie Ray negligent. A damn shame. It wasn't that boy's fault. But the all-powerful U.S. government said that it was, so they gave him a general discharge and sent him back here. He didn't challenge it on the advice of counsel. Don thought he should have. The Army said the shooting was, quote, 'a case of extreme negligence.' The Army thought he should have known he was behind the patrol, but damn, think about what had happened.

Think about it—out there in the middle of nowhere, head all messed up from shooting someone the night before. He already had PTSD before he shot Lucy Sherrill. By the time he go back to St. Vincent, he was messed up real bad. Obsessed with that girl he shot. He wrote her family a letter, but they never answered. Don said he had a picture of her he'd gotten somewhere. He used to talk to it. Don even caught him a few times. We got him in counseling at a place over in Apalach. I guess the military threw him a bone. He still had some benefits to cover it.

"Don and Betty didn't want their one son to be the talk of the town. You understand that, right? Don's a military guy. Conservative, just like me. Believes in America. Believes in honor. He didn't need this town whispering about Donnie Ray. And Donnie Ray didn't need to deal with a bunch of people whispering about him, talking behind his back. So not long after Donnie Ray got home, Don called me one night. Asked if I'd come out to his house and bring Mack with me. I didn't know what he wanted, but I went out there to Bay View. He asked us if we'd help keep it quiet, you know? Asked us to look after Donnie Ray. He thought that his son deserved another chance at life. I thought I owed Don that much. Mack and I agreed. We talked to Davis Malone, too. He served. He understood. Mack even talked to the folks down at Clawson's to get Donnie Ray that job.

"And then, when he died, and you started poking your nose around and running your own investigation, we all tried to keep it from you. We knew you'd been through hell. We could see the way you staggered in and out of work. Believe me. I know what it's like to have insomnia. After Janey died, you fell apart. So Mack stayed off your back and Davis and I tried to keep you away from the incident report. It wasn't any of your business. It didn't have anything to do with you. I was just trying to keep a promise to a friend."

Cowboy and I stood by my truck, staring at the night sky. We'd not spoken for a long time. After he'd finished the story, we sat in silence for a few minutes. Then, I got up and walked around the side of the house. Cowboy followed me. I found the Big Dipper and pointed, dragging my finger up to the North Star.

"Did you learn to use a sextant when you were in the Navy?"

Cowboy nodded. "Yes. We all had to. It was part of it."

"Is it hard?"

"Not if you know what you're doing."

"I always wanted to know how to use one." I opened the truck's door and put a foot in. "I'm sorry," I said.

"For what?"

"This is none of my business. You were right. I just wish that I'd known."

"You couldn't have known." Cowboy leaned against the side of my truck. "That's sort of the point. How did you know about the friendly fire incident?"

"I tracked down Lucy Sherrill's daddy."

He looked at me and shook his head. "I guess I should be mad at you for poking your nose in where it doesn't belong, but you seem to be good at it. You should have been a detective."

I pulled myself up in the truck and put my keys in the ignition. Cowboy stood in the doorway, his hand resting on top of the truck. "Justin, listen to me. I need you to understand something."

"I know," I said. "I won't say a word. I get it."

"It's not that. But, I would appreciate it if you kept this all quiet." He rubbed his face and pulled at his mustache. "Listen. When I was a teenager, joining the military was just something that you did. No one really talked too much about it, not really. My daddy was in the Army. My brother joined the Navy two years ahead of me. We didn't really see it as a sacrifice. We were just serving. That was how it was. I didn't see myself as a hero. I don't know that any of us at the time did. I liked the Navy. I enjoyed it. But I knew that it wasn't for everybody."

"I'm glad you joined, Sergeant." I wasn't sure where he was going.

"That's not what I mean. That's not what I want you to say. After 9/11, so much changed. I mean, I can remember when none of these roads out here had names," he said and waved an arm out at the empty highway. "They were all informally named after landmarks and families who lived on them. Then, after 9/11 and then the Patriot Act, we had to name everything. Down at the sheriff's department, we had a shit ton of paperwork to do. How many firearms we owned. How much ammunition. That kind of thing. After 9/11, a bunch of folks like Donnie Ray joined the military because they thought they were supposed to sacrifice. And I guess they were. The sons of bitches that flew those planes into the World Trade Center probably thought they were sacrificing, too. But at the end of the day, it's service. Being a deputy is a kind of service, too. This war is different. You're not a coward for not joining the military, Justin. You need to understand that. Don't carry that around with you. Don't indict yourself that way."

I gripped the steering wheel, unsure of what to say, uncertain that I needed to say anything. "Thank you. I'm sorry that I bothered you at home."

"Don't worry about it. Go home. Get some rest."

I turned on the truck. The dash board came to life, and classic rock played loud and fast though the radio. I turned the volume down. "Thanks,

Cowboy," I said and put the truck in gear.

"I guess I'm not ever escaping that nickname, am I?" he said.

He watched me from the yard as I backed away, did a three-point turn, and coasted down the gravel driveway. As I turned south on the highway, the porch light winked off. I passed dark houses set way back up off the road. Porch lights glowed. Mailboxes stood empty. I rolled the window down and smelled the air—a mix of salt and stench from the paper mill. If in some future place, I awoke one morning and walked out into say, a forest of virgin pine, and inhaled, the pollen and morning dew would enter me, fresh and wet and life-giving, and still, I'd yearn for it, that stink, that decaying, dying smell of home.

20

The mill shut down the week after New Year's. No hoopla. No big protests. One evening, the lights didn't come on, and they never would come on again. A few lucky men who worked there took jobs at the mill in Panama City, mainly because they knew someone who knew someone. Others headed north to look for work in the mills of Alabama. Some hung around town. You'd see them, tooling around in old pickup trucks, the paint faded from years of parking in the ashen fallout. They all had the same look on their stone-carved face: stunned, a shell-shocked stare. My father would have rallied the troops. Maybe he'd have pulled a Wayne Childress and tried to sue the new owners.

By February, Wayne was locked into a fierce court battle with Clawson's, which had shuttered in late January. Both sides had turned to the newspapers and television to fight their battles. One evening, I watched Wayne Childress, now clean-shaved and wearing a three-piece suit, talk with a reporter outside of the state courthouse in Tallahassee. He talked about worker's rights and the people of Apalachee County. He played the part of an angry young man well, but since he'd confessed to me that his work at Clawson's was just a school project, I suspected that he craved the limelight as much as Clawson's lawyer, a young, Ivy-league-looking guy who appeared on the same news program a few nights later. He railed about how the country was turning against self-made men like Frederick Clawson, how the country had become a bunch of people who didn't want to work, who were sitting around waiting on a handout.

The displaced fishermen and unemployed mill workers in Apalachee County would disagree. From Bay View to Stink Town, you'd see them, aimless men and women. How do you find a job when there are no jobs?

I was unemployed, too. I'd not taken Cowboy's advice and applied for a job in Bay County. The city manager and the mayor passed down some harsh budget cuts, and some deputies lost their jobs. I wasn't on the hatchet list. Neither was Chris. But my absence kept some folks from getting cut. Last I heard, all the deputies were still working twelve-hour shifts with only one day off a week. No overtime.

I wasn't sure what I was going to do, but I did know that my time as a law enforcement officer had come to an end. Without really even deciding to do so, I found myself packing up the house, working room to room and boxing things I intended to give to Mama or to Janey's parents. I took down maps and pictures of lighthouses. I wrapped protective cloth around candles and framed photographs. I found an eight by ten photograph in a manila envelope buried beneath clothing in the bottom drawer of the vanity in the bedroom. It was a shot of me and Janey after our wedding. She looked stunning, still, her bridal veil pushed up to reveal those doe-brown eyes, her long arms draped around my neck. I looked happy. Not tense. I held the photo for a long time and stared at me, wondering who that guy was, wondering if I could ever be him again.

I cleared out the hall closet. In it, Janey and I had once stored gifts we received that we didn't want: gaudy scented candles, crystal bowls, cheap dinner ware. After our wedding, we stored all the unwanted gifts in the closet, promising ourselves that one day, we'd return them. We never got around to it. Instead, we began to stockpile unwanted gifts. Every time we needed a present for someone, we'd plunge into the gift closet and choose a gift and give it to the unsuspecting recipient, some friend or relative who was never the wiser.

Janey had cleaned out most of the presents when she left. A few random gift bags stuffed with shirts and socks for me lay on the closet floor. I reached up and took down an oversized folder, stuffed with papers. Financial stuff, I thought. Old bills. Credit card statements. I knelt down and spread the folder's contents on the hallway floor and found maps instead: Pensacola, Atlanta, Birmingham, cities and neighborhoods. The maps had been printed from the internet, and Janey had circled several locations. With the maps, she'd collected a stack of ads for houses and apartments. She'd written notes on several: *Cheap. Good location. Near hospital.* I found a list of phone numbers on the back of a map of Gulf Breeze, Florida. Local utitlies. Comcast cable. Bank of America.

I flipped through the maps and stopped when I noticed the date the printer automatically imprinted at the bottom of each sheet. Janey had printed many of these maps and brochures over a year ago. She'd been planning to move almost since the day we got married. I dropped the blanket and picked up the map of Gulf Breeze. It had been printed six months after our wedding.

I stacked up the papers and put them back into the folder and closed it, not knowing what emotion to feel. Of course, I'd known that she wanted to move. I thought back to those early months of marriage, which now seemed like twenty years ago. We were happy, right? We were doing married couple things. We went to friends' houses. We went to Panama City and saw movies. We went to the beach sometimes. But she'd been planning on leaving St. Vincent from the beginning.

My phone buzzed one afternoon a week into February. I was out in the backyard, going through things in the shed. I'd been stacking cardboard boxes in the back of my truck. I'd planned on making a trip up to Decatur Valentine's weekend to see Mama and Aaron's family. Dad had left a bunch of old tools, assorted wrenches, half-filled toolboxes, and a cordless drill. I planned on giving them to Aaron. Maybe he could do something with them, build something that would last.

I opened the phone. Chris had texted. *You home?*

Backyard. Come on by.

A few minutes later, the gate rattled and he came into the backyard. He wore a camouflage jacket and a black baseball cap with an American flag on it. His hands were buried in the jacket pockets.

"What's up, man? You planning a yard sale?"

"Getting rid of some junk," I said and dusted my palms on my jeans. I stuck out my right hand and we shook hands like old men. "What's up with you, partner? I haven't seen you in a coon's age."

He smiled. "Same old, same old. Guess you heard about the cuts."

"Yep. Economy's in the toilet."

"You're done?"

I nodded. "Yep. I'm starting work at the credit union next week."

"Really? Doing what"

"Security guard. It's part time," I said.

"You been looking?"

"For a job as a LEO?"

He nodded.

"No. I'm—I don't know what I'm going to do. I guess it depends on how this thing with Denise turns out."

"How's that going?"

I thought, unsure of how to answer the question. Since our trip to Georgia to see Lucy Sherrill's dad, we'd been more or less an item. She spent some weekends at my house, and we sat in the den watching scary movies. She was working cleaning rooms at a motel in Panama City, but she'd been dropping hints about going back to school in Pensacola. I didn't know if those plans included me.

"Good," I said after a moment. "I'm taking it day by day."

He began to help me work, and we spent the rest of the afternoon, packing boxes and cleaning. He climbed up on top of the shed and swept off years of pine straw. He helped me with some hedge clippers and an edger around the backyard. We cleaned up around the fire pit, straightening the old cinderblocks. Chris picked up a plastic lawn chair and looked at me questioningly.

"It's dry rotting," I said. "But I'm going to keep it until it falls apart."

"Figured you would," he said and grinned. "You cheap son of a bitch."

Later, we drove down to the Swifty and got a six pack of Yuengling and came back to the house. We lit a fire. I sat on the old chair and Chris on an oversized log I intended to burn.

"You could probably get on over in Bay County," he said after a while. He took a long pull off the beer. The green glass glinted in the firelight. The sun had sank over the bay, out of sight of my backyard. Light twinkled through the pine needles.

"I need to do something else with my life," I said. "I'm just not sure what. Is that what you're doing? Cowboy said you got a job with Bay County."

"I did, but I quit," he said. "I joined the Coast Guard."

"Are you serious?"

He nodded and reached into the plastic bag between us for another beer. He twisted it off and threw the cap into the fire. "Yep. I talked to the recruiter in Panama a few weeks ago. I told him that I might have to come back to Freddy's trial to testify. He didn't seem to think it was a problem."

"You think you'll like it?"

He nodded. "I do. It's regimented time. I'll be able to see a lot of the world. Hell, man, we're going to turn around one day, and we'll be forty. I don't want to be living here then, doing the same damn thing. Do you?"

"No. I definitely do not." I finished the beer I was drinking. "Will I hear from you?"

He picked up a handful of pine needles and began tossing them one at a time into the fire. "Oh yeah. Of course. I'll email you when I can." He paused. "Listen, there's something I've been meaning to tell you."

I studied the green, yellow, and blue flames flickering in the pit. "What's that?"

"You know, when I said that I'd gone to a couple of Treadless meetings, I had no idea what Freddy was going to do. I didn't know Rich was going to try to kill you. You know that, right?"

I nodded. "Of course, man. I know."

He shifted so he could look at me directly. "It's just that I've got to believe that we can disagree about politics—or whatever—and still be friends. I mean, hell, you're the closest thing I've ever had to a brother."

"Man," I said, "of course, dude. Of course." I meant it, too. My throat had swollen.

He stood up. "It's getting late. I need to go." He stuck out his hand and I took it and he pulled me to a standing position.

We walked around the front of my house. He'd pulled his truck all the way up into the yard, the way he always did. When we were teenagers, he'd done the same thing with a piece of crap S-10 he had when we were in high school. It drove my parents crazy. Now, his over-sized gray Chevy with its giant mud tires looked like the little blue S-10 had grown up and grown old. He opened the door and pulled himself up.

"You take care of yourself, man," he said.

"You, too. Love you, buddy."

He looked at me. "You, too, man. You, too."

The truck backed out, and Chris drove down the street, the truck's tail lights fading out in the evening darkness.

One Saturday morning in March, Denise and I drove to Charlie's for breakfast. She'd spent the night, and we were planning to spend the day together. We were going to fish and then come back to house to clean what we'd caught and cook dinner. She had the weekend off. I was off from my new job, a security guard at the credit union. I worked four nights a week and escorted the closing tellers out to their cars. It wasn't a full-time gig, but jobs were scarce, and I wasn't exactly qualified to do anything else.

We ate at Charlie's and chatted with him about the future of St. Vincent. "Always been here," he said. "I guess it always will."

"In one form or another," I said, thinking of St. Vincent's past, how the original town lay submerged beneath the bay, the pioneers' and Aplachee Indians' bodies long since dissolved in the briny water.

"Where are you two headed today?" Charlie said. He was sitting with us, drinking a cup of coffee. His fingers wrapped around the thick beige mug. Though spring was in the air, a chill wind still blew from the south. It was hard to get used to not smelling the paper mill stench in the air.

"We're driving out to Sand Gnat Beach," Denise said. She'd ordered a cup of fruit and black coffee. She wore a heavy pull over shirt with a Florida State Seminole head on it and pair of white shorts. I enjoyed watching her legs as she crossed and uncrossed them.

"What for?"

"Fishing," I said. "See if we can catch some dinner."

Charlie nodded. "There are worse ways to kill a day. Tell you what. I've got a twenty-two foot center console parked at the house. Go get it. You remember how to launch a boat, right?"

"Yes," I said. "Are you sure?"

"Sure thing. You'll catch bigger fish," he said and smiled, the edges of his eyes wrinkling. "I nearly called you 'deputy,' Justin. You still working at the credit union?"

I nodded. "Part time."

"What's next?" he said.

I took a breath, unsure of what to say. Denise had been talking about going back to school in Pensacola, and I wanted to get out of town. Since I'd packed up the house, it looked like a storage shed, each room empty save for a few cardboard boxes. I'd taken a lot of things to Mama's house when I'd driven up to visit in February. I'd dropped the rest by Janey's parents' house, leaving boxes on the walkway after dark so I didn't have to talk to anyone.

"I don't know," I said. "I guess I'm going to have to figure that out." I caught Denise's eye, and she cocked an eyebrow, playful, waiting to see what I was going to say. "I guess we'll have to figure that out."

Charlie looked from me to Denise and smiled, his mouth disappearing beneath his bleach-white mustache. "You kids will be fine."

We settled up, and for once, Charlie let me pay full price. I ushered Denise out the door with my hand on the small of her back, and she huddled against me as a sudden wind blew. The air smelled like the bacon and eggs cooking in the restaurant's kitchen. We got in my truck and pulled out onto the street. I turned left on Main Street, the road running parallel to the highway, and we passed by empty storefronts and dying mom-and-pop's. Yank's Subs. The Video Den, a place that kept its name when the owner switched all of the video cassettes for DVDs a few years back. A nail and styling salon place, Nita's. At the end of the block, I turned and took the road down toward the old oil docks. We crossed the highway, which was empty. Usually, this time of day, you'd have to wait for a line of log trucks to pass.

Denise had turned the radio on, and we listened to someone sing about a bay and a job and the impossibility of escape. She knew the words and sang along, her thin, high voice a descant to the singer's low baritone.

"Let's try the fish down at the Docks before we get the boat," I said.

"Sounds good," she said.

I pulled up to the edge of the waterfront, the same place I'd come the night Janey died. We got out, and I went around the back of the truck and got the fishing poles. We walked down to the edge of the sea wall. "You see that?" I pointed out at the old stairway down to the bay.

"I do," she said. "Why?"

"What was it for?"

"What do you mean?"

"Why's it there?"

She looked at me. "You don't remember? Eighth grade history? Mr. Washington's class? This place used to be a deep water port."

"I know that."

"That was for tugboat crews to board," she said. She'd sat up in the seat. I loved it when she got this way, enchanted by history. She loved the past and all the stories that went with it. "The tugboats pushed barges in here and helped to guide them back out of the bay. There used be a platform down at sea level, but it collapsed years ago. I think it was a hurricane back in the 1970s." She looked around. "My daddy used to come fishing down here when I was kid. He'd bring me and sometimes Big Don came with Molly and Donnie Ray."

"Ancient history," I said.

"I guess," she said. "But I can still see us out there, running along the sea wall."

I scanned the crushed oyster shell lot running up to the concrete seawall. The salt wind blew. If I closed my eyes, I could see smoke and smell the paper mill. She was right. If you looked hard enough, the past was still right there in front of you.

Epilogue

If you drive far enough, everything looks new, even landscape you've seen before. Sand dunes, long leaf pines, palm scrub, sea oats, salt water inlets—all the coastal things I grew to love. They exist up and down the coast, all over North Florida and all over the world.

There's a road just south of Bayard's Bayou just off of the highway, maybe six miles east of Donnie Ray Miles' old trailer. If you turn off that road, the asphalt will quickly give way to sand. If you drive far enough down that road, the sand itself gets so soft that your vehicle will sink to the axle. So, you have stop and get out. Walk up the side of the dune and lean into your stride. Otherwise, you'll fall back down the hill. When you crest it, you'll look down over a stretch of virgin beach that seems to run a million miles in either direction. Look out at the Gulf of Mexico, for this is the Gulf, not the bay. This is the other side of Cape San Vicente. Look east, and you'll see a barrier island that has no name. No one lives there. It's home to crabs and coyotes, herons and bats.

Now, walk down to the edge of the water and walk along the shore. Kneel there and take a palm full of the sea. Feel the warmth in your hands. Put the tip of your finger in your mouth and taste the salt and brine that binds us all. Think of the Natives who must have done the same. Think of the periwinkles just beneath the sand, their lives a wash of salt and sand. Walk along the coast and feel the wind on your face. You'll smell the salt later when you take off that shirt. The footprints you leave will be washed away by the tide.

A Native of the Forgotten Coast, Jeff Newberry lives in South Georgia with his wife and two children. He is the author of *Brackish* (Aldrich Press) and *A Visible Sign* (Finishing Line Press). With fellow Gulf Coast native Brent House, he is the editor of *The Gulf Stream: Poems of the Gulf Coast* (Snake Nation Press). His website is http://www.jeffnewberry.com.

CPSIA information can be obtained at www.ICGtesting.com
Printed in the USA
LVOW07s0424190216

475653LV00002B/42/P